Across the Border:

Interview with a Refugee

I0664998

I.C. Rivera

EI YUNQUE
PUBLISHING

This novel is a work of fiction, spiced up with a hint of my own personal experiences. And though many of the characters, places and events mentioned in it are real, the names of certain individuals have been changed to protect their privacy.

To God, for the precious gift of life.

To my loving parents, for always believing in me. To W. Khoshaba, because you are my biggest inspiration. And to all the refugees in the world, who risk their lives crossing seas and deserts in search of a peaceful future;

I pray you may all find freedom at last.

Amen.

CONTENTS

ACKNOWLEDGMENTS

God called upon me for a mission and purpose, and a single conversation with a random stranger completely transformed my perception of the world. This opened a wide door of curiosity, motivating me to look deeper into many social issues I ignored. There's much to learn and discover still. But for now I'd like to recognize some great individuals, whose hard work and dedication to speak the truth inspired me to complete this novel; Dr. Noemi Caraballo Lopez, thank you for your guidance and for correcting me when I need it (countless times, I know). You're forever my pastor, and my spiritual mother. Dr. Nidhal Garmo, you are an inspiration to us all and a light for the Iraqi Christians. God-willing, I will join you in your humanitarian missions someday. Dr. Nicholas Al-Jeloo, your articles on Assyrian history have opened my eyes, and helped me in this journey to discover the wonders of a hidden world. Author Ian Buruma, your book *Murder in Amsterdam* helped me understand many situations I faced in the Netherlands. Authors Paul Marshall, Lela Gilbert, and Nina Shea, your book *Persecuted* is a priceless gift to the Church of this time. Artist and illustrator Javier Rosa, thank you for your support, your friendship, and your amazing talent. It's only the beginning.

PREFACE

How would you react if you only had five minutes to flee your home, in order to save your life from a terrorist attack? What would you do if you were persecuted for your ethnicity, your beliefs, and were threatened with death for refusing to renounce your Faith?

It sounds appalling, doesn't it? And still, this is the horrific reality of countless human beings in many regions of the world today. Unfortunately, situations such as these aren't covered by the media in their entirety. And even if we happen to hear about them in the news, or read some article shared through a social network, it is sometimes not enough to shake us out of our comfort zone, and motivate us to help those who are suffering.

There are times in life when we are put in situations that make us reflect upon ourselves, and on our priorities. Lessons may come in the form of direct experiences, but also through the people we encounter on our path. Whenever we are told to "walk a mile in other people's shoes," it is only for the best of reasons. And if we manage to develop some level of empathy for others, then it will be possible to unite in solidarity for their cause. Let us learn to be more spiritual, more grateful, and more loving. I believe those are the first steps towards changing the world we live in.

This is a novel about a woman's search for identity, life purpose, and love. But this is not her story only.

1

NOT ONE OF US

She stood naked before a long mirror, and her demeanor was neutral, steady, and emotionless. There was nothing camouflaging the thin dark lines underneath her eyes, nor the one stubborn blemish at the corner of her left brow. She was a natural beauty nonetheless, perhaps not flawless, but real.

She sighed, "Good morning to you too, Spotty."

She gently placed her right hand on one of her breasts, pressing her thumb into it, followed by her index. The mechanical fondling was merely a routinely habit, something she'd learned in a health course, and often read about in women's magazines. The purpose of it was for her to feel something under her fingertips. Then again, doing so would have signified only chaos.

Nada.

She took a closer look at every part of her body; from the top of her head, to the bird-shaped birthmark painted over her ankle. But this time, she looked for something more than dangerous abnormal tissue— she searched for answers.

What does my tan skin say about me? What can they assume by looking at the natural curl of my light brown hair? Could anyone figure out who I am, just by exploring the roundness of my hips? Could they call me by a pseudonym, just by studying the fullness of my lips? I wonder…

Her name was Isabel Alvarez. By the spicy sound of it, it was easy to conclude that she was a Latin girl. Still, she wasn't exactly the kind who fitted the common stereotype of the sociable bombshell, owning every other chick at the Salsa club on Friday nights. Instead, Isabel was an introverted, elegant woman in her mid-twenties; not overly loud like many of her Hispanic counterparts. And to everyone's surprise, her Spanish language skills certainly left a lot to be desired.

Although she was originally born in Caracas, to a Puerto Rican mother and a Venezuelan father, her mother—Amelia Guevara—took her out of the country when she was just a toddler. They went to settle in Florida with a sister of hers named Lydia, who was a distinguished art dealer and gallery owner. Isabel never really heard much about her dad, except for a few stories her mother used to tell her; about them having met during a resistance protest, or having worked together as columnists for a left-wing newspaper. The only explanation she ever gave her daughter concerning her father's absence, was that he'd gone to work one day and never returned home; thus leaving her with no choice but to flee to the United States. After all, due to her Puerto Rican background, Amelia was also an American citizen, and she knew that up in the North her daughter could enjoy of certain privileges and commodities they could never acquire back in Venezuela.

From a young age, Isabel was given expensive gifts; videogame consoles, all the latest gadgets, and her first computer. Business was good for her mom and aunt, and they would spoil the girl at any given opportunity. But Amelia never wanted to admit the actual motive for overindulging her daughter. After some bad experiences while living in Caracas, including a strenuous divorce, she'd become overly-protective of Isabel, doing anything in her power to keep her out of danger and inside the house at all times. However, she never considered the serious consequences of denying Isabel the opportunity to assimilate with other kids of the Latin community.

For this and other reasons, High-School was a lonely place for the young girl. Most students in the building sorted themselves into different groups. The Latinos usually kept close together, yet they rejected Isabel, for she was seen as an outsider who didn't even speak her parent's tongue. But after mastering the introverted lifestyle, she could always overcome solitude by integrating with the only friends she ever had; her collection of contemporary and renaissance romance novels—secretly fantasizing that one day she would meet one of the dreamy European monarchs she so often read about. Isabel was also able to beat isolation by listening to songs from all over the world, assuming to have discovered the true beauty of music. Because, while she didn't understand the language of the lyrics, she could still embrace the melodies, and be enchanted by the sounds of all the exotic instruments.

Later on, when it was time to leave home for college, the issue was not to find a group to gather with, but to find real direction and purpose in life. Isabel recalled going through all the different prospectus in search of anything that matched her interests—journalism, literature, languages, and other liberal arts—all which most people said would lead her nowhere in the current economy. Her mother, though previously encouraged her to major in what she loved most, also worried that she wouldn't be able to find a prominent job in any of these fields. Needless to say, the skepticism was so contagious that she decided to look into a career that could be financially-promising, at the very least. Four years later, she obtained her degree in Hospitality Management at UCF. And while she couldn't say this was even remotely close to her passion, a career in the Tourism industry was certainly the safest ride to take in the Sunshine State.

But whenever the subject of culture surfaced, Amelia would speak about her Puerto Rican heritage with great pride—unconsciously leaving out the fact that Venezuelan blood ran through her daughter's veins as well. Every so often, Isabel wished to have the same affinity with her ancestral roots, as most Latinos did, but she just didn't know how. She felt that neither Venezuela nor Puerto Rico represented her, just as she didn't think she represented them either. All she knew about both countries came from the stories that others told her, or whatever she would read about in books and travel magazines. Many times, during her college years, Isabel considered enrolling in a study exchange program at some university, either in San Juan or Caracas, but her mother always discouraged her from the idea. She argued that both countries were far too dangerous for someone who didn't understand the language—something Isabel always blamed her mother for. Amelia would also criticize the relentless crime, the constant political revolts, and other negative details that ultimately managed to kill her daughter's desire to discover where she came from.

2

THE PARTY CRASHER

Isabel had been working for some time as an Event Planner at La Porte D'or—a five-star, lavish neoclassical-styled resort. And while she was in charge of all events taking place at the luxurious facility, she would also get hired to co-manage larger-scale activities at several other venues. Still, despite earning an enviable salary and receiving competitive benefits, she was not satisfied with her dynamic career. She enjoyed the challenges and creativity behind her job, but her ambitious mindset lead her to aim for higher grounds. Coincidentally, there'd been rumors about the General Manager position turning vacant that same year. Upon hearing these news, Isabel came to set her pretty hazel eyes on what she thought could be the ultimate job in the Hospitality field.

Being promoted to business executive soon became her newest and biggest goal, and she wouldn't stop talking about the possibility. Some of her coworkers often said she took her career too seriously, and suggested she'd get involved in other and more entertaining activities; such as dating. But they seemed to ignore the fact that, as an Event Planner, Isabel was often surrounded by lots of interesting people. She would meet clients from all corners of the world—be it at conferences, festivals, or the conventions she organized. During many of these events, Isabel had the opportunity to share intelligent conversations with sophisticated, rich men—even possible bachelors. Oddly enough, her romantic experiences never got much further than the usual dating exercises; dinners, plays at the theater, and seldom, other overnight affairs.

But then one day, during a conference dinner held at her hotel, she met a charming and smart businessman from The Netherlands who filled her vivid imagination with wonderful stories of his life in Europe. His name was Lennert de Graaf—a tall, classy Dutchman, with great ash-blonde hair that slightly fell over his bright, green eyes. He worked as a Management Analyst, spending most of his life meeting with various clients at a different location almost every week. While this may have sounded like a dream job for many, for Isabel it seemed rather exhausting. Surely, the idea of frequent traveling and seeing new places was intriguing, not to mention culturally-enriching. And yet, she felt that his lifestyle left absolutely no room for the stability she'd always been searching for.

Nevertheless, on his last evening in Orlando, Lennert and Isabel went out on a romantic date, and he left his business card in case she'd ever consider the possibility of "…gaining some experience within the Dutch hospitality industry," as he'd put it. And when Isabel got home later that night, she admitted that it wasn't a bad idea to have those exact same words printed on her résumé.

"Maybe," she thought out loud.

"Huh? Maybe what?" asked her roommate Veronica, who was the Sales manager at the same hotel, and one of those annoying colleagues who often criticized her workaholism and overly-corporate taste in fashion. She was, however, the only one who knew about Isabel's week-long Dutch affair. But apart from the passive-aggressive bullying, Veronica had always been like family to her, and her only true friend. They were so close to one another that even the universe conspired to keep them together; for when they met in college they never expected to get an internship at the same workplace, followed by a permanent contract upon graduation. Just a lucky coincidence, some people said.

"Oh, you know, I've just been thinking about...Holland," Isabel said.

"Holland? Or perhaps you mean...Lennert?" her roommate giggled.

"Also," she laughed along.

"Well, you've worked at La Porte D'or for nearly four years and have never taken a vacation. Why don't you plan something for the Holidays?" Veronica suggested.

Though the idea sounded appealing at the time, a short vacation was not exactly what Isabel had in mind. There were moments when she couldn't seem to ignore a certain side of herself. It was like an undiscovered part of her nature that secretly yearned for new and strange experiences—accompanied by a little voice in the back of her head, telling her to take the chance of moving away for a while; a chance to broaden her horizons, just like Lennert had proposed. She too wanted to see other parts of the world, but not as a regular tourist. Instead, she was curious to meet new people, explore new places, and have the opportunity to listen to all her favorite foreign songs, right at their place of origin. Then again, she also considered it insane to leave now that she had a secure job—especially one with a good, steady pay. Not to mention there was still that possible promotion around the corner, and all her hopes were resting on it.

It was soon the midst of the Holiday Season, and just like it occurred at many theme parks in Orlando, business was always booming at the hotels during that time of the year. The bookings for special events, seminars, conferences—and even a couple of glamorous winter weddings—seemed to never stop. Isabel had actually been working harder than usual, and with good reason. At long last, all of the rumors concerning the retirement of the current General Manager, Monsieur Jacques Duclerc, were to become a reality. And due to the positive feedback she'd been receiving from the Board, Isabel felt pretty confident about her chances of being promoted. She knew there were a few other hopeful candidates in line for the job, but was certain that none of them possessed her drive or experience.

This gig is mine, she would tell herself.

Back home, at their apartment in River Park—in which they'd been living since having met during their sophomore year—Veronica and Isabel discussed the latest gossips from work; who'd been fired, who'd been hired, who'd been cheating on who, and at which suite. Her bold roommate was always one of the first to know about a scandal in the city; probably an advantage from frequenting the hottest clubs, and spending most weekends away in Miami among infamous celebrities. As an event coordinator, the last thing Isabel wanted to do on her free time was to attend even more parties, or be someplace crowded with drunken tourists. Instead, she preferred a more Bohemian atmosphere—such as poet cafés or exhibits at her family's gallery—or simply relaxing in her own bed with one of her corny romance novels.

"You know, they'll be announcing the new GM in about two weeks," said Veronica.

"What?! Already?" Isabel jolted. "But the applications came out this week. How is that possible?"

"Babe, Le Directeur signed his resignation over two months ago. I thought you knew that."

While eavesdropping behind every door wasn't exactly one of her habits, Isabel did find it strange that her roommate never told her anything until then.

"Well, not really. But...um, who are they choosing?" Isabel asked with a shaky voice.

Veronica shrugged. "Oh, that I don't know. Why don't you speak with Monsieur Duclerc tomorrow?"

Taking Veronica's suggestion into action, Isabel headed straight to the GM's office on the following day, with the excuse of turning in a performance report. In the meantime, she would start a casual conversation with her haughty boss.

"He'll be with you in just a moment," said his secretary. "You must be excited!"

8

"Excited? Why?" queried Isabel, trying to act clueless.

"Oh come on! You know you're one of the top managers around here."

"Claire, please send Miss Alvarez in," commanded Jacques, through the speakerphone.

"Success," Claire whispered as Isabel walked in.

The bureau was spacious and neat, with an overall minimalist style, contrary to the extravagant Louis XV layout seen throughout the rest of the building. The flooring had been recently polished, and it was made from the finest hardwood. On the right side of the room was a gorgeous white lounge, with contemporary furniture that contrasted perfectly with the office's grey walls and the cherry blossom paintings mounted on them. Isabel found the place quiet and private, ideal for a reserved and organized woman as herself. It was not her first time inside that place. But at that moment, she scanned every corner of it with a different set of eyes. In her mind she'd already made it her own; picturing herself placing a lovely divan by the French windows, from which she'd enjoy the relaxing view of Lake Eola Park.

The Parisian executive sat behind a rectangular glass desk, placed on the opposite side of the office. He stared at Isabel with a puzzled expression, as she appeared stunned before him, still fantasizing.

"Mademoiselle? Are you listening?" called her boss.

"Yes, sorry!" she cleared her throat. "I just came by to bring this report," she added, handing over the piece of paper—which had been squeezed so hard it almost looked like origami.

"Ah? Isn't your assistant supposed to do this?" he asked. "Anyway! You're precisely the person I want to see."

"Me?" she acted up. "What can I do for you, sir?"

"As you must already know from the hallway rumors, I'm retiring, which means that the GM position is open."

Oh my God, this is it! she thought, sitting up straight and trying to keep a serene and uninterested look on her face.

"Yes, of course. Everyone has been...talking about it," she rolled her eyes, chuckling.

"Right! And I also know how close you and Miss Veronica Adams are," he said.

"Ah? Well, yes, she's like a sister to me—"

"Indeed! Which is why, I've specially chosen you to be in charge of her promotion party!"

Isabel's voice dried up under his previous words. "Her...what?" she barely mumbled.

"Just like you heard it! Veronica Adams is the new General Manager of La Porte D'or!"

Her voice stuttered. "Oh...that's just...that's great news, sir"

"Oui, bien sûr!" he exclaimed. "She's the perfect candidate for the position. She's outgoing, spontaneous, and she speaks very good French, which is important in my hotel, of course."

Isabel felt herself shrink inside the cold leather chair, crushed and overwhelmed, and sensing that she'd just been betrayed by the person she trusted the most.

"Claire has a document with the guest list, and other information you may need. Make sure to ask for it on your way out."

"Yes, Monsieur," she muttered as she got up.

"Oh, and, Isabelle?" he called again.

"Sir?"

"I know you'll do a great job, as always," he winked.

Isabel turned her face away immediately, biting her lip to keep herself from responding in an impulsive manner as she made her way to the door. She couldn't understand what had just happened, or why

Veronica never told her she'd been considering the same job as her. When she walked out of the office, she noticed that Claire's initial amused expression had changed into a pair of large, confused eyes. But Isabel darted right past her desk without asking for the document, nor even saying a word. Instead, she quietly guided herself into one of the empty conference rooms.

A big presentation had taken place there, early in the morning, and she groaned from noticing that the maintenance staff hadn't showed up yet. There were water bottles lying around—all labeled with the hotel's golden logo—and several flyers were scattered over the carpet as well. She sat in silence on the last row of chairs, unable to decide whether she was sad or just plain pissed off. She began to take the situation a little too personally; mostly by resenting Veronica's secrecy over her professional aspirations. Either way, Isabel still couldn't figure out why her friend would be interested in the position, and there was a reason. For a long time, Veronica had been considering a transfer offer to another luxury hotel in New York City, making the radical twist of events look absolutely pointless. At that moment, the only thing that Isabel understood, was that it didn't matter how hard people worked to meet the expectations of their superiors, life was still full of bitter surprises.

That morning's presentation happened to be about new hotels from their franchise that have recently opened abroad. She leaned forward and grabbed one of the brochures from under her feet—it showed pictures of different popular cities around the globe. And as she studied the flyer, she recognized one of the pictures immediately; it was in Amsterdam. She let out an ironic scoff while tapping on the folded piece of paper. Their brand had just inaugurated a hotel at one of the greatest cities in Europe, making her think that perhaps the one person destined to transfer elsewhere was herself. But just as she was submerging deeper into impulsive possibilities—surprise, surprise—her *treacherous* friend walked into the room.

"Hey, are you alright?" asked Veronica, looking concerned.

"Seriously?" responded Isabel.

"Look, I—"

"Not now, Veronica, please."

Her roommate's presence completely irritated her then. And the lump growing inside her throat became her cue to avoid eye-contact as she left the salon in a haste. While she got away, Isabel hoped that every thought concerning the promotion would disappear from her head— especially her manager's praise for Veronica, which wouldn't stop echoing in her ears. And yet, as frustrated as she may had been, she still had a job to do. Because—as she was taught by her college professors— even when the world seemed to be shattering underneath her feet, she had no choice but to hold her personal feelings back and put her best hospitable face on.

The angry event planner made her way downstairs to her office, to occupy herself with as much work as possible; confirming catering orders, sending follow-up emails to clients, and verifying the schedule for upcoming events. That's when she noticed that her assistant, Becky, was doing the impossible to avoid her gaze. Choosing to focus on her tasks, she tried paying little attention into the matter. But as she went to the restaurant to speak with the head-chef about a wedding reservation, she saw that some employees were glancing at her awkwardly, and the room was filled with an annoying symphony of clearing throats.

"Alright, what the hell is going on?" asked Isabel as she returned to her office.

"Nothing!" Becky replied with a tense tone.

"Ehh, any plans for this weekend?" she added, in an attempt to distract her supervisor.

"Aha!" Isabel exclaimed. "You all knew, didn't you?"

Once again, Becky acted like she had no idea of what her boss was talking about. And yet, every single employee at the hotel did know about Veronica's promotion—everyone except for her supposed best friend. Isabel felt the blood boiling inside her veins as she slammed a stack of folders on her desk, startling her jumpy assistant.

"Isabel, I swear I didn't know…at least not for sure."

"Sure you didn't…"

Amidst sarcastic responses, Isabel cleared her small office up in blooming rage. She discarded all photos in which she posed with Veronica, and emptied a file crate to throw in anything she considered of value.

"Wh—what are you doing?" Becky asked.

"What does it look like?" Isabel glanced at her. "It's time for a change, isn't it?"

Isabel then grabbed a blank sheet of paper from a drawer, and hand-wrote a letter addressed to Monsieur Duclerc. A rush of adrenaline started building up inside her body as she signed it.

This is so impulsive, and yet so liberating!

Carrying the large crate, she strutted across the grand and flamboyant lobby, and out towards the parking lot. She could feel the eyes of her colleagues follow her steps as she walked further away, but she didn't look back at them. In the same arrogant fashion, she took her keys out, and with utmost determination she scraped Veronica's red mustang from hood to trunk as she walked past it. Parked right in front of it was Isabel's new black BMW x6—in which she proudly hopped in.

Isabel drove faster than usual that afternoon, and her cell-phone kept on ringing non-stop inside her blazer. She didn't care who it was, nor did she wish to hear anyone's voice at that moment. All she looked forward to was getting back home, where she hoped to have enough time alone to think of what she would do from that day on. But just before taking a sharp right-turn through River Park Boulevard, she stopped at a convenience store to purchase a bottle of wine; assuming it would help ease her tension, and perhaps even enable her brainstorming.

As she walked into the establishment, her ears were caught up with a rhythmic Arabic pop song. The attractive sounds came from a TV screen hanging on a corner above the checkout counter, which was set on a channel featuring foreign music videos. As she hummed along with the tunes, Isabel went on to select two bottles of white wine from the fridge, a frozen key-lime pie, and a bag of gummi-bears—a mix that didn't make sense, just like her entire day. She then stood in line to pay for her groceries, glancing at the TV once again. Without noticing, she began to be entranced by the gentle flutes and violins that played in the current song, both which—accompanied with a sentimental chant—created a melody that was both melancholic and romantic.

"Excuse me, Miss?" spoke a woman standing behind her, patting her on the shoulder. "You're next."

"Oh, sorry!" Isabel jumped, rushing forward, and drawing her attention away from the screen.

The male cashier—who was Palestinian—glanced at her groceries suspiciously, then directed his light coffee-colored eyes back at her.

"Anything else?" he asked in a rough, foreign accent.

Before she responded, the handsome Middle Eastern placed a toothpick between his teeth, twirling it sultrily with his tongue while keeping his gaze fixed on hers. She lowered her face coyly, portraying a tight-lipped smile as she slid her card through the debit machine before her.

"Nope," she said, feeling sheepish under his penetrating and disarming stare.

"Is there a problem?" a waiting customer protested, as the cashier took a ridiculous amount of time to pack her few items.

"No, no problem," he said while handing Isabel the paper bag. "Just want to keep admiring this woman's beauty for as long as I can."

When Isabel tried to react to his remark in a phony posh accent, she couldn't hold back a sudden burst of laughter, and neither could the smug Arab.

"How'd I do this time, Belle?" he asked in a different, much friendlier tone.

"Not bad, Rachid," she said with a chuckle. "Rehearsing for a new audition, I assume?"

"Yeah man, I really hope to get the role this time!" he sighed. "I've been trying so hard, you know?"

"I know exactly what you mean," she exhaled, "but, you never know."

Rachid Khaled was the eldest son of the shop's owner; who was a kind, hard-working immigrant, but also a really conservative father. He didn't approve of his first-born trying to pursue an acting career, considering it both a waste of time and a humiliation to his people—possibly due to the type of roles that had been given to Arabs over the past decade. His son, on the other hand, was determined enough to try changing the stereotypes within the film industry. And while rehearsing or not, he was still a natural charmer—so much that Isabel admitted that his few flirtatious words had been the highlight of her day.

Getting home at last, Isabel began undressing from the moment she shut the door behind her. She kicked her black heels off her tired feet, and stripped out of her sweltering wool blazer and pencil skirt. She also did not wait another second to rip her stockings off.

Oh how I hate these!

To have her legs imprisoned inside the itchy piece of black nylon, day after day, was probably one of the worst parts of her job. She left traces of clothes all the way from the living room to the bathroom, opening her bottle of wine as she went to fill the tub. She let out a soft moan, as the warm water embraced her skin with provocative grace. One by one, all of her troubled thoughts vanished from her head, and they were replaced with the same childish thrill she used to feel on the last days of school; right before the Summer Break.

Isabel stayed in that exact position for nearly an hour, getting out only when her glass had dried out, and her fingers and toes looked like they were a century old. But when she looked around her, she'd come to the silly realization that she'd left her towel back in her room. She then gave a mischievous glance at a pink one hanging on the rack, which belonged to her roommate, deliberately wrapping it around her dripping body.

"Ye take mah job, and I take yer shit!" she slurred before scuffing across the hall, laughing.

"Oh my God! Isabel!"

The tipsy woman flinched halfway, and turned around to see Veronica standing in the middle of the living room.

"I've called you like fifteen times! Did you seriously key my—hey! Is that my towel?!"

"Oh mah bad," Isabel mumbled, "I thought mi casa was su casa. But here, take it back!"

She then unrolled the cloth off herself, throwing it at her roommate, who stared in shock as Isabel swayed away towards her room, carefree and soaking wet. She slammed the door shut and threw herself face-down on the bed, able to hear her friend's noisy heels approaching, just before she started knocking on the door with great persistence.

"Isabel, open the door!" she shouted.

"Go away!" Isabel yelled from underneath her pillow.

"Please, just let me explain!" Veronica insisted, but her roommate wouldn't respond anymore.

Isabel slept soundly throughout the rest of the afternoon, unbothered and completely numbed out by cheap liquor. And as she lied unconscious in a well-deserved nap, she also had a long and strangely detailed dream:

> *She appears lying down, sunbathing in a one-piece white swimsuit by a luxurious hotel pool. Next to her is also Veronica, along with several other employees from the hotel where they worked. Though they all seem to be enjoying themselves, listening to tropical beats while engaged in chit-chat and laughter, their eyes are completely covered with a yellow ribbon, tied up in the back of their heads. Isabel then hears a loud noise that sounds like a gunshot. She becomes startled and gets up from the pool lounge, reaching out with her arms while toddling toward her colleagues. But no matter how hard she calls out for them, they all ignore her. All of a sudden, when she finally decides to take the blindfold off, she is shocked to see that no one else is there, and notices that her lips and ears are then concealed by the exact same ribbon. However, she is further alarmed to see that the previously-blissful scenario had changed into a ghastly panorama. Rubbing her newly-uncovered eyes, she sees herself standing all alone in the middle of the resort's deserted patio; in which the pool had become nothing but a large, dried up hole in the ground. There are no trees, no flowers, and no sunshine. And the moment Isabel removes her gag and screams, she discovers that she has lost her voice.*

The grim, vivid images of what turned out to be a nightmare, caused Isabel to sit up on her bed in one sharp impulse. She held her head and groaned, followed by reaching out for her bathrobe. It was already the evening, and she could hear the sound of the TV out in the living room. She then groaned once again, only this time from recalling the events of hours before, as well as from the pain of having to speak to her roommate about it.

While Veronica sat watching her favorite dramas, Isabel walked right past her and straight into the kitchen to pour herself a glass of water. They glanced at each-other awkwardly for a moment, then turned their faces away once more. It was like middle-school all over again for both of them. However, it was also a little hard for two women to play the silent treatment card on each other while they shared the same couch.

"Alright, could we just talk about it like two adult women?" asked Veronica to break the ice.

Isabel chuckled. "What is there to talk about? You got the job, so congratulations!"

"Yeah...but—"

"But why couldn't you tell me you applied?" Isabel added.

"I didn't, ok?" her roommate said. "I wanted to go to New York, you know that."

"Then why...how?"

Veronica hesitated for a moment and mumbled towards the ceiling, as though trying to find the right words to explain herself.

"Ok...you remember the guy I told you I've been dating for a while?" she asked while squinting.

"Aha, the guy whose name I still don't even know," Isabel said. "What about him?"

"Well, it's Astor...Astor Duclerc," Veronica replied, clearing her throat and looking in another direction.

Isabel dropped her jaw. "You're sleeping with Jacques' son!?"

Veronica coughed. "Well, we're also—"

"Wow! That's not unethical at all!" Isabel exclaimed with mock shock. "I can't beli—"

"We're also getting married."

Veronica's second confession made Isabel take a sharp breath. She'd suddenly lost all ability to speak, and retired back to her room a minute later; where she remained locked for the rest of the night. Lamenting her situation, she tried to find any gaps she may had forgotten to fill along the way.

Where did I go wrong?

She'd been a responsible citizen, a good student, and an outstanding event planner. She'd tried her best to meet all of the standards imposed by society; all of those which were supposed to grant her a life of success. But looking back at her day, she realized that following the rules of the game didn't always guarantee victory. That night, all she wanted to do was disappear.

Upset, Isabel opened her closet to look through her clothes, wrinkling her nose as she realized she owned too many uniforms, blazers, pencil skirts—all in black, gray or dark blue—admitting that she needed some color in her life again; just like during her college years, wearing colorful and eccentric boho skirts like a Spanish tarot reader. Letting out an annoyed moan, she pulled half of the clothes off the rack and threw them on the bed, followed by the second half. She then grabbed a large plastic bag and stuffed most of the outfits in it. In less than eight minutes, Isabel had emptied almost her entire closet; keeping only a blazer, a few cocktail dresses, a maxi gown, some jeans, and casual tops. She also cleaned her purse and wallet, in a desperate attempt to find Lennert's business card. They hadn't been in contact since that week he spent in the city, and Isabel was clueless of where he may had been at the time. For all she knew, he could have well been on an airplane right at that moment. But she still had to try reaching him.

"De Graaf," a sharp male European voice spoke.

He'd identified himself with his last name; a typical Dutch custom.

"He—hello Lennert, it's me...Isabel."

"Pardon?"

The embarrassing impression of him not remembering neither her voice nor her name, pushed her to hang up immediately. She felt like a fool for even considering calling such a busy man at such odd hours, especially to ask for a favor. But less than a minute later, her phone started ringing in her hands.

He'd returned the call, but she couldn't find the courage to answer this time. She let it ring four times until it fell silent, and when she thought he'd given up, the startling sound resumed.

"Hello?" she ultimately answered, taking a deep breath.

"Isabel Alvarez," he chuckled. "I just checked the caller ID and noticed the area code. Why did you hang up?"

Ashamed to tell him the truth, she made up the ridiculous excuse of having dialed a wrong number.

"And you managed to accidentally call an old friend in the Netherlands? Now I'm impressed," he replied with humorous sarcasm.

To her pleasant surprise, he was in Holland at the time to spend Christmas with his friends and relatives. But for a man who usually spent months traveling the world, it only made sense that he'd chosen to be home for the Holidays.

After catching up on dull, work-related subjects, Isabel diverted the conversation toward the real purpose of her call.

"I've been thinking about your suggestion to move over there," she said.

"Ah, over...here?" he asked, "You want to come to Holland?"

The doubtful tone of his voice was once again discouraging, but she stayed on the line and tried to explain her sudden urge to change of location.

"I tell you what," he said, "if you really want to come, you're more than welcome to stay at my own place."

"Are you serious?" she asked in bewilderment.

"Natuurlijk! As a matter of fact, I'll be leaving for a business trip at the end of January, so you could be like...my house-sitter!"

A house-nanny?

Isabel became frozen on the line, until she realized that, if she accepted his conditions, she could be exempt from paying for lodging. She agreed to everything without having a second thought. And she began her expat research that same night, somewhat thrilled about the random turn of events in her life.

3

AN IRONIC TRUTH

The next couple of days went by swiftly. Jacques Duclerc had grown tired of trying to contact Isabel, leaving voice messages until realizing that she wouldn't go back to work at the resort. From another side, and after long hours of investigation, Isabel found out that applying for a job overseas wasn't as simple as she'd initially assumed, nor as simple as applying for the resident permit; since they had different rules that she could only figure out once she'd arrive in Holland. Nevertheless, she was still preparing for her big move, and there was nothing that could ever stop her.

Luckily for her peace of mind, Veronica had left the apartment for a while, which gave her enough time and space to analyze the current situation on her hands. Being able to count on Lennert's hospitality was reassuring. It granted her a firm base to start from, and she would be living from her savings until she was able to work. That same week, she went shopping for thick winter clothes, as her future host warned her that Dutch weather was dreadful during that time of the year. It wasn't long before her suitcases sat all packed in a corner of the living room, almost ready to be strolled over the spacious halls of Orlando International Airport. And though her trip wasn't happening for another week, she wasn't planning on staying alone during her last days in America.

Apart from her clothes, Isabel boxed all other personal belongings carefully, leaving the apartment immaculate and with no trace of her existence—except for a letter addressed to her roommate and her copy of the apartment's key. As she loaded her luggage into the trunk of her car, she was astonished to see Veronica arriving at that exact moment, along with the presumptuous Astor—who gallantly got out of the vehicle and rushed to open the door for her. The phony grace with which she stepped out of his white convertible—flipping her pharmacy-blonde locks in the process—was quite an irritating sight. They approached Isabel promptly, both dressed in white tennis outfits, and carrying a friendly expression on their faces that Isabel wasn't moved by.

"I just came to say goodbye," Veronica said to her.

"Perfect timing!" Isabel replied sarcastically.

"Look," said Veronica, "I can imagine how you must be feeling now, but I'm actually glad you're leaving."

Isabel nearly choked at her roommate's comment. "Excuse me?"

"I mean, you really need this change, this new journey in your life. You've said it yourself," Veronica added.

For as much as she hated to admit it, Isabel knew there was truth in those words. It was time for her to stop living by the book, sucked into a meaningless routine. It was time to start living an actual life. There was a great amount of empathy in Veronica's eyes as she spoke. It was the kind of look that would have inspired trust on anybody, except on Isabel. Sadly, trust had become a privilege she could not grant her roommate anymore.

"Very well, Veronica. Good bye."

Biting the inside of her cheeks, Isabel got inside her car and drove away. Everything she had left to say was written down on that piece of paper lying on the kitchen counter. Isabel loved Veronica—they'd been best friends for far too long for her to say otherwise. But on that day, a betrayed woman's pride showed to be much stronger than forgiveness.

Packing and boxing things up was a time and energy-consuming task. But fortunately for Isabel, her mother lived just half-an-hour away, and she was certain that upon arrival she'd be spoiled with a hot meal of classic *arroz con gandules*, *mofongo*, and grilled skirt steak. Adding a chilled glass of sangria on the side would have made her day, but her mom was a devout evangelical Christian and forbade alcoholic beverages in the house. In contrast to the young and bold revolutionary she once was, Amelia had now turned into a traditional, religious Puerto Rican woman in her mid-fifties. And apart from working at the gallery with her sister Lydia, she also volunteered at a shelter in the weekends. She argued that helping others and speaking to them about the Lord, gave her a sense of true fulfillment.

Albeit briefly, going back to her old home was somewhat relieving. It was Isabel's custom to drop-by every two weeks and check on her mother—mostly to indulge in her cooking—but this one return felt like taking a long step back to push herself forward.

"Hola, mi niña!" her mom greeted.

"Hey ma'," Isabel said. "I missed you."

Amelia's home was traditionally-decorated for the Holiday season— with a bouquet of bright poinsettias sitting in the middle of the table, and a chubby Christmas tree standing next to the window. Like many Christian Latinos, she also collected Nativity figurines, which she placed on every surface of the house during this time of the year. Amelia wanted Isabel to be a strong believer like herself, and often spoke to her daughter about God, quoting passages from the Bible whenever she found a chance—basically in every phone call, email, and any other form of communication. And though she used to bring her to Church as a child—and even a few times during her high-school years—by the time Isabel started college she gradually separated herself from it all. She respected Amelia's ideas, but at the same time believed that religion caused too many problems among people. For that reason, she opted to reject it completely. Nevertheless, to her it was sometimes a mysterious thing; how her mother somehow managed to find some Biblical answer to all her questions and concerns.

In the cozy living room were two sofas made of wicker, assembled with blue cushions and cream-colored pillows. The walls were all painted in a sweet pale peach tone, and on each one of them hung replicas of famous paintings from two Puerto Rican artists—Oller and Frade—depicting the folkloric memory of Puerto Rico, which often intrigued Isabel. Her mother also owned another masterpiece that she valued greatly, for it was an original made by painter Luis Germán Cajiga. It was the portrait of a bronze-skinned man, displaying a serene countenance and a hopeful gaze. His name was Pedro Albizu Campos, an all-time national hero of Amelia's.

Just like every afternoon when Isabel visited, mother and daughter sat together to have a cup of coffee while enjoying of the peaceful atmosphere inside her home; created by the gentle sunlight peeking through the curtains, and the melodic sound of wind-chimes hanging by the window. All of these elements combined served to remind Isabel of what it was like to be home. As expected, Amelia brought up her daughter's impulsive decision to move abroad, listing all of her concerns. Like any loving parent—with exaggerated overprotective issues—she feared for her child's safety while on the other side of the world. Isabel was going to a place she'd never been to before, and where she knew no one except for the charming businessman. In any case, she was not a child anymore.

"Is Lennert at least interested...romantically?" her mother asked, showing great interest in the matter.

"Mom, please, don't start," she groaned.

Amelia shrugged. "I'm only saying, you need to meet someone eventually."

"I will, ok?" Isabel sighed with annoyance over the repetitive subject. "Just let me figure my life out for now..."

"Don't wait too long! I mean, what is he, like 40?" her mother asked.

Isabel groaned. "He's 38."

"Same thing!" Amelia joked.

Not wanting to continue rambling about her slow love life, nor the fact that she was still single at 26, Isabel changed the subject into one much more appealing to her ears and lips; Puerto Rican food. As soon as she sat at the table, her mom brought her a mouth-watering serving of one of the best traditional dishes from her country. It was colorful, and with an incredible saucy texture and spicy aroma she swore she could never find in another cuisine. But even though Latin food was wonderful to the taste, it was also devastating for the figure. It was the kind of food Isabel wouldn't indulge in more than once a week—unless she could spend an hour on the treadmill afterwards.

After a decadent, yet delectable meal, Isabel brought her suitcases inside the room where she spent her childhood and lonely teenage years. Weary from a busy morning, she lied face down on her bed, noticing that her old tribal-print sheets smelled like fresh lavender. Amelia had an obsession with cleaning, and Isabel saw that there wasn't a single trace of dust on any surface. Everything was perfectly neat and in order, almost as if she'd never left the house in the first place. The decoration in her room was pretty alternative and abstract, nothing had ever been changed. Looking around, she would take solace in knowing that she was never surrounded by an explosion of pink walls and boy-band memorabilia.

She turned her laptop on for a video-chat with Lennert, just to make sure he wasn't having any second thoughts about their deal. To her peace of mind, his sweet, green eyes looked sincere through the computer screen. She trusted him. And while he insisted that it wasn't a problem for her to stay at his place, for Isabel it was a huge step outside her comfort zone. She felt excited nonetheless, not just for the pleasant company, but also for the new journey ahead of her. The flight ticket had already been bought, and she prepared a file with her most essential documents, to be handy whenever required. Moving to Holland out of the blue was like throwing her dice up in the air; an insane decision after having her primary life plan stolen from her hands.

To collaborate with her list of silly first-world problems, the countdown for the big day had almost ended but she still had no clue of what she'd wear for the trip. Her bags were packed with sweaters, coats, long-sleeved shirts, and thick stockings—much too warm even for a few last hours in Florida. But just out of curiosity, one morning she opened her closet to see if there was anything more suitable for the occasion.

"Perfect!" she exclaimed, after finding the same black leather jacket that accompanied her throughout her senior high-school year.

"Feliz Navidad, mi amor!" exclaimed her cheerful mother, walking in with a lovely breakfast tray.

"Aww mom, I should have done that, not you."

Without hesitation, Isabel grabbed the cup of coffee, and took a long sip of the warm, creamy delicacy she couldn't live without. Next to the buttered toast and scrambled eggs, was also a festively-wrapped present. Taking it in her hand she could feel that it was a book, and immediately guessed which one.

"Because man shall not live on bread alone, but on every word that comes from the mouth of God," Amelia quoted.

Isabel smiled tight-lipped, unable to mouth anything except for a generic expression of gratitude. She then browsed inside of her purse, and drew out a silver envelope adorned with a red bow. With all the rush of preparing for the trip, Isabel had forgotten to do any Christmas shopping. However, since she did have great social connections, she managed to get last-minute accommodations at the Ritz for a whole spa-weekend; for her mom, her aunt Lydia and two other friends.

"And for the woman who's already found spiritual balance, here's a little fancy physical treat," Isabel said.

Amelia appeared thrilled as she received the certificate, but the expression faded a second later when she read it.

"Oh, honey this is quite nice and...extravagant," said Amelia. "But you know I have the shelter in the weekends. Can the date be changed, perhaps?"

Isabel groaned. "Ma', come on! You deserve a break from all that work. Let someone else feed the poor for once. Live a little!"

Amelia frowned upon her daughter's cold remark and returned the envelope. "I didn't raise you like that, Isabel."

Her daughter rolled her eyes skyward. "Please mom, you know what I meant."

"I still can't accept it, I'm sorry," Amelia insisted.

"You're seriously rejecting my Christmas present?" Isabel scoffed. "Look, fine. I'll give them a call later to change the dates. Happy?"

With an agreeable smirk, Amelia wrapped her arms around her daughter. They embraced for an entire minute, not allowing the misunderstanding to cause unnecessary tensions between them.

"So, what are you up to, dear?" Amelia asked.

"Trying to find an outfit to wear for the trip, actually."

Isabel picked out a white tank top, a gray scarf, and a pair of light-blue jeans. She wanted to put together a simple European look, but noticed there was a missing element.

"Um, have you seen those leather boots I had?" she asked her mother.

Amelia scratched her head. "Hmm, I think I put them in one of those boxes above the closet."

"Why all the way up here?" Isabel asked as she tried to reach for the box, standing on her toes and barely able to brush it with her fingertips.

"Okay...being 5'8" is definitely not...tall," she mumbled.

"Watch it!" her mom shouted.

In one strong impulse, Isabel managed to pull the container, bringing two other boxes down in the process, and causing all their contents to scatter over the floor. Isabel picked the long black boots up and wiped them with her hand, glad to see they were still intact.

"Oh my, sorry," said Amelia as she dropped to her knees, hastily placing the items back into the box. "I should've left all this old junk back at Lydia's place."

"Wait! What's all this stuff?" Isabel asked, crouching over the mess on the ground, and grabbing a vintage Polaroid camera that caught her attention.

"Wow, I've never seen one of these up close before," she added as she examined it.

Apart from the camera, there was a blank journal, a dried-up pen, old photographs, and a yellowed folded document. Isabel was shocked to have found such old photos of her mother and father among the things, and wondered why she was never given a picture of him before. Amelia, however, seemed rather uneasy to see that her daughter had found a forbidden treasure she hoped to have kept buried forever. And she even tried to snatch the document off Isabel's hands.

"Oh, I'll take that—"

"No! Wait a minute!" Isabel said as she opened.

Her shifty eyes scanned the paragraphs with great intrigue, only making sense of the words the moment she discovered it was a letter from her own father.

"What...is this?" Isabel asked with a drying mouth.

Amelia remained silent, with her brows scowled and her lips folded inward.

"Mom!" Isabel shouted.

"Oh, just read it!" her mother sighed with defeat.

Dear Isabel,

I want you to know that it was not my decision for you to leave my side, but your mother's, and I don't blame her. I understand her wish for you to live a better life in the tranquility that perhaps I couldn't offer you over here. It truly pains me to see you go, knowing that you'll be living in a country I swore to never land on. But despite my feelings towards that decision, I can still admit that you'll be getting a good education and better chances to become the fierce journalist I always dreamed you would be. I tell you this, because no matter where you go, you must never forget where you've come from, nor who you are. And you, my sweet Isabel, are the daughter of a revolution. Make no mistake, the pen is the most powerful weapon of all. And if you follow this path you will see how both your spoken and written words will help many people—especially your people.

The words written on this letter may seem strange to you now. But I'm sure that when you return home, your heart will lead you to the truth. Please don't ever think that I don't love you or your mother. She chose another path, and I respected it. But you, my child, don't be dragged into her irrational religious ideas. You are a freethinker, as am I. I look forward to the day we'll be reunited once again, here at Barrio 23.

¡Patria o Muerte!

Te amo,

Tu papá, Julio Alvarez.

"And now you know everything," her mom whispered, keeping her eyes steady on the ground.

Isabel let the piece of paper fall off her shaking hands, seeming breathless for a moment, just before a short burst of laughter escaped her throat. Amelia stared at her with confusion, astonished by her peculiar reaction from discovering why she'd truly grown up without a father.

"Why?" Isabel asked. "After all these years!"

"It's compli—"

"Complicated?" interjected Isabel. "Did you ever plan to tell me the truth?"

Feeling judged under her daughter's burning glare, Amelia tried to mouth an explanation for her prolonged secrecy. In her motherly mind, it was all a noble attempt to protect Isabel from some kind of danger, in this case, her father's expectations. There were far more things Amelia kept her daughter from doing—as she was growing up—than she ever allowed her, fiercely believing that it was all for her own good. Isabel, however, felt that both her parents were to blame in this matter; Amelia for keeping the secret, and her father Julio for choosing his devoted patriotism over his own family.

"You know what's crazy about all this? Isabel lamented. "That long before I went to college, I knew that I wanted to write."

Amelia dropped her saddened gaze further.

"And now I can see why; it's in my blood," Isabel added.

"Yes, I know," Amelia said. "But I couldn't let him drag you into his political ideas!"

"Funny," her daughter scoffed. "You always try to drag me into your own Church circus, though."

"Hija, don't speak like that. Remember, only God has a per—"

"Perfect plan?" Isabel retorted. "Yes, you've repeated that so many times it's exhausting."

Isabel picked the letter back up from the ground, placing it inside the journal as she wiped a tear away. She then focused back on the old cardboard box, looking through the rest of the items with childlike endearment; as though they represented the Christmas gifts her father never gave her. An asphyxiating lump started to build up inside her throat, but she couldn't tell whether it was from nostalgia, anger, or mere regret for not having taken the initiative to find her dad—regardless of the negative stories she was told. But even in her developing remorse, Isabel admitted that it seemed highly unfair to be entrusted with tasks of any kind; as if it had been something mysteriously predestined. In any case, the timing of these revelations couldn't have been more inconvenient; for she was leaving America in a few days, and there was absolutely no living force on Earth that could have made her change her stubborn mind.

4

TUS OJOS NEGROS

Isabel's last hours in Orlando went by almost in slow-motion. She could have used the tranquility of the morning to engage her mother with questions about her father, but opted to begin her journey with a clear, unrattled mind. Amelia offered to drive her to the airport herself, spending the whole ride ranting about the dangers of the outside world, like she was instructing her daughter on how to cross the street for the first time. But basing her wisdom on shallow internet research, Isabel assured her that any European country was a million times safer than the entire United States of America. Amelia continued to insist on her fearful assumptions, but upon seeing the control tower of Orlando International Airport in the distance, Isabel was convinced that she was already past the point of no return.

"Please, just take care of yourself," Amelia said, hugging her.

"I always have," replied the future expat.

After waving goodbye to each other one last time, Isabel walked away overjoyed, strolling her two suitcases over the long terminal; in which she carried more expectations than personal items. Fortunately, her flight was on time and the passengers were already boarding. After the disillusions of the past weeks, all she wanted to do was lounge in her spacious first-class seat, and be handed a glass of sweet, sparkling wine. That indulgence alone gave her a sense of freedom she never experienced before. She laughed within herself, realizing that she hadn't done anything so spontaneous since the time she posed nude for a figurative art course at UCF.

I needed the extra course credit...

"Good Morning ladies and gentlemen, this is your captain speaking. We'd like to welcome you aboard KLM Airlines flight 1625—service to Amsterdam. Flight duration will be around eight hours and twenty-five minutes, and uhh...we may be experiencing some slight winter turbulence today. Once again, welcome aboard and have a pleasant flight."

As they finally announced their takeoff, Isabel was thrilled to imagine that in only nine hours she'd be walking over European soil for the very first time. She felt just like a child on her way to Magic Kingdom; except in Cinderella's Castle she wouldn't find amiable flight-attendants with googly blue eyes, bringing complimentary cocktails.

To begin her expatriate adventure, Isabel took out her dad's blank journal and wrote that day's date on the second page—December 29th, 2013. But apart from a month, day, year—and an extensive narrative about how ecstatic she felt on her first time inside an airplane cabin— the only other words inside her mind were those written on her father's letter. Then again, that was precisely what she didn't want to be thinking about during her journey toward freedom. And yet, she couldn't help to wonder if her dad was truly waiting for her somewhere in Caracas, or even if he was still alive.

After five minutes of doodling and tapping her pen on the page— and failing to find anything interesting to watch on the in-flight entertainment—Isabel figured that surrendering into deep slumber was all she could do then. For a person with a mild case of anxiety disorder, sitting around for that many hours seemed like absolute torture— especially during a slightly-turbulent flight, making it difficult for her to find the inspiration to sleep. But when she did manage to fall into Morpheus' mighty arms, she also crashed right back into her bizarre realm of dreams.

And just like in her first dream, Isabel appears lying down—this time over a carpet on the ground—moving from left to right, and looking anything but rested. The distant cries of small children awaken her, and she groans with great discomfort from the anguish noises that come from all directions. Her throat is sore and dry from thirst. And as she opens her eyes she sees that both her arms are covered in dried clay—giving the impression that she'd been crawling over mud. Looking over at her surroundings, Isabel grumbles from realizing that she is sitting inside an old, white tent.

God, how I hate camping, she thinks, finding it hard to believe that someone has actually managed to drag her along to some isolated park, or to a cay in the middle of the Caribbean. She hates the idea of being at a beach. And at that moment she's repulsed by the sensation of sweat and sand sticking all over her body. When she stands up from the hard ground, she notices that she's barefoot, wearing dirty torn jeans and an oversized t-shirt.

What the hell is this? she asks herself, approaching the opening of the dusty tent. But as she steps outside of it, what is revealed before her eyes leaves her completely appalled. She was not at a camping site in the tropics, but standing in the middle of a hot desert, and surrounded by what seemed to be thousands of crumbling huts and numbered tents. While it seems like there is not a soul around but hers, she can still hear the bizarre infant wailing from afar. As she begins to follow it, the faint rumble of a large crowd becomes audible as well. Isabel then tries to figure out where it comes from, tiptoeing with pain, for the sand burns her soles with every step she takes forward. Nevertheless, the muddy tents sprawl far across the land creating a gigantic maze, making it impossible for her to find the end of it.

Where am I? she wonders, falling on her knees, and feeling as though she were to pass out from the excruciating heat. She tries to breathe through the thick hot air, slowly lifting her head when she hears an array of tiny steps closing in. Right in front of her—merely three feet away—appears a little girl in white and pink pajamas. She is no older than five; with pigtailed light-brown hair, and an expressive pair of amber eyes that resemble Isabel's in a way that is almost eerie. The child says nothing, but reaches out to hold Isabel's hand, pulling on it as if asking to be followed. The confused woman does not hesitate, and after a long stride they finally reach the end of the labyrinth. But the new scenario before them is just as dreadful, perhaps even more.

A multitude, nearly as numerous as the grains of sand underneath her feet, suddenly materializes right in front of Isabel's eyes. They were shouting desperately and pushing forward, trying at all costs to climb over the ten-foot tall, heavily barb-wired fence that surrounds the entire site. But as frightening as it appears, Isabel is still unable to guess what kind of place it is. For her, it looks like an outdoor prison of some kind—a prison in hell itself.

"Hello? Are you alright, Ma'am?"

The phony, sweet voice of a flight attendant pulled Isabel back down into her actual setting. About ten minutes had passed since the plane had touched European soil, and she'd slept right through the bumpy landing.

Thank God, it was just a bad dream…ufff

Realizing she was the only passenger left in her section, she quickly picked her carry-on luggage up and rushed out of the aircraft; with a tad of embarrassment displayed over her flushed cheeks as she waved at the staff.

The suspense to see Lennert again was overwhelming, and it was imperative for her to retouch some of her make-up before meeting the handsome Dutchman. She walked into a restroom and looked at herself in the mirror, making sure she was neat, presentable, but most importantly, approachable. She turned from left to right, checking all her angles, but feeling there was still something missing in her overall appearance.

"Come on, you're an Alvarez-Guevara," she murmured, unzipping her jacket and rearranging her bust—letting out a bit of the Latina spice she kept hidden within.

"Just be spontaneous," she added, as she reached for the top of her ponytail and pulled on the tight band, to let her long caramel hair fall like a cascade over her back and shoulders.

While smirking at her new reflection, she'd come to the conclusion that if she wanted to portray a renovated version of herself, she had to start out by looking less corporate, and more outgoing, inviting, and sexy.

Isabel walked out feeling a bit more secure about herself, strutting her way toward the enormous baggage claim hall. There were fourteen belts in total—all identified with a large, yellow cube on top. In the distance, she could see lots of people gathered in front of large glass windows, which separated the hall from the rest of the airport. All of them seemed to be friends and relatives of the passengers, who waited impatiently to greet their loved ones. Isabel tried not to look too hard in that direction, so that anxiety wouldn't disrupt her current poise character—an inner fight she was already losing. Following a few strolls around the place, she found her red suitcases riding on the fourth belt, hurrying after them before they would go back into the walls. After loading them into a luggage cart, she took a deep breath, and made her way toward the exit that read; *Nothing to Declare*, located before a narrow, green passageway. But as she looked through the curious crowd outside, she saw no familiar faces.

He's probably just late, she thought, and kept on walking through the masses.

Though slightly absent-minded, Isabel couldn't help noticing the looks some men were giving her as she paraded around Schiphol's shopping centre. They would smirk, wink, and whisper inaudible words as she passed them; all while she tried concealing her own bashful grins behind her silky hair. She was not a stranger to receiving compliments, but there was definitely something special about flattery when it happened in a foreign country, and in a different language.

However, Isabel soon grew tired of walking around without direction; crashing onto people and their suitcases, for not paying attention to where she went. Almost everyone in the terminal seemed to be in tremendous hurry—for the trains, for the planes, and for the crowded subways. Isabel had become a little disoriented, to the extent that the entire hall was starting to resemble one of Edvard Munch's paintings. She shook her head, walking closer to the main entrance, where she found a large, red checkered structure; known as the Meeting Cube. She had no choice but to sit there, and wait patiently for Lennert's arrival—unable to keep herself from speculating the worst;

What if he changed his mind?

Suddenly, she heard her full name being called by a deep, commanding voice that was closing in. And as she lifted her head, Isabel's fretful gaze was caught by a pair of furious eyes that were as dark as pools of raw Arab oil. They belonged to an exotic, handsome man, wearing a crisply-pressed black suit and black leather gloves. Isabel stood up muddled, scanning the area for any signs of Lennert, just before the man in front of her spoke her name once again, and with a sharp question mark in the end. He was about half a foot taller than her, broad and athletic, with striking and unmistakable Middle Eastern features. His full Syrid nose, furrowed thick eyebrows, as well as his neatly trimmed goatee and neckline, made Isabel guess his ethnicity right at first sight. In his hands he held a white cardboard with her name written on it, but she continued to appear confused.

"Are you Miss. Alvarez, yes or no?" he persisted.

"Ye—yes, it's me," she said. "Is Lennert de Graaf with you?"

"No, Mevrouw. I drive you back to Rotterdam. This way, alstublieft," he hurried.

"Rotterdam?" she asked.

The chauffeur grabbed both her suitcases and hurried toward the exit. And not having a chance to ask anything else, Isabel had no choice but to follow him. Though disappointed from not seeing who she'd expected, it was still reassuring to know her host had arranged decent transportation for her. The whole traveling experience started to feel pleasant and welcoming, up until the second she stepped on the other side of the large glass doors, and a gush of freezing wind slapped her across the face. Isabel flinched from the cold struck, speeding up her pace to escape the frightful winter she was so often warned about— immediately regretting not choosing to travel in the summer. Parked about fifty meters away, just in front of the tram-stops, was an immaculate black Mercedes with tinted windows and sparkling rims.

"Get in, it's open," the Arab-looking man said, leaving her in a state of surprise as he got in the driver's seat; coarsely slamming his door shut.

The lack of gentleness in his maneuvers was unheard-of, but Isabel tried not to make a big deal of it. However, she did ask herself—and him too—how he knew who to pick up at the airport in the first place.

"They give me your picture, look," he replied as he handed her his phone.

It displayed a photo Lennert had taken during the convention back in Florida. She couldn't believe he still kept it, and that alone brought a smile to her face.

"Happy, yes? Now be relax. I take you to Mr. de Graaf and you can ask him what you want," he added with an annoyed tone, snatching his cellphone back.

For as much as she tried not to be judgmental, Isabel was competent in the hospitality business, and could not ignore the unprofessional attitude coming from this man. It was a behavior one could perhaps expect from a taxi man during rush hour in New York City, not from a luxury chauffeur in Amsterdam. She directed her attention toward her surroundings instead, curiously staring out the window like the day she first arrived at the gates of Walt Disney World—she thought the scenery back at the theme park seemed much more appealing, anyhow. Through the glass she saw nothing but foggy roads and grey skies, giving the impression that she'd just fallen into a scene from a Tim Burton film. And yet, it was just a common cold and ghostly afternoon in the Netherlands.

I hope it isn't always like this, she thought, looking at what would become her environment from then on.

From left to right, in the far distance, she saw country-side gabled houses; sitting on extensive fields covered in snow and dirt, and some of them placed next to old windmills. The far-reaching plains were adorned with long rows of naked oaks and elms, perfectly but unnaturally lined up next to one another.

Isabel turned her head to the front for a moment, looking through the rear-view mirror and noticing the same angry expression in the driver's eyes—catching him glancing over at her a few times even. Still, he wouldn't mouth a single word, and the silence inside the vehicle was beginning to feel uncomfortable.

"Could you perhaps turn the radio on, please?" she urged.

He furrowed his eyebrows further but complied nonetheless, tuning in to a random station that happened to be playing Holiday classics. She noticed that not even joyous Christmas melodies helped change the driver's mood, as he continued on portraying a sternness that was just hard to ignore.

The main road towards Rotterdam was a long strip, which continued in a straight line almost throughout the whole drive. On the way, they passed a few popular cities that could be seen from afar; The Hague and Delft were two of them. The first one was the home of the Binnenhof—or House of Parliament—the International Court of Justice, as well as many important museums. And then there was Delft; the historic and vintage-looking hometown of painter Johannes Vermeer. This last one was easy to recognize for its two notorious Church towers, sticking out above the snowy rooftops—one of them having a bit of a Pisa complex.

Isabel and the cranky driver soon began approaching an area with diverse buildings situated on every side; car dealers, factories, apartments, and hotels. And all of the previous grasslands had been replaced by various parks and football fields—some which even had teams playing heartily in sweaters and shorts, regardless of the mortifying cold winds.

"Are we close?" she asked.

"Almost, this is Schiedam," answered the chauffeur, glancing fiercely through the mirror once again.

All of a sudden, he began accelerating, and cutting other cars off like a Middle Eastern Dom Toretto—while Isabel braced herself to a grab handle above the door.

"Sorry about that," he said as he slowed down, "I hate traffic."

Though she was tempted to return the cheap apology with stereotypical racial slurs, she became distracted by the new view outside her window. There were bridges and elevated train tracks, as well as several recreational areas; parks, frozen lakes and canals, courts, and even a zoo. The roads became narrower, divided into different lanes; for automobiles, trams, pedestrians and cyclists. These last ones were impossible to miss, for they rode their bicycles with tremendous joy and enthusiasm, as they would on a hot summer day. Most buildings around this urban site were made out of red bricks, adorned with white window frames, no taller than four or five stories. They were different from the traditional, Dutch stepped-gable houses one would normally see in travel magazines. Instead, these inner-city buildings were all merged together, as one long superstructure that went all the way down the road. The majority of them were in fact residences, but some had restaurants and other public establishments at the ground floors as well. This particular area was called the *Blijdorp District*; Isabel's new neighborhood.

"We're here," said the driver, as he parked before a long apartment complex.

It was located at the corner of Statensingel Street, and right in front of a far-reaching iced canal. The second Isabel stepped out of the fancy vehicle, her nostrils hurt from inhaling the freezing air. She could even see her own breath translated into puffs—quite a spectacle for someone who was raised under the tropical sun. Most of the trees in the zone appeared leafless, except for a few tall firs covered in frost. And the ground was slippery, and powdered with snow, just like every other surface that was exposed to the frigid weather. It was surely not the most convenient season to visit. But on a more positive side, Rotterdam Central Station was located just ten minutes away by foot. Though she would miss driving her own stylish car, she was still glad to have good public transportation available nearby.

Isabel approached the front door of the building, eagerly searching for Lennert's name on the resident caller panel. She pressed the button several times, but no one answered. Right at that moment, the chauffeur appeared behind her and drew a set of keys from his jacket pocket, followed by opening the door for her.

"Oh, thanks," she said.

He shrugged, pushing through with both her suitcases.

The apartment was located on the second floor—first floor, according to the Dutch point of view—and it was no average bachelor pad. The living room was fully furnished with two well-stocked bookshelves, a long leather couch, a matching black armchair, and a cool vintage trunk that was being used as a coffee table; all resting on polished, dark wooden floors. Right across the sitting room was a four-person glass and steel dinner table; beautifully combined with contemporary, red tall-backed chairs. She could tell that Lennert was a man fond of art and culture, for on the pearl-colored walls he'd displayed an impressive collection of world artisanry; tribal masks, antique swords, and several abstract paintings. And as expected from any guy, he also had a gigantic flat-screen TV mounted on the wall, right above an old, decorative fireplace.

As Isabel approached one of the windows in the living room, she had a clear view of nearly the entire neighborhood. It was a sight she wanted to contemplate better once the snow was gone, making way for the colorful beauty of spring. But as amused as she felt with her new surroundings, she was suddenly startled by a loud thud right next to her.

"I leave this here," said the ever-improper driver, letting her suitcases fall hard on the ground.

"Ugh! Do you have to be so rude!?" she shouted, unable to contain her frustration any longer.

"Listen woman, today was my free day!" he replied in a foul mood. "But because of you, I am now late for my appointment."

With a gaped mouth, Isabel reached into her purse to tip the ill-mannered fellow so that he would finally leave. But then, she changed her mind completely.

"You need to learn how to treat your clients," she responded with arrogance, drawing out an empty hand.

"Thank you, you may leave now," she added with a grin.

Her tone was ice-cold, but his glare even more so. The chauffeur left the apartment moments later, snarling, and slamming the door on his way out. It wasn't like her not to give gratuity for a service, and yet his rough actions revealed that he didn't deserve any of it. Her only regret was not having asked for his name, in case she felt like writing down a review on his bad attitude.

Seeing that she was all alone, Isabel gave herself a tour of the flat; starting out with the kitchen. It was a comfortable space, accompanied with a small balcony overviewing the bottom neighbors' landscaped gardens. The petite culinary playground was fully equipped; with stainless steel appliances, and a spotless stove that made her wonder if Lennert even made use of it at all. Placed on the dark granite countertop, Isabel found two wine glasses, and a note tied up to a single red rose. It read;

For later tonight. See you soon, L.

Though his absence was disappointing, she was still reassured of her host's prompt return, using the quiet time to get more familiar with the place. She dragged her suitcases through a narrow hallway that had several doors. One of them lead into a walk-in closet, another into a bathroom—so tiny that it also looked like a closet—the next one lead into a small office, and lastly, there was the bedroom. It was not the most spacious of chambers, but cozy nonetheless; with light-gray walls and a queen-size bed wrapped in sheets of burgundy satin. Isabel went to take a pleasant, long shower; feeling overwhelmed with joy and excitement about her new life. She could hardly wait to attend her first job interview, and learning the local language was something she looked forward to as well. Coming out of the bathroom, she quivered from the cold that surrounded her, and immediately checked the heater's control panel on the wall—turning it up all the way to 25°C. At that moment, Isabel couldn't deny the hot South American blood running through her veins, being unable to withstand temperatures lower than 20°C.

Looking through her suitcases, she couldn't find a single piece of clothing that could warm her up, and at the same time make her feel sexy for when Lennert returned. She then stepped into the large closet, finding entire racks of impeccably pressed shirts and pants, all organized by color. Twisting a lock of her hair, she pictured herself parading around in one of Lennert's shirts, just before she'd seduce him into a passionate evening of lovemaking. Following her novel-inspired fantasies, Isabel slipped into one of her sets of white lace lingerie, and grabbed a baby-blue dressy shirt from the rack. She was delighted by the soft texture of fine Italian cotton; precisely the way she imagined Lennert's pianist-like fingers would feel when caressing her skin.

Clueless on how long he'd take to return, she went on to lie on his bed and closed her eyes for a little while. But lately, closing her eyes for too long had been causing Isabel to have strange visions with hidden symbolism. She'd been dreaming about faceless multitudes, disastrous environments, and unknown places she didn't even know if they existed.

This time, her unconscious mind sends her to walk aimlessly, through what seems to be a Middle Eastern town in the midst of war. The roads are dusty and deserted, and the blazing cars on every corner make the place look like a post-apocalyptic city. There are many abandoned shops and empty beige edifices on every side; all of them built over a hot sea of sand, mud and rubble. At one point, exhaustion causes her to cease moving forward, and she stops before a tall, vandalized building with Arabic words spray-painted all over its outer walls.

It looks like an old Catholic Church...

The cross appears to have been forcefully removed from its large dome, and its windows have been completely shattered by thick bricks and stones. But it only takes seconds for Isabel to confirm that it was in fact a Christian place of worship; for in front of its chained doors lied pieces of resin saints and a headless statue of the Virgin Mary.

Precisely an hour later, the noise of a shutting door—along with the sound of keys being thrown over a hard surface—awoke Isabel from yet another incomprehensible, eerie dream.

Lennert had finally arrived. And Isabel suddenly became so nervous she couldn't decide between strutting out in her teasing outfit, or lying back in bed pretending to be asleep—for a phony, sweet effect.

"Isabel? Are you here yet?" he called out.

Her heart raced at the sound of his sophisticated European voice. She felt thrilled, for she was about to reunite with the kind of man she always fantasized about. And as she swayed out into the living room, she saw him standing by the window, looking out into the street.

"I'm here," she said softly.

The Dutchman turned his face around, scanning the sensual Latin woman as she sultrily approached him. He wore a long wool coat, layered with a long-sleeve navy cardigan. Around his neck was a thick grey scarf, matched with grey pants and black leather shoes; accenting his chic and smart look. Like the ideal gentlemen of classic literature, he reached for her hand and kissed it, without taking his eyes off hers for even a second. In her mind, Isabel strongly disagreed with Monroe's choice of cold rocks over the ever-charming Continental gesture. But as his lips parted from her skin, Lennert spoke a set of words that caused Isabel to blush in embarrassment.

"You look great in that 200 euro shirt," he remarked with a smirk.

"Oh my God, I'm sorry. I was just...um..." Isabel cut her own words mid-speech, squinting and grinning, unable to formulate a clever explanation for her rather conspicuous intentions. He, on the other hand, continued to behave hospitable and cool about the matter.

"Haha, it's no problem," he added. "Let's see…Chardonnay, wasn't it?"

"You still remember," she sighed amorously.

As he took the bottle of wine from the freezer, flashbacks of that date in Florida flooded her mind. He was still the same charismatic and charming European man; the one who'd taken time off from his business trip to spend it with her. They drank and chatted for a while, and even listened to sappy Guus Meeuwis love songs. Isabel then rested her head on his shoulders during a slow dance, and it was a new experience she hoped would last forever. But as their kisses turned more passionate, Lennert started holding back, grabbing Isabel by the wrists.

"Isabel," he said, "before this goes any further, I want to be clear about something..."

"Okay. What is it?" she asked, looking into his eyes with concern, not imagining that her expectations of a cozy evening would be shattered underneath his following confession.

"I'm married," he said bluntly.

She backed off in an abrupt manner. "Wait...what?

"Isabel—"

"When were you planning to tell me?!" she claimed. "And what will your wife say when—wait a minute!"

Isabel scanned the living room once again, realizing that there were absolutely no wedding photographs, nor any evidence of female presence except for her own jacket and scarf resting on the sofa. That apartment was in fact Lennert's realm during his days as a single man— or whenever he needed an escapade from his marriage. She noticed him drawing a small object from his back pocket. It was a gold band, which he deliberately put back in its righteous place. The embarrassment she felt over wearing his pricey shirt had now been multiplied by a thousand. But this time, she found herself trapped in her own foolishness.

"I feel I owe you an apology," he said with a soft voice. "I wasn't completely honest with you from the beginning."

"You think?" she replied, excusing herself to go change back into her own clothes.

For the first time in her life, Isabel saw herself without a contingency plan—one of the vital aspects of Event Management—for not having taken any intelligent measures before setting foot on the other side of the world.

"How could you be so stupid?" she mumbled.

"You aren't," said Lennert, who stood by the door frame, staring down at the girl with a face of empathy. "But now I have to ask you; why did you come to Holland? For me, or for yourself?"

His question, though logical, placed her between a hot sword and a spiked wall. He sounded like he wasn't taking her feelings into consideration, and more like an entrepreneur giving a motivational speech to an audience.

"So when you said I would be house-sitting, you meant—"

"I meant my old place, yes," he interjected. "Nicoline and I live in Amsterdam."

The name alone made her picture his wife as a tall, long-legged blonde gazelle—most-likely uptight—with great posture and an enviable sense of style. At the sight of her evident disillusion, Isabel could immediately tell that his intentions for that night had shifted entirely. But even then, he reassured her that he would do whatever he could to help her get around in Holland, until she could figure it all out on her own. As he said this, he took a piece of paper from a drawer and wrote down a number and address.

"This is the immigration office. You must go and register for a working visa as soon as possible. I hear it can be a long, dull process for foreigners," he explained.

She took the paper from his hand and nodded as a sign of gratitude. For as much as it bothered her, she had to recognize the validity of his earlier inquiry, and it was one she'd already answered in the back of her mind. Although she had to strike *European Romance* off her list of New Year's resolutions, nothing else seemed to really change in her future plans. She still had the opportunity to write a new chapter in her life, a new culture to integrate to, and was fortunate enough to have been offered a free and secure place to stay for as long as she needed.

"So I guess you won't be here tomorrow night either," she said, realizing that she'd be spending the last evening of the year all by herself.

After all, there was nobody else she knew in the entire country, and going out into the freezing streets alone was a risk she wouldn't take.

"Hey, did Gregory treat you good at least?" he queried.

"Um, who's Gregory?" she asked.

He scoffed, "The driver I hired to pick you up, of course. Polite, old Brit?"

Isabel stared at Lennert with puzzled eyes; for the man she drove with earlier that day was anything but old or British—and most definitely not polite.

"Wow, Gregory the Arab. That's a new one," she said sarcastically.

"What do you mean?" he persisted.

Isabel rolled her eyes, and told him everything that had occurred since the moment of her arrival in the Netherlands. With an expression of disbelief, the Dutchman took his phone out of his pocket and made a call. And like a hopeless romantic—even after being led down by him— Isabel still couldn't help admiring Lennert's articulate speech, as he spoke the complicated and tongue-twisting language she was supposed to learn in the near future.

"Well, it turns out that Greg has been sick with the winter flu since yesterday," Lennert said as he hung up. "I just called the car company, and it seems they sent a new guy this time; Sayid, Sarmad, or something like that."

Isabel shrugged, having little opinion on the matter, except for remarking that the so-called new driver had been rude and unprofessional. Despite the uncomfortable circumstances, Lennert de Graaf stayed with Isabel for a couple more hours. They ate delivered pizza, and finished their chilled wine. But when the night was at its coldest, Lennert got into his car and made his way back to his actual home; and into the arms of his naïve, pregnant wife.

5

NEW YEAR. NEW STRANGERS.

The next morning, Isabel was awakened by a low whistle, accompanied by a breeze so sharp that her entire body crunched the second she slid a leg out from under the covers. The cold made it impossible for her to concentrate back into her sleep. And after ten minutes of rolling around in bed, she developed enough courage to get up and look for the problem. Shaking with each step, she followed the noise that was coming from the bathroom, finding out that a small window had opened overnight.

"Whoa!" she exclaimed, witnessing her very first blizzard.

Despite feeling lucky for being safe and sound inside the apartment, she'd also realized how upsetting it was going to be spending such a cold day all by herself. She closed the window and remained staring at the magical, yet melancholic scene, while silently telling herself that it was way too late for any regrets. Alone or not, she had to focus on the real reasons why she'd moved to Holland in the first place.

"For new experiences, to see a new culture, to speak a new language…"

She continued to chant these words throughout the morning; while underneath the shower, and even later on as she stood before an empty fridge. In the entire kitchen she found nothing to eat except for a bag of white bread, half a jar of peanut butter, and a box of colored sprinkles.

"What the hell is this?" she asked aloud.

Right then she could understand why the kitchen was so immaculate; it had probably never been used. Connecting her laptop to Lennert's Wi-Fi, Isabel did a quick research on the neighborhood, and prepared her very own *expat survival guide*. Trying to find a supermarket nearby was the first task on the list, and there was one just around the block with the name of Albert Heijn. She changed into a gray knitted dress, a pair of thick leggings, and jumped into her black leather boots. Despite wearing a wool scarf and a matching knitted hat, she had the feeling that her clothes weren't going to be warm enough to face the environment outside. However, when she opened the front door she noticed that the sharp, cold winds had decreased, and it was the perfect chance to do her groceries before the storm came back.

"Here we go," she said, taking a first step into a thick layer of fresh snow, and wobbling forward over the bumpy sidewalk.

What could have been just a five-minute walk under normal conditions, on that day it turned out to be a struggle that lasted three times longer—but she made it. The store itself was packed with customers; most of them stocking up on snacks and beer for the upcoming celebrations. Isabel, on the other hand, went directly to the meat section to select a pound of their best beef.

"Sancocho it is," she told herself, while browsing for all the ingredients necessary in order to cook a hearty stew; tomato sauce, maize, potatoes, onions, pumpkin, carrots, cabbage, peppers, and many, many spices. She only hoped that upon returning to the apartment, she would find a pot large enough to cook it. Isabel was also determined to stock up on enough food to survive for a week, not wanting to face the harsh weather again for a bite to eat. As she pushed her cart through the alcohol section, she was shocked to see how people had almost cleared all of the shelves. Not being a fan of beer herself, she moved on and checked out the wine section, indiscriminately grabbing the first bottle with the word *chardonnay* written on its label. After picking a bunch of seedless grapes and several cheeses, she stood in the kilometric checkout line, making a mental picture of her single-person party later that night.

While carrying two large and heavy grocery bags, she fought her way back home once again. It was only the start of the afternoon, and being locked between four walls was causing the hours to pass rather slowly. After preparing her savory Puerto Rican dish, Isabel selected a random DVD from Lennert's vast collection. She never imagined herself spending New Year's Eve all alone in a foreign country. And for a moment she even started to miss Veronica, and the times they lounged before the television to watch Dexter and Sex and the City; an odd combination only she and her friend could have enjoyed simultaneously. But that night it was just her, a flat-screen, and a large bowl of highly-condimented soup.

Minutes away from midnight, Isabel grabbed the house-phone to call her mother; considering that Lennert never established any rules on long-distance calls.

"Hey ma'," Isabel whispered.

"Mi amor! I was waiting for your call. Is it twelve in there already?" asked Amelia, sounding thrilled to hear her child's voice.

"Yeah, almost," said her daughter. "How are you? Not alone, I hope."

"Oh, I'm good, dear. A few sisters from Church are here with me. Are you with Lennert? Is he treating you well?"

Isabel sighed. "Yes mom, he's great. Um, anyway, I just wanted to say Happy New Year."

"For you too! I love you and miss you!" Amelia replied.

"Me too, mom."

Hearing Amelia's voice through the telephone was soothing, and made her remember the importance of having loved ones close by; a privilege she wouldn't be having for a long time. Still, she knew that even in the distance she could always count on the incomparable comfort of her mother's loving words. That privilege gave her just enough energy to keep her head up, while looking forward to the upcoming days.

The following week was crucial for Isabel, for she'd be attending her first appointment at the IND; the Immigration and Naturalization Service bureau. Through her pre-travel research, as well as from Lennert's advice, she learned that it was mandatory to register in that office upon arrival into the Netherlands. Since the last thing she needed in her life was to get in trouble with the international *migra*, she made sure not to waste any time. After one large cup of coffee, and wrapping her body around five layers of winter clothes, Isabel was once again ready for the snowy streets of Rotterdam. Taking a short walk out of Blijdorp, she arrived at Rotterdam Central Station—from where she took a tram toward Coolsingel Road, after being told it would stop near the City Hall. Fortunately, the weather conditions had changed for the better, allowing the city to be packed with people; many of them on bicycles. Isabel found this particular practice amusing, and wondered how anyone would dare ride a bike with the risk of falling over the slippery roads.

It must be a Dutch thing.

Scanning the area carefully, she found herself surrounded by tall buildings from every side, unable to figure out which of them was the actual immigration bureau. She was beginning to feel impatient, and her fingertips were starting to hurt from the cold. But at that exact moment, her attention was caught by a person in a thick white hoodie and jeans, walking in her direction. Anxious to find her way, she stopped this random stranger to ask for some emergency guidance.

"Sure! How can I help?" he replied in perfect English.

As he uncovered his head, he revealed a pair of ice-blue eyes that were absolutely bewitching. Isabel felt like she'd lost her ability to speak, as she took a good look at him. The young man before her was utterly beautiful, almost a vision; tall and broad, with perfect mid-length golden curls, a scruffy blonde beard, and a masculine jaw.

"Are you like...a Viking?" she asked with childish wonder.

His rosy thin lips parted in laughter.

"No, but I shall take that as a compliment," he replied. "But that wasn't your question, was it?"

"Oh gosh no, I'm sorry. I was just...well, I'm lost," she said.

"I see. Now the question is; do you know where you need to go?" he asked.

As she showed him the piece of paper with the address, he kindly offered his arm to escort her to her destination himself—and she did not refuse. While she hoped it would have been a longer walk, the place was actually located closer than she'd imagined; through an alleyway in the back of the old City Hall.

"Here you go, milady," he joked.

"Thank you so much, really," she said with a smile.

"No problem. Veel succes!" replied the lovely guy as he went on his way.

Now that's what I call a charming European...

Before going inside, Isabel checked for her ponytail and outfit to be in place, making sure she looked presentable even under all the layers. She then took a deep breath and reached for the door handle, and all of a sudden she was startled by a group of people that stormed out at the same time, almost hitting her right on the face. It was a large Arab family—she could tell from hearing their language—and for some reason they seemed to be quite upset. But as Isabel stepped inside the building, she was even more alarmed at the new sight before her eyes.

"You've got to be kidding me," she whispered.

Through the large, rotating doors were over three-hundred people. They were sitting on chairs, on the floors, and standing about, and all of them looked pretty foreign. The place itself was just like any social services office, but gigantic; with dozens of information desks and cubicles, and large screens displaying the number of the waiting customers.

"Appointment? First visit? Information?" asked an irritated security guard.

"Uh, yeah, appointment," she replied with puzzlement.

The officer then pressed a button on a small machine, from which a ticket popped out with her very own number; 625. After picking her jaw off the ground from the shocking view, she moved around searching for a spot to sit and wait. She couldn't help to overhear that most of the people present were refugees from Gaza, Kabul, and Damascus. Many of them were accompanied by their relatives, who were already established in the Netherlands. Rather curiously, as Isabel sat among some of the Middle Eastern women, she seemed to fit right into their group, for they possessed the same sun-kissed skin, curvy figure, and expressive eyes. After waiting for over two and a half hours, the three digits on the big monitor finally matched those printed on her wrinkled ticket. The place had gradually emptied, and the deafening screams of unattended children—and some people's lamentations—had finally faded as well. Overwhelmed with anxiety, Isabel then made her way into one of the private offices, where she was assisted by a stern, blonde woman.

"Goede Middag, may I have your passport, please?" she asked immediately.

It was like being at the airport customs all over again; she took Isabel's ID and sat behind her computer to find out who she really was.

"Ah, you're American. Are you here by yourself?" the woman asked.

Isabel stuttered, "Well I...ye—"

"Who is your sponsor in the Netherlands?" she added.

"My...sponsor?" Isabel asked, confused.

In this case, a sponsor served as a guarantor that could support and act on behalf of the new resident if necessary.

Well, that's the damndest thing, Isabel thought, trying not to laugh from the irony.

Fortunately, Isabel was told she could apply for the visa as an individual, and was handed a couple of forms to begin the process. After sorting out her paperwork, she left the building and grabbed another tram towards the Municipality office—or Gemeente, as they called it—to register for the Dutch-language courses. Though it had been a very productive day, she was still anxious for having to wait a whole month for all her applications to be processed.

Once she arrived back to the house, Isabel gave Lennert a call to ask him for some professional advice; as he'd initially agreed to provide. He didn't pick up, but a minute later, she received a short text from him;

Out with the wifey. Can't talk.

Her whole face flushed from both embarrassment and shattering pride, coming to the bitter conclusion that she was indeed all alone in The Netherlands. Despite having an education, work experience, and having done plenty of research, Isabel still looked empty-handed if she didn't have any connections in that country. All she had left to do, in order to keep herself busy during those weeks, was to continue learning as much as she could of the Dutch culture.

After having experienced some of the coldest days of her life— which translated into slothing around the house, watching marathons of old TV shows—she thought it was time to get off the couch and go out to explore the city. For just one day, she wanted to forget all about her concerns and developing frustrations, allowing herself to discover the real beauty of the country she was living in; famous for being a culturally-diverse, contemporary utopia. All wrapped up in knits and wools, Isabel made her way to the station, picking one of the subways at random, clueless of where it would lead her to. She wanted to see a new side of Rotterdam, besides of the crowded Centrum and her dead-quiet neighborhood. But what she never imagined, was that she would end up stuck at one of the most dangerous parts of the city; Rotterdam South.

For some reason, there had been a problem at the subway tracks, and all passengers had to get out while it was being fixed. Everyone seemed annoyed by the small incident. But unlike the rest, Isabel had no important appointments to attend, nor someplace else to be at the time. What signified a bump on the road for others, to her it was an opportunity to get familiar with her new environment. But after ambling around for a couple minutes, Isabel felt as though she'd been stranded in the middle of Pine Hills—also nicknamed *Crime Hills*—a ghetto in downtown Orlando that never left the local headlines. Rotterdam Zuid did not resemble the North in the slightest bit. Some of the roads were cracked, and parts of the sidewalks were covered in all kinds of rubbish—not to mention, the air around the area reeked of pot and uncertainty. Walking alone through such places was not something Isabel was accustomed to. And the further she went, the more nervous she became. But there she was anyway; attempting to hide her chilled face behind her hair and an oversized red scarf, all while carrying on with her aimless stroll. This was definitely not her idea of cultural integration.

"Hoi dushi, ben je verdwaald?" asked a random guy.

He was sitting on a bench in front of a football field, along with two other dusky teenagers that resembled him. They all wore sweat-pants, tacky black jackets, white sneakers, and each of them sported the same dark semi-mohawk. Isabel eyeballed the small posse as they called her attention for a second time, but she didn't understand a word they said. Between scoffing and taking sips from their energy drink cans, the group of young men figured this out, and one of them asked her again;

"Are you lost, cutie?"

The harsh January weather was beginning to pierce right through her fingertips, spreading to her joints and taking over her head. At that point, she remembered the pain of sunburn over unprotected skin—how it stung, how it peeled off—and the current cold was just as unbearable. Considering her circumstances, all she wanted to do was to get back to the station, and being uptight wasn't going to get her that.

"Hi! Yes, it looks like I am," she chuckled. "Could you guys tell me how to get back to the metro?"

As she stood there waiting for an answer, the young men started speaking to one another in roughly accented French, but fluent nonetheless. Isabel smiled at them, finding it somewhat reassuring to hear the lovely and sophisticated language in that part of town. And just as she was beginning to feel comfortable around them, the whole group started to run away when a police car showed up on the scene. Isabel froze up with fright, watching as two tall officers chased them through the field, managing to catch only one of them. The unfortunate detainee jerked heavily, and began yelling slurs at the policemen while they handcuffed him—having his face pinned down hard against the damp, cold grass. Alarmed by the brutal display, Isabel rushed over toward the disturbing brawl and called upon the cops.

"Excuse me, is this truly necessary?" she asked.

"Step away, Mevrouw!" one of the cops shouted.

"What did he do to be treated like that?!" she insisted.

"What they always do; breaking into people's homes," said the blue-eyed officer, as he helped his partner drag the detainee into their vehicle.

"Kom op jongen, even rustig aan!" he added.

Isabel remained static, with her eyes and mouth gaped wide from having witnessed her first Dutch arrest. Internally, she told herself not to be so unwary the next time she'd wander the city alone—or at least that part of the city. As she went to sit on the newly emptied bench, she looked around and tried to figure out in which direction to go. She feared walking further away, and encountering even more troubling situations along the way. But as if God himself had listened to her silent plea—for somebody to pass by and give her truthful guidance—she heard the sound of a rough and oddly familiar male voice closing in.

"Looks like you took the wrong train," he mocked.

"You!" she muttered, jumping off the bench at the unexpected sight of the same man who'd picked her up at the airport; the same discourteous chauffeur who'd managed to ruin her touristic mood on her first day in the Netherlands.

"Yes, me," he said with smug.

"Right...so what are you doing here?" she asked with a tad of arrogance.

He clicked his tongue three times, "I live in this country for two years, and a tourist come ask me what I am doing here. Are you crazy?"

Isabel flushed at his clever response. And while softening her mien, she confessed having lost her way in the area, taking the opportunity to ask him for directions.

"This is no place for you. Come," he uttered firmly.

His tough appearance and commanding tone of voice made her dubious of his intentions. And judging from the recent incident, the stubborn girl wasn't too inspired to oblige.

"I'm not going anywhere with you," she returned. "Just point me in the right path."

"I go also to station, same thing," he added.

"I don't care," she retorted.

The off-duty chauffeur—who looked like the Middle Eastern version of Wolverine himself—reached into his thick leather jacket, and drew out a pack of cigarettes. He placed one of the smokes between his lips and glanced at the stuck-up woman in front of him, squinting, as if trying to figure her out.

"Okay, stay. Good luck," he said.

Isabel remained in the same rigid pose, with her arms firmly folded, watching as the fitness jock marched away. But as he got further, almost out of her sight, she found herself alone in the shady sector all over again.

"Fine, whatever," she muttered to herself. "Hey mister! Wait up!"

The vacillating woman hurried her pace, and caught up with the mysterious fellow. He was standing at the edge of the sidewalk; patiently waiting for the pedestrian stoplight to display the little green man— though from his sturdy looks and rowdy behavior, Isabel could have sworn he was a regular jaywalker. As she approached, he looked over his shoulder and smirked at her.

"You...again," he taunted.

"Look," she sighed," just help me get back to the station, okay?"

"Okay your Majesty. Yallah," he replied, pointing forward with his head.

They walked side-by-side for over twenty minutes, making her realize she'd gone much further from the station than she'd initially imagined. She attempted to share a bit of small-talk on the way; starting out by mentioning the sudden police incident. On that particular matter, he asserted—in his rather rudimentary English—that arrests were a common phenomenon around that district.

"Marokkanen, yes?" he asked bluntly.

"What?" she queried with daze.

"From Morocco, I mean," he cleared up.

"Oh! Well, I...I don't really know. Why?" she asked.

He shrugged, "Just asking."

He remained silent throughout the rest of the stroll; leaving Isabel with a large, neon-green question mark dancing above her head like a

Sim's plumbob. As they finally arrived at the station, she was both thrilled and relieved to see that the metro was running again. Stepping inside, she opted to sit on the row opposite to her short-term street companion—which allowed her to take a better and longer look at his striking foreign face. He sat quietly with his arms folded, raising a skeptical brow at the stunned expression on Isabel's visage.

"How did you recognize me so quickly?" she broke the straining silence.

His earnest demeanor faded into a sarcastic grin. "I can't forget your face…"

Isabel blushed at the unexpected remark.

"Oh…thanks. I—"

"Because you didn't tip me," he added with mockery.

She cringed, "Well! You shouldn't have pissed me off then!"

"You make me I lose my appointment!" he retorted with a fierce glare.

"Wait, how was that my fault?" she asked. "And you should learn how to speak!"

"It was my free day!" he added, rudely pointing his finger at her.

Isabel turned her heated face away from his, noticing that a few onlookers appeared highly vigilant over the boiling conversation. Both the expat and the annoyed Middle Easterner switched their attention toward their cellphones; as an ordinary tactic to ease their thriving tension. But for as much as she tried to divert her thoughts, the fervent desire to continue arguing wouldn't vanish from her mind. It was not in her nature to remain quiet, without a chance at defending her point of view. And as she lifted her head for a second time—with a sharp, impulsive remark hanging at the edge of her lips—her gaze was caught red-handed by the man's bewitching eyes. A single piercing glance with just the right amount of determination; that's all it took for Isabel to be captivated by his steadily-vexed countenance. Three seconds didn't go by before her strong-angled brows unfurrowed, as she felt defeated before the resentment depicted all over the driver's face. He stared at her unrelenting, while she remained baffled by the unexpected effect his intimidating scowl seemed to have on her. She suddenly felt lightheaded and feverish, as though she were sitting right in front of an intoxicating, unquenchable pillar of fire.

Who is this guy, really?

Her coy, brisk glances mixed into the hush surrounding them throughout the rest of the ride. And after four stops, the metro finally made it back to the center of the city; Station Beurs. She stood up with anticipation, but noticed that he remained in his seat—pensive and ever solemn. His journey wasn't over, unlike their unforeseen encounter. And as she stepped out of the subway car, she realized there was one remaining blank she needed to fill.

"I didn't get your name, by the way," she said.

"Samir," he replied firmly.

"Well, thank you Samir, for helping me out there. Oh, and I'm Isa—"

"Isabel. I know," he added, as a tiny curve appeared at the corner of his lips.

The wagon's door shut before she could react to the fact that he still remembered her name, even though they'd not been too polite to one another—not even on that day.

Upon returning to Lennert's place, Isabel's only goal was to dive into the soft, warm couch, engulfed in relief for getting out of the most troublesome part of town—with a bit of assistance, she had to admit. And as she thought of the handsome stranger who'd brought her back to the station, she couldn't overlook the bizarre sensation she had while sitting before him.

"Samir…" she whispered.

She sort of regretted not having apologized for her attitude, but knew she wouldn't have done so anyway; not if she truly considered herself innocent. But after having looked directly into Samir's dark eyes, Isabel had noticed something strange. Aside from evident anger, she saw deep melancholy. Then again, that day she was intrigued by much more than just the intense way this man stared at her. She couldn't help to wonder why Samir had so randomly assumed that the young detainee was of Moroccan background, as though his nationality could have had something to do with his abrupt, and violent apprehension. Curiosity kept on poking at the back of her mind, and seeing that she had nothing better to do that day, she decided to look deeper into the matter.

Her first move was to browse the internet for articles on Moroccan youth in the Netherlands, and the results were utterly distressing. Despite having heard about the low crime-rate in the country, Isabel was appalled to find out that most of the offenses that actually occurred, were specifically attributed to second and third generation Turks and Moroccans. It was odd to learn that, within such a culturally-diverse country, the local media focused so passionately on these particular minorities. However, the issue was far more serious and complicated than Isabel had anticipated. The debates on an increasing immigration issue were endless—especially concerning the latter group. And there were certain politicians stating that a part of the Muslim youth living in Holland—and other European countries—showed a defensive, aggressive, and criminal behavior that was supposedly triggered by their religious beliefs.

"Oh sure, because all Christians and Jews are angels, of course," Isabel mocked.

It was no secret that Islam had been causing a great deal of controversy throughout the past decade; the extremist views and practices of a sector were responsible for it. And yet, linking a religion to each and every petty crime that took place seemed completely absurd and unjust. After all, whenever people from the Latino community breaks the law, they are usually identified by the full name—sometimes their nationality—but never as a Christian, despite having a crucifix hanging from their necks, or La Virgen de la Guadalupe tattooed across their arms.

How ironic...

Amidst her research, Isabel came across a short film titled *Kop of Munt*, or Heads or Tails—as in the tossing of a coin. It was basically an eight-minute video presenting what the Netherlands would look like without its Moroccan population. Isabel found it quite compelling, as it reminded her of a movie she once watched called; *Un Día Sin Mexicanos*—A Day Without Mexicans. Both films sent pretty much the same message; with immigrants gone there is no one left to do the unwanted jobs; no maids, no gardeners, no nannies, and so on. In the Dutch version they showed what would happen if this particular group of foreigners wasn't present to fill certain stereotypical positions; such as chauffeurs, newspaper distributors, and garbage collectors. However, from all the images displayed on her laptop screen, the scene that Isabel found most bizarre was one in which a barber—the last Moroccan to leave the country—carries a TV satellite dish along with him as part of his luggage.

What's the symbolism behind this?

The strange phenomenon stroke her curiosity much further, as she felt urged to understand the cause of the evident prejudice against these groups. And yet, it merely took a quick read for her to verify her initial assumptions; the issue with the Moroccan youth was not quite related to Islam. By disregarding all details concerning religious beliefs and ethnicity—which were so prominent in the country's crime statistics—Isabel considered that the young guy arrested in Rotterdam Zuid was no different from a Hispanic delinquent back in the States. She thought it possible that both sides endured the exact same struggles; little or no opportunities of development available for them, deficient education, lack of family values, as well as having grown up with absolutely no sense of belonging. Merged together, there was a high chance that all of these factors managed to trigger some serious resentment within these communities. And reading of far more extreme and recent cases, Isabel learned that each one of these components had also caused young men and women to become more susceptible to joining radical militias abroad—all while being offered what they believed no other system or entity ever could; identity and life purpose.

On the following week—during a chilly late afternoon—Isabel was returning home from the supermarket, and was greeted by her downstairs neighbors for the first time. They were a lovely, young Chinese couple; Mei and Xiang Chen. And after introducing themselves, they kindly invited the newcomer over for a meal that same evening.

"Consider it a welcome dinner," the gentle wife said.

Looking down at her heavy bags, and relieved to be saved from eating alone that night, Isabel found no reason not to accept their invitation. After putting away the groceries, she went on to change into a nicer outfit—by simply throwing a black blazer over the same shirt and jeans she was already wearing.

As gratitude for their gesture, she stood before her neighbors' doorstep with a bottle of white wine in her hands. Xiang smiled as he invited his guest into his home. But the warm expression on his face faded immediately into one of awkward surprise the second he received the potentially-inebriating gift. He remained polite nonetheless. And a soon as Isabel walked in, the sweet smell of vanilla filled her nostrils delightfully, reminding her of her mother's own house. There were scented candles lit around their cozy living room, as well as several vases full of fresh white lilies. Stepping further into their home gave her a feeling of absolute peace and well-being; almost like she was standing inside of a sacred Asian temple. Apart from the warm-hearted couple, Isabel was greeted by two beautiful children; an 8 year-old boy named Jun, and a 2-year old baby girl named Bo.

"Sit wherever you like. I'll be right back," said Xiang, guiding Isabel toward the dining room.

Moments later, Mei reappeared with a large bamboo steamer and sat it in the middle of the table, while her husband returned with a big pan of fried rice. Mei went on to place little Bo inside her playpen, then gathered around the table with the rest.

"Let us say Grace," Mei said, reaching out for Isabel's hand, "Miss Isabel, would you like to lead us in prayer?"

Isabel was momentarily paralyzed, clueless on how to mouth the kind of words she hadn't recited since she was just a child—recalling that it was usually her mother who said the prayers out loud before each meal. She then cleared her throat and closed her eyes, feeling like she was in the middle of a stage, with a gigantic spotlight melting her face right off her skull.

"Hello...dear...God? Um, thank you for this lovely family, and for the meal we are about to have...uh…"

She paused and opened one eye slightly, noticing that the family was still in absolute communion.

"Ah, bless them for their kindness, and help those who are less fortunate. In Jesus' name, Amen."

"Amen!" exclaimed the family in unison.

"That was very sweet, dear," said the mother, causing Isabel to blush a darker shade.

"Thanks...I guess?" Isabel murmured.

The big, bamboo pot before them was divided into four parts, and within each of them was a different dish; mixed vegetables, steamed meat buns, chicken dumplings, scallops and salmon fillets. Isabel was asked whether she wanted a fork or a pair of porcelain chopsticks. And having mastered the technique after many sushi nights back at her previous home, she chose the latter option with great enthusiasm. But the banquet wasn't tempting only through her eyes, for in the first bite she could also taste the love and selflessness with which it was prepared.

"Miss," spoke Xiang, "your wine is in the freezer, if you'd like some."

"Oh...sure, but I brought it for both of you as well," Isabel replied heartily.

"Thank you, dear, but we choose not to drink alcohol."

As Isabel suspected after the sudden prayer request, she was sitting inside a devout Christian home. Even still, the loving couple offered her the drink, for they weren't too bothered by her having one glass among them. And yet, the red-faced guest considered it far more appropriate to respect their values.

After the succulent sweet and sour Chinese meal, all of them gathered in the living-room for tea and a warm dialogue. Isabel learned that Xiang used to be a cardiologist back in Beijing. But having been unable to get his license approved in the Netherlands, he had no choice but to accept a job as a supervisor of an East Asian supermarket. Mei, on the other hand, used to be an orchestra cellist in her country. She confessed not having made an effort to retake her career, but admitted feeling happy nonetheless, by offering private music lessons to children at the comfort of her own home. Isabel felt at ease among them, and didn't hesitate to speak about her own life in the United States. She also spoke of her impulsive decision to move to the Netherlands, and of her false expectations with Lennert.

"Oh, sorry to hear that," Xiang said. "We thought he was renting the apartment out to you as...well...as a regular tenant."

Isabel shrugged, "Yeah, well it kind of feels like it right now."

"You're still a brave woman for taking such a leap of faith," said the loving mother, as she zealously embraced her cute baby girl.

"This little angel is the reason why we came to Europe," she added.

But as Mei started to elaborate on the matter, Isabel felt her mouth turn dry. Two years back, Xiang and his loveable wife were pushed to abandon their homeland, along with their young son. They both explained how the authorities threatened to murder their unborn second child—by forcefully performing a late-term abortion—due to China's extreme one-child policy. Isabel recalled having heard of this issue before, but never imagined she'd meet someone who'd suffered under such a cruel regime.

"God saved our baby!" Mei said with joyful tears.

It was a heart-warming scene, and Isabel watched the family in admiration for their courage and faith. Still, she wondered how they managed to stay united—even through the critical circumstances—while her own family was not as fortunate.

"I think you guys deserve the award for bravery, not me," Isabel said.

But that story was not the only one the Chens had for sharing that night, for they also confessed having been victims of persecution due to their Christian faith.

China, as a Communist country, rejected all religions; each one of them historically-branded as an *opiate of the masses*. Believers were also labeled as being superstitious, to the point where Chinese Christians weren't even allowed to express official political opinions in their own land. However, due to the fast growth of Christianity throughout the decades, the Communist Party came up with the idea of allowing people to exercise their faith, but in a restricted manner.

"What do you mean by restricted?" Isabel asked. "You can't go to Church, or what?"

"Well, it depends on which Church," replied Xiang.

He explained to Isabel that during the Maoist regime, the communists created something called the Three-Self Patriotic Movement—a system of over fifty-thousand places of worship designated by the government itself. It was merely a twist from the initial aim of eradicating religion, into accommodating it according to the interests of the leading political party. In these so-called churches, Christians were allowed to worship under surveillance, with State-regulated sermons, and cherry-picked Scripture. But there were many people, like the Chens, who strongly opposed this organization. And instead of attending the State-assigned temples, they gathered in 'illegal' places of worship; known as the *house churches*.

"What happened to secularism?" Isabel asked.

"That doesn't exist," Xiang replied.

According to the couple, it was estimated that there were around two-hundred million Christians living in China at the present time. Despite the mentioned restrictions, Isabel thought that Chinese Christians were lucky to have their religion grow in such a rapid manner, and somehow backed up by the government. And yet, the two former members of the underground congregations didn't seem to agree with Isabel's opinions.

"Well, the Three-self thing doesn't really sound too bad," Isabel said.

"Oh, but it is bad!" expressed Xiang.

"Why?" Isabel scoffed. "At least you can worship. Besides, cherry-picking Scripture happens everywhere."

Xiang shook his head. "The head of the TSPM-Church is the Communist State, not Christ."

"What do you mean?" she asked

Xiang explained, "TSPM requires that all believers show absolute obedience and submission to the State. You're not allowed to preach outside of the assigned places, and they don't even let foreign missionaries come speak of the Gospel in China. They would be immediately deported if they tried."

As Isabel swallowed back her own words, Xiang continued explaining that there was a lot of oppression against those who chose to worship in freedom, as they tried to do in the house-churches. These gatherings were strictly forbidden, and often punishable by law under the excuse that they "disturbed public order". The Chens were proud to say that their faith in Christ kept them strong, even throughout the persecution and constant harassment. Nevertheless, he also admitted that the moment Mei became pregnant for a second time, they felt pressured to make a drastic decision.

"But God heard our prayers!" added the mother. "We wrote to an international Christian organization, and they helped us out of the country within a couple of weeks."

Isabel took a long sip of her mint tea, as she meditated on every word that was spoken. She found it hard to believe that so many people could be attacked or condemned simply over their religious beliefs—especially in the twenty-first century.

"It really sounds unbelievable, all this," Isabel said. "And, no offense, but I'm better off living as an agnostic."

"Well, Jesus himself warned us that there would be persecution," Mei said.

"Can't persecute me if I don't believe, or can they?" Isabel added with snob, noticing a small frown drawn on their faces as she said this.

It was not her intention to offend them, as she simply aimed to point out her own personal views on the matter. She agreed, however, that what the Chinese government did was awful. And yet, she also believed that religion was the cause of most problems within every society.

It was nearly midnight when Isabel went back to Lennert's apartment. Regardless of the evident ideological differences between them, she still felt fortunate to have met such an interesting and inspiring family. By spending time with them, she realized two things; the world was in fact a small place, and in order to hear an incredible story, all you had to do was step outside your door and listen.

6

"MEERVOUDIGEPERSOONLIJKHEIDSSTOORNISSEN"

At long last, halfway through February Isabel received her first letter from the City Hall. She was excited to learn that her paperwork was in order, and that she could finally begin the Dutch-language courses. They were scheduled for Tuesdays and Thursdays, from 13:00 to 16:00, and the classes were offered through the *IVIO Integration Program*—and their offices were located in the eleventh floor of a building known as Katshoek. This was in a street called Heer Bokelweg, situated right in front of a subway station; which made it possible for Isabel to get there without getting lost.

On her first day, she strived to get to school a little before the hour; looking to get familiarized with the building, as well as its surroundings. Walking down a narrow hallway, she heard a man and a woman arguing inside an office. Seeing that no one else was around, Isabel started eavesdropping on the conversation—barely understanding anything they said. All of a sudden, the door opened forward and nearly caused her to fall over. The couple flinched at the minuscule incident, while Isabel remained frozen with embarrassment. The blonde inside the office was tall and elegant; wearing an impeccable black pantsuit and red heels. The slim fellow had a more casual-classy style on him. He wore a gray shirt and a blazer, along with a pair of blue jeans and dressy shoes. His distinctive features revealed that he was originally from South-East Asia, but his strong and fluent Dutch made it obvious that he'd been living in the Netherlands for a long time. The stern woman turned her attention back to the man before her, leaning forward and muttering something at him. She then grabbed a stack of papers from a table, and abruptly headed out of the room. She looked over her shoulder as she passed Isabel, eyeballing her with arrogance before disappearing behind the closing doors of the elevator.

"Well, isn't she friendly?" Isabel remarked.

"Tell me about it," said the man behind her.

His name was Ray Pelengkahu; a classic rock and jazz singer of Indonesian descent, who also happened to be her new language instructor.

When the rest of the students started to arrive, Isabel noticed that most of them seemed to know the place like the back of their hands. They proceeded to get inside their assigned rooms, and the new girl followed her group with anticipation. The classroom resembled an ordinary hotel meeting salon; with a long white table in the middle, surrounded by cushioned metal chairs. The walls were painted a light crème color, and on one of them hung a rectangular white board with a list of long Dutch words and impossible tongue-twisters—these were quite a frightening introduction to the foreign language. The group itself wasn't large, with a total of nine people, including Isabel. But an interesting quality about it was that each of the students came from different countries and cultural backgrounds; Jamil from Tanzania, Fatima from Tunisia, Dorina from Romania, Amaité from Mexico, Sarah from Kurdistan, Amina from Morocco, Aiko from Japan, and Pete; a bohemian Englishman.

Mr. Pelengkahu asked everyone to sit in pairs, as he wanted the students to get acquainted with each other through a casual conversation. Since they were an uneven number, Isabel was left to sit with the professor to engage in the culture-sharing dynamic. While listening fascinated to his personal story, she could tell that he was enthusiastic about his work, and passionate about knowing people from other regions of the world. He possessed a voice that was smooth, European, and with absolutely no trace of an Asian accent. But his

Dutch was not always fluent. For in the late 1970's he'd migrated to the Netherlands to pursue a Master's degree in music. And then, after falling madly in love with a golden mane and a sapphire gaze, he'd gotten married—thus deciding to make Holland his permanent home. Unfortunately, the marriage wasn't as permanent as he'd hoped.

Though some of the students spoke English with difficulty, it was relatively easy to overhear and comprehend their conversations. Jamil was the youngest of all; a teenager who'd been adopted by a Dutch family of Christian missionaries. They'd taken him around the world many times, and he'd lived in more cities and learned of more cultures than he could remember. Such a life could have seemed amusing to many people, but he expressed being glad to be settled in one place at last. Sarah, Amina and Fatima had all migrated for marriage, while the rest of them were people who simply wanted to find better work or study opportunities abroad—except for Pete, who'd left a perfectly stable job as an accountant, to pursue his dream and become an artist in Holland.

"And what about you, Miss Alvarez?" asked the professor.

"I...I don't know. I guess I needed a break from Florida," she answered, catching the attention of everyone in the room the moment she mentioned having come all the way from the U.S.

"You have American passport?" asked Fatima.

"Yes, of course," Isabel said, taking her passport out of her bag and handing it to her.

The hijab-wearing girl examined the I.D. like it was an alien artifact she'd never seen before, and even passed it on to another student. Isabel squinted dubiously as she studied the scene, which made little sense to her.

"Lucky you," said Fatima.

"Why?" asked Isabel. "Don't you all have passports?"

"Some people don't," added the hijabi, "I still wait for mine, two more years."

Isabel looked unsettled by her words.

"But why leave America?" asked Jamil. "You didn't have work?"

"Oh, I was an Event Coordinator. I still am...maybe," she replied unsure.

"But...?" Jamil added.

"I—I'm just looking for something better right now, I think."

"You don't sound too sure about that," mocked Pete.

A momentary awkward silence filled the entire room. And then, Amina asked Isabel why she'd left such a *perfect* life behind, just to have new experiences in Holland.

"You think my life was perfect!?" Isabel asked, throwing her head back in mild laughter. "Sure, until the day my best friend stole my future out of my hands."

At that moment, the pensive professor could no longer ignore the tension building up around them, commenting that there was nothing wrong with searching for better opportunities abroad—for he'd done the exact same thing.

"Easy for her to say...pinche gringa," spoke Amaité, in an arrogant tone. "The only Latino thing about you is your face...maybe."

Amaité was the kind of person who wore no masks, but who certainly built high walls around herself. She was an indigenous Sinaloan beauty, with a college tomboy style, and features almost as tough as her character. Her remarks were always sharp and frank, and she possessed an attitude that Isabel resented from the very first day they met.

"What's so good about being an American anyway?" asked Pete, making scornful noises with his mouth, and causing another heated debate among them.

Fatima seemed to take Isabel's side in some way, not to applaud the fact that she was an American citizen, but to express her own personal wish to live in the *Land of Freedom*. Like millions of other people, Fatima also believed in the unrealistic idea that moving to the United States automatically translated into instant prosperity and notoriety.

"Now, now, that's enough," interrupted the teacher. "Everyone's story is different, but all deserving to be heard and respected. Is that clear?"

The students nodded at Mr. Pelengkahu's strong statement. But after listening to the stories of her fellow expats, Isabel felt embarrassed for not considering the many procedures some of them had to endure, before being able to set foot in the Netherlands. These were procedures and fees Isabel was exempt from by default, just because she was a holder of an American passport—not to mention that, unlike some of her classmates, she was lucky to be living at a house for free.

Intrigued by the commotion displayed before him, the professor started writing some new words on the board. They were instructions for the last course assignment. And for this project, the students were to work in pairs once again, in the form of an interview. They had to learn each other's immigration stories, then write an essay to turn in by the end of the term. To Isabel, it sounded like an interesting project her father would've strongly supported her in. She contemplated this, recalling that he'd already given her the genes and materials necessary for the job.

Despite her solitude, Isabel managed to keep herself busy during most days; between studying the new language, exploring other and safer areas of the city, and attempting to do home-based exercises— using Lennert's workout DVD's. She'd even found a park close to her neighborhood to jog in the mornings, but the cold weather wasn't always helpful. She'd wear a full tracksuit, along with a sweater and thick leggings underneath, as well as a wool scarf to cover her neck and mouth. But the freezing air piercing through her nostrils, still managed to give her sharp headaches with every breath she took. Unable to carry on with the finger-numbing torture, Isabel searched online for a Gym where she could train during the winter—finding the perfect one just behind Rotterdam Central Station.

Jackpot!

The fitness center was three-stories high, veiled behind wide glass windows that allowed by-passers to see those breaking a sweat on the cardio machines. The bottom level was spacious; with comfortable changing rooms, lockers, and even a small café-bar with a cozy red lounge. As Isabel took the stairs to the second floor, she was impressed by the quantity of machines—some of them completely new to her eyes. There was also a darkroom with blasting music, in which the Spinning lessons were given. Coincidentally, indoor cycling happened to be one of the few sports she'd been curious to try out. They also had a tanning room, a third floor used for aerobics, a spa, and an extensive weightlifting hall. But what she enjoyed most throughout her guided tour, was the vast diversity of nationalities marching up and down the large building— from native Dutch, Antilleans, Surinamese, Hispanics, Middle Easterners, to Asians. It was almost like roaming around the training camps for the Olympic Games.

During her first afternoons at the gym, Isabel gradually got familiarized with some of the equipment and exhausting routines. While at first she'd expected to easily blend into the colorful panorama, her presence in the gym didn't go unnoticed. It is said that Latinos can spot one another effortlessly, anywhere in the world. And that day, as she was approached by a guy from the Dominican Republic, Isabel was able to prove that theory.

"So, are you Dominican too—or Colombian, Mexican perhaps?" he asked.

"Half Puerto Rican and half Venezuelan, actually. But you were pretty close!" she replied with a warm smile.

"Whoa mami, I knew it!" he exclaimed with conceit.

She scoffed. "Aha? How so?"

"You got that hot swing goin' on when you walk," he added with a suggestive grin.

"Wow—that's...very observant of you," she remarked with a raised brow.

"Come on, it was a compliment. I'm Miguel," he said while extending his hand.

She stared at him indifferently. "Right...I'm Isabel."

"¡Bonito nombre!" he exclaimed. "So...you're new in town, or what?"

Just a she was about to respond, Isabel suddenly became startled by a loud thud nearby. It sounded as if a large metal boulder had been slammed on the ground, causing the entire floor to shake. To her surprise, no one else jolted except for her, as though extreme noises were a common phenomenon around that place. She looked over her shoulder immediately, scanning the background for whatever or whoever had caused such ruckus. But as she glanced at the brute culprit, standing just across the hall, Isabel gasped sharply when her eyes were caught by the same dark gaze she'd been unable to forget.

"Samir," she whispered, slowly raising her right hand just a little above her shoulder; sheepishly waving at the intriguing man who'd left her puzzled at the edge of a subway platform.

He responded with the same gesture, but then turned his hand around, beckoning her to walk over to him.

"Anda el diabloooo—don't tell me that's your boyfriend!" exclaimed the sturdy Latino, snapping his fingers in disappointment.

"What?!" she turned to face her new acquaintance again. "Oh Lord, no! Haha."

But Isabel's laughter was phony and insecure; like she were contemplating the bold assumption inside her head.

"Just a second," she said, before walking toward the enigmatic Middle Eastern man—and feeling somewhat self-conscious of her sultry walk as she went. For reasons she ignored, this time he portrayed a rather delighted demeanor at her unexpected sight. He wore long, black sweatpants, and a grey tank-top displaying his massive arms and shoulders, as well as a bit of his protuberant pectorals.

"Well, this city isn't so big after all," she said in a pleasant tone. "And I see you're still throwing things around."

He smiled confidently and offered his strong hand in greeting.

"Nice to see you again, Isabel."

The sound of her name in his deep, husky voice gave her shivers she couldn't help to feel running all over her body. His eyes were fixed steadily on hers, and he wouldn't let go of her hand just yet.

"Who's your friend?" he asked, tightening his grip and signaling Miguel with his head.

"Who—ow! I don't know, I just met him!" she responded.

He looked at her with intense determination, deeply studying her words and dubious countenance.

"Um, could I please have my hand back? You're crushing it!" she protested.

He then let her go once again, arching a sly brow as she twirled her wrist and stretched her finger joints.

"Sorry for that," he added.

Isabel stared at him with amazement for his rough manners—nothing she'd not seen before, however.

Moments later, another Middle Eastern man approached them both. His aspect was a little softer than Samir's, but both were nearly as brawny. They spoke in rough Arabic, sounding almost like they were quarrelling with one another. Isabel stood-by perplexed, unable to decipher even their hand gestures.

Are they talking about me? she asked herself, for they smirked at her in every glance.

Without clarifying her suspicions, the pair of jocks excused themselves to carry on with their training. A moment later, a small curve appeared on the side of Isabel's mouth, as she unconsciously gawked over Samir's ripped physique.

"Show-off," Isabel murmured with a grin, watching him perform a set of heavy bench presses.

He's rude and egocentric, keep walking...

"I think I'm going to check out the Spinning class," she said upon returning to her fellow Latino expat.

Miguel squinted and stroked his chin, then turned his face toward the area where Samir and his friend trained.

"Yeah...go right ahead," he spoke in a suspicious tone.

Not delaying her workout any longer, she grabbed her towel and water bottle from the ground and scurried out of the hall; heading toward the small darkroom where the stationary bicycles awaited. While she'd expected a real-life trainer to give the class, Isabel soon learned from Marcelo—the friendly Antillean staff member who'd given her a tour of the facilities—that it was actually a virtual instructor displayed on a screen the one who'd be guiding the group. The program was rather interesting, and it offered several amazing routes from different locations around the world, through which users could 'ride' as they cycled lined up before the large flat-screen. Only five Spinning enthusiasts, including Isabel, were taking the lesson at the time, and the majority voted for a scenery of the south of France. Seeing that the rest of them had more experience in the sport—not to mention very solid calves—Isabel watched attentively as they adjusted their saddles and handlebars, attempting to do the same with her bicycle. She struggled to find the right setting, feeling either too tall or too short as she tested every option. And in the background stood Marcelo, unable to hold his laughter back as he witnessed the comical scene.

"Do you need some help?" he asked in a chortle.

Isabel gave a sigh of defeat, "Yes, please."

After adjusting Isabel's saddle, Marcelo turned the lights off to create the ideal ambience for the energetic, yet artificial journey. The virtual instructor appeared on the screen, sitting ready on his bike and introducing himself as Evert—who was in fact an actual person, and a well-known fitness trainer in the Netherlands. He wore a skintight white shirt zipped in the front, and a pair of black lycra shorts, showing off his perfectly toned legs and thighs. He was tall, blonde, athletic, and possessed an ebullient spirit. And though he spoke mostly in Dutch, it was easy to understand his sharp and exciting body language.

The scenery before them was breathtaking. It displayed a simulated ride through the majestic French Alps on a sunny day—a sight far more inspiring than the actual frigid environment outside of the building. Virtual Evert faced the indoor cyclists, cheering on them while he pedaled vigorously himself. He would shout stimulating remarks during a heavy hill climb, then tell silly jokes about the panoramic view, as though they were all enjoying of the lovely weather in it. He made the entire workout feel fun and entertaining, aiming to make the participants push themselves even through the burn in their thighs and the fatigue in their lungs. His motivational skills managed to encourage Isabel significantly. And though it was her first Spinning lesson ever, she gave it her best and followed all commands as though he were really there, supervising them closely.

When the hour-long class ended, everyone in the room clapped their hands in victory and relief. Despite appearing exhausted, Isabel was complimented by one of the experienced cyclists, and was invited to join the group's weekly spin; a suggestion to which she nodded with enthusiasm. As the sore-legged girl walked out of the hot darkroom, the sharp sunlight in the main hall stung her eyes, just as much as the sweat running down her forehead. Isabel dried her face with her towel, and stood before the reflection of a glass-framed poster to fix her ponytail back in place. She then noticed another and much larger silhouette getting closer from behind. When she turned around, she couldn't help to flinch in surprise at the sight of Samir standing so close before her.

"Is this yours?" he asked in a languid tone, holding a white Samsung Galaxy and a pair of earphones she'd accidentally left in the other room.

"Oh my God!" she exclaimed while taking her phone back. "Thank goodness nobody took it—well, except you."

She wiped the screen with the towel and asked him where he'd found it, noticing that there were a few tabs open—including her photo gallery and Facebook profile.

"That man you speak with...he had it," he said.

She raised an eyebrow. "Oh, and he just gave it to you? That's weird."

"Uh, not exactly," he added, avoiding her eyes for merely a second.

She looked at him bug-eyed, taking a step back to balance herself amidst a sudden assumption. Samir folded his strong arms under his chest, standing erect and self-assured, while Isabel placed her hands around her waist, shaking her head in disbelief. He kept looking at her with conceit, and she found his expression so humorous that her initial look of disapproval evolved into a cheeky laugh she could no longer keep under control.

"Well, alright. Thanks," she told him.

He nodded. "You're welcome."

"Anyway, I should get going now, so..." she added.

Isabel reached out for his hand in farewell, and Samir returned the gesture by pressing his grip just as he'd done earlier. She tried to let go, but he grasped her just a little harder, piercing his dark, magnetic gaze into hers.

What is he doing? she wondered, noticing something in his expression that she didn't see before.

This time it was neither resentment, anger, nor melancholy—but true, relentless longing. He eventually released her hand, slowly, causing their fingers to brush against each other's for a second. It was a miniscule, yet electrifying friction that made Isabel gasp; unsuspecting that her own eyes would suddenly fire up, creating a yellow ring that glowed bright around her iris.

"I'll...see you later...Samir," she said, nearly stumbling as she made her way toward the stairs. Before heading down, she looked over her shoulder one last time, savoring every second of the gratifying attention. Without knowing, a part of her yearned to go back and bask in that man's intense stare—his onyx eyes said far more than his lips ever could.

Having changed back into her warmer attire, Isabel stood before a tall mirror and smiled at her latest memory. Something in Samir's behavior seemed uncanny, but it also started to make her feel better about herself, particularly after healing from her previous disillusion.

But how could he like me? she debated inside her mind, considering their first, and other awkward encounters.

She highly doubted that all of their misunderstandings and arguments could have somehow translated into some random attraction. In an attempt to divert her thoughts, she checked her phone for unread messages or missed calls, noticing that a new contact had been added into her list.

"Oh, sneaky mother—agh!" she exclaimed, trying to conceal a bashful smile.

Eager to demand an explanation, Isabel rushed back upstairs to confront the audacious bodybuilder; but appeared disgruntled to find out that he'd already left the building. She pouted her lips in disappointment and left the gym as well, hurrying to Rotterdam Central in hopes to catch him at the subway station. She stood by a yellow information booth, looking in all directions as she tapped her fingers on the counter. But it seemed useless at the time, to try spotting Samir's face in the middle of one of the most crowded places in the city.

"Mag Ik u helpen?" asked a man behind the glass booth. Isabel turned around and shook her head, smiling faintly, just before making her way back to Lennert's house. She tucked her hands inside her jacket pockets, camouflaging half of her face within her scarf when she came out the back tunnel of the station, and out into Spoorsingel Street. This was a straight passage, with both modern and traditional apartment buildings situated on every side, divided by abundant willow trees and a long waterway. Isabel crossed the road to take the scenic path next to the freezing canal, staring oddly at some gleeful locals who threw bread crumbs at greedy seagulls—all while sitting on cold, damp wooden benches. She secretly wondered if one day she could also learn to enjoy the chilled weather—or if she would stay in the Netherlands long enough to grow used to it.

She saw that it was around 16:30; almost her favorite time of the day. The sun would be setting shortly, creating a majestic, and golden glow in the skies that she adored. Isabel hurried home to watch it all from the living-room window; grabbing her phone to snap a photo of the artistic panorama. It satisfied her to keep a vivid memory of the wonderful view, in case any other storm decided to hit the region during that season. That afternoon, the skies were clearer than on most days of winter, and she was able to wallow in the picturesque beauty above the water canals.

In that same tranquility, Isabel retired to take a long, pampering bath. She lied back in the tub, listening to a romantic melody of Spanish folkloric guitar. With a soft cloth she spread the silky foam over her skin, closing her eyes, unconsciously submerging herself in thoughts much more pleasant than the warm, bubbly feeling all over her body. As if the universe itself had planned it, the shuffled tunes coming out of her phone's speakers turned faster and more intense; featuring a combination of flamenco beats and enchanting arabesque music. It happened unexpectedly, but at that point her thoughts had been invaded, pillaged and sieged by the kind of men on which that music had been inspired. In a matter of seconds the entire room was filled with the unmistakable sound of chalice drums, combined with the sweet lament of the oud and violins. Isabel was suddenly sucked into an epic fantasy; for her ears had become seduced by each and every note that was being played. She had found some harmony and contentment within herself at last. And would have remained at ease much longer, if it wouldn't had been for the rapid pitch of a wild darbuka; pushing her to open her eyes wide and fall back into reality with one sharp breath.

"I must be out of my mind..." she panted.

Later that evening, Isabel made herself a cup of her favorite hot drink, and looked for something to distract her mind throughout the night. She sat before the TV and zapped through the local channels, finding nothing of interest—or at least not in a language she could understand. She sighed frustrated as she walked to the bedroom, and the air coming out of her lips was the loudest sound in the entire apartment. She lied down and tried to fall sleep, but it was useless. And after a couple of minutes of spiraling around a tempting idea, she did what she'd been trying to hold back from doing; texting Samir. She sent only a few words through the messenger; merely a comical remark on the boldness he'd shown earlier that day. She then fixed her eyes on the phone screen, waiting impatiently for a response of any sort. The second his avatar switched to online, she sat up straight on the bed, eager to find out what he was going to say. But he didn't reply any words at all, and instead limited himself to sending a winking emoticon. Isabel rolled her eyes and tossed the phone aside, plunging back into the covers like every other lonely, silent night.

7

MAID IN ROTTERDAM

Fortunately, it didn't take much longer before Isabel received an anticipated letter; reading that all her permits had been processed, and that she could finally pick up her working visa. She danced around the apartment, thrilled to start hunting for a job. She felt pretty confident about herself, reassured that she possessed all the right qualifications and experience to find a similar position—if not the same—as the one she had in Florida. Raiding through the job-search engines, she could see there were plenty of vacancies available that matched her profile, except for one detail. All of the positions on the list required the applicant to speak fluent or native Dutch, which Isabel obviously didn't—at least not yet. However, she recalled having one last playable card under her sleeve, and decided to give Lennert a call that same day.

Despite assuming that he was out of town, she still hoped he could spare at least five minutes to help her out. She dialed his number very slowly, while practicing a sweetened speech that could convince him straightaway. The classy Dutchman picked up after the fourth ring, speaking in a soft and stealthy tone, making it evident that he was not alone.

"I hope my house is still in one piece," he joked.

"Of course, Lennert. I'm calling because I need your help with something else."

After thoughtfully explaining her concerns, she sent him an email with links to the vacancies she was interested in. Through the phone he sounded eager to give her a hand, and this made Isabel feel as though a huge weight had been taken off her shoulders. She really needed someone's support at the time—especially someone with professional connections such as him.

That week at the Dutch course, the group discussed the final project—which Isabel hadn't even begun thinking about—and they also chose each other's partners for the interviews. Being the last one to pay attention into the matter, and recalling that the number of students was uneven, Isabel saw herself without a partner, yet again. Luckily, the professor pointed out that the interviews weren't limited to the people in that classroom, granting her the opportunity to find a partner somewhere else. Mei and Xiang were the first people to come to her mind, as they were the only other immigrants she knew in Holland, apart from her classmates.

During a brief coffee-break, Isabel felt her phone vibrate in her pocket, and noticed she'd just received an email from Lennert. She opened it hastily, assuming he'd already moved mountains in her favor. But her hopeful smile faded into a grin of disappointment in a fraction of seconds. In the beginning of the email, he apologized for not being able to accommodate her in the Event Management position she desired, explaining that all he could do was get her a job as a common hotel maid.

"What!?" Isabel shouted in the middle of the break lounge, dragging all attention to herself in the process. She eyeballed the other students as they wouldn't stop staring, then she retired to take her matters elsewhere. Once outside of the building, she looked for Lennert's number in her contact list, nearly piercing her fingers into the screen as she pressed his name. This time, he answered without delay.

"Look," he said, "I know you're upset, but—"

"Upset? I left everything to come here, Lennert! I need a real job! How can you even suggest I work in housekeeping?!" she yelled.

"First of all, stop shouting! Secondly, it will only be temporary until you can speak Dutch fluently," he explained.

"But what if I send them my résumé?" she insisted.

"I already did. But they are still very strict about the language factor. I'm sorry."

Flustered by his disappointing statement, Isabel felt like she was losing her temper—not realizing that she was about to mouth an array of hurtful words that she'd end up regretting forever.

"Listen to me! I didn't study and work so hard all these years, just so I could come to Europe to clean toilets like some penniless, wetback immigrant!"

"Oh schatje," he scoffed with pity, "and what do you think you are, if not an immigrant?"

His rhetorical question felt like a solid kick to the face. But it didn't feel as terrible as the many judgmental eyes that watched her the second she turned around. Standing before the entrance of the building, were her entire class and professor; as they'd come down to check on her after her abrupt departure. They portrayed a look of both disgust and disappointment, while Mr. Pelengkahu mostly appeared saddened by the scene.

Isabel was overwhelmed by embarrassment, with her eyes shifting from one classmate to another. And just before they could see a tear of shame running down her cheek, she turned the other way and fled far away from their judgement. She crossed the road and reached the marketplace at Binnenrotte Square—a maze made out of long rows of kiosks and tents; most of them managed by Turkish, Indian, and Arab merchants. It was completely organized by aisles and sections of fruits and vegetables, clothes and shoes, rugs, antiques and countless other household items. It seemed like a diverse and multi-ethnic place;

crowded, colorful, and rowdy. And all that Isabel could hear around her was the tumultuous sound of vendors shouting the prices of their products. The nerve-racking noise was coming from every side, and it was suddenly combined with the deafening call of dozens of seagulls, and the blasting bells of St. Laurent Church. Isabel was paralyzed right in the middle of the pandemonium, feeling lightheaded as she struggled to breathe normally. But soon her sight began to blur, and a minute later there was nothing but darkness.

Later that afternoon, when Isabel managed to reopen her eyes, she was startled to find herself lying on a bed inside a hospital room. She flinched even more from seeing her arm connected to a long cable, which lead to a serum bag hanging on a stand next to her. Just as she was about to pull the syringe out, Mr. Pelengkahu stormed into the room and prevented her from doing so.

"Professor, what happened?" she asked, placing her hands around her head from feeling a sudden migraine.

"You don't remember?" he queried. "You fainted in the middle of the marketplace, Isabel."

All she remembered was having felt dizzy and weak as soon as she reached the square, never imagining that she would cause a dramatic scene in public. She was fortunate, for her professor had witnessed the whole situation from a distance, calling for an ambulance almost immediately. He'd canceled the rest of the lesson right after she'd ran off—following her all the way to the market—wanting to find out why she'd become upset during the break. Isabel was astonished, for she'd never experienced a blackout before; and she couldn't figure out the cause of it. She looked at Ray Pelengkahu with deep endearment and gratitude, for that day he demonstrated to be much more than her language instructor. He was the father she'd been needing throughout her entire life.

"I'm so sorry about what I said earlier," she whispered, with her eyes glistening in shame. "But right now I need to get out of here."

Taking a deep breath, Isabel pulled the syringe out from her arm and got off the bed. She then put her jacket back on—ready to flee from the scene as she did earlier—just before another familiar fellow walked in, stopping her once again.

"Whoa! And where do you think you're going?"

Isabel gasped softly, smiling at the lovely face of the same guy who'd escorted her to the Immigration Bureau.

"Oh, hey! I remember you. You're—"

"The Viking! Arrrgh—wait, no! That's a pirate sound, isn't it?" he joked.

Even amidst her distress, Isabel couldn't help to giggle at his innocent humor, nor could she help admiring his heavenly eyes and lively expressions. She noticed, however, that his scruffy beard was gone, and that he was wearing a set of blue scrubs, as well as a stethoscope hanging around his neck.

Do all doctors in Holland look like this?

"You gave us a scare out here, missy. Have you been eating well?" he spoke in a more serious tone, while reading a chart.

"Sure, I have. Why?" she replied.

"Well, you need to eat enough, and get your hypoglycemia under control."

"Wait—I have hypoglycemia?" she asked confused, sitting right back on the bed.

Learning about her apparent condition came as a surprise, especially since her mother never mentioned anything on the matter before.

"So that explains why I feel shaky so often," she commented.

"Indeed. Try to carry snacks in your purse from now on, ok?" said the friendly medical intern.

"I believe you're in good hands now," said Mr. Pelengkahu, as he politely excused himself from the room.

"I think so too," Isabel added with a warm smile. "But I still don't know your name, Doctor...?"

"Oh it's Maikel, or Michael for you, my American friend."

Maikel's caring attitude and genuine friendliness, were traits that Isabel highly appreciated to see in those surrounding her—particularly at the current stage of her life. Then again, as she recalled the previous events of the day, she wasn't sure to deserve any kindness from anyone at all. After receiving further advice from the handsome doctor, Isabel was finally discharged from hospital care. And when she walked out into the hallway, she found Mr. Pelengkahu sitting on a chair, waiting.

"Sir, I don't know how to thank you for what you did today," she said.

"Well, I wasn't just going to leave you lying on the ground," he replied, arching an eyebrow and grinning slyly.

Isabel chuckled at his remark, but her smile faded into a hard circle as she came to a new realization.

"Oh God, how much is the hospital bill?! I'm still not insured here!" she said anxiously.

"Ah! Don't worry about it, it's been taken care of," said the professor.

"What? How?" she asked.

When they reached the waiting room, Isabel gasped in surprise to see her entire class standing around. She placed her hand over her mouth, turning to face her teacher, who portrayed a loving, fatherly demeanor. She knew there were no words good enough to express her gratitude for their selfless gesture—particularly after all the inappropriate expressions she'd shouted that afternoon.

"Guys...I'm—I'm so sorry. I really don't know what I was thinking," she said with shame.

"It's all good, we just hope you're feeling better," said Jamil.

Isabel nodded vigorously, unable to contain her tears as she walked up to them for a warm group embrace. All of the students joined in, except for Amaité; who stood in the background with a face of strong displeasure. Despite this, on that day Isabel learned the meaning of selfless love and unity. She was an immigrant just like any other, and this was something she couldn't deny or try to embellish with her credentials or previously privileged lifestyle. The frightening experience of that afternoon served as a great lesson to trigger her humility. She could finally see that she was not completely alone in the Netherlands; because her classmates had become her new family away from home—a multicultural family of expatriates.

Back in the house, Isabel analyzed her circumstances a little more calmly, and realized that she had to accept Lennert's suggestion for the time being. As she opened her purse to get her phone, a small, white envelope fell out of it. She'd never seen it before. But as she turned it over, she smiled at the words written above;

Here's some sugary food for your mind and spirit.

-Dr. Maikel, le Viking.

She then proceeded to open the envelope curiously, and inside she found a small card with Biblical Scripture on it; Jeremiah 29:11, written in gold ink:

"For I know the plans I have for you, declares the Lord,

plans for welfare and not for evil, to give you a future and a hope."

A long, peaceful sigh left her lungs as she read the ever-encouraging words on the card. And though his gesture was sweet, it also made her feel a little nostalgic, for it was usually her mother who'd share uplifting Bible quotes whenever she felt preoccupied. Even when Isabel wouldn't admit it, these verses truly improved her mood every time. She placed the note inside her wallet, making sure to keep it accessible if she ever needed a little motivation later on.

Setting her pride aside, Isabel showed up for a job interview that Lennert had arranged. It was at a hundred-room boutique hotel situated by the *Oude Haven*—just around the corner of the place where she'd blacked out. As she stepped into the lobby, she had the notion of having walked into the set of an Austin Powers film mashed up with Pulp Fiction. There was a mix of both modern luxury and retro memorabilia all around; abstract European furniture, funky decorations, black walls, fluffy rugs and whatnot. It was nearly impossible to figure out the decade on which the whole place was inspired. But all of her dazzlement soon faded away as she was escorted to the service area, and into the office of the Housekeeping supervisor; a fifty-something year-old, small Portuguese woman named Luisa.

"So, have you ever done this kind of work before?" she asked, staring at Isabel with a bit of skepticism.

"No, but I've worked in the Hospitality business, and I'm familiar with the tasks."

Luisa nodded at her confident response. "Very well. Can you begin on Monday?"

"Certainly," Isabel said, smiling as she signed a couple of documents provided.

Despite that folding towels wasn't something she'd hoped to be doing in Europe, she still felt grateful for having found a job. She told herself that it was just going to be a temporary deal—remembering the words written on Maikel's card—reassured that better things would come soon enough.

On her first day at work, the supervisor appointed another maid to show Isabel around the hotel, in order to provide her with some training in the 'art of housekeeping'. The woman giving her the tour happened to be a refugee from Uganda, and her name was Ebele; a big, round lady with a grouchy face and a tight hair bun. At first, Isabel considered it a ridiculous waste of time for someone to be instructing her on how to make a bed. However, the minute she started to get her hands dirty, she realized that housekeeping was in fact a really tough job. Ebele held a timer in her hand while she waited for the anxious newbie to dress each bed. She would have to do it neatly and fast, followed by arranging the pillows in a way that made them look flawless and plump. Judging for the way the Ugandan woman twisted her lips and shook her head, Isabel feared not being able to impress Luisa any more than she impressed her. Having only about ten minutes to clean an entire room—twenty if it was one of the bigger suites—made the task seem arduous and exhausting, and had even caused her terrible backaches. An entire week went by before Isabel could figure out the systematic technique, in which a maid was supposed to sweep a hotel room. She'd finally managed to do her work on time; without accidently leaving traces of dust over the TV screens, and enabling Ebele's nagging in the process. By the end of each day, Isabel had to admit that even the simplest of jobs had very strict rules to be followed.

On the other hand, she found it difficult to approach her fellow colleague outside of work, having no success whenever she tried to make a connection with her. Still, there were times when she could hear Ebele singing, softly but beautifully, in her distinctive native dialect. She did so while she cleaned; perhaps imagining that no one was listening, or that Isabel was too busy in the other room with her headphones on. But it was impossible to ignore such a sublime melody, and quite difficult to believe that it was coming from the exact same humorless person. One afternoon, before signing out of her shift, Isabel sat down to speak to Luisa about her coworker's strange behavior, finding out that Ebele's tough character had its reasons.

"Her entire family is still back in Africa," explained Luisa. "She came here so she could support her sick mother and her two children."

The brave matriarch dreamed of bringing her loved ones to Europe as well. Unfortunately, her salary was barely sufficient to cover her own basic expenses in Holland. Now Isabel understood why—while all employees gathered to eat lunch—Ebele would sit all by herself, with a pack of saltine crackers and nothing else. She chose to have a scarce lunch every day, in order to send most of her earnings to her children. It was a heartbreaking, yet truly admirable story worth reflecting upon.

Isabel's weekly schedule gradually began to fill up with various activities. She worked Mondays, Wednesdays, and Fridays from 8:00 to 16:00—a little less if she finished her rooms faster. It was only on the remaining days when she could squeeze in her workout routines and Spinning lessons; and when she also managed to clear her head from stress. Getting up in the early mornings for any sort of physical training, would have seemed like a huge effort to most people. But for the past week, Isabel had found a much larger and good-looking inspiration to crawl out of bed and hop into her spandex leggings. After crashing into him several times at the gym, Samir had offered to become her very own personal trainer. Judging from his incredible physique, it was evident that he possessed enough expertise on the matter, and she accepted his offer without thinking it twice.

From the first day of training, Samir introduced his new client to his closest workout buddies; Ali and Adnan. They were polite to Isabel, but rather distant, and they greeted her with Arabic words every time. Out of all the guys at the fitness center, Samir was the most outstanding, and Isabel noticed that most other men respected him. He was also a strict coach, ruthless perhaps, and he wouldn't waste his time chit-chatting or resting more than it was necessary. Nonetheless, when Isabel first entered the labor world, she became the type of competitive woman who bragged about being self-sufficient, always too proud to ask anyone for help. For that reason, she wanted to show Samir that she didn't need him hovering around at all times during her workout.

"Seriously, I got this," she said to him, while positioning herself in the middle of the Smith machine.

Isabel stepped in front of the long barbell, letting it rest on her shoulders as she held it tightly on each side. Standing firm, she lifted it out of the security hook, then carefully took a step back, separating her legs about two feet from one another. As she began squatting—with a 20kg plate around each end of the bar—Samir and his friends curved their lips into an impressed moue. For the self-proclaimed, ever-independent woman, the exercise felt relatively easy during the first two sets. She was proud of her strong thighs, and wanted to show the big Arab men that she could be as tough as them. But just like a desperate soul trying a little too hard on a first date, Isabel nearly made a fool of herself when she decided to add another 20kg to the barbell.

"One...two," she breathed in and out, "...three...fo—ahh!!"

Right on her fourth attempt to lift herself, Isabel's knees had given out in strength halfway. All of her weight, and that of the heavy iron, would have lost the battle against the laws of gravity, if Samir wouldn't have been standing close to save her from an imminent accident. He did not hold on to the bar, however, but rather wrapped his great arms around her slim waist; pressing her body hard against his.

"You got this," he whispered into her right ear, with his lips slightly brushing the back of her helix. Isabel closed her eyes and breathed out an unconscious moan, feeling as though he'd somehow transmitted part of his own energy into her. She tried to ignore the sultry scent of his cologne, directing her eyes toward the mirror in front of her, and focusing back on her primary goal. With his appreciated, and rather compromising assistance, she managed to complete her routine of squats. Once again, Isabel learned the importance of having someone give her a hand—or pair of strong arms—admitting that there was no shame in asking for a little help from time to time.

8

ONE CUP OF CURIOSITY. TWO TEASPOONS OF PREJUDICE.

As April completely flourished throughout the country, the freezing afternoon winds were replaced by a gentle breeze of spring. Isabel welcomed the new and warmer season with open arms and shorter sleeves. But being familiar with the unstable local weather, she still kept her favorite jacket nearby. It happened to be April 30th, and the Dutch were celebrating one of their most important national holidays; King's Day—formerly known as Queen's Day. Isabel was particularly excited about this celebration, for it was rumored by other expats that one could feel real Dutch pride everywhere in the country, or anywhere in the world where two or more Nederlanders would gather to honor Holland's monarchy.

Or to honor the Heineken, Isabel thought with a chuckle.

All of the streets and homes were decorated with orange flags, balloons, banners, ribbons, and anything else painted in their flashy national color. From locals to visitors, everybody was enthusiastic about *Koningsdag,* and many people traveled to the Netherlands from all over the world just to take part in the annual event. Isabel excelled in speed that day while doing her housekeeping chores, just so she could go out and enjoy of the amusing scenarios and famed 'free-markets' scattered all over town. Though she wore her regular, casual attire; skinny jeans, boots, and a strappy, white top, she bought a pair of orange bunny ears to avoid feeling left out from the extravagant fashions of the occasion.

The temperature outside was lovely and fresh, and the afternoon sun rays felt gentle on her skin. She swayed happily all the way into the city center, admiring the fun and creative costumes of every person she passed. Those who chose not to disguise completely, opted to embellish their heads with flashy orange hats and large sunglasses. The Dutch became excessively agitated during events such as this one, just like whenever there was a match between Feyenoord and Ajax—their two major football clubs. It was an amusing sight, and the energy in the atmosphere was inescapably contagious. Isabel mixed through the multiplying crowds, yearning to be infected with their raving euphoria, then made her way to Binnenwegplein; another large Square surrounded by diverse shops, and packed with eccentric street performers. In there she found a food kiosk known as Bram Ladage, from which she bought one of Holland's most popular snacks; *patatje pinda*—fries with spicy peanut sauce, served inside a paper cone. Isabel heard of the greasy treat from her Dutch-language professor, during an introduction to the local culinary customs. The thought of salty fries dipped into a sweet mix repulsed her at first. But one day, Mr. Pelengkahu challenged all his students to try the inexpensive delicacy, proving that experiencing something new wasn't always a bad idea.

Unexpectedly, as if she'd just summoned him with her thoughts, Isabel recognized Samir coming out of the subway station, and walking in her direction. He wore a tight, black t-shirt—in which he miraculously fitted his massive arms—a pair of blue jeans, and black Italian sneakers. But spotting him amidst the throngs was not difficult, since his tough swagger and mean demeanor could easily make everyone else disappear into a cloud of smoke. As he got closer, she could tell from the gleam in his onyx gaze that he'd also noticed her. That thought alone caused a strong, but pleasant chill to run all over her skin; like she'd just been shot with a high dose of adrenaline.

"Well, this sure is a surp—"

"You're eating *patat*, in a costume." he interjected, crossing his arms firmly. "Look what this country does to people..."

"Oh come on, coachey. It's cheat day!" she replied in a childish manner.

He smirked. "Really? I will make you be sorry for this tomorrow."

His tone was both threatening and somewhat tempting. And his alluring expression made Isabel think of everything except dumbbells and treadmills.

"Anyway, you want to get coffee?" he asked as he noticed her nerves. "I know a nice place very close."

Isabel agreed without doubt, considering they could finally engage in a conversation that wasn't related to protein bars and supplements. They passed through a beautiful, historic street known as the *Oude-Binnenweg*. All over the long trail were many independent shops; petite bistros, diverse bars, exclusive boutiques, and vintage record stores—some of them closed for the holiday. Walking side by side, Isabel couldn't stop contemplating the unchanging seriousness on Samir's face, for he kept his head straight, facing toward their destination and nothing else.

Why does he look so angry all the time?

The populous café was located at a corner facing Eendrachtsplein; a public Square right in front of a large, black statue of what—at first glance—appeared to be a troll holding a giant phallus. And though the piece of art actually represented Santa Claus holding a Christmas tree in his right hand, it was still commonly known by locals as the Buttplug Gnome. It was quite the inside joke.

When they entered the establishment, Samir ordered a large cappuccino for Isabel and one espresso for himself, then they sat together at a table in the furthest corner.

"So, where are you actually from?" she asked.

He took a deep breath, "I am from Iraq. What about you?"

"Oh shi—wow!" she coughed. "Well, I'm half Puerto Rican and half Venezuelan, but I lived in the United States most of my life."

"Puerto...Rico...ah! Then you know Marco Antonio," he replied with excitement.

"Oh, you know Marc Anthony, I'm impressed!" she said.

"Of course! He's a great singer. What you think? That Iraqis only listen to bombs all day?

She gulped, "What? Samir, I never said—"

"Relax, I was kidding," he chuckled.

"Funny," she muttered behind her cup.

As shocked as she may had been by his crude sense of humor, Isabel was somewhat pleased to watch Samir laugh out loud at his own joke. He was the kind of man who displayed the deepest solemnity most of the time, even as they trained at the gym. Seeing him chortle with such spontaneity was a welcoming sight. Their first, and rather uncomfortable encounter was an event they still discussed, but luckily, one that they could finally dismiss.

"This sure is a pleasant irony," she said.

Even as he portrayed an agreeable smile, the fierce longing in Samir's eyes was unyielding. He demonstrated great interest as she described her experience in adapting to Dutch culture, as well as in learning the local language—which he confessed to have found absolutely dreadful the moment he started learning it himself. But after having exhausted most general subjects, silence and tension slowly began to grow around them. Isabel took a slow sip of her coffee, as her mind pasted together all of the information she knew about Iraq, in a hopeless attempt to show a bit of savviness on his country.

He knows Marc Anthony, and you don't know a single Iraqi singer, she thought.

The saddest part about it all, was that most of the details popping up in her memory were inadequate for such a colorful day. They were headlines; all related to wars, explosions, dictatorships, and dangerous, armed terrorists. The Arab world was a mysterious place Isabel still had not discovered, even in the slightest way. And most Arabs she'd been close to in the past were store-owners, and thobe-wearing Saudi guests who never addressed her at the hotel in Orlando.

"So, how did you end up in Holland?" she finally asked.

He stared down at his untouched drink for a few seconds.

"I am...refugee," he said with a reluctant tone.

"Oh...because of the war, no?" she asked.

"Yes," he cleared his throat. "And you?"

"Oh God, long story," she remarked as she rolled her eyes.

"Not longer than mine, I am sure," he added.

Not going deep into detail, Samir explained that he'd been born in Mosul—Iraq's second largest city—but had to flee the country due to the relentless violence that had broken out during the U.S. occupation. But then, he fell silent once again.

"Hey...you don't have to talk about it if you don't feel like it," she said.

"Shokran," he bowed slightly. "Really, not a good subject."

Samir's deep, manly voice was somewhat distracting, and his sharp pronunciation of some words made him sound exotically charming. Then again, after listening to a mere introduction to his life's story, Isabel was left curious, yearning to hear more of it. But she continued speaking about herself instead. She told him about her uncertain professional goals, and even about her missing father. To share some of her concerns felt somewhat liberating. Samir was attentive to everything she said. English was not his first, or even second language, thus at times he would ask her to slow her speech down. But even with the slight language barriers, he was polite and understanding. At that moment, a terrific idea came to her mind, realizing that he was the perfect candidate for the class project. While she'd initially been considering writing about her neighbors' inspiring testimonies, it seemed that Samir kept far more intriguing tales inside his head that Isabel just had to listen to.

"Samir, could you help me with a class assignment?"

"What assignment?" he asked.

"I need to…well…interview an…immigrant…about his journey into this country, the culture shock, and so on…" she tried to explain.

"Why you speak like this?" he smirked.

She tilted her head to the side. "Hm?"

"When you said 'immigrant', like it was something bad," he added.

"Oh no, it wasn't like that. It's just…I don't know," she said, crossing her arms under her chest and looking in another direction.

"I mean…I am an immigrant too, right?" she chuckled, the skin on her cheeks and chest turning crimson.

He stroked his chin and studied her expressions with curiosity.

"Hmmm, we can speak about it in the week," he said.

Isabel nodded, and smiled satisfied with his firm answer. A minute later, Samir received a call, which he answered as soon as he glanced at his phone screen. He spoke in Arabic, sounding calm in the beginning of the conversation, but gradually raising his voice, and his expression aggravated to the point that it seemed almost threatening. He slammed the phone against the table when he finished, taking a deep, slow breath, and closing his eyes as he exhaled. Silence surrounded the two of them for another ten seconds, before he came to gaze upon Isabel once again. She had her lips slightly parted, and her eyes had become discouraged and confused by his abrupt change of mood.

"I have to go. Sorry for that," he said as he got up from his chair, reaching out for her hand in farewell, as he usually did. Isabel looked in his eyes, noticing they still reflected a bit of rage. She hesitated to extend her own arm for a moment, yet ultimately obliged to the frigid salutation.

"Yeah...maybe I should leave also," she added as she got up herself, noticing that he'd not even taken a sip of his coffee—something she pointed out deliberately.

"I don't like it. I prefer tea," he shrugged.

"And yet, you invited me to a café. Very clever," she returned with sarcasm.

"All the women I meet like coffee," he said confidently. "I was sure you would accept."

How presumptuous...

"And I guess you've met plenty," she said as she pursed her lips.

A tiny smile dangled at the corner of his lips, accompanied by an inviting wink that made Isabel gulp.

How can he be so alluring, funny, and scary, all at the same time?

As Isabel arrived back to the Blijdorp district, she noticed that the lights in Lennert's living room were on. She rushed inside the building, and going upstairs she could hear soft piano melodies coming from his apartment. She opened the door carefully, tiptoeing inside to find the Dutchman sitting on the couch, and holding a beer in his hand. Like many other locals in the city, he wore two orange leis around his neck that contrasted humorously with his navy-blue suit. However, he also sported a rather annoyed expression on his face.

"Hi...I didn't expect you here. Are...you ok?" Isabel asked.

"Well, excuse me for coming to my own house uninvited—which by the way, I can see you have not been taking good care of."

During the first ten minutes after her arrival, Lennert pursued Isabel throughout the apartment, as she tried to organize her little mess. He nagged about the few items left out of place around the flat; shoes, empty coffee mugs on the surfaces, as well as books and stacks of papers from the Dutch classes. Isabel had been exhausted from her long shifts at the hotel, unable to keep the place tidied up as she used to in the beginning. He had a point, and she was aware of it. Yet his voice tone was draining and his arguments repetitive. Deep inside, she felt the urge to repay his annoying words with spiteful remarks, as a pretext to blame him for every situation that wasn't going according to her primary expectations. Carrying the dirty cups back to the kitchen, she noticed five empty beer bottles on the counter. Lennert had been drinking throughout the entire day—celebrating King's Day with his colleagues—but it was clear that the party was still going on for him. He opened the freezer and took out another six-pack he'd brought, soon reaching a point of intoxication where he could no longer hold back some of the most common side effects; grabbing the nearest woman by the waist and grinding up against her body.

"I think it's time for that raincheck, Miss Alvarez," he whispered in her ear, as he attempted to run his hands under her top.

Isabel jerked fiercely until he stumbled from his own drunkenness, falling forward and banging his head against the counter.

"Kutwijf!" he shouted, as he sat on his knees and placed a hand over his aching head. The batter had been so rough, that the skin of his eyebrow had been cut open. And he started calling her by many other foreign names, using adjectives she still could not even pronounce.

"What is the matter with you?!" she asked enraged. "You are not the Lennert I met back in America."

As he got himself back together, he grabbed a napkin to wipe the blood off his face, then started to laugh with irony. He took a moment to fix his shirt and blazer, then faltered towards the front door while mouthing the very words she feared to hear.

"Maybe you should start looking for your own place."

The exact moment the door shut behind him, all of her built-up frustration burst out at once. She stormed back into the kitchen, and one by one she slammed the empty Heineken bottles against the wall, while screaming and losing even her last nerve. Isabel's life had been taking a series of strange twists—precisely from the day that she assumed to have become the boss of that resort in Florida. And now, in her attempt to find new experiences and better opportunities, she found herself just as unlucky. She felt lost, and believed that not even her mother's words could comfort her that night.

When she finally calmed back down, and the tears in her eyes had dried up, Isabel began picking up all the pieces of broken glass from the wooden floors. She continued cleaning the living room, placing all of her study papers inside a folder, and finding the instructions to Mr. Pelengkahu's assignment in the bottom of the stack. Though the due-date to turn the project in was around two months away, she thought it a good idea to sit down and begin preparing the query. And on a piece of paper, Isabel wrote what she'd learned about Samir so far, and her mind was soon diverted away from her previous tantrum.

"He's an Iraqi refugee," she said. "He speaks Arabic...hmmm...he must be a Muslim too," she concluded.

Isabel wondered why he'd never mentioned anything about his religion before. After all, the subject of Islam had become the talk of the whole decade, and most likely of many more years to come. She remembered having heard that devout Muslims were generally strict and proper, and the men usually kept their distance from strange women, as part of their religious values. In contrast, Isabel and Samir had become good friends at the gym, and the circumstances pushed them to become rather close—or close and personal, depending on which exercise they did.

"Well, maybe he's not so devout then," she chuckled.

As she submerged further into her brainstorm, she started to see another purpose to the whole project. The list of questions had gone over three pages—much more than she'd anticipated—making her realize how little she knew about other people's cultures. She began thinking of all the individuals she'd encountered in the past months. Each one of them was unique, molded by strong traditions and intriguing customs. Isabel was excited about the interview, and hoped to learn more about the ethnic diversity within the Netherlands. Nonetheless, she'd come to the staggering conclusion that at the end of the course she'd know far more about somebody else's culture than her own. For Isabel, it had always been easier to speak about her life as any other American citizen, than to explore any subjects concerning her sense of national identity.

Browsing through her things, she found the old journal her father had given her.

"Perfect!" she exclaimed, finding it useful for the assignment.

She could write the whole interview on it, without necessarily creating another mess of scattered papers in Lennert's living-room. Apart from the general details she already knew about Samir, she also wrote down his physical description, as a way to make his character come alive on the pages;

Intense midnight eyes, enticing full lips, and the solid arms and legs of a warrior, all attached to a perfectly sculpted torso...

Isabel remained in that line of thought for a few minutes, unsuspecting that her memories of him would turn into another vivid fantasy. But all of a sudden, her engaging mental trip was interrupted by a phone ring, causing her to jump in absolute spook. Isabel groaned, but as she checked the home-phone's caller ID, she was delighted to see her mother's number displayed on it.

"Ma', so glad you called," Isabel sighed.

"Hello dear," Amelia said, "You haven't left my mind all day, and it got me worried. Is everything okay?"

"Yes, of course. Why wouldn't it be?" Isabel let out a forged chuckle.

"I don't know, just a feeling. Have you found a job yet?" she asked.

Isabel delayed her answer for a few seconds, then completely embellished her current reality, stating that she'd started working in the same field as she did back in the States. Amelia reacted with joy at her daughter's false words—while on the other hand, Isabel felt ashamed for lying to her mother. Even still, she knew it would have been far worse to fill her head with unnecessary concerns. Unfortunately, a mother's fears could often discourage children from taking risks in life, and she was certain that Amelia would have begged her to return home immediately if she knew the truth. Now that she'd finally received her visas, such an idea was surely out of the question.

On the first week of May, Mr. Pelengkahu brought tickets to all his students to see a local Brit-rock band called *Scarlet,* for which his own Frank Zappa tribute band would be opening. After everything that had been going on, Isabel was more than thrilled to go on a night-out and watch a performance of any sort. Her personal tastes in music usually varied from Indie rock, world beat, to a selective list of Spanish ballads. And though she was Latina, Isabel hardly ever listened or danced to Latin music. She found it a fortunate coincidence for the show to take place on May 9th; the same date of her birthday. She wanted to look and feel good that night, and resolved treating herself to some new clothes. After getting off her shift, she passed by the shops in Rotterdam Centrum, to find an outfit that could be both trendy and adequate for the event. H&M usually carried that *alternative* look she searched for, and with little effort she found a *Ramones* tank-top, and a pair of faded skinny jeans to combine with her boots. Strutting back to the nearest metro station, Isabel stepped into a crowded subway car, and her evening was brightened even further, at the sight of a beautiful and unforgettable face.

"Hello again, Viking Maikel!" she greeted him with childish enthusiasm.

The young doctor lifted his head, diverting his heavenly eyes away from a thick book he was submerged in, and smiled at her with the same level of joy. He invited Isabel to sit by him, and she complied without delay. She thanked him for his deep and meaningful card, and even praised him for his dedication and genuine concern for people. Talking to him was comforting, and though it'd been just the third time they'd met, it felt like they'd always known each other—or at least like he knew her, entirely. She told him about that evening's concert, expressing her excitement for spending quality time with the same generous students who'd paid for her treatment at the hospital.

"I'm glad you don't feel so alone anymore," he remarked. "By the way, Happy Birthday!"

"Wha—how did you know?!" she gasped.

"Well, back at the ER I kind of borrowed your passport to take your information, so..."

"Oh, right! Thanks!" she giggled. "It's nice to hear someone say it."

"Then you're very welcome!" he said. "And don't be discouraged, dear. Use your time in the Netherlands as an opportunity to grow. Learn from everything and everyone around."

She looked into his peaceful, cerulean eyes, completely mesmerized by the sound of his voice and the encouraging words that came out of his lips.

"And trust me on this," he added, "trials are inevitable. But in the end, everything happens for a reason. The key is to keep on believing."

His advice filled her heart with a hope she thought she'd lost— especially after her last day inside Monsieur Duclerc's office. And as he kept on speaking, she felt engulfed by a strong current of positive energy.

"Alright, I'm off here," he then said.

But before leaving her side, Maikel gave Isabel three tender kisses; one on each cheek, and the last one planted softly on her forehead. As he stepped out into the platform, Isabel peeped through the window and sighed with pure endearment. Waiting for him by the escalators was a lovely, young woman. She was a true Celtic beauty; with long, red hair, and big eyes as clear as the Caribbean skies.

"And so the Norse god has a goddess," she whispered with contentment, watching them walk away hand-in-hand.

Later that night, Isabel arrived at a concert hall known as *The Lucius Theatre*. Walking up and down Kruiskade Street, she looked for her classmates and spotted them waving from the middle of the crowd line. As she approached them, she noticed the absence of the Muslim women in their class, except for one; Sarah. She was a Kurdish woman who'd been living in Denmark most of her life, but who'd recently moved to the Netherlands to get married with another Kurdish national. In contrast to the other Muslim girls in the group, Sarah never wore the hijab; always keeping her long, black hair lose. She was a professional makeup artist, fashionable, and really beautiful.

"Where are Amina and Fatima?" Isabel asked as she scanned the area.

The rest of them chuckled at her question, and explained that their religion forbade them from participating of such activities.

"It's *haram*, forbidden," said Sarah.

Isabel apologized for her ignorance, and once again expressed being glad for not affiliating to any religion. In her mind, she tried to comprehend why anyone would submit to such a repressive lifestyle, having the slightest of freedoms snatched right off their hands.

The venue was not as large as others located around the city. But judging by the length of the line, Isabel could tell that it was going to be a full concert. Knowing little about the band, she took her phone out and looked them up online, discovering the most unexpected of details; two of the band members were Puerto Rican.

Well, this is random.

Isabel was then stung by curiosity, impatient to find out what could happen if they'd let two Puerto Ricans play British rock, inside a local Dutch band. Either way, she would have to wait until after her professor's performance to find out.

When Mr. Pelengkahu came out on stage, his students cheered louder than anyone else in the hall. He wore his usual work attire, keeping his medium dark-brown hair lose, and his chilled beer close by.

"Who's ready for some rock and blues!?" he asked the whole audience, just before the group started playing Zappa's *Trouble Every Day*.

Isabel then closed her eyes, submerging in the mellow sound of the saxophone and bass, which blended gracefully with her professor's sultry voice. Deep down, she wondered if he'd chosen that song on purpose—which criticized sensationalist press, racism, and social injustice—as a way to send his multi-racial students a clear message.

Veronica would have loved this, she thought, recalling the many festivals and cultural fairs they attended together in college.

When it was time for the main band's performance, Isabel spotted her fellow Hispanics almost immediately; both sharply dressed in a Geekish-elegant style. One of them was a guitarist, while the other rocked hard behind the drum set—their caramel skin and dark hair gave them away instantly. Right in the middle of a song, Isabel was again fascinated by the music; this time by the rhythmic combination of a bongo-solo with the entrancing cry of the electric guitar. Despite that she was one of the very few people in the crowd who didn't know the lyrics, it didn't stop her from enjoying herself throughout the entire gig. At the end of the show, Isabel approached the guitarist and congratulated him for his work and amazing skill. His name was Ramiro; a natural of the city of *Mayagüez*, who'd already been living in the Netherlands for several years. He was also polite enough to share some quick advice, and tips for adapting to Holland as smoothly as possible.

"It's difficult at first, but you've got to learn from the culture and pick up the positive things it has to offer. Trust me, there are many," he said, as he ran his fingers through his long, brown hair.

Though it might have been easy for a rising star to make such optimistic statements, she still had to admit that he had a point—which reminded her of Maikel's own words. But as far as adapting to the Dutch culture, Isabel described it as herself attempting to ride a bicycle, while balancing two other people on the rear rack and handlebars. And if she failed the difficult maneuver, life in Holland was going to be like a big chunk of bittersweet licorice she was never going to be able swallow.

After leaving the hall, the group decided to continue the party at Stadhuisplein; a spacious plaza full of bars, restaurants, and a vast *multi-culti* crowd. Standing out in the square was deafening, as every pub was placed right next to the other, playing a mix of the loudest and tackiest techno songs of all time. Having scanned the whole area, the students picked a place at random and sat around the tables outside.

"Alrighty, time for some bitter! Shall we?" exclaimed Pete, in his natural classy accent.

While Isabel started out with her usual sweet chardonnay, the rest of them opted for ordering beer and strong spirits. The glasses and large jugs kept on coming. Their laughter became louder, and the evening seemed a lot livelier. But right after the third round, Isabel started to feel a mild headache, and recalled that she'd been roaming around with an empty stomach. Then again, she didn't want to interrupt her classmates' fun chatter, for it'd been long since the last time she'd actually gone on a night out. But then, as she feared it would, the conversation shifted to one she couldn't contribute in; her national identity.

"Tell us, Isabel, what do you miss most about your country?" asked Sarah.

"Which one?" Isabel replied humorously. "I told you, I was raised in the United States. I don't recall anything about South America."

"Yes, we remember," spoke an annoyed Amaité. "But don't you know something about your Latin roots?" she scoffed.

Isabel scratched her head, unable to think of anything except for dull historical facts she'd read on Wikipedia, as well as some cultural trends, and the recipes her mother taught her to cook. At that moment, she felt left out once again, just like she did in school as a young girl, being unable to elaborate in such an important subject.

After one more round of booze, they decided to hop into another pub, but Isabel was exhausted and just wanted to jump into bed.

"Come on girl, it's your birthday," Sarah insisted, making the peer pressure too intense for her to resist.

"Fine! One last drink!" Isabel lastly agreed.

They sang classic rock songs, while lurching and rambling the whole way to a popular bar called *De Witte Aap*—or The White Ape. Once again they sat down in front of the establishment, gradually relaxing after an exciting night.

"I don't want to sound racist, but—"

"Stop it Pete! Nothing good ever comes after that!" exclaimed Jamil as he burst out in laughter. "No, I'm joking, go ahead."

Pete shook his head, slightly annoyed by Jamil's mockery.

"I'm only trying to understand why Arab blokes always look like they're about to give someone a good kicking," he remarked, while stealthily pointing at a group of Middle Eastern men that stood across the street.

"Be quiet!" whispered Sarah, popping her eyes at the bold Englishman. "One of them is glancing this way! He looks kind of familiar too..."

"I think he's actually looking at Isabel," said Dorina, adding a cheeky smirk. "Do you know him?"

Due to her mild level of intoxication, Isabel couldn't help to look over her shoulder in a rather abrupt and obvious manner. While the rest of the group groaned and threw their heads back from her lack of discretion, she gasped in both surprise and glee from locking eyes with her mysterious friend and personal trainer. Without thinking twice, she got up from her chair and approached him—displaying a struggled but coquettish strut as she went.

"Hey coach! Guess how many calories are inside a frozen daiquiri." she joked.

"Better don't tell me," he replied, greeting her with a confident grin and a firm handshake.

He then turned around for a moment, and addressed the men that accompanied him.

"We go eat. Come with us, I think you need it also," he said with a commanding tone.

"Uh, who are they?" she asked, staring at the group skeptically.

"Cousins," he answered plainly.

"Ok, well, I'm actually with my classma—" she gasped as she turned her head towards the bar. "Guys?"

The table where she previously sat was empty, and all her classmates had left the square. Seeing that she had no other people to run back to—and that she'd been dizzy from both hunger and the alcohol in her system—Isabel agreed to join Samir and his fierce wolfpack. She listened curiously as they spoke among each other in Arabic, then walked with them around the corner of *Coolsingel*, finally crossing the road until reaching another row of bars and food establishments.

"You like *döner*?" asked Samir as they entered a small Turkish restaurant. She had no idea what he was talking about, but judging from the delightful smell, she could tell it was going to be a tasty meal. And the first thing that caught her eye in the entire place, was the large piece of meat being roasted on a vertical rotisserie.

"Oh! Gyros!" Isabel exclaimed, as she recognized the Mediterranean dish.

"No, no! This is Turkish, not Greek!" protested a man with a thick black moustache, who stood behind the counter. Samir and his relatives chuckled at the scene, while their female companion feared having said something offensive. But as they gathered around a table, Samir explained that it was easy to confuse the names, for many dishes around that region were very similar.

"Greeks and Turks just won't admit it," added one of the guys. "Sorry, I'm Rami."

"Nice to meet you," she replied, glancing curiously at the thick cross pendant hanging around his neck.

A crucifix? That's odd...

"And these are my brothers, Rabih and Rahim," he added.

Rami, Rabih, Rahim...I'm already confused.

When the food was served, Isabel watched amazed as the primarily stern expression on their faces shifted into one of full enjoyment. The four Iraqis clearly shared plenty of similar bodily features—*the* nose, raven hair, and deep, dark eyes—but Samir was the only one with the overly-muscular physique. Apart from that, Isabel also noticed that his table manners were a bit more primal in contrast to his cousins' ways.

"Are you going to make me do extra cardio for all this?" she asked Samir, while stuffing her mouth with cheesy *pide* slices.

"I will tell myself this night never happened," he said as he stroked his finely trimmed chin, portraying a phony look of introspection.

She tittered at his comical expressions, as they were always rare and unpredictable. But having finished their delicious meal and entertaining chat, she realized that it was almost three in the morning, and feared that all public transportation had stopped for the night—except perhaps for the after-hour buses. She then thanked the intriguing men for their lovely company, just before rushing outside, and into the predictable rain of the Netherlands.

"Perfect!" she blurted angrily, and took a few steps back to find shelter under the outer roof of the restaurant. As she continued to reflect on the ugly panorama, she heard a metallic click next to her. Samir had gone outside to light yet another cigarette. He glanced skyward and then at the frustrated girl—who groaned as she recalled how her group had abandoned her earlier.

"Don't worry, we take you home now," he said calmly.

"Oh, really I don't want to give you guys any trouble," she replied.

"No trouble, you're welcome," he said politely, adding one of those teasing winks of his.

Don't laugh, Isabel.

They waited safely and dry under the roof for around ten minutes—until the intensity of the rain had diminished—then made their way to Rami's car. It was a small two-door silver Peugeot, in which she didn't expect all five of them to fit comfortably. And while Samir should have opted to call *shotgun* on the rest of them, the sturdy fellow chose to squeeze himself into the back seat, next to Isabel and Rabih. She sat in the middle, but with much difficulty. And her only breathing options were to lean forward and risk flying out the windows—due to Rami's reckless driving—or try sitting back while leaning hard against either Samir or his cousin. She felt a tremendous urge to laugh at the situation; analyzing what the odds were of her ending up inside a tiny car, with a bunch of Middle Eastern men, and at such strange hours.

"I really must be out of my mind..." she whispered.

"Are you ok?" asked Samir with preoccupied eyes.

"I can't...sit right," she replied, trying to make her Latina hips fit between the two men.

Samir had noticed her discomfort from the moment they got inside the car, and yet he waited until they'd hit the road to actually say something about it—and do something about it too. Without a warning, he pulled Isabel close against him, causing her to lean almost on top of his body.

"Better?" he asked, while putting his arm around her.

She could only nod slowly, in a state of both disbelief and heavenly daze. The rest of them didn't say anything about the peculiar scene, nor did they even stare—except for Rami, who asked for her home address. The ride wasn't too long, but interesting nonetheless. The Iraqis seemed to party harder inside the tiny vehicle, than what they did back at the notorious bar street—singing out loud in Arabic, and clapping along with the melodies coming from the radio. And when Isabel was finally dropped off at Lennert's place, she was moved to see that the men didn't drive away until she was safe inside the building. Even though she'd been deserted by her whole class earlier, she could still say that it'd been the best birthday of her entire life.

The next day at IVIO, however, she wanted to ask why they'd left her in the first place. But then, as she entered the classroom, she was the one being interrogated and made fun of.

"Well, well, well, how was your time with Samir?" asked Dorina, in her strong Romanian accent.

The rest of the students began laughing as she imitated Isabel's tipsy and sultry cat-walk from the previous night.

"Guys, I wasn't thinking clearly, ok?" Isabel assured them.

"Oh, sure you weren't," continued Dorina. "You are the most conspicuous person I've ever met!"

"What are you talking about?" asked Isabel, feeling attacked. "And how do you know him?"

"Well, unlike you, Miss USA, some of us had to take the Civic Integration Courses," interrupted Amaité, rather sarcastically. "That guy was in the same group."

"He always looked kind of dangerous, all quiet and serious," spoke Jamil.

"What's your problem? Maybe he just prefers to keep to himself," Amaité returned at him.

Isabel's squinty eyes shifted from one arguing student to the other, trying to make sense of what they were saying.

"I still think he was weird," reaffirmed Jamil. "Mr. Pelengkahu always let him be."

"Just as you all should," added the professor, as he walked in on the awkward conversation.

Some of the students pouted in disappointment, left yearning to hear more of the heating discussion.

During class, Isabel tried hard to focus on learning how to conjugate dozens of unpronounceable Dutch verbs. But all of her thoughts spoke to her in raw Arabic. Memories of Samir made her lose absolute focus of the course, and her classmates' odd reaction to her growing friendship with him was something she couldn't seem to ignore. She took her phone out, and hid it under the table to send Samir a text message. She asked if he could meet her for another coffee that same afternoon, using the class project as a pretext.

I told you I prefer tea. Where?

His instant response excited her. But she didn't want to meet him at a public spot; like every other day they happened to be near each other. For the purpose at hand, they needed a private and quiet place where they could speak. She took a minute to consider her options, then told him to find her that afternoon at the subway station in *Beurs*. Isabel kept an excited grin fixed on the phone screen, not noticing the silence that had suddenly filled the classroom; nor the many pairs of eyes closing in with skepticism.

"Guys, it's really not what you think," Isabel said, unable to contain her laughter.

As they were dismissed, Sarah approached Isabel to ask about her relationship with Samir. They never spoke much, but she was the only Iraqi girl in class—which could have possibly been the reason she was so curious about the matter.

"So you really don't think he likes you?" she asked.

"I don't know," said Isabel, unconsciously twirling a lock of her hair around her index finger, and digging into her most recent memories. "I mean...we train together, we had coffee once, and last night we ate something called döner."

"Oh honey," she said as she rolled her eyes mockingly, "first comes the coffee, then the spicy dish, and after that comes the baklava."

Confused by Sarah's double entendre, Isabel took out her father's journal and showed her the real intentions for meeting Samir. The beautiful Kurdish woman was then unable to contain her laughter.

"You really don't know Iraqi men, do you?" she asked, while biting her lip and frowning her eyebrows.

Once again, Isabel didn't know what to respond, and limited herself to shrug her shoulders, trying to appear as uninterested as possible.

"Well, if you ever change your mind…" continued Sarah, handing Isabel a business card with the words *Ishtar's Fantasy* written on it; it was a dance academy.

"You will find that very useful, our men love it," she said with a seductive tone.

"Dancing?" Isabel asked while raising an eyebrow.

"Not just dancing, love. Belly dancing! Like this…"

Suddenly, Sarah extended her arms above her head, and gracefully began twirling her hands while shimmying her hips in a sensuous manner. The moves were provocative and enchanting; like the perfect weapon of seduction no man could ever resist. But this was indeed not just a dance, it was pure art.

"And take this also," she added, handing Isabel a tiny roll-on flask she took out of her purse.

"What is it?" Isabel asked, examining it curiously.

"It's scented oil with pheromones. Very powerful, but only for special occasions," she said with a suggestive wink.

As Isabel left the building, she tried to shake all of Sarah's speculations out of her head, as well as her snaky moves and witchy behavior. Instead, she made her way to the station to meet up with the Iraqi in question. She walked up and down the platforms, but there was no sign of him anywhere. A minute later, her phone rang in her hand, and the startling vibration caused her to drop it hard on the ground. A small crowd stared at the scene with curious eyes, as she embarrassedly picked the device back up.

"Hello?"

"Where are you, Isabel?" asked Samir with a firm voice. "I am here in Beurs."

"Ow, where? I'm here too and I don't see you," she responded, scanning her surroundings anxiously.

It turned out that Samir was on the other side of the station; located at the *Koopgoot* shopping site. Beurs was exceedingly swarmed—as most people were getting out of work at the time—but Samir had asked her not to leave her spot for a second. The tension of the moment was causing Isabel to feel dizzy and panicky—just like back at the marketplace—and she'd become suffocated by the growing masses, crashing onto her in their rush to get home.

"I've got to get out of here," she muttered in an attempt to breathe.

Her anxiety was taking over again, making the urge to flee that crowded place seem unbearable. She rushed to the exit, looking above the stairs towards her freedom and fresh air. But then, just as she was halfway through the steps, she crashed onto Samir who was coming down from the opposite direction.

"Isabel, are you okay?" He asked while holding her in his arms.

"Hi! Yeah…I just felt sick for a minute," she replied, taking a deep breath and supporting herself against his strong frame.

"Do you want to sit down for a moment?" he inquired, in a genuinely preoccupied tone she'd never heard from his lips before.

"Yes, but not here," she said, guiding him back to the subway platforms, from where they took the metro heading towards Blijdorp.

He sat with his arms crossed firmly as usual, saying nothing, but portraying his typical sternness. Throughout the whole ride, Isabel tried concentrating her thoughts on the list of questions she'd written down for the assignment. However, her classmates' opinions about her relationship with the Iraqi stud continued to reign in the back of her mind.

9

THE INTERVIEW: PART ONE

They got out at Central Station, and took the back tunnel towards Spoorsingel. This time, the view was much more promising than before. The terrain surrounding the previously frigid canal was now embellished with lush trees and a far-reaching emerald carpet, and bunches of dandelions and red poppies had bloomed scattered all over the fertile ground.

"Oh look!" she exclaimed with enthusiasm, pointing at a pair of majestic swans that floated close against one another, almost engaged in a romantic waltz. She'd never seen these lovely creatures up close before, and wanted to take a picture of them in their natural embrace. The giant lovebirds moved under the arched bridge of the canal, and Isabel stalked-on carefully to avoid startling them. She bent her knees down in a perfect squat, balancing her body as she held her phone steadily, in an attempt to snap the perfect shot.

"What are you doing?!" Samir inquired roughly, as he sneaked up from behind, alarming not only the precious animals, but also Isabel; who fell forward on her hands and knees.

"My phone!" she shouted, watching her mobile slip right into the lake.

Samir mumbled an array of foreign words, just as he crouched over the edge of the channel and reached into the shallow water.

"It's ok, I get it for you," he said in a cool tone.

A moment later, he retrieved his soaked arm; holding the dripping phone in his hand like nothing major had happened.

"What do you mean 'it's ok!'? It's ruined!" she ranted on, snatching the damaged device from his hands, and attempting to dry it up with her shirt.

"Khalas, woman! It's only a cellphone," he said.

She gave him a cold stare and shook her head, then continued on walking towards Lennert's house in a slightly-foul mood.

As they arrived, Xiang Chen happened to be putting some letters inside the mailbox at the edge of the sidewalk. He greeted Isabel spontaneously, as he always did. But as soon as he saw the strange buffed man next to her, his jolly expression changed into one of surprise and curiosity. It was a bit of an awkward moment for the three of them. Not stopping to chat with her prying neighbor, Isabel guided Samir into the apartment—though he already knew the way in. As they stepped into the living room, Isabel heard him chuckle while he scanned his surroundings.

"See something funny?" she asked.

"The first time I come here I was angry, and now I'm back for chai," he said ironically.

"Oh, that reminds me..." Isabel said, as she drew a 20-euro bill out of her purse. "Now that tip is settled."

She winked at him in the same devious manner he normally did. And he looked at her with humorous skepticism, while placing the money inside his wallet. As he waited in the living room, Isabel went to the kitchen to make him a cup of green tea, and one black coffee for herself. She sat down by the solemn man and contemplated his moves, capturing every detail to write the perfect paper later on. Arching a brow of disbelief, she watched him add seven cubes of sugar into his hot drink, and flinched in disgust from imagining how sickeningly sweet it must have tasted.

"Can I ask you something?" he spoke out, breaking the library-like silence in the apartment.

"Sure," she said. "But don't get too excited, I'm the one asking the questions today."

"Ok, what is your relation with Mr. de Graaf?" he asked. "I know this is his house, but where is he?"

Isabel tilted her head to the side.

"Well, that's quite bold of you," she said, clearing her throat. "However, he's a friend that I met in America, and he lent me this house for a while. He lives elsewhere with his wife."

This time, she spoke in an aggravating tone, recalling how Lennert had been acting from the moment she arrived in Holland.

"Wow, good friend to let you live here for free," he added, folding his lips into a small moue.

"Sure he is!" she cackled. "Can we begin with the interview now?"

Samir noticed her discomfort with the subject, but said nothing further about it. Instead, he nodded in agreement, followed by asking if he could smoke inside the house.

"Yes. Now let's begin," she added.

His name was Samir Ishmael Youkhana; the eldest of three brothers. And according to the man himself, the most rebellious of all. He was then thirty-five years old, and he'd spent nearly eight of those years trying to live through warfare and uncertainty, until losing everything he had. From what he'd mentioned back at the café, Isabel assumed that Samir had left his country primarily to escape the occupation, just like countless Iraqis did. But after ten minutes of story-telling, she became confused as he kept on mentioning the persecution against *his people*. Nonetheless, she continued to write every word he said—gasping in horror the moment he confessed having received several death-threats. Like many locals in Iraq, Samir had been employed by American

I.C. RIVERA

soldiers—particularly assisting them as a translator—and such a move was considered treason. In exchange for their services, the U.S. government had promised the interpreters special visas into the United States. But to this day, hundreds of Iraqis are still waiting for these permits.

"They even sent someone to murder me," he added, "but one of my brothers said I was out of the country."

"That's so sad! Arabs killing other Arabs for—"

"Isabel, I am not Arab!" he shouted, breaking her speech halfway, and causing her to drop her journal on the ground. She pressed her hand against her chest and breathed heavily, shocked by Samir's impulsive and unexpected reaction—though it hadn't been the first time. He immediately got off the couch, and went on to stand by the window. She could hear him inhaling and exhaling systematically, like he was trying to pace himself down. He leaned against the window frame in silence, looking out at the late-noon sunset that Isabel cherished daily.

"I'm sorry...I didn't want to shout at you," he then spoke.

"And I'm sorry for my ignorance, but why do you need to get so mad?" she asked, slowly approaching him.

"It's not that I am mad," he said, looking over his shoulder and into her bright amber eyes. "It's about my identity."

"Your identity?" she added, waiting for him to elaborate on his confusing remark.

"Isabel, I am Assyrian," he then revealed, in a tone that was almost philosophical, causing Isabel to squint in further bewilderment.

"You mean, you're...a Syrian?" she asked, assuming he may have mispronounced the words. "Didn't you say you were Ira—"

"Have you ever opened a history book, or even a Bible!?" he asked boldly.

124

The usually lore-presumptuous Hispanic flushed from feeling ignorant on yet another relevant subject. Unable to formulate a clever response, she went to sit back on the couch, with her face humbled down on the ground. She then remembered her mother's Christmas gift—still lying somewhere inside her suitcase. But even then, she couldn't understand what Samir really talked about. All of a sudden, he began speaking in a strange dialect, totally different from the regular Arabic she commonly heard him speak with his friends and relatives. She kept a mesmerized gaze while listening to the words, as though she'd been enchanted by some ancient hymn or poem.

"This is Aramaic, the language of Jesus Christ—my real language," he said clear and proud—his profound voice sending chills down her spine.

"Oh," she murmured.

Oh; that short, empty answer that escapes a person's lips when they've just learned something incredible, or when they don't have the slightest idea of what they're being told. Isabel was right in the middle of both definitions.

Maybe I should have paid more attention in Sunday school.

Standing with a firm and erect posture, Samir continued on explaining that ancient Assyria was once a powerful nation. Unfortunately, it had now been forgotten by nearly the entire world— turned into a collection of relics resting behind the glass displays of foreign museums. Although they were often confused with, and compared to other ethnic groups settled in the same region, this Semitic people were actually the indigenous inhabitants of the Nineveh Plains of northern Iraq—and they happened to be Christians as well.

"But because we are Christian, they persecute us. They bomb our churches and homes, our shops," he added. "It's really difficult to live in the Middle East if you're not a Muslim."

"Difficult? Are you sure that's the word you want to use?" she commented, her eyes wide in disbelief. "This sounds horrendous!"

"Yes, but this is our truth, from many years ago." he shrugged.

He spoke about persecution like it was their daily bread; a normal situation they were used to enduring since the beginning of time. Isabel remained silent and attentive, while a fast movie of her entire life started playing in her head simultaneously. She wondered where she'd been all those years before that afternoon, ashamed to admit that the worst Middle Eastern issue she repeatedly heard about was the conflict between Israelis and Palestinians. Never for one second did she consider the many other groups and minorities that suffered heavily under terrorism, barbaric regimes, and in many cases, foreign interventions.

"Maybe you don't believe this, but I swear in God that Iraq was once a great country," he affirmed with a scolding finger.

Samir was defensive in his remark, as he resented how the media continuously portrayed a negative image of his homeland and fellow countrymen. It was the same prejudice-inducing propaganda that Isabel had been following throughout her entire life. And for too long they'd made Iraq seem like a forsaken land, incapable of inspiring love and wonderment. But Samir didn't need to place his statement under oath, for the sincerity in his eyes was more than convincing.

"So, did you leave because of the religious persecution, or the war?" she queried.

"Both, of course," he said.

"And what about the Christians that choose to stay behind?"

To answer her question in a graphic manner, Samir ran his thumb horizontally across his throat, while portraying a snarly look on his face. Isabel inhaled a sharp breath. The gruesome message couldn't have been any clearer. He admitted that life had already been, for centuries, troublesome for Assyrians and other minorities in Iraq. But then, he added that it was right after the U.S. Occupation when these communities became intensely harassed and threatened by radical groups. Their only chances at surviving were to escape their ancestral lands, or to renounce their Faith in order to become Muslims. As his lips kept on moving, Isabel began questioning everything she ever learned growing up; including the sole definition of democracy—so *peacefully* introduced in Iraq by the United States—which should advocate for the protection of everyone's human rights. But that Western idea of democracy had failed miserably, and the oil-rich country was left completely broken apart, unstable, and brought back over a thousand years.

By the time the evening fell, Isabel felt as if her conscience had been awakened for the very first time. But what she didn't know, was that these facts were merely the warm-up of Samir's story and heartbreaking revelations.

"They killed my best friend in front of me," he said softly. "They took his head...and—"

His voice was shaky, and the momentary sepulchral silence that had filled the room was broken by the abrupt sound of cracking porcelain. Isabel jumped from her chair when she realized what had happened. Samir had become extremely angry—so much that he grasped his cup with all his strength, causing it to break in a dozen pieces. A thin stream of blood started to run down his hand, and Isabel hurried to find a towel to stop the bleeding—while he stayed in the exact same position, behaving as if feeling no pain at all.

"It's ok, Isabel, don't worry," he said calmly as she returned.

"Are you insane!? We have to wash your hand, come on!" she said with urgency, guiding him toward the bathroom.

Luckily, he did not have any pieces of glass stuck in his skin, and the wound wasn't as deep as she'd initially feared. She looked inside the cabinet for some bandages, while in her mind she reconsidered the entire school project.

It must be painful to recall such horrid memories...

"Maybe this interview is not such a good idea, I'm sorry," she said with regret, gently wrapping the thin piece of cloth around his palm.

But as she finished her sentence, Samir grasped her wrists and pulled her closer to him—embracing the shaken girl at such inviting proximity that their lips slightly brushed against each other's.

"You want me to go?" he whispered.

She was stunned, quivering under the fervor of his gaze and the warmth of his powerful frame. She shook her head in slow motion, her own yearning body giving him the answer to his ridiculous question. He smirked, pleased and sure of himself, slowly letting go so that she could recover her breath.

"Good," he added in the same soft tone, just before turning around and sauntering back to the living-room.

An electrifying rush of euphoria filled Isabel's veins right that instant, and she found herself urged to liberate the long-suppressed energy before reappearing in the presence of the enchanting Assyrian. She locked herself in the bathroom for a couple of minutes, looking for something to ease the maddening thrill growing inside her. Grabbing a towel from a rack, she pressed it hard against her mouth to scream stealthily, until she managed to put her impulses under control. By the time she went back to the bold Iraqi, she found him sitting on the sofa, with her open journal in his hands.

"I see you have many questions," he commented as he turned the pages.

"Well! I told you, if you don't wan—"

"I will help you with your work, Isabel. It's just...a lot to remember," he said, licking his bottom lip as he scanned the living room. "But...if you have something stronger than tea..."

"Um, didn't you just say you were a Christian?" she asked.

"Tsk," he clicked his tongue. "Is ok, I am Catholic."

His phony-sounding remark caused Isabel to chuckle awkwardly, assuming that he'd just thrown another one of his strange jokes on the table. Nevertheless, his anticipating eyes said otherwise. Isabel checked the kitchen and the rest of the apartment, in hopes to find any other alcohol besides her wine—unsuspecting that she would shortly hit the biggest jackpot in terms of fine liquor. As she opened a tinted cabinet between the bookshelves, she found a small stash of bottles and whiskey glasses. She examined them carefully, unsure of which one to choose—ultimately selecting the one that caught her eye the most. Despite her years organizing events for hotels, she was still a little inexperienced when it came to choosing good drinks.

"Will this be ok?" she asked naively, while holding a bottle of *Macallan* right at his face.

Judging by the twinkle in the corner of Samir's eye, she could tell that it was a good one. He eagerly poured himself a glass—just about two fingers in quantity—then brought it closer to his nose to delicately inhale its aroma.

So he eats like a beast, but drinks like a gentleman…interesting.

"Maybe I should write this peculiar detail down as well," she spoke out in amusement, granting him a few minutes to savor his drink, before proceeding to the next question on her list.

"So, what did you do in Iraq? Apart from the interpreter job, of course."

He sat back comfortably, throwing his left arm behind his head while hovering the glass of fine whiskey before his face.

"Different things," he said in a contemplative manner, "But I was studying to be an electrician, before the war fucked everything."

"Ok, let's just…move on to the next one, shall we?" she suggested nervously, not wanting him to recall other painful events of that time.

"Come on, Isabel, ask me what you want," he said deviously. "And I will try not breaking this glass also."

Isabel took a moment to review her questions, in hopes to find one that was adequate and not too bold. However, she saw that most of them seemed rather basic or irrelevant, almost resembling the typical questionnaires found on common social networks.

She groaned, "You know what, Sam? Just tell me everything."

He nodded gallantly.

"That's better," he added as he took a sip of his drink.

Samir and his whole family had a relatively-good life back in their native land. They were humble people who lived modestly, but never lacked a plate of warm food at the end of each day. For this, he was grateful. His mother was a school teacher, and his father a baker who was loved by everyone in their village. His youngest brother was in elementary school, while the other one coursed at the University of Mosul. Their circumstances weren't perfect while Saddam Hussein was in power, but according to Samir's own perspective, they were a lot better. Isabel lifted her eyebrows in surprise as he said this, having recalled hearing about Saddam's *Regime of Terror*—among other intimidating titles—in which he was described to be a vicious, brutal dictator. Samir, on the other hand, portrayed him as a strong leader, who maintained peace and order among the different communities in Iraq; an allegation to which Isabel nearly choked.

"You see? You people of the West only speak the same things about Iraq; terror, evil!" he roared.

"Samir, that's not—"

"Really, if you don't know anything, better don't say anything!"

The truth in his words, and defiant tone of his voice made her wish to be swallowed by the earth at that exact moment. Like a misinformed debater, she'd made the mistake of arguing about a subject she knew little or nothing of, upsetting him yet again in the process. She waited about a minute for his heated demeanor to ease down, then remained silent to let him proceed with the story-telling, specifically on the whereabouts of his family. This particular subject caused his serious face to change into one of both astonishment and sorrow.

"One of my brothers is in Turkey," he spoke softly. "Thanks to your America I don't know where the rest of my family is."

My America? U.S.? I am Latina…why is he attacking me?

Isabel inhaled deeply as she wrote this, wondering how he was able to sustain so much pain in his heart, without turning into a mindless vessel of hatred and hard feelings. On the other hand, she then began to comprehend Samir's constant mood-swings and his steadily-furrowed eyebrows. Not wanting to continue opening old wounds, she decided to ask him about his journey into the Netherlands instead. This, however, was another series of shocking and even more painful revelations.

"I was smuggled out," he said.

People smugglers; they were like a mafia in charge of supposedly helping people escape into a better and safer country. Then again, those who placed their lives in the hands of human traffickers were vulnerable to further risks, even death.

Due to the constant kidnappings and killings of Christians, during and after the Occupation, many Assyrians had no other choice but to leave their homes and flee to foreign lands. That's why, in the middle of one chilly night, Samir and his whole family hurried stealthily towards a covered cattle truck, stationed just outside *Qaraqosh*; Iraq's largest Christian city. They carried only one backpack each, containing some food, water, and two changes of clothes. They weren't allowed to bring anything except for the most basic of things, in order to prevent being slowed down during the seventeen-hour journey to Damascus. Right before departure, while Samir was paying an advance for the transport, a series of gunshots were heard in the distance, causing the family and other people inside the truck to cry out in fear. The driver hurried them into the vehicle, driving off hastily before being caught by any insurgents or soldiers. At the checkpoint of the Iraqi-Syrian Border, one of the smugglers sneakily paid an officer with a roll of dollar bills and a box filled with bottles of scotch. This exchange of favors would keep them from undergoing a vehicle search, or being asked too many compromising questions. In the back of the truck, amongst a herd of bleating sheep, hid another family with two young sisters between the ages of seventeen and twenty-five. The eldest had been crying without comfort throughout the night over the death of her fiancé, who'd been killed in a terrorist attack inside Sayidat al-Nejat; a Syrian Catholic Church located in Baghdad. Around her neck hung a golden crucifix that symbolized their engagement, as it was the tradition within the Assyrian community. On another side was a young couple who'd decided to run away together, defying their family's rules as well as ignoring the ongoing sectarian war; he was a Shia Muslim and she was Sunni. There was also another man sitting alone in a corner, but he kept all to himself the entire time.

The truck continued its long course, causing the refugees to feel anxious and impatient, while the strong odors and the excruciating heat in the compartment made the whole ride seem endless. Unexpectedly, they felt the truck slowing down before the appointed hour, causing the group to become even more uneasy. Samir peeked cautiously through a small air duct, noticing that they'd stopped at a remote area. He watched with suspicion as the driver received a package from a masked man; armed and all dressed in black like a Shinobi. While he obviously couldn't see his face, he gasped in horror the second he recognized the white symbols displayed on the man's headband. Alarmed by the sight, he whispered what was going on to the other men inside the truck, plotting and preparing to attack if necessary.

"Oh my God! What happened then?" Isabel interrupted, hugging one of the couch pillows hard against her chest.

"We couldn't do anything...they all had guns," Samir continued.

The hope of these families was taken away too soon. For the moment the back doors opened, a group of four armed men started firing warning shots in the air. The uproar caused the cattle to scurry, pushing the refugees out of hiding. The insurgents yelled as they fired, threatening to kill anyone who dared confront them as they grabbed all the young women—even shooting a pleading father on the thigh when he tried to prevent them from taking his daughters. Samir and his brothers tried to hush their crying mother, forming an embracing circle around her and their father. The horrid scene was over quickly, but the pain and cries of the two parents and young Shia man continued on helplessly. The vehicle started moving again shortly after the atrocious crime—for another eight hours—before finally approaching Syria's capital city.

On the way, Sam and his middle brother took some bread out of their bags and shared it with the remaining people inside the truck. The young Muslim took it in his hand and just stared at it, as he was still trapped in a prolonged state of shock. But then, the grim silence surrounding them was interrupted once again; this time by the screams of a heartbroken mother who'd realized her wounded husband lied dead in her arms, as he'd bled out through his femoral artery. Samir's mother gently reached out for her hand and pulled her away from the body, and into the embrace of her family, in an attempt to comfort her after an entire day of tragedy and loss. The deafening cries made the driver hit the brakes abruptly. A moment later, one of the traffickers reopened the back doors of the truck and ordered the small group to come out of the vehicle. With little regard, the crooks dragged the bloody corpse out, and threw it on the side of the dusty road for vultures to devour. And right after, the newly-widowed woman ran over to the body and fell on her knees in anguish, pleading to be left behind with the latest fatal victim of human smuggling.

"She had nothing left to fight for..." Isabel sobbed. "How could you trust those men? They betrayed you all."

"For them is only business," explained Samir. "When someone dies in the way, they don't care. They already have payment."

The smugglers made some phone calls, while remaining stationed in the same isolated place. A farmer's fruit truck appeared in the distance about half an hour later; it was their next ride. After another series of shady trades, between the new traffickers and the previous ones, the first two men drove back the same way they'd come from. The new dealers carried fully-loaded AK-47's, and with an aggressive tone of voice they urged the remaining refugees to get inside their truck. Moving several crates of tomatoes, they uncovered a wide hollow space in the middle, just enough to fit Samir's family and the other two displaced persons. The smugglers glanced at the crying woman for a moment, but just as unmindfully they got inside the old vehicle and left her behind with her haunting mourning.

The arduous journey continued for another twelve hours. They were restless, but far too overwhelmed to catch any sleep. It was precisely dawn when they'd finally made another stop. They couldn't see anything from their hiding spot, but they could still hear a lot of fuzzy chatter, car honking, and the unmistakable melody of the *Adhan*; the Muslim Call to Prayer. For this reason, they concluded that they'd arrived in Istanbul at last. The two armed men parked inside a warehouse near the marketplace, as it was the only relatively-safe place to come out of hiding undetected. In there they met another group of refugees from different countries; among them a young Iranian couple, three Syrian men, and a Pakistani-Christian woman with two little children. Just as though they were mere pieces of merchandise, Samir and his family, as well as the other two guys, were all delivered into the hands of yet another gang. The only difference was that this time they were treated with a little decency. They were all given soup, water, and coats that were donated by certain members of the local community. Many people were fully aware of the tough circumstances endured by countless immigrants, but very few took the initiative to help them out.

The man in charge of the operation was of Armenian descent, and his name was Sarkis Nazarian. He was a former refugee who'd previously planned to cross into Europe, but changed his mind after learning about the risky, yet profitable smuggling job inside Turkey. In contrast to the other cold-blooded dealers Samir had encountered, this man seemed more compassionate, and promised to do his best to get them all into Greece safely.

"Armenians are Christians too, aren't they?" Isabel interrupted once again.

"Yes, how did you know?" Samir asked.

"Well, the Kardashians are Christian too, so I assumed..."

"The what?"

"Nevermind, please carry on…"

Though the refugees were frightened from the risk of being discovered by the authorities, some of them were also relieved to be able to rest for several hours before getting back on the road. By late-loon, two passenger buses leading to Athens had parked just outside the warehouse. Their driver was already aware of the operation, but the buses were nearly full, and the group had to be divided in order to try accommodating at least most of them. All of a sudden, the young man whose girlfriend had been kidnapped got up from the ground and assaulted one of the gangsters, snatching his handgun in the process. He'd gone completely mad from the pain of losing his future bride, and in his desperation he placed the gun inside his mouth and pulled the trigger without having second thoughts. The tension of the gruesome scene caused a revolt between the traffickers and the anxious group of immigrants, as they started to run outside and towards the vehicles.

They pushed and pulled one another in an attempt to find a place to sit, provoking the drivers to beat each one of them indiscriminately, for there was not enough room for all. Throughout the confusion, Samir and his brother Yasir were separated from their parents and little brother, but the three of them soon managed to find a safe spot inside one of the vehicles. Samir pushed forward, approaching their side of the bus to make sure they were alright. Just a moment before departing, Samir's mother took her gold crucifix necklace off, and drew a Bible out of her bag as well. She handed them over to her eldest son through a small window, telling him to; "…keep looking toward the heavens." He took the items warmly, then hurried back to his brother. The two

Assyrians then forced their way into the other bus, where they paid for the rest of the long, precarious ride.

"How much did you have to pay in total?" Isabel queried.

"Hmm, like six thousand dollars," he said plainly.

"For a whole family?"

Samir shook his head. "For each person."

Her mouth dropped at his casual reply. "What?! Where do people get that kind of money?!"

"Isabel," he sighed, "just like my family, these people sold everything they had for one last chance to survive."

His courageous statement made Isabel drop her face in embarrassment, admitting that she couldn't even imagine what she would have done in the same situation.

"But," he continued, "like you heard, things don't always happen like we expect…"

When both cars started driving away, Sam glanced over his shoulder a few times, making sure the other bus was still in range behind them. He and his brother continued to do this for a while, until they ended up dozing off from their exhaustion. By the time they reopened their eyes, the other bus was gone. Anxious for losing sight of their family, they asked Sarkis what was going on, and the Armenian explained that the other driver had taken a different route in order to prevent calling unnecessary attention. Though it made sense, Samir still felt preoccupied for his family's safety in the open road of a foreign and somewhat dangerous country.

It was nearly sunset when they finally reached the appointed drop-zone, just outside the town of Edirne, but there was no sign of the other group anywhere. The driver hurried the refugees out of the bus, as he needed to continue his way towards Athens along with his actual passengers—the legal way. Sarkis opened the luggage compartment, taking out a large gray bag and two retractable orange paddles. To comply with Samir and Yasir's plea, he waited for another twenty minutes, but the other vehicle never arrived. In a tone of regret, he approached the two Iraqi brothers and explained there wasn't anything he could do; not even reaching the missing chauffeur through the phone. It was already past 22:00, and the group of nine people—Samir, Yasir, Sarkis, the Persian couple, the Pakistani family, and a silent fellow Iraqi—started making their way through bushes, and toward a swampy terrain leading to the dreaded Evros. They hiked carefully and as quietly as possible, trying not to startle any border guards who may had been patrolling the area. As they reached the edge of the river, Sarkis asked the men to help fill the 10-feet rubber dinghy. It took time and a lot of energy, and all the while Samir only hoped that the rest of his family would pop out of the wilderness to continue the journey together, but they didn't.

It was then time to move forward, time to get in the yellow boat and look towards the horizon; Europe. Ironically, reaching the other side of the river normally took just about ten to fifteen minutes. And yet, they were the longest and most nerve-wrecking minutes of these refugees' lives. The task itself sounded simple enough; Sarkis would tie a rope to the boat, then he would swim to the other side and tie the other end around a tree, pulling the boat while another person paddled against the current—easier said than done, of course. The women and children started getting inside the boat first. But all of a sudden, the young Persian woman slipped and fell into the water, causing a major splash that alarmed the rest of them. She was instantly washed far away from the shore, and into the cold, raging currents of mid-November. Her desperate husband jumped in to save her, successfully reaching her hand and pulling her over a fallen log. Unfortunately, he too was dragged away by the waves. The young veiled bride screamed his name uncontrollably, helplessly crying out for help as she watched her man disappear in the deathly dark depths. Samir jumped back on the shore and ran towards the area closest to her, pulling her back over firm land. He covered her mouth with his hand, pleading her to stop crying, for they were in a situation so vulnerable that there was no time to grief for any accidents. Stopping their mission for just a second could have risked them getting caught, arrested, or worse.

"He died for her...oh my God," Isabel whispered as she wiped a tear off her cheek.

"Many people die in that river every year, all trying to reach Europe," Samir added.

To their misfortune, and as they'd feared, the remaining runaways saw the beam of a flashlight in the distance, and heard the frightful barking of dogs. They hurried back to the boat, where the children cried uncontrollably. Yasir tried to row faster, but struggled to keep the oars in place while Sam attempted to push the vessel forward. To make things worse, one of the Turkish officers started firing from afar, and the range was just close enough to catch Samir right in the chest.

"They shot you?!" Isabel roared in bewilderment, jumping from her lounging position when Samir pulled down his t-shirt collar; showing her the evident scar that was on his right, and very pronounced pectoral.

"Can I continue now?" he asked as he arched his eyebrow.

"Sorry, sorry! Go on…"

The boat was then too far away for him to reach, and the pain inflicted by the wound made it impossible for him to swim towards it. He desperately looked around for a way across, but was surprised once more by the attack of a patrol K9. Samir shouted and growled, kicking the dog hard on the head, yet the rabid animal continued to pull strongly on his leg and the bottom of his jeans. The rest of the group yelled his name as the guards got closer to the scene, but the Assyrian still couldn't shake the canine off him. To everyone's surprise—and like a heroic gargoyle who'd suddenly been awakened to save the night—the other Iraqi refugee jumped into the water, swimming back to the Turkish side to aid his compatriot. He was strong in will and athletic in built, and he made it back to land with just enough power in his hands to snap the German Shepherd's neck in one single twist. He quickly helped Samir back up, and with heavy effort they managed to reach the edge of the vessel. The guards resumed their firing with even more deliverance, but the darkness of the night, and the faith in the refugees' hearts served as a cloak against their bullets of hatred. When they reached firm soil again, they began to run as fast as they could, away from any border control, knowing that it wouldn't be long before they'd be surrounded by more officers.

Their goal was to reach a small village near the border, where they would be picked up by another vehicle. But after an hour of running, Sarkis began to feel concerned. The town should have already been visible in the distance. And yet, before them lied nothing but plains of plowed fields that extended way beyond their sight. Samir had lost a lot of blood on the way, turning weak and unable to keep up with the pace of his companions. Overwhelmed, he fell on his knees and pleaded his brother to leave him there on the cold ground. Yasir tried to pull him back up, but Samir refused to cooperate. Instead, he ordered his younger brother to save his own life and find their family for him. The saddening picture created even more anxiety among the distressed refugees, causing Sarkis to lose his initial calm. He knew that Sam was slowing the group down, and couldn't put the rest of them at risk of being discovered by border control. Should this occur, they would all be dragged into a detention center in the village of Fylakio; which wasn't too far from their location either.

"Oh my God, don't tell me they left you alone in there!" Isabel exclaimed.

Samir groaned, and hammered a clenched fist on the coffee table. The continuously-interrupting woman flinched, finding the rough reaction more comical than frightening. The Assyrian looked at her with annoyance, and she sat back with her lips pursed inward, attempting not to laugh.

"Woman, do you not see me sitting in here!? Let me finish!" he said aloud.

139

They did indeed leave Samir behind, but half an hour didn't go by before the group returned for him. Surprisingly, it was his same fellow countryman who'd convinced Sarkis of going back. He strode towards the wounded Iraqi, roughly grabbing him by his blood and sweat-drenched shirt. He shouted at the refugee's weary face, encouraging him to keep on walking, as they were almost at the gateway to the West. Slowly, Samir began to lift his head, and his eyes were deep red and full of compressed tears. "Ya Allah!" he cried out, while gazing up to the starry skies. He yelled in great pain, not over his open wound, but from thinking about the whereabouts of his family. It was at that moment when he made a pact with God himself; that if He would grant him enough strength, and helped him find his relatives, he would serve Him throughout his entire life. And right after declaring such determined words, a strong wave of energy and willpower began inundating his mind and heart, pushing him to get back on his feet and finishing the dangerous race he'd begun.

"Wow...this is all amazing, Samir," Isabel spoke in awe.

"Yeah, amazing," he replied uninterested, as he took another sip of his fifth glass of scotch.

"But...why did you pray to Allah?" she asked, tilting her head sideways.

"Isabel, Allah is the Arabic translation of 'God'. It has nothing to do with Islam, like you're thinking," he cleared up, making her flush in embarrassment.

"Oh, right," she murmured. "And what's his name?"

"Who?"

"I mean, the man who went back for you," she added.

"Asim, great friend," he replied with half a smile.

"He really sounds like it," she sighed in admiration. "Hmm so, what happened next?"

Samir then checked the time on his phone, saying some words in Arabic while shaking his head. Isabel glanced at her laptop screen for a second, realizing that it was nearly midnight.

"We continue another time, I have to work in the morning," Samir responded, as he got off the couch to put his leather jacket back on.

Isabel groaned in disappointment, yet admitted that she also needed to get up early the next day. As she walked him downstairs to the main entrance, she asked Samir one last question that night;

"By the way, what was that appointment you had when we first met?"

"Ah, yes, I had a meeting with a lawyer from immigration. I'm trying to bring Yasir into Holland."

Isabel gasped. "Oh no! I'm so sorry! You missed that because of me?"

"It's ok. Anyway...good night Isabel," he shrugged, stretching his arm toward her for a polite handshake.

She stared at his hand for a few seconds, then directed her golden gaze back into the darkness of his Middle Eastern eyes. She smirked flirtatiously, then took a step forward and planted a tender good-night kiss on his left cheek.

"Thank you for your help. I'll be looking forward to the sequel," she whispered.

Displaying clear smug on his face, Samir lit a cigarette and made his way down the sidewalk, falling back into his introverted-self. Isabel stood by the door until he disappeared into the night, wondering how far he lived, and with whom; the latter question causing her to unconsciously pout sideways. She then hurried back upstairs, and a minute after shutting the apartment's door she heard a soft knock. She turned back to reopen it immediately, only to find her Asian neighbor standing right outside, and carrying a suspecting countenance.

"Oh, hey Xiang. How can I help you...at this hour?" she asked.

"I know it's none of my business, but you should be careful with who you bring into Lennert's house."

Isabel's eyes burned furious from her neighbor's intrusive behavior.

"You're right, it's none of your business, Xiang," she retorted. "And he's not a stranger. We're working on a class project."

"Yes, I see that... " remarked the family man, as he glanced over at the whiskey bottle sitting on the coffee table across the room.

Surprised by the breach into her private affairs, Isabel tried to send him off in a polite manner, not letting him notice her growing outrage. She leaned against the door, telling herself that nothing should ruin her good mood, particularly after such an intriguing evening. And with those pleasant vibes, she pranced back to the living room to review all her notes.

And to think that it's only the beginning...

10

CHRISTIAN FAITH. ASSYRIAN IDENTITY.

Back at work, Isabel tossed the vacuum cleaner aside to query Ebele about her own journey into the Netherlands. The Ugandan refugee looked at her skeptically, as if unsure of why her co-worker would be interested in the matter.

"It's for a class project," Isabel explained; words to which Ebele rolled her eyes rudely. She then contended that journalists often interviewed refugees across the world, supposedly as a way to raise awareness on their cause, but that it rarely made any difference.

"The people on this side of the world don't care about us," she continued to argue.

Judging by the rough manner in which she'd suddenly begun to fold a pair of towels, it was easy to tell that the subject made her rather uncomfortable.

"Well, I do," Isabel affirmed in a compassionate tone.

"Yes, because your teacher asked you to do this," she replied with sternness. "But have you ever thought about refugees before this day?"

Isabel felt besieged, and cornered by a question that felt as solid as a punch in the gut.

"You're right," she whispered, glancing away from her coworker's confronting expression, "I never did."

Ebele sighed. "Look, it's not how we got here what's important, but what we do with our lives from the moment we arrive."

"Which means, what?" Isabel asked.

"Means that the real journey of a refugee begins across the border, not while hiding in the back of a cattle truck," Ebele added.

The strong matriarch marched away proudly after her firm statement, pushing her service cart and humming one of her distinctive tunes; leaving Isabel speechless and pensive in the middle of the hotel's hallway.

Later at the apartment, Isabel washed the dishes after a gym-friendly meal of steamed broccoli and lean chicken fillet. She'd been trying to follow a meal plan written down by Samir himself, despite the fact that he was free to eat whatever he wanted. He would also come into her mind more often, and in many different forms; as her fitness coach, her interviewee, and a friend with whom she'd started to bond in a very special way. His story, along with her coworker's own declarations, had left her head full of unanswered questions.

She sat on the couch to watch V for Vendetta—one of her favorite films—but her mind was compromised with her unfinished classwork. She couldn't focus on the moving pictures before her, constantly biting on her nails and glancing over at the flashing laptop next to her, every five minutes. When her right foot started shaking from anxiety, she threw her arms in the air, surrendering to her need for knowing what was going on. She placed the computer on her lap, opting to do further research on the refugee issue, and the results were far more astonishing than she'd imagined. According to the UNHCR, the number of asylum-seekers and internally displaced people worldwide had exceeded fifty million—most of them coming from the Middle East and Africa.

"My God, this is a disgrace," she said, opening her journal to take notes of what she'd found out online. She also searched for reports of refugee sightings surrounding the Evros River, learning of the several routes that people used to get to the Greek side. She found out there was even an unofficial graveyard nearby—in a village called Sideró—for the many immigrants who drowned in the attempt to cross the strong currents. While Isabel tried to imagine all the dangerous scenarios, she was unable to decide whether it was better to end up dead, or inside a detention facility; to be held up for months, without safety, medical care, or even the slightest dignifying conditions for human beings to live under. She read interviews made to immigrants like Samir, who'd lost their family members on their way; many times in the hands of untrustworthy smugglers. Instead of receiving any help from the authorities, they were put in these horrible prisons that were much worse than dog pounds. The horrid detention center in Fylakio, for example, was even labeled the Guantanamo of Greece. Sadly, all these jails, camps, and high barbed wire fences, seemed to be the only answer from the West towards the evident humanitarian disaster unfolding all around the world.

Isabel's eyes began to hurt from going through dozens of articles. One of the last pictures she saw online had been taken from an airplane; it was a massive refugee camp in Jordan. It looked oddly familiar, but she couldn't remember where she'd seen that dreadful maze of tents before. At that point, she took her reading glasses off and held her nose bridge between her fingers.

"I so need a break..." she whispered.

She then turned the TV back on, wondering if there was any media coverage for the refugee issue. But as she zapped through the channels, she saw nothing but game shows, old films, American reality TV, infomercials, and a lot of pornography. When she was about to turn the television back off, one channel captured her eye just in time; Al Jazeera. A Middle Eastern anchorwoman appeared before the camera, just before they started showing strong images of the ongoing conflicts in both Syria and Iraq. They were live reports of civilian casualties caught in the middle of battle, as well as raw footage of uniformed militants shooting rebels, and vice versa.

"This is crazy," Isabel said, unable to tell one country from the other, unless she'd pay attention to the symbolic differences on their flags. She couldn't stop looking at the screen, almost holding her breath as she watched a newscast resembling some kind of endless war movie. However, these violent, distressful images were very much real. She took notes of this as well, but felt there were many details she still missed. Her interest on the heavy issue began surpassing her obligation to write an essay. And speaking to Samir suddenly signified having peeked into Pandora's Box itself; slowly discovering all the wrongs of the world which had been concealed from her ignorant sight. And realizing what had been awakened in her, she remembered her mother's words—or better said, King Solomon's words;

"For with much wisdom comes much sorrow;

The more knowledge, the more grief."

But even if it hurt to know the truth, it was too late for Isabel to abandon her assignment; she was too involved in the matter. She was determined to arrange another meeting with Samir, not just to get off the cliffhanger of his life's story, but also to learn more of who he was.

"But it will have to be somewhere else," she said to herself, wishing to avoid any unnecessary trouble with Lennert, or her snoopy neighbor. She wanted to ask Samir about a new date and place right away, but as soon as she grabbed her phone, she threw her palm flat over her forehead in exasperation.

"Damn it!" she groaned, placing the damaged device back on the table, watching as drops of water still came out of it.

As if seeing herself without her smartphone wasn't critical enough, there was another important element missing in her daily routine; her fitness instructor. He wasn't waiting at the gym the next morning as he always did, thus pushing Isabel to train all by herself. Without him present, she didn't feel the same energy and drive to lift even a 5-kilo dumbbell. She sat on one of the benches annoyed, considering leaving the gym for the day, but her thoughts were interrupted by a warm and familiar voice calling her over—in a bit of a tacky manner, though.

"¿Qué pasó, mami?"

"Oh! Hey Miguel, long time no see. How are you?" she greeted heartily.

"Bien, bien," he responded in the same cheerful way. "So this is why I never see you anymore, you're training early.

"Yeah, my schedule changed a little. I have a coach now," she bragged. "But it looks like he didn't show up today."

"Some coach he is—wait!" He squinted furtively. "Don't tell that crazy Arab is your trainer!

The Dominican's disapproving tone and eyes rolling skyward upset her. He'd reacted exaggeratedly, as if she'd just spoken the most outrageous words he'd ever heard.

"First of all, he's not Arab," she said. "Secondly—"

"Whatever, they all look the same to me," he interrupted. "Those guys are dangerous, and my advice is to—"

"Stop!" she shouted.

His xenophobic and disrespectful behavior made her bury her fingernails into the cushioned seat underneath her, feeling extremely defensive of her Assyrian friend.

"Tell me, why is he dangerous exactly?! Because he's Iraqi?!" she added with eyes that gleamed from anger.

"Well...yes?" he chuckled. "The crazy part is that you know where he comes from, yet you still hang out with him."

Miguel frowned in disappointment, patting his hands in the air to disregard her opinion, then left her side arrogantly. This caused the blood in her veins to boil into hellish temperatures.

Idiot!

Later that same day, Isabel arrived at the IVIO building for her Dutch classes, and noticed that her classmates were all gathered at the main office.

"What's going on?" she asked perplexed.

"Man, they're threatening to fire Mr. Pelengkahu!" shouted Jamil.

Isabel felt a sudden ache inside her chest, recalling a course evaluation that had been done at the school recently. She was not worried at the time because she knew how dedicated her professor had always been; making sure all his students understood the lessons thoroughly. He often brought additional books and worksheets, and even took the group out on field trips so they would have a closer look at Dutch culture and Holland's historical sites. Needless to say, he was an exceptional teacher, and Isabel couldn't figure out what had gone wrong.

"They claim he wasn't following the school's regulations," spoke Amaité. "But I know what they're trying to do."

The rest of the students turned to face the fierce Sinaloan girl; notorious for her activist spirit and sharp frankness on every matter.

"Which is?" asked Pete.

"Don't you see? They're angry because our teacher is helping us integrate easier!" she added. "Their goal is to discourage us immigrants, so that we choose to leave their country!"

Her strong statement seemed unbelievable. But after analyzing it for a minute, and recalling all the immigration issues in the Netherlands, the logic was pretty clear.

Mr. Pelengkahu then emerged from the meeting room, along with the same woman who was in charge of the evaluations. Isabel gasped as she recognized her, for it was the same long-legged blonde she'd seen in the building on the first day of class.

"Students," Ray said," as you are now aware of, there has been a controversy over my ways of teaching, and they have decided not to renew my contract. Therefore, starting next week you'll be having a new teacher for the remaining part of your course."

His voice was serene and unchanging, as he calmly accepted the decisions of the organization's council. A second later, an intense feud exploded inside the room, almost resembling a brawl at the United Nations Parliament. And like that wasn't amazing enough, a larger group of multi-ethnic strangers suddenly stormed into the office to join the discussion. At first, Isabel assumed they were students from his morning class that she'd never seen before, but it turned out that they were alumni from previous years; men and women who'd already passed the class and all the exams. It was thanks to Mr. Pelengkahu's instruction that they managed to speak fluent Dutch in just one year. This naturally translated into them growing professionally, as well as giving life to their own immigrant success stories. As soon as the rumor of Ray's dismissal reached the ears of a few pupils, a chain text message was sent to every person he ever taught in the past few years. Without delay, each one of them placed their daily routines on hold to advocate for their teacher. Isabel watched the group with admiration, internally praising their selfless determination to fight for somebody else's rights. She felt privileged to be taught by a man loved by so many. But who wouldn't love him? He was like a father to the expatriates; always offering his advice and a shoulder to cry on whenever they faced struggles, or when cultural shock was far too consuming. Fortunately, the problem was solved in a more diplomatic manner, right after a vote was called for; one that the hostile evaluator was certain to lose. The students roared victorious, and Isabel was compelled to join the wild cheer.

Bravo!

"You can't always go easy on them, Ray," the blonde argued. "Just look at what the Netherlands has turned into."

"Don't forget I am one of *them* too, Anneke," he replied firmly, just before she stomped out of the room with her haughty nose risen upwards.

Later in class, Ray Pelengkahu showed his gratitude by extending the due date of the project another week. He laughed amused from hearing his students sigh in relief, as they were just a month away from turning their work in. Isabel was a little nervous herself, for she still didn't have Samir's whole story written down, nor had she started to type the first draft down on the computer.

"May I take a look?" spoke a sweet and gentle voice.

Isabel turned her head to see her Japanese classmate, Aiko, who'd noticed her handling her broken cellphone.

"Oh, this thing. Yeah, sure," she scoffed. "It doesn't work. I don't know why I keep trying to turn it on."

"Well, don't lose hope!" she giggled. "I can take it to my husband's repair shop if you like."

"Yes, please!" Isabel nodded heartily. "I've tried every YouTube tutorial with no luck!"

"Very well," Aiko chuckled, handing her a piece of paper with the shop's address.

On the following weekend, the entire Netherlands was graced by sunshine and heat; an uncommon but highly welcomed phenomenon. Missing her warm days in Florida, the Latin-American expat took advantage of the beautiful weather by wearing a sleeveless maxi-dress she still kept inside her suitcase. Its soft fabric wrapped her body sensually, accenting her curves without seeming overly fitted. After combining it with a pair of strappy sandals and a brown cross-body hobo bag, Isabel was ready to strut through the city, carefree and willing to treat herself with some new and fresher clothes.

Despite the shifting temperatures each month, she could tell that it was going to be a hot summer in the region. The streets were packed with both locals and tourists alike, all wearing their best fashions for the sizzling days. Isabel stood right in the middle of Beurs for a minute, just to admire the colorful sight of the multi-cultural society she lived in. She also used her reflective moment to open her ears to the many different voices, accents, and languages that blended all around, as rhythmically as a Putumayo World Music album.

Holland is truly a magical place...

Coming up from the highly populated, Koopgoot shopping passage, Isabel was approached by two jolly teenagers who were collecting funds for a social cause. She wanted to hand them a ten-euro bill, but was told by the couple that the organization only accepted bank account numbers—from which they'd retrieve a specified low amount each month. Her forehead wrinkled as she stared at the charity volunteers in disbelief, having expected them to draw out some labeled jars, or even an envelope.

"Well, I could give you my American credit card number." Isabel said. "Would that be ok?"

The pair glanced at each other with uncertainty, and ultimately shook their heads. As they continued their path, Isabel told herself that opening a Dutch account should probably be her next small step as an expat.

On her way back to the subway station, and walking across the Lijnbaan, Isabel noticed a man standing in a corner, speaking frantically through a wireless microphone. He was about sixty years old, with the appearance of a history professor—except that he was a Christian preacher. Next to him stood two women holding signs displaying Bible verses—Matthew 5:10-11 and Hebrews 13:3—written with a bold, red marker.

"Wij moeten voor vervolgde Christenen bidden!" the man shouted continuously through the mic. It translated to: We must pray for the persecuted Christians.

The impression from hearing such words was heavy, as she immediately thought of Samir and his missing family. It was the first time she'd ever heard of this plea being transmitted publicly. Not even as a young girl, when her mother dragged her along to Church on Sundays, did she ever hear the word 'persecution' being mentioned during a sermon. Isabel sat her bags down on the ground, and folded her arms over her belly while she listened to the moving message. However, while shifting her eyes around she noticed being the only person standing-by, paying the slightest attention. It made her feel sheepish and out of place, wondering why most people didn't care for the cause. But then, the reasons suddenly became evident. These were days in which almost everybody lived wired to their earphones and smartphones, completely and deliberately disconnected from reality. Having her own mobile broken gave Isabel an excuse to actually realize this. The preacher waved at her, and she waved back shyly while portraying a tight-lipped smile.

Her next stop was at a small electronics repair shop in *De Meent*; a trendy shopping street in Rotterdam. Aiko was already waiting for her classmate, holding the fixed device in her hands.

It's almost like new!

A minute later, a young boy walked out of a room located in the back of the store. He was no older than ten years old, quite tall for his tender age, with long almond-shaped eyes and shiny brown hair.

"Oh, this is my son, Taiyo-chan," Aiko said.

The sweet kid gave Isabel a polite handshake, then spoke some Japanese words to his mother. She replied back in her native tongue, and the boy ran outside to meet with other two children.

"He's so cute!" Isabel exclaimed. "I love the mix!"

"Yes, he has a lot of me in him, but he's going to be very tall like his Dutch father," Aiko added proudly. "By the way, I believe you have some new text messages."

Could they be from Samir?

These last words nearly made Isabel jump off her sandals. But she held herself back and paid for the services, making no eager move to verify her inbox just yet.

Back at the apartment, she went on to confirm her assumptions by finding several messages from the Assyrian. They were about two days old, and in them he apologized for his abrupt absence, hoping that she would contact him soon. After brainstorming for something to respond, Isabel only asked him where he'd been in the past few days. She then went on to make herself a large cup of coffee, and sat down to review her journal.

"I really need to work on this thing..." she told herself, while going through the pages.

For her, it was shameful to know so little about Samir's culture and heritage, as well as being ignorant on the relentless harassment against his people. Then again, it was a confusing situation, for the Assyrians were facing a double persecution; for their Christian faith, and for their national identity.

Who are they, really?

"Alright, alright," she sighed, internally convincing herself to dig into her suitcase, and begin feeding her knowledge on Assyrians with one of the oldest collection of books ever known to man. She carefully took her Christmas gift out of her bag, then read the words that her mother had inscribed on the first page;

The answers to all your questions.

But Isabel was still too skeptical about the old Bible to use it as her sole reference. Instead, she opted to keep both online and paperback resources side-by-side, to get a clearer historical picture of this wonderful ethnic group.

Looking through images on the internet, Isabel admired their ancient fortifications and citadels—some of them with gates guarded by great stone deities depicting a lion's body, eagle wings and a human head. These majestic creatures were known as *Lamassus*. All of their sculptures, reliefs, and bizarre graphics—painted all over their alabaster walls—made it evident for Isabel that she was dealing with a nation of fierce warriors. From the ninth to the seventh century B.C., Assyrians were the protagonists of the most relentless and barbaric acts of war ever imagined. Their power was such that they ruled over lands way beyond the Nineveh Plains, and their armies controlled the major trade routes of the entire region. Isabel then read, in the tenth chapter of the book of Isaiah, how God made use of an Assyrian king's mighty sword to punish His own people in Israel. However, the ancient Ninevites were not exempt from Divine penalty either, as stated later on in the book of Nahum. For in the end, God Himself brought the menacing nation to judgement, precisely due to their endless cruelty, sorcery, and harlotry—ultimately allowing its total destruction in 612 B.C.

"Naughty, naughty..." Isabel murmured with amusement.

Despite the constant butchery on the battlefields during the much, much previous centuries, Isabel learned that these Semitic people—Assyrians and Babylonians alike—were deserving of infinite merit for their many contributions to civilization. They were pioneers of a functioning governmental structure, the first writing system, and Hammurabi's code of law. They were also the inventors of the wheel, aqueducts and canals, as well as the designers of incredible architecture.

And breeders of really handsome men... she giggled.

Browsing further into the bottomless pit of the internet, Isabel came across an even older piece of literature; The Epic of Gilgamesh. This fine masterpiece also spoke of battles and the savagery of these Mesopotamian men. From the very first page one would come across the raw description of the story's mighty protagonist; an epic hero with a dominant character—traits that were impossible not to attribute to the one Assyrian who kept on controlling her thoughts. And yet, it wasn't the first time she'd wondered if this exciting portrayal was based on truth, or if it was mere, provocative poetry.

Surely, it has to be true... she thought, and flashes of Samir automatically appeared in her mind once again.

She recalled the bold way in which he threw his arm around her, as they rode in the back seat of Rami's car. She also couldn't deny how he weakened her knees whenever he stood close to her—when training, talking, or simply walking silently side-by-side—nor could she forget the warmth of his body when he embraced her in the hallway of that same apartment she lived in.

"Most definitely, it is true..." she whispered, taking another sip from her cup.

After an introduction to these ancient empires, Isabel searched for more recent information on their descendants. She was keen to know about their actual culture, their traditions and art—though she figured it would have been easier just to spend more time with Samir and study him instead. She also felt curious to learn how and when Assyrians came from being polytheists to embracing Christianity. They did, after all, have quite a list of deities—*Ashur, Ishtar, Adad,* and many others. Out of all these, she recognized *Pazuzu,* the king of demons, after having seen his frightening statue in a horror film.

"Just when I was already over it!" she groaned, slamming her eyes shut.

To divert her mind from the movie's eerie images, Isabel decided to play some music, thus creating a pleasant ambience. She rapidly came across notable Assyrian artists, both contemporary and traditional; Ashur Bet Sargis was one of them. There was an endearing sentiment in his voice that was enchanting. And the fact that she could not understand Aramaic didn't keep her from being hypnotized by the timeless melodies. She even attempted to sing along, but failed miserably, as she was unable to reach the high, long notes.

Better stick to the research, Isabel...

As far as their religion, Assyrians—along with the Armenians—seemed to have been among the first people to accept Christianity, from the 1st to 3rd century AD. It was puzzling for her to imagine countries like Iraq or Syria covered in churches and crosses, in contrast to the existing Islamic power that prevailed in that region. This was the main reason why she'd assumed Samir was a Muslim in the first place.

"I really should have taken Mesopotamian History as an elective course..." she sighed.

But then, her amused and curious expression changed into one of absolute distress. Isabel suddenly fell into a pile of disturbing articles, with headlines reading the same words over and over again; Genocide, Massacre, Ethnic Cleanse, Holocaust, Persecution. These reports and essays described a series of genocidal assaults, and episodes of harassment endured by the Assyrians since the 1890's—under the ruthless Ottoman Empire—up until the present day.

"My God, what are they doing to these people?" she spoke aloud.

At that moment, Isabel was certain that the so-called interview she'd began with Samir was much more than just an immigration story. This was truly a man's testimony of survival, while escaping an ongoing persecution that was both religious and ethnic. For a woman who often complained about her circumstances, all of these revelations gradually served as life lessons that would start changing her perspective of the world. She brought her hand over her forehead, feeling a headache from all the alarming news she'd read. But even then, Isabel was sure about one thing; she needed to know more. She suddenly yearned to understand what was happening around her, and why she never heard of these Assyrian and Armenian Holocausts before, happening at the shadow of the First World War. But more importantly, Isabel wondered what the Western Church was doing to defend the oppressed Christians in the Middle East, as well as in other regions of the world.

"Probably too busy building bigger stadiums for their hypocrite preaching," she said annoyed.

And yet, Isabel felt that losing Jesus followers in the Middle East wasn't the world's biggest problem. For a real shame would be to have the wonderful Assyrian nation slowly disappear; along with their rich culture, irreplaceable heritage, and unique language. After all, the Assyrians were the ones at risk of extinction, Christianity obviously was not.

Later that night, while relaxing after a light dinner, Isabel received a surprising call from Samir. He wanted to see her again, and by his mild stuttering she could tell that he was a little anxious.

"If you want to go on a date, I accept," she chuckled. "Just tell me where."

"Next Wednesday? I can take you from your work," he proposed.

"It's settled, but...where are you, Samir?" she added.

"I'm in Berlin for a job. See you soon."

Non-speculative of what he may have been doing in Germany, Isabel focused her thoughts on the one date she'd been needing for a long time. It was evident that she'd grown totally fond of the Iraqi. She admired him, not just for everything he'd endured in his life, but also for what he'd done for her—being the only man who'd managed to open her eyes to the real world, by pulling her out of the cushioned comfort zone of ignorance.

That night, Isabel had a deep urge to dance, just the way Sarah taught her to. And after a minute of browsing for the right music, she found an old but popular song by the Egyptian superstar Amr Diab. She laughed with utmost delight, not wasting a second to move her body to the exotic rhythm. She lifted her blouse atop her belly button and tied it in a firm knot, followed by letting her luscious hair down over her shoulders. She then raised her arms above her head, twirling her wrists in a slow, seductive motion while swaying her hips in the very same manner. Closing her eyes to savor the trance, she felt an overpowering desire to have Samir's body close against hers. The sensual beat of the eastern drum brought all her memories of the fervid Assyrian back to life, along with the need to feel the weakening touch of his perfect, strong hands.

11

WE'RE GOING SOUTH

In the middle of the following week, Isabel spent all morning begging Ebele to cover her at the end of her shift, while she used one of the vacant rooms to get ready for her highly-anticipated date. The stern Ugandan woman refused in the beginning, but after several hours she couldn't stand Isabel's annoying and desperate plea any longer.

"You have ten minutes!" she added with a commanding tone.

"Thank you so much!" Isabel exclaimed, planting a kiss on her coworker's cheek. "I promise to do five of your rooms for a whole month!"

"Mhmm..." Ebele mumbled, twisting her lips.

Later that afternoon, Isabel locked herself in one of the suites, taking a quick shower, then throwing her outfit on in a hasty manner. She wore a new knee-length, black lace dress, combined with a pair of jeweled nude pumps and very simple make-up; a little powder, the classic cat-eyeliner, and a reddish gloss over the lips. And as for her hair, she opted to let her natural curls bounce freely. Counting her last moments of cover, Isabel stuffed her maid uniform and previous outfit inside a bag, then rapidly scanned the room to make sure everything was left in place. When she walked out of the suite, she was startled to see Luisa speaking to Ebele at the end of the corridor. Luckily she stood on her back, and her loyal colleague distracted the supervisor while Isabel took another way out of the floor. Inside the guest elevator, she stood among a small group of German tourists. They all gawked over her while mumbling sexual remarks among one another. Isabel scoffed when she understood some of the words—which she'd learned not too long ago from a former colleague at La Porte D'or—and resolved to amuse the *tudescos* even further as soon as they reached the lobby. The Latin expat sensually swayed out of the lift, looking over her shoulder and waving at them flirtatiously. The cheeky Caucasians immediately began wolf-whistling like animated cartoons. But just a few seconds later, their dirty grins shifted into plain displeasure.

"Auf Wiedersehen, schmutzige Schweine!" Isabel growled, as she turned her hand to flip them off.

Taking advantage of her supervisor's absence, Isabel sneaked into the tiny changing-room by Luisa's office. She threw her laundry inside her locker, just before rushing out the door, and stealthily across the wide-open lobby. It was just about 17:00 in the afternoon. Many chauffeurs were dropping off guests while some picked up others, but none of them were her beloved Samir. All of a sudden, she spotted the unmistakable black Mercedes coming from around the corner. It parked right in front of the hotel's entrance, making her feel as though she were in the spotlight at a red carpet event. Onlookers contemplated the gorgeous Latina as she approached the vehicle in anticipation, witnessing her face lightening up at the sight of the handsome man stepping out of the driver's seat. He looked as neat and sharp as the first day they met, only this time he was smiling joyously.

"Mevrouw...you look amazing," he expressed with loving admiration.

She lowered her gaze and coyly tucked a lock of hair behind her ear. And he opened the back-seat door, reaching out for her hand to gallantly guide her inside.

"Dank U wel, Meneer. So do you. But…"

Isabel closed the door once again, skipping over to the front, and letting herself slide into the passenger's seat. Samir smirked complacently, rushing back into his own side of the car. She didn't' know where he'd take her that evening, but she could already tell that it was the beginning of an interesting date. She also couldn't help noticing that he'd tamed down his reckless driving, riding carefully and patiently, getting caught on each and every stoplight almost on purpose.

"Is it far?" she asked.

"It's very close to my place, actually, not too far."

His voice did not tremble one bit as he said this, and Isabel swallowed hard at the possibility of going back to his house after dinner. At a red-light halt, there was complete awkward silence around them. She tried to figure out what to say or talk about, but a rush of teenage nerves had suddenly overwhelmed her. She then turned her head to the left for a glance at Samir's face. But to her surprise, his own eyes had been set upon her right from the moment she'd started daydreaming. Unable to resist the tension of their closeness any longer, Isabel slowly leaned to his side, beckoning him closer for a first kiss. She placed her hands around his head, and his skin felt as though it was burning in fever. Samir breathed heavily through his nose, impatient, yet allowing her to make the first move.

This is torture!

Her eyes were glowing a bright golden, mad with desire and anticipation. And just like opposite poles of powerful magnets, their lips locked with savage determination. Time had ceased to have any meaning at that instant, and the traffic lights had turned green, yellow, and back to red, all while their ongoing passion caused a symphony of car honking right outside their doors.

But they did reach their destination, eventually. It was a beautiful Mediterranean restaurant, situated right under an eight-story apartment building at the corner of Nieuwe Binnenweg. It had the layout of a Greek garden; with leafy trees, lush pink bougainvillea, and blooming grape vines hanging over the enclosing fences. The weather was perfect to sit out in the terrace, facing the placid canals and overlooking traditional Dutch houses scattered in the distance. A friendly waiter approached the intriguing couple moments later, warmly welcoming them with two complimentary shots.

"What is this?" Isabel asked Samir.

"It's a drink from Greece. It's nice, try it," he replied, grinning self-assured.

Placing her trust on his confident words, she threw the liquor down her throat right after Sam did, followed by being instantly repelled by the strong taste of anise. To her, it tasted just like the dreadful licorice gumdrops. And from witnessing her reaction, Samir laughed out loud while clapping his hands on the table.

"God! That is awful!" she exclaimed, unable to contain her own laughter.

Shortly after the humorous display, they began their feast with a small tray of some spinach pastries called *spanakopitas*. Of these, the Hispanic food enthusiast couldn't have enough. Later on, they delighted in their main dishes of lamb and a side of spicy pilaf rice. Their wine glasses were refilled over and over again, triggering Isabel's merry little laughs and ridiculously bashful glances.

"Ok, ok! So this is your part of town, isn't it?" she queried. "Where is your house then?"

"I live right after the bridge behind me, just a five-minute walk," he responded casually.

"Just a five-minute walk, huh?" she chortled playfully, gradually pulling her lips close together at the sight of his rather suggestive, smug nod.

She felt her cheeks blushing hot while looking in the direction he'd pointed out, realizing that his place really wasn't far at all. She took a deep breath, attempting to calm her rising nerves, and swiftly turned her face away from his. But then, she gasped sharply at the touch of Samir's warm hand on hers.

"Another time...if you prefer," he said gently.

Though a part of her applauded his courteous response, Isabel wasn't sure if those were the words she wanted to hear that night.

"Yeah...maybe another time," she replied with a hesitant tone, but portraying a content smile.

They stayed at the establishment nearly until closing time, discussing part of Isabel's research on Assyrian culture, and sharing some of their most memorable anecdotes while living in the Netherlands. Despite that Samir had already been in Holland for a little over two years, he still found it difficult to assimilate to the Dutch way of life. He admitted that his love for his country and his people was too strong; much stronger than his will to become one of the West.

"Tell me something more about your customs," she said enthusiastically.

"Hmm, like what?" he asked.

"I don't really know...ah! What's your traditional dance like?" she queried.

He scoffed, "Assyrian dance?"

She nodded with an amused countenance.

"No, I don't tell you," he said.

Isabel sighed. "Come on, why no—"

"I show you. Wait."

Samir went on to pay for the restaurant bill, then reached out for Isabel's hand.

"Come," he commanded.

He guided her back to the classy vehicle, and they drove slowly past the street where he lived. But it was dark at that hour, and she couldn't see the area clearly.

The handsome Middle Easterner took a sharp left-turn through a long, narrow road, driving by a port swarmed with old-fashioned sail boats and classical architecture—almost resembling Johannes Vermeer's *View of Delft*. He then parked the Mercedes on a small hill above the Nieuwe Maas River, and held Isabel's hand as they stepped down a grassy slope toward the harbor. Right there, at Havenstraat 53, stood a red loveseat in the shape of a heart.

From afar, it looked just like a large metal cradle. And yet, being an expert in tourist attractions, Isabel soon realized she was standing before one of Europe's Love Padlocks locations. This was a popular, world-renown tradition, which encouraged people to affix colorful locks around bridges and other public structures to symbolize their *everlasting love*. Neither of them had a padlock at the time, however, nor could they define their growing attraction for one another as being anything else but that. They ignored the artsy landmark at this point, and continued walking until reaching a clear space in the harbor, where Samir drew a white handkerchief out of his pocket.

"Now, watch," he said, just before he began twirling the piece of cloth in the air, while shrugging his shoulders, and stomping rhythmically.

Isabel swung one arm across her body, to support the other arm as she held her chin steadily, curiously studying the silent Iraqi dance displayed in front of her.

"I'm sure that looks quite impressive with music," she tittered.

Each time they were together, Isabel could notice a new change in Samir's temperament. He seemed more open and outgoing. And that night, he demonstrated having a surprisingly spontaneous side.

"We have the music inside, come join me," he beckoned.

"But I don't know how!" she responded.

"First, take off those shoes!" he urged.

Isabel did as he asked, thrilled for trying something fun and new. Samir then lead her on a cyclic dynamic of line-dancing. They held hands first, kicking forward a few times, followed by swinging their arms and shifting to the side in a rhythmic march that went forth and back, almost like a two-way *cha-cha*. This was called the *Khigga* dance. They had no drums nor melodies to accompany them, except for the beating of their hearts, which became stronger after every passing second. And Samir's energetic way of sharing his culture, only came to an end when Isabel couldn't jump or breathe anymore.

They sat at the edge of the port to catch their breath, admiring the bright city lights and the Euromast tower standing grandly in the far distance. It was a sublime starry night in the Netherlands, worthy of being immortalized on a fresh canvas all over again. For a moment she thought it was all a dream, and feared that any minute she would wake back up at her Florida apartment. Because despite all of the challenges she'd encountered in Holland, the last thing Isabel wished was to be awakened by the deafening blasts of her alarm clock, marking the beginning of a day like every other.

"This is wonderful..." she whispered.

"What is?" he asked.

"You...and this evening, those lights, and even that corny heart over there," she chuckled. "I don't know, I just feel at peace right now."

Samir nodded to her remark, slowly pulling her body closer against his for another passionate embrace.

But just like the fairy-tale curse of a ticking clock, at the end of that same week, Isabel's entire perfect scenario crumbled underneath her maid slippers. She'd arrived to work early and with a lot of energy, and stepped inside the locker room to change into her uniform. Suddenly, Luisa walked in, followed by a gloomy-looking Ebele. She hadn't the slightest clue of what was going on, up until the moment her supervisor harshly threw a piece of red lace at her face. Isabel recognized the underwear immediately, for it belonged to her.

"You're fired," Luisa spoke in an acrid tone of voice, giving Ebele a stare of antipathy before storming out of the room. Isabel remained standing still, shaking as her eyes turned reddish and watery. Her next reaction was to check the laundry bag she'd left inside her locker, browsing through her wrinkled clothes in hopes to find the alibi she needed. But her attitude of denial was useless.

"I don't know how this happened," she sobbed. "I swear I checked the room!"

"One of the other maids found it under the bed," her colleague explained.

"I can't lose this job, Ebele!" she cried out while slamming the locker's door shot.

But she'd already lost it. In her eagerness to impress Samir, she hadn't thoroughly checked the red-carpeted floors of the suite, overseeing the eventual cause of her dismissal—nor did she consider that there were surveillance cameras in the hallways. The introverted Ugandan woman felt moved by her apprentice's tears, and offered her arms and shoulders for a comforting embrace that Isabel couldn't possibly reject.

Leaving her uniforms behind, Isabel made her way back to the subway station in absolute silence and introspection, as she tried to figure out what she would do for money from that moment on. She knew there were plenty of other hotels seeking *kamermeisjes*, yet she thought about using her layoff as an opportunity to find a better job. She continued meditating on the encouraging possibility, walking on with her shoulders slumped and her hands inside her pockets. But as she approached Lennert's place, she never considered that her circumstances could worsen. She noticed that a black Audi was parked just in front of the building, and behind it was a small branded truck from a moving company. When she got closer, she noticed a gray-haired, finely-dressed man in the front seat of the car, calmly reading a newspaper. The elegant fellow turned his head to the left, and automatically stepped out of the car to greet Isabel in a polite manner. His overly-proper accent rapidly made her assume that he was British.

"Good morning, Miss Alvarez. How do you do?" he asked with a slight, gentle bow.

"Um, who are—"

"There you are!"

Another European voice disrupted her speech. And as she looked past the suited man, she saw Lennert emerging from the front door. He was followed by two other men who carried Isabel's suitcases outside of the building, along with a crate full of her groceries and many other items she owned.

"What is this?!" she demanded with great surprise in her eyes.

"What does it look like?" responded Lennert in a sarcastic tone. "My keys, please."

Isabel felt her throat closing tight, and the air around her was suddenly so thick it could barely reach her lungs. But she wouldn't allow herself to completely break down in front of that man's arrogance—she couldn't give him that kind of satisfaction. With a trembling hand, Isabel drew the keys out of her purse and threw them at him.

"Take them! I don't need anything from you!" she muttered, fiery-eyed and determined.

"Sure you don't," he scoffed. "Oh, and before I forget..."

Lennert then handed the exasperated girl a yellow envelope, in which she found both the phone and gas bills. The international calls to her mother, and the constant use of the heater during the previous months, had all amounted to a total of three thousand euros.

"Make sure to pay every cent, unless you'd like to find out what a Dutch court looks like from the inside," he threatened.

The other two men kept unloading a few pieces of furniture from the truck, followed by what appeared to be a large painting—partially wrapped in parchment paper. It almost looked like Lennert was moving back into his old apartment.

Or perhaps he's just redecorating...

Isabel's shifty mind speculated on this for a moment, then rapidly refocused on her current, and more critical situation.

"Let's go, Greg!" commanded the cocky Dutchman—who was escorted back to the vehicle as though he were some kind of political party leader.

"Good day, Miss," added the old chauffeur.

Isabel snarled back at him. And just before they drove off, Lennert lowered his window and called her over one more time. When she came up to him, he unrolled his tongue to unleash another series of cutting words that made her feel further responsible for her circumstances.

"You know why I do this?" he asked, rubbing his face with his hand. "It really wasn't the bills, nor your bad housekeeping skills."

She shrugged, "Why, then?"

"Because I know it wasn't you who drank my best scotch."

His last words left her stunned and with a fiercely-pounding heart. She glanced over to the sidewalk, where lied everything she had left. Quietly, she sat atop one of her suitcases, trying to think of any clever solutions to her problem. She considered that the safest way out of her mess would be to take her bags, grab the next train to the airport, and return home pretending none of it ever happened. However, the harsh threat inside the yellow envelope in her hands was one she wouldn't easily escape. Coincidently, Mei walked out the front door, holding her baby in her arms. She was on her way to take little Bo to the Rotterdam Zoo. But seeing her neighbor in such condition, made her put her plans on hold.

"Come inside, I'll make you some tea," she kindly offered.

Mei respected Isabel's silence, asking nothing about the scene she'd witnessed outside. She quietly sipped from her porcelain cup, giving her former neighbor the chance to speak if she chose to.

"I guess it was just a matter of time..." Isabel whispered.

The poise Chinese mother sucked her lips inwards, just as though she were ashamed to agree with what she'd heard. Isabel suspected that Xiang may have had something to do with Lennert finding out about Samir's visit, but that would had been a premature allegation. The now-homeless expat slouched deeper into the couch. But her heartache was soon replaced by a burst of the purest love, when the adorable toddler wobbled towards her, handing her a picture she'd drawn and colored.

"Oh, how cute!" Isabel exclaimed in a high-pitched, childish tone. "Is dit voor mij?"

Little Bo nodded rapidly as she understood the question, coyly putting her hands over her smiling mouth. Isabel took the child in her arms and cuddled her, captivated by her tender innocence.

"You will make a great mother someday," added Mei, as she watched the sweet display.

"I don't know about that, but Bo is truly a miracle child," Isabel said. "I'm already starting to feel better."

"So, what are you going to do now?" Mei asked.

Isabel thought about the question for a moment.

"Well, there's one thing I could try..." she sighed.

Placing the child next to her, she took her cellphone out of her bag and browsed through her contact list, pressing the name of the only other person she trusted in Holland.

"Hello, Isabel." spoke Samir in a silky tone. "How are you?"

"Not so well," she said. "Are you busy?"

"Parked outside a hotel, waiting for a client. What happened?" he inquired.

"Lennert just kicked me out. I didn't know who else to call."

"What?!" he growled. "Listen, I come to get you now."

"No! Wait! But you're worki—"

The call was disconnected before she could finish her sentence. Isabel stared at her phone with a dropped jaw, fearing Samir would get himself in trouble for her cause—yet again. And just like he'd said it, he appeared in front of the apartment building in less than fifteen minutes, parking the shiny Mercedes right in the middle of the road. Isabel ran downstairs and out of the premises, rushing into his strong arms and secure embrace.

"You come live with me, yes?" he murmured, looking fondly into her eyes, just before he caught her round lips with the inviting warmth of his mouth.

The two of them engaged in a toe-curling, passionate kiss that even caused her neighbor to clear her throat. And just as if they'd pressed an imaginary rewind button, Samir once again loaded the red suitcases into the trunk of the car. The moment Isabel slipped into the impeccable, leather front seat, she felt somewhat relieved from her distress. She then waved at Mei and her beautiful child, not just in gratitude for their love and hospitality, but also to say goodbye. For that was the very last time Isabel wandered around the streets of quiet, little Blijdorp.

12

A HOT SLICE OF MOSUL

Samir and Isabel left the Northern side of the majestic city, driving once more towards the same borough where they'd had their first official date. The sun seemed to shine brighter in that part of town. But as Isabel looked out the window, she wondered if she was still in Rotterdam at all. From left to right she saw nothing but Middle Eastern clothing stores, Muslim *halal* butcheries, sidewalk fruit markets, Turkish restaurants, electronic shops, travel agencies, and plenty of money-transfer establishments. As Sam continued to drive up Schiedamseweg, Isabel boldly asked him where all the Dutch people had gone, and he laughed at her random question.

"We have some, but almost everybody here is an immigrant," he explained.

There was a festival of hijabs and vibrant tunics on every direction, as well as a rather scandalous chatter all around. Samir then parked the car in front of a red-bricked building, stepping out swiftly to open Isabel's door. It was a simple four-story apartment complex—just like most other residential blocks around the city—with the difference that this one was oddly accessorized with plenty of satellite dishes, installed outside almost every window.

Oh my God, so it is true...

Samir helped her bring her bags up to the third floor. But before he opened the door to his apartment, he turned to face her one more time.

"I should tell you, my house is small, and maybe not what you're used to," he said.

His words caused Isabel to pout her lips and scowl her brows in disapproval.

"That's the most ridiculous thing I've ever heard you say, Samir."

She stepped through the door right after him, following the kindhearted Assyrian toward the bedroom, where he gently placed her suitcases. Standing underneath the door frame, Isabel couldn't stop staring at the neatly-made queen-size bed, imagining that later that evening she would also be lying on it, right next to him. The idea of resting her head over his solid chest was thrilling, and she could feel her heart racing to the fantasy. She wanted him from the very first time he held her in his arms, but she was embarrassed to admit it. Then again, her secret desires were irrelevant if she couldn't even conceal the reddish glow spreading over her chest and cheeks.

"I guess you only have one bed, huh," she spoke nervously.

He sighed, opening the closet and pulling out a blue, foldable mattress.

My God, I've had yoga mats thicker than that thing...

"Choose wisely," he hinted with a wink.

"Ok, I got it," she snickered.

"Make yourself comfortable," he added. "I must go back to work now."

"I understand," she said, pouting childishly, and batting her lashes to convince him otherwise.

"I come back at 18:00," he added, "Oh, and here's a copy from the apartment key."

For a moment he felt hesitant to leave, smiling warmly at the beautiful woman before him. But then he kissed her one last time, before rushing out into the hall and down the stairs.

Once again, Isabel found herself alone inside an apartment. It was smaller than any of the other residences she'd ever lived in, but cozy nonetheless, and very organized. The layout was simple as well; one black couch placed against a tan wall, and a cushioned chair in the same color on the opposite side. There was an oval tea table in the middle, and on it was a laptop, a remote control, and a small, shapely glass with a tiny silver spoon inside. Mounted on the opposite wall, across the sofa, was a large flat-screen, installed together with a home theater system. Isabel grabbed the remote and turned the TV on, hoping to break the nerve-wracking silence in the room. But suddenly, she became startled by the blasting sounds that came out of the speakers; they were literally the sounds of bomb strikes and gunshots from a live news report.

"Jesus Christ!" she screamed, turning the TV off immediately, and repeating the exact same last two words—only this time with a big question mark at the end. Above Samir's dining table sat two resin figures that Isabel didn't notice earlier; Jesus and the Virgin Mary. This naturally helped prove that he was in fact Catholic.

The neat appearance of his apartment not only made obvious that he was a great housekeeper, but also that he'd not been living there for long. This awakened Isabel's curiosity. She took the intrusive liberty of looking into his cabinets and drawers, noticing that most of them were empty, while others contained only personal documents and Dutch-language books. She continued her prying back in the bedroom, and started browsing through a wooden armoire that stood next to the bed. Between scattered papers and folders was a red backpack. Inside, Isabel found a Bible written in Aramaic, with a gold crucifix necklace wrapped around it. All the hairs on the back of her neck stood up, realizing that those were the same items Samir's mother had given him, just before they were separated prior to fleeing Istanbul. To hold the family heirloom, made Isabel feel as if the words written in her journal had suddenly materialized in her own hands.

"What the hell are you doing?" she asked herself, placing the priceless gifts back where she'd found them.

She then proceeded to unpack her suitcases, making space for her own clothes inside his closet. In it, she found two black suits, uniforms, many dark-colored t-shirts and several pairs of jeans. He was truly a simple man when it came to wardrobe; a trait that he and Isabel seemed to have in common. When she went on to check the kitchen, she saw that it was just as neat as the rest of the apartment, but was missing the most essential of appliances; a coffee machine.

"But of course…" she whispered, noticing a tin can full of English-tea bags.

She then opened the cabinets, hoping to find something more than what she'd discovered at the previous bachelor pad, and she was amazed. The cupboards were stocked up with bags of basmati rice, boxes of pasta, as well as cans of garbanzo beans and tomato sauce. In the fridge she found a variety of fresh vegetables, olives, bottled cream cheese, a tub of plain yogurt, and a drawer full of ripe pomegranates.

"So the man can cook too," she said, biting her lip. "We shall see."

Isabel took advantage of her time alone to start looking for other viable options of employment. Since she'd already lied to her mother about finding work in the Event Management field, she thought it a good idea to give it an actual try. She also wanted to prove herself in the Dutch language, for she'd already begun to master the sharp and rigid pronunciation of the words. Browsing through a job-search database, she found several notices from clubs and pubs in the city, mostly looking to hire bartenders and waitresses. The ambitious event planner continued scrolling down uninterested, eventually coming across an advertisement from a Latin restaurant, where they needed a new assistant manager. Isabel tapped her fingers on the table and pursed her lips sideways, ultimately concluding that she was not in the position to be picky. She then went on to write them a cover letter, self-assured that her CV alone would catch the employer's attention.

A moment later, she received an email from her mom, in which she shared photos of herself getting mani-pedis together with her friends, all while sitting by a luxurious swimming pool. It pleased Isabel to learn that her mother had finally redeemed her Christmas gift. Seeing her smile brought her joy, though it also made her feel a little nostalgic. As postscript, Amelia wrote being concerned over Isabel's BMW. She'd already used every last cent left behind by her daughter for the monthly bill. The main purpose of her email was to ask Isabel if she could transfer the upcoming payment that same week. Reading this was alarming for the unemployed expat, and nearly caused her another panic attack. Being completely overwhelmed by frustration and embarrassment, she decided not to reply to the email, for she couldn't find the words to tell Amelia the truth of what she'd been going through.

"I'll figure something out," Isabel told herself.

Later that evening, Samir returned to his apartment carrying a bag with groceries. He seemed excited, and eager to prepare a special meal for his new guest.

"Be sure, tonight I make you fall in love with Iraqi food!" he warned humorously.

Curious of his culinary skills, Isabel accepted the food-tasting challenge. However, he insisted in doing all the work on his own.

"But it's a little bit warm, so I hope is ok with you…" he added, just before taking off his blazer and unbuttoning his shirt.

Isabel intended to look away. But her eyes became automatically fixed on Samir's monumental physique. She felt herself melting from within at the sight of him, gawking over his solid bare chest for the very first time.

"No—it's...not at all," she mumbled, contemplating him intently as she leaned against the wall. She never imagined that a man could look so attractive inside a kitchen, showing off his perfectly-shaped pecs pulsating as he moved about.

That evening, he was preparing a dish called *Lis'an el qa'thi*, or simply put; lamb-stuffed eggplants. Isabel studied his moves with great attention, surprised to witness him prepare the meal with utmost craft. He would rinse the vegetables thoroughly, then proceed to chop them in even measures, almost in a ritualistic manner. Anyone would have sworn that he'd been a professional chef in his past life. He stewed the tender meat in a saucepan, carefully filling the eggplants next, and later setting them on a glass container to bake. For the side dishes, he cooked basmati rice and made a light cucumber-yogurt salad.

"Ok, we wait in the living-room now," he said as he washed his hands. But Isabel remained stunned by his presence, and from being intoxicated amidst the warm scent of exotic spices.

"Oh, yes, of course," she chuckled.

They sat close to each other for a while, watching a Turkish TV series that he liked. During a commercial break, Samir turned his head towards Isabel, gently closing his hand around her chin. And without saying a word, he pulled her face up and kissed her with impassioned pace. He then began running his lips over her neck, while lowering her top's straps off her shoulders. Between her own moans of delight she could hear his breathing accelerating, and the grip of his greedy hands became tighter around her slender waist. Before she could take a new breath, Samir pulled her down to the classical-patterned rug on the ground. He crawled on top of her in seconds, devouring her lips while his longing fingers found their way underneath her shirt.

"Samir, wait! The oven!" she gasped.

Both of them jumped off the floor alarmed, for the entire room suddenly smelled like burned food. Luckily, the eggplants were still their normal aubergine color.

"That was close," he remarked in relief.

Samir then asked Isabel to help him serve dinner, giving her certain instructions that she found to be quite peculiar. He first demanded to have all the rice poured over a large tray, where they could both eat from.

"This is normal in my country," he added.

Then, he asked her to place a stack of *markouk* on the table.

"We use this better than a spoon, or fork," he continued.

As they finally sat to eat the aromatic meal, Samir parted one of the flat breads and dipped it within the saucy eggplants. He gave Isabel the first bite out of his own hand, and she was blown away by the exquisite taste as soon as it passed through her lips.

"I must say, I thought I was a great cook, but this is fantastic!" she exclaimed.

"Good! Next time you make something, and we will see," he teased.

"You're on!" she replied.

Later that night, after a long and relaxing shower, Isabel stood dripping wet over the bathroom rug, thinking about what had happened in the living room earlier.

Or what almost happened...

Wrapping herself in a towel, she tiptoed towards Samir's bedroom and collapsed flat on his bed.

"What is the matter with you?" she asked herself, feeling embarrassed for being intimidated by the man waiting in the living room.

She later browsed through his drawers, which she'd recently occupied with her own clothes, and picked a short nightdress to wear that night, hoping to resume the intimate magic-carpet scene a little more appropriately. The silky champagne camisole beautifully accentuated the natural tan of her skin. And she smeared a shimmering lotion over her legs and arms to make them smoother. She then took one last glimpse of herself before a mirror, becoming startled as she heard footsteps approaching the room, and pausing right behind the door.

"Can I come in?" asked the Iraqi, in the sultriest and deepest version of his voice. The anxious gal sat right back on the bed, pretending to brush her hair as she cursed inside her head.

Damn it, calm down already!

"Sure, I'm just—come on in!" she stuttered.

But there was no use for any more words the second Samir Ishmael Youkhana stepped into the bedroom. The carnal tension between them had grown so strong that if their lust would have had a voice of its own, it would have wailed in anguish long ago. He approached her like a tiger stalking his prey, and cornered her just the same, pouring his zealous intentions deep into her gleaming eyes. Samir made this woman nervous in a way that fascinated her beyond her imagination. In him, she saw a bearer of pure masculinity who needed not pretend being dominant before the opposite sex. There was no doubt that before her stood the living image of the same men described in the ancient poems of Mesopotamia; beautifully endowed, yet terrifying like great, wild bulls. Just like these epic characters, Samir possessed a physique that seemed to have been forged by Sumerian deities themselves. And everything else about him was equally as extraordinary; the rawness in his speech, his legendary features, his whole enthralling, hypnotizing ethnicity.

"You can't be real..." she whispered in awe.

"Shhh!" he hushed.

His powerful Middle Eastern gaze disarmed her immediately, leaving her with nothing left but a faint breath that was stolen mercilessly with a long, ferocious kiss.

"Hold on," he whispered into her ear.

Before Isabel could even react to his command, the handsome bodybuilder was already holding her body about seven feet in the air. Seconds later, he started to perform an acrobatic act that sent her on a maddening odyssey between pleasure and delightful torment. He effortlessly sustained the squirming female over his broad arms and shoulders, as though she were a weightless bird resting atop the thickest branches of an olive tree. But no matter how entrancing the moisten twirls might have been, they could never ease the torturous desire that she felt for him. Spellbound by her passion, Isabel willingly submitted to Samir's foreign regime of Ashurian erotism. His skilled fingers were as devious as horned cerastes, which later crawled smoothly through her radiant hair. He used his serpentine touch to both indulge and tease her, ultimately pulling her frenzied lips away from his sweet paradisiac essence, and leaving her to die of thirst at the very edge of the mighty Tigris. He then beckoned her with his midnight eyes, and she could feel her heart dancing to the beat of the zamboor as he pulled her up against him one more time. He spoke to her with strange words she could not understand, but words that enchanted her nonetheless. He was like no man she'd ever seen in this world; sort of like a hero from an epic tale one would only read about in ancient tablets and forbidden scrolls.

"Samir...I want you so much," she whispered, bewitched by the flawless bareness he exhibited.

"Tsk, tsk..." he uttered, gently lowering the strings of her chemise, and letting the delicate silk drop soundlessly on the ground. He then lifted her up once again—just high enough to have her legs entangled around his robust torso—firmly cupping her round derriere with his large hands. He took her out into the living-room, and lied her down on the soft tribal rug, just as he did before, contemplating her precious nakedness before slowly crawling over her body.

"It's like you're on fire," she breathed, running her fingers over the fervent skin of his chest.

Parting his lips, he spoke another line of foreign words. But the meaning behind his expressions was irrelevant under the enigmatic sound of his voice. The molten fire that ran through his veins had long been flowing in her honor. And yet, Samir still wouldn't give into Isabel's agonizing urge.

"Samir!" she groaned, but he hushed her again, and more intensely.

The purpose behind his suppression was grand, just as it was sadistic. For that night, Samir was determined to make Isabel discover the mysterious and wild side of herself. The corners of his mouth dampened in delight atop her rich breasts, and the ticklish brush of his tongue caused her to stagger underneath his herculean frame. She arched her back in abiding trance, while he savored her body zealously, as if it were smothered in pure honey. He then slithered all the way down, until his lips reached her ticklish toes. At this point, Isabel drew her sensitive feet away from his grip.

"Khalas!" he shouted, his nostrils flaring in anger.

Her self-conscious move had upset him. And he pushed himself forward abruptly, until his heated face hovered right above hers.

"Let me!" he said rabidly.

Is he trying to make me go mad?

Samir yearned to siege every part of her, but she wouldn't allow herself to surrender underneath his touch. This, he greatly resented.

"You Western women always want everything fast," he continued to argue.

"That's not true," she muttered, feeling a little insulted.

"Then let me do what I want...in my way," he murmured in a tone that made her shiver—though not as much as his warm solidity gliding over her abdomen.

Samir lowered his head to kiss her again, but backed away just before their lips could touch. She wanted to cry in frustration, unaware that a second later she'd be succumbed to Samir's devoted hunt for each of her sensuous regions. Isabel moaned in escalating ecstasy, squeezing the smooth fabric she rested on while praising the gifted hands and lips that possessed her. He watched over her sweet defeat and grinned complacently, moving up to lie on top of her weakened body once more. Conscious of the effect caused by the sound of his voice, he brushed the tip of his nose against her right earlobe, and invaded her blown mind with more Aramaic phrases of love.

"You're killing me…" she whimpered breathlessly.

"Not yet…" he said, continuing to tease her until he saw that she'd finally dropped all defenses, until he concluded that she was already on the edge of madness.

With one hand, he held both her wrists down above her head. And with the other he anointed himself with the naturally flowing springs of her lust. Her eyes flashed in desperation, and she felt forced to turn her impassioned face away from his sadistic gaze.

"You want it?" he whispered.

Isabel nodded as a single teardrop ran down the side of her eye. He then released her hands again, slowly, gradually settling amidst her dampish limbs.

Damn it, just take me!

With overwhelming suspense and longing, Isabel secured her tingling arms around her lover's neck. Samir let out a soft growl as he leaned in, inhaling the exhilarating fragrance off her bosom one more time, just before seizing her yielded body in a long-lasting, demented rapture.

13

CULTURE SHOCK

The following morning, Isabel was awaken by an array of noises she never heard back at her previous neighborhood. It was a combination of child laughter, car honking, and rowdy neighbors initiating a hot and busy Saturday. Despite all of the fuss, she delighted greatly at the sight of the beautiful man lying next to her. It was both a charming and comical display. For Samir slept soundly, with his brows furrowed and his arms firmly folded on his stomach, looking just like a mythical warrior in vigilant slumber. She slowly moved away from him, browsing over the ground for something to cover herself with. But as she got further, Isabel discovered that he was not a heavy sleeper at all.

"Where are you going?" he asked in a deep tone, keeping his eyes closed.

"Oh, hey!" she flinched. "I think I'm going to buy some coffee."

"Hmmm, ten more minutes," he said, pulling her back against him, to embrace her between his beastly arms a little longer.

Later on, Samir and Isabel strolled throughout the historical town, enjoying the soft summer breeze and the picturesque scenarios on every side. Locals stared at the Hispanic girl with curiosity, easily recognizing a newcomer roaming freely around their community. To be in this multicultural district was like falling into another dimension within the Netherlands. Ironically, Delfshaven was considered the most traditionally-Dutch borough in Rotterdam, as it was sanctuary of classical architecture left untouched by WWII.

When the eye-catching couple walked into a Middle Eastern supermarket, the Arabic music coming from the ceiling speakers reminded Isabel of the corner-store near her old apartment. This time, she felt like she was truly in the Arab world. Every product on the aisles carried labels which were unreadable to her eyes, but that still didn't prevent the java enthusiast from recognizing the coffee bags on the shelves.

"I will need a machine for this," she said.

"No broplem, we can get one," he added.

"Don't you mean, no 'problem'?"

Isabel couldn't help impersonating him after listening to the comical solecism. And as response to her innocent mockery, Samir playfully grabbed her from behind, attempting to find any ticklish spots around her abdomen. She jerked fiercely, unable to control her laughter and causing them both to nearly stumble to the ground. As they engaged in a warm kiss, a mature and conservative-looking couple walked before them, gasping at their loving spontaneity. The man hurried his partner out of the store, portraying a strong impression of outrage and offense, then instantly called out for the owner of the establishment. A manager walked into the scene a minute later. He seemed baffled by the exaggerated ruckus, all while Isabel stood in the background, completely lost as she witnessed Samir arguing with the two men in rough Arabic.

"Come, leave the food. We get it from another place," growled Samir, grabbing Isabel by the hand, and pulling her out of the shop. He marched forward in silence, almost stomping, and she could feel him squeezing her hand harder every second.

"Aren't you going to explain what happened back there?" she demanded.

"Forget about it," he muttered.

"No, I want to know now, please," she insisted, letting go of his strong grip.

He paced down and rubbed his face.

"Look, this part of the city is not like the rest. Some people here have strange rules..."

She stood tall and firm in the middle of the sidewalk, raising her eyebrows so he would elaborate on his remark. Seeing that she wouldn't dismiss the issue, he continued to explain that most store owners in the area were very religious. For this reason, they had established strong rules against Public Displays of Affection, which Isabel and Samir had apparently violated.

"That's just ridiculous!" she retorted. "I mean, it was just a kiss!"

"Clearly you've never been to the Middle East," he remarked sarcastically.

As they continued their way down Schiedamseweg, they stopped by a small convenience store and butchery; from where Samir would purchase fresh lamb, ground beef, and several packets of spices. Isabel stayed outside the shop, browsing through the fruit stands and filling a small plastic bag with ripe, plump peaches.

"Well, look who it is; Miss United States of America."

Isabel turned around at the sound of the familiar voice, finding Amaité standing by with a dubious expression.

"Oh, hi!" Isabel greeted. "How are—"

"Cut the bullshit. What are you doing here?" asked the Mexican tomboy.

The other Latina appeared dumbfounded by her classmate's hostile expressions.

"What's your problem with me?" she asked.

"Nothing. I just didn't expect people like you to hang out in these areas," replied the Sinaloan.

All of a sudden, Samir called out for Isabel, asking her to get inside the store.

"Ah, you're with him. It all makes sense now," Amaité added.

"Actually, I live with him now," Isabel said with smug. "So if you'd excuse me..."

Stepping into the store, she found Samir speaking to another handsome Middle Eastern man.

"Isabel, this is Yousef. He is my friend."

"Hola señorita!" greeted the friendly store owner.

He was a tall, thirty-something year-old Lebanese fellow with a cheerful personality. And for the way he gallantly kissed her hand, Isabel could tell he wasn't too driven by regulations regarding personal space. Nonetheless, he did follow a code that was even stranger. For as soon as Isabel reached for her wallet, Yousef shook his head and stuffed his hands inside the pockets of his white apron.

"It's ok, he will take care of it," he said while pointing at the Iraqi.

"No, I want to pay, please," she stressed, trying to hand over a five-euro bill.

Even still, both men refused her money over and over again, leaving her with no choice but to accept their offer. As they left the establishment, Isabel commented on the bizarre issue, considering it just as odd as the whole PDA drama. This time, Samir explained that a woman paying for something was slightly frowned upon if her man was also present.

Oh, wow. Does that mean that I'm his woman now?

Isabel snickered softly.

"Hey, no laughing." he added, moving his right hand up and down, with his fingertips huddled together. "Is my culture, okay?"

Gee, sorry...

His firm statement made her comprehend that she'd indeed stepped into a whole new world—Samir's world. But then, all of her inner questions dissolved the moment they stopped by a Turkish baker, where Isabel nearly drooled over the colorful treats guarded behind the glass displays.

"You want some?" asked Samir as he noticed her big, hopeful eyes.

"I don't know what they are, but yes!" she exclaimed.

"I know the perfect one," he said confidently.

The unusual couple arrived back to the apartment with full bags, and a box of sweets known as *baklava*. Isabel had heard the name before, and couldn't wait to try them. While Sam prepared his ultra-sugary tea, she made herself a rich and creamy cappuccino. Seeing this, the self-proclaimed food connoisseur opened the cupboard, and took out a bottle of a brownish powder.

"Can I?" he asked, attempting to add it in her drink. "You will like it."

"Sure. Is this also part of your culture?" she joked.

"Yes, this is cardamom," he replied.

The second she placed her lips around the cup, she was delighted by the warm and sweet aroma of the strange spice, and the way it enhanced the flavor of her coffee. She then indulged in the soft, flaky pastries, which tasted just like almond strudels drenched in warm honey. She took bite after bite rather eagerly, entranced by the orgasmic taste of the sweet liquid running down the side of her lips. It was nearly impossible to stop.

Sarah was so right about everything!

It also didn't take much longer before she'd forgotten about that morning's culture shock experience. In fact, all it took to turn her day around for good, was a suggestive glance from the alluring Assyrian man. Despite all of the customs she still didn't understand, everything that Samir said or did was absolutely fascinating; from the incredible stories he told, to the delicious dishes he prepared, up to the devout and impassioned manner he made love to her. But while they thought nothing could possibly ruin their intimate afternoon, they were suddenly interrupted by the deafening buzz of the doorbell. Jolting in surprise, Samir rushed to look out the window of the living-room.

"Shit, really, shit!" he said, jabbing a tempered fist against the wall.

"Isabel, please stay inside the bedroom," he hurried.

"What's going o—"

"Just do what I say, please!" he insisted.

His tone aggravated, and his serene expression had turned noticeably tense, as he hurriedly dressed himself back up. Judging by the preoccupied look on his face, Isabel figured there was someone downstairs that Samir clearly didn't want her to discover.

Is it a woman?

Her brows frowned at this upsetting assumption. But before she could even react to his command, he'd already stormed out of the apartment. She nipped briskly towards the window, and observed with attention as he argued with another man downstairs.

Who's that?

The unexpected visitor insisted on getting into the building, but Samir pull him away, and they ultimately walked in another direction. Isabel then put on some clothes herself, hoping that her mysterious host would soon return with an appeasing explanation to yet another unusual incident.

She sat on the couch with her legs brought up against her body—waiting impatiently for over two hours, before finally recognizing the sound of dangling keys closing in. As the door opened, Isabel nearly exploded out of the sofa, unable to decide whether she should stay in the living-room, or hide in the bedroom as Samir had primarily urged her to. But she remained casual instead, not letting herself become overwhelmed by the dilemma.

"Isabel! Come meet my cousin Petros!" exclaimed Samir, in a surprisingly pleasant tone.

"Hello," she said, debating between greeting him with a handshake or a kiss on the cheek—not wanting to do anything that could be regarded as disrespectful. Fortunately, Sam's cousin was warm and gentle, as well as really talkative. He grabbed Isabel by the arm, and hugged her as though she were family.

Well, this was unexpected...

Petros was fairly thinner than his relative, lighter-skinned—not to mention clean-shaven, unlike the stereotypical bearded, Iraqi male. His loudness was also hard to ignore, and his speech contained a mix of Dutch, Arabic, Syriac and English words that sounded both amusing and puzzling—even to Samir.

With drinks in hand and a merry heart, the three of them spent the afternoon making jokes and listening to contemporary Greek songs, transporting Isabel's mind across the Mediterranean sea. Petros emphasized feeling a deeper love for Greece than he ever did for his native land. He'd fled out of Iraq many years before the war had begun, and went to settle down in Athens—where he lived for almost a decade—becoming fluent in the Hellenic language, as well as a superb Zorba dancer. That evening, he performed a traditional dance for them, known as the *Zeibekiko*. Following Samir's instruction, Isabel got in one knee next to him, clapping her hands slowly and rhythmically, while Petros did a series of graceful twirls, poses and kicks—all around a glass of ouzo that sat dangerously in the middle of the floor. The Greco-

Assyrian himself then kneeled—leaning backwards with incredible flexibility—to pick the shot glass up with his teeth, drinking every last drop of the heavy liquor.

"Wow! That's amazing!" exclaimed Isabel, applauding heartily.

As they proceeded to play Dabke songs next, Isabel entered a deep, contemplative mood. She felt herself submerging into a manifestation of many cultures that fused perfectly in one single place. There was a Latina and two Iraqis dancing to Greek music in the Netherlands. The world as she knew it suddenly seemed way too small.

Later on, after an entertaining night of mesmerizing music and culture-sharing, Samir walked his tipsy cousin back to the subway station. In her brief solitude, Isabel thought of her host's odd behavior earlier, not hesitating to bring it up upon his return.

"Why didn't you want him to see me?" she asked calmly.

"Don't worry about it now," he replied, avoiding her sight.

"Samir..."

"Isabel, I said not now!"

Her persistence had begun to irritate him. And she saw herself with no other choice but to let the issue turn into the large elephant nobody would speak about. Fighting with Sam was the last thing she needed then, admitting it would had been foolish to ruin the pinnacle of her splendid evening with petty arguments.

Within a few weeks of living together with the enigmatic Middle Eastern man, Isabel could already conclude that cohabiting with him was going to be both complex and interesting. The more time they spent together, the deeper she studied him, soon realizing that he wasn't like most other immigrants she'd met in the country. He, for instance, only hung around people of his own ethnic background. She found this strange at first, seeing that he hardly integrated to the local culture, nor kept a close connection with any Dutch people. Even still, being a bit of an 'indoor person' herself, she greatly enjoyed his familiar idea of quality time. This last one was basically to gather at home with his closest friends, setting a table with peculiar snacks; black olives, dates, pomegranate seeds, pistachio nuts, and some sort of chickpea soup. Then they would sit down and chat for hours, with a hot cup of tea in hand. On one occasion, they even taught Isabel how to smoke the hookah, not warning her about the buzz side-effects, though. Either way, all of this made it evident that Samir was still fully wired to the land he was born in. Everything he did somehow lead back to the Middle East; his cooking, his favorite TV shows, his buddies, the places he shopped, even his barber. Nevertheless, Isabel admired him for being an authentic Iraqi man who could never be influenced or changed by anything that was foreign. He was faithful to his culture and customs, absolutely reluctant to be anyone but himself. These facts, however, also complicated their confusing relationship. Even though Isabel was living inside his world, she was still not part of it.

Due to his heritage, Samir grew up to be a real patriarch. This was not to be confused with being *machista*, though it could be a matter of debate among some groups. And for some reason, living with a woman for the first time seemed to have triggered his possessiveness of her. He began asking Isabel to dress more modestly; to wear less fitted yoga pants at the gym, and tops with higher necklines. None of this was an issue for her, for she understood that—Catholic or not—he came from a Muslim country with highly conservative values. And instead of questioning his singular ways, she opted to keep an open mind around the whole situation.

At least he knows where he comes from...

Nevertheless, Isabel noticed something about Samir that truly preoccupied her; his drinking. At first, she thought it was okay for him to occasionally enjoy a glass of whiskey or a beer—especially after a long, hard day of work. But then, she saw that it'd turned into a daily habit of his. There was an evident pattern, accompanied with a serious case of insomnia. She'd been awakened on several nights by strange noises, finding herself alone in bed, and catching Samir looking out the living-room window. Sometimes he'd be smoking a cigarette, or holding a glass in his hands. He would get annoyed when confronted about it, and avoided the subject at all costs. But Isabel suspected that his vice and restlessness were both related to his family's disappearance, as well as to his impotence to help his brother. She'd also heard him scream in his sleep once or twice, unable to do anything except for watching the sweat run down his scrunched forehead, as he remained trapped in his own nightmares and horrid memories of war. And yet on each following day, the reticent Assyrian acted like nothing was troubling his mind, trying his best to go on with his day just like everybody else.

14

MAD WORLD

"Good morning," spoke Samir, walking into the bedroom still wet from the shower, and with a towel wrapped around his waist.

Isabel looked at the time on her phone and squirmed between the sheets.

"Morning..." she whispered.

"What are you doing today?" he asked.

"Um, interview...at a restaurant...at 9:00," she mumbled amidst a long yawn.

"Oh, yes. Good luck," he said.

"Thanks. By the way, my project is due very soon," she hinted.

"We speak about this later," he responded, "I go now."

Samir rushed to put on his impeccable dark suit and shiny shoes, hurrying so he could get the company car in time to pick up his first client of the day. He then leaned forward to kiss her lips goodbye, and she returned the gesture tenderly. As for her own routine, it merely took a large cup of cardamom-flavored coffee to get all her senses running.

"You'll never know if you don't try," she told herself, right before going out into the city.

The restaurant she applied for was located in Schouwburgplein—a lively and spacious area, close to one of the city's main movie theaters and casinos. From afar, the establishment looked fairly vibrant and familiar, and so dramatically flashy that it could have been confused with a Bollywood movie-set any day. The outdoor furniture was made of brown wicker chairs, embellished with colorful pillows and orange cloths. And the tables carried glass centerpieces, adorned with lovely fresh daisies and river stones.

As Isabel admired the outer layout, she could hear a girl's indistinct cries coming from the inside. Holding onto her purse, she walked through the wide doors, and saw a man arguing heavily with a young woman.

"Please Hector, just give me another chance!" she begged.

"I won't tell you again!" he shouted. "Leave my business or I report your skinny ass to the authorities!"

By listening to the blonde girl's heavy accent, it was easy to assume she was of Eastern European descent. And judging by the blue apron around her waist, Isabel figured she must had been one of the waitresses as well. The couple ignored Isabel's presence completely, and for business' sake, the restaurant was still free of customers at the time. Standing awkwardly by the door, the hopeful job-candidate tried to find a polite manner to interrupt the heated dispute. But as the yelling continued, she chose to keep quiet and wait for the dramatic scene to end. A moment later, the male arguer grabbed the weeping woman by her shoulder, and dragged her forcefully towards the exit. His vile and vicious move caused Isabel to react instinctively, by pushing him away from the victim, and standing before him in a defiant pose.

"Who the hell are you?!" he bellowed furiously.

"I'm your 9:00 appointment...or was. Screw you and this whole place!" she retorted.

Isabel helped the girl outside, portraying an expression of disgust as she looked over her shoulder. Both women clumped over the metal flooring of the large public Square, ultimately reaching a long, wooden bench. They sat side by side for a couple of minutes, in silence, while Isabel brainstormed for comforting words.

"May I ask...what happened?" she inquired.

The young woman slowly lifted her gaze, wiping the tears and traces of mascara around her large, blue eyes. Her name was Irina; a delicate and beautiful eighteen year-old Ukrainian, who'd traveled to the Netherlands in pursuit of an illusion. Back in her homeland, Irina was a professional ballet dancer, and a promising rising star in the Fine Arts. Just before graduating from secondary school, she'd already been offered several scholarships at renowned dance academies across the country, including the opportunity to try-out for a part in Tchaikovsky's Swan Lake—which would then be performed at the National Opera House of Ukraine. Her parents were thrilled about the opportunity, and so was she. But despite that she'd evaluated every option carefully, Irina felt it was also time to explore new and foreign terrains. Prior to making a final decision, she applied for a few ballet schools throughout Europe. And a few weeks before the revolution exploded in her country, she was selected to audition at a prestigious dance conservatory in Amsterdam.

"The email looked official," she sobbed. "And I was happy because it was going to be my first trip abroad."

Irina arrived in Schiphol at around 22:00 on a Saturday. She waited for long hours to be picked up by a guide, but no one from the dance company showed up at the hall. She then received a private phone-call from a man, indicating that her ride to the hotel was waiting for her across the exit. Blinded by her ambitions, she pranced outside unhesitant, naively following the waving hand of the stranger on the other side of the line. Sadly, Irina never imagined that the second she'd sit inside the tinted car, she would be kidnapped on gunpoint. Her frightful eyes dilated as two masked men in the backseat held her down; gagging her, and tying her arms and ankles until she was unable to move a muscle. While one of the thugs threatened her, the other looked through her handbag and confiscated her passport, along with all of her personal documents. However, the true horror of her evening began the moment they showed her a photograph of her entire family.

"They downloaded it from a social network," Irina said, "and...they knew exactly where I lived."

After a long and petrifying ride, the kidnappers parked at the corner of a busy and boisterous place; where the streets reeked of piss, beer, and vomit. Trashy techno music could be heard all around, just as loud as the laughter of countless degenerates, intoxicated by much more than their wicked licentiousness. Irina jerked heavily as the thugs dragged her out of the car, then through a door in an alleyway. She was then pushed against the ground of a dimly-lit room with red walls, where there was a round bed covered in tacky animal-print sheets. Inside the room was also another female—of Latin descent and no older than twenty years—who seemed poised and unruffled, as though she'd been there for a long time. When unbound, Irina crawled towards her and pleaded for help, but the girl remained emotionless and wouldn't look at her in the eyes. Seconds later, a stout dark man walked into the room, handing the kidnappers a bag full of cash and two kilos of marijuana, quickly sending them away after the exchange.

"They...sold you into prostitution?" Isabel whispered with a shaky voice.

"They did much worse than that," responded Irina. "They threatened to kill my family, so there was nothing I could do at that point..."

The young Ukrainian dancer cried out for help twice in a row. But her wailing was abruptly silenced by the hard blow of a slap across her porcelain cheeks. The unexpected beating was induced by the same man who'd just paid for her in cash and drugs—as though she were nothing but cattle, or a mere piece of furniture. He then commanded the second girl to get Irina cleaned and prepared, forcing her to wear a set of skimpy lingerie, a pair of crimson lips, and two weary, smoky eyelids.

"...then they gave me some pills..." murmured the sobbing girl.

"What pills?" Isabel asked.

"Like...Valium or Xanax, I don't remember..."

As she became slightly sedated by the drugs, Irina was escorted through a narrow corridor, and into a vestibule infused with bright-red neon lights. And right in the middle of it stood a pair of padded bar stools, on which she was ordered to sit. The second woman reappeared after a minute or two, wearing similar trampy rags and clear high heels. Unlike Irina, this woman showed no particular expression anywhere on her face, nor did she glance at the anxious girl next to her. Instead, the unsubtle prostitute opened a curtain, revealing the notorious tall glass doors and windows which would confine the Ukrainian girl for nearly four months.

Isabel's mouth dried before Irina's painful words, feeling powerless to even hold her hand in solidarity, for this was a situation she could never imagine to experience.

"But, h—how did you escape then?" Isabel uttered nervously, absorbed by the sorrowful story.

It turned out that one morning, Irina and her unusual coworker were scheduled for a mandatory medical examination at a clandestine clinic for immigrants, located within the neighborhood. As they sat inside a small waiting room, the man escorting and supervising the two women turned up the volume of a wall-mounted TV. There was a film playing at the time, but it was suddenly interrupted by a *breaking news* bulletin, reported directly from the city of Sloviansk. Irina lifted her head the moment she heard the name of the place she was born in. And though she was fully aware of the conflict going on back in her country, watching footage of hundreds of her own people being evacuated in military trucks was staggering. She tried to keep calm in front of the guard. But inside, she was panicking at the thought of her parents and little sister being taken to a swarming shelter—or them being exposed to an assault in the attempt to flee the city. Nonetheless, a little voice in the back of her mind made her realize that the present calamity was in fact her salvation.

"How so?" interrupted Isabel.

"Well...if they don't know where my family is, they can't threaten me anymore."

But escaping her distressing reality required much more than taking away the brothel-keeper's leverage. She needed someone to distract the thug accompanying her that day.

When it was her turn to go into the examination room, the nurse on shift instantly noticed Irina's uneasiness—primarily suspecting it had something to do with the large venipuncture syringe she was preparing. The highly anxious teenager beckoned her to lean closer, whispering the truth of her condition right into her ears. The caregiver's first reaction was to take a deep breath, as she tried to figure out how she could help the young sex-trade victim sitting in front of her. Realizing that she had scarce time on her hands—perhaps less than five minutes before the doctor would walk into the room—she did the only clever thing she could think of.

"She gave me her car keys, and showed me a back exit where she was parked...and then…"

Slamming her eyes shut, the heroic nurse grabbed the needle and stabbed herself in the middle of her right thigh. She gasped sharply, holding back a dramatic cry, up until the moment she heard the engine of her car being turned on.

"She drew all attention to herself and I managed to escape," Irina sobbed. "Oh God, I just hope she's okay!"

Isabel shook her head, stunned and speechless, while she continued listening to the heartbreaking tale. For the past few weeks, Irina had been hiding in a local hostel, paying for her fare by cleaning the rooms and bathrooms of the lodge. She later started working as a waitress at the Mexican restaurant, in hopes to save up enough money to purchase a fake ID and a train ticket back to her country. However, Hector feared being fined over hiring illegal immigrants, and fired Irina due to her inability to provide legitimate documentation.

"Is there anything I can do?" asked Isabel. "We could go to the City Hall, or find the Ukrainian Consula—"

"No!" she yelled. "These gangs have people everywhere! You don't know what they will do to me if they find me."

The beautiful ballerina—whose emotional instability was more than evident—got up from the bench and crossed her arms around her stomach, displaying an amount of fear and paranoia that Isabel had never witnessed before. She felt compelled to aid the troubled girl, but as she tried to approach her once more, Irina stepped back in distrust.

"Let me help you, Irina. Don't go like this," Isabel pleaded.

"If you really want to help me, don't mention that you saw me...ever!"

Irina's last words echoed in Isabel's ears, as she hastened her pace further away from the Theater Square. There was an industry of international crime and modern-day slavery, exposed right in front of her eyes. And to know of the serious matter, but be unable to say a word about it, made her feel like nothing but an accomplice. All she could do was carry the heavy weight of awareness on her shoulders, unsuspecting that Irina represented merely one out of approximately 30 million women currently trapped in the sex-trade enterprise; as victims of scams and false promises of great opportunities. When Isabel snapped back into her own scenario, she took a last glance at the restaurant, and sighed.

Moving on...

She took a shortcut through an alley leading towards the Westersingel canal, right by the trendy Mauritsweg path. Her mind was distracted with concerns, but her sight was seized by a brown four-story building standing on her right. It was of abstract shape—sort of like a gigantic, truncated octahedron—made out of numerous triangular copper plates that formed a futuristic piece of architecture. Isabel walked up to the front to see it closer, discovering that the peculiar structure was actually a Christian Church.

"Well, this is new," she said, being generally accustomed to seeing cathedrals, and more traditionally-built places of worship around the city. As she peeped through the glass window, she was greeted by a black man in his early-thirties, who'd suddenly emerged from the front door. He wore a blue sweater, tattered jeans and sneakers. In his hands he carried a stack of magazines, titled *De Straatkrant*. He kindly handed one over to the curious woman before him, and by this gesture Isabel figured that he was a homeless man. She looked eagerly inside her purse, hoping to find some euros to give him, but he was not willing to accept her money. Instead, he invited her inside the strange building. Isabel hesitated for a moment, contemplating excuses to refuse his offer in the most polite way possible, yet unable to think of a good reason to.

"Alright, why not?" she ultimately said.

Behind the strange geometric walls was a spacious hall, but it looked nothing like the kind of churches she was used to visiting. In fact, it almost resembled one of Google's amusing offices. Apart from the booth displaying pamphlets and prospectuses, it also had bright and colorful table sets, a small café-bar, and an information desk with amiable volunteers. The friendly stranger introduced himself as Ulan, and he was kind enough to give Isabel a short tour of the premises. The equally-stylish nave was located on the second floor, but there were no sermons or Bible studies scheduled for that day. Ulan pointed out that the edifice was equipped with two kitchens, a dining room, several offices, a library, and that on the fourth floor there was even a shelter with twelve bedrooms. Isabel wasn't sure why he'd so randomly decided to tell her this, but that last room was precisely where he'd been sleeping for a couple of weeks, along with a group of fellow asylum seekers. She nodded to every word he said, and tried her best to seem intrigued.

Alas, her mind was already overwhelmed with other people's issues, and stories she couldn't completely understand.

Great, more drama...

As they took the stairs back to the lobby, Ulan then introduced her to a clergyman who was present at the time.

"This is Minister Jansen," he said proudly.

When Isabel turned around, her eyes enlarged in surprise, realizing that he was the same street preacher she'd seen in the middle of the shopping district. Nonetheless, in contrast to the passionate speaker she'd witnessed that day, the man before her appeared gentle and loving, and he welcomed her with a tender smile and a polite handshake.

"We're always happy to receive new visitors," he spoke with glee. "How can we help you?"

"Actually...I was just passing by," Isabel replied with a bashful shrug.

"There are no coincidences, my dear," he added.

His assertion reminded her of words that her own mother often repeated; nothing in life happened at random. Their warm hospitality made Isabel feel at ease, as the three of them then sat down to have a chat, accompanied with a cup of tea. That's when Isabel learned that Ulan was actually a refugee from Sudan, who'd been smuggled into Europe to escape a death sentence.

"But...what did you do?" asked Isabel.

Ulan scratched his head.

"It's ok, Ulan. You're safe here," said the minister.

"I know, pastor," added the Sudanese. "I was sentenced for being homosexual."

Isabel froze her expression at a puzzled stage.

"O..k, and that's a problem, because...?" she added.

"Homosexuality is illegal in Sudan, and punishable with death," spoke the pastor.

What!?

"Oh, wow. I had no idea, I'm sorry," she said.

Persecuted by the authorities, Ulan lost everything—including his consensual partner, who'd been lashed in public a hundred times before being thrown in jail. Even though Islam was the official religion in the country, Ulan couldn't find it in him to embrace it, for he feared the barbarism that was lived under something called *Sharia Law.*

"But Islam is different in this country," he said. "Muslims here can live in peace with others, and nobody interferes."

And yet, with the help of Dutch missionaries that were stationed in Khartoum, he soon discovered a new Faith, as they spoke to him about Jesus Christ.

"I didn't understand then, but now...I do," added Ulan.

These same missionaries helped him out of the country as well. And he admitted that the moment he stepped into that Church in Rotterdam, he was received with open arms and a secure roof above his head. But most importantly, he was received with utmost love and compassion.

Why do I need to know all this?

"But most of all, I thank God," he added with a hopeful sigh. "I finally found some peace in my life!"

"Peace? No offense, but you're...homeless. How can you feel so relaxed?" Isabel asked with a skeptical demeanor.

"I'm not sleeping on the street, am I?" he riposted.

"No, but—"

"Then I'm not homeless," he finished with contentment.

Isabel swallowed her own words with bitter embarrassment, wondering if she could have shown the same level of optimism, while placed under the same circumstances. She couldn't presume about having a place of her own, yet she also couldn't deny that it was due to the kindness of others that she too had a place to sleep each night. But Isabel still had a big doubt in her mind, and she couldn't easily shake it off;

"I don't mean to be disrespectful, but I find it hard to believe that you're suddenly...straight."

The clergyman appeared immersed in thought as he observed the controversial conversation. He was sitting across Isabel and Ulan, with his elbows firmly placed on the table, and both his hands clenched together in front of his lips.

"I didn't say I was," responded Ulan. "It's a process, a painful one, but I will try my best."

"Why?" she asked. "Because a three-thousand year-old book says it's a sin?"

Ulan frowned upon her question. "Because I believe God saved me from death, so that I would live for Him."

The pastor continued listening to the discussion, up until the moment silence wrapped the vibe around the table, making him feel obliged to ask Isabel the most significant question coming out of a Christian mouth;

"Do you know Jesus, dear?"

"Well, yes. My mother is a Christian, actually," she responded confidently.

"Amen, but that doesn't answer my question," he added.

Isabel meditated on the cleric's words for a moment, figuring he must have referred to whether or not she was a practicing Christian like her mother. To this, she awkwardly and hesitantly shook her head, while he smiled with tightened lips, as though implying sympathy.

"I'll tell you what," he continued, "why don't you come to one of our services? I promise you will not regret it."

As he said this, he handed her a bulletin featuring future Church activities. She thanked him for the invitation, making no particular promises until she read the subject of an upcoming sermon. And right at that second, something inside her told her to reconsider her answer.

"Persecution of Christians Around the World—oh wow, I've been reading about this a lot lately."

"Like I said, there are no coincidences," he lastly emphasized, retiring in the same polite manner, and turning his attention toward a group of visitors that walked into the building.

Touché...

While sitting in the metro, on her way back to Delfshaven, Isabel continued asking herself why so many strangers felt compelled to share their stories with her.

What's the meaning of all this? And what am I supposed to do about it? I can't even comprehend Samir's own story...

"The interview..." she groaned, recalling all of the work she still had to cover for the assignment. Once again, she realized that the essay couldn't possibly be written about Samir's testimony alone. Being conscious of the sad reality surrounding her, truly changed her primary idea of what it meant to be an immigrant in that country. But this type of knowledge was bittersweet. Because knowing so much about other people's struggles somehow made her feel responsible. Even still, her hunger for social awareness was starting to turn insatiable. And that day, she'd indeed lost her chance to getting a job for doing what she considered just. It was merely a minor sacrifice in the name of righteousness, or perhaps simple common sense. Either way, there was a great feeling of solidarity flourishing within her that she could no longer ignore.

Isabel leaned against the subway window, and closed her eyes to sink in deep, introspective rest. She couldn't stop thinking about Irina's situation, nor on how powerless she felt before the matter. She wanted to help, and found it difficult to accept that she couldn't reveal the girl's whereabouts, as it would had been counterproductive and prejudicial to her safety.

There has to be something I can do…

Her cloud of reflection suddenly vanished as she felt a vibration coming from her purse. Samir was calling to announce that they'd be having a guest over for lunch that same afternoon.

"An old friend," he said. And it had to be someone important enough for him to take the rest of the day off.

Isabel became excited to hear these words, which brought her great joy after a stressful morning. This was the one opportunity she'd been waiting for; to make him a special recipe from his very own homeland. Sort of like the old saying, Isabel hoped to find a direct way into the man's heart, by working her magic amidst pots and spices. Once back in the multicultural borough, the kitchen enthusiast hurried to the apartment and did a brief research on popular Assyrian dishes.

"Well, this might be costly." she said, realizing that she'd have to use part of her emergency cash reserve, in order to purchase all the necessary ingredients to make a rich, savory-looking dish known as *Dolma*.

From what she read, she learned that it was a popular meal in many Middle Eastern countries, but with some variations. The recipe she found most appealing consisted of a large stew made with several stuffed vegetables—while the original one was prepared using vine leaves as shells.

Finding the greens and condiments at the local supermarkets was easy, but the preparation was not as simple as it sounded, however.

"Alright, let's do this!" she inhaled sharply. "But first..."

Before getting her hands covered in seasoning, Isabel took her phone out to make a playlist of Linda George songs, creating the perfect *Atouraya* vibe in the background, while she also followed the recipe's YouTube tutorial on her laptop.

Assyrian Dolma
by Mabel Younadam.

Ingredients for the stuffing/seasoning:

1 lb ground lamb meat
2 cups of basmati rice (cooked)
a bunch of fresh parsley
a bunch of fresh dill
a bunch of scallion (spring onion)
a handful of fresh mint leaves
1 tbsp of minced garlic
200 grams tomato puree
1 tbsp of paprika
1 tbsp of black pepper
1 ½ tbsp of sea salt
1 tsp crushed chilli (might make the dish a little too hot for some)
1 tsp chilli powder
the juice of three lemons
1 cup of olive oil

Ingredients for the shell:

3 medium eggplants
2 red bell peppers
2 green bell peppers
6 tomatoes
1 cabbage
3 courgettes
3 large onions

To begin, she took a large pot and boiled both the onions and cabbage for softening. She then cut off one end of the aubergines, courgettes, tomatoes, and bell peppers. And using a spoon, she scraped out all of their insides, leaving the sliced pieces to be used as lids. In a large bowl, she mixed all of the spices and part of the oil and lemon juice, as well as the meat and rice. As soon as she began stirring the ingredients for the filling, the aroma of them combined became more delightful and mouth-watering by the second.

"I could indeed eat this whole thing raw!" she said, echoing a remark made by the spirited cook on the laptop screen.

The next step was to fill each one of the vegetables to the limit, using toothpicks to keep them closed. On the other hand, both onion and cabbage layers were prepared a lot easier, rolled up as though they were lamb wraps. She then placed all of the stuffed greens inside a large soup pot, and poured over them a broth made with the remaining elements. Finally, all she had to do was turn the stove on and let the heat do the rest. After spending two hours locked up inside the hot kitchen, the Latin cook leaned against the wall to catch her breath, only to groan in exhaustion as she scanned her surroundings. The kitchen looked like it'd been raided by Nebuchadnezzar's army—with tomato sauce dripping from the counter for a more dramatic effect—and Isabel saw herself with no other choice but to roll her sleeves back up, and clean the entire place before Samir's imminent arrival.

The aforementioned king of the castle appeared just half an hour later, calling out for Isabel who was in the bedroom changing her outfit. She walked out of the room wearing a long summer dress and sandals, pleasing Samir's sight as soon as she appeared before him. However, just as she'd suspected, he walked up to her and adjusted the neckline on her dress, concealing her prominent cleavage.

"You look beautiful," he complimented, "but—"

"Yes, Sam. I can wear a scarf..." she said with a deep sigh embellished with a sarcastic smile.

"Thanks habibti, because my friend will be here," he added in a fatherly tone.

Isabel turned back around, and browsed through the closet for a cotton stole. She fixed it over her back and showers, then tied it loosely in the front. Through the mirror, she saw that the new accessory suited her, admitting that being a little covered wasn't that big of a deal—especially when it symbolized respecting somebody's culture. In the same thoughtful state of mind, Isabel looked at herself directly in the eyes and gulped from a sudden realization.

"He called me habibti…" she whispered, aware of what the sweet word signified; *my beloved.*

At exactly 14:00, the ear-splitting buzz of the doorbell resonated through the apartment, like a thousand vuvuzelas during a World Cup match. While Samir unlocked the main entrance downstairs, the over-excited girl went on to set the table, impatient to see the two men putting her Iraqi-Rican food the test. Through the door then came a tall and strongly-built man, with short dark hair, light-brown eyes, and a distinctive, prominent nose. Just like Samir, he was a mouth-gaping Mesopotamian stud, and the kind of man nobody would ignore, even if he were walking in the middle of the city during rush hour. Isabel tilted her head in endearment, watching as the two guys hugged firmly. But then, her eyes widened in surprise when their brotherly embrace was complemented with four cheek-to-cheek kisses. While working at assemblies and other diplomatic events in America, Isabel had witnessed greetings such as these between men of other cultures—such as Spanish or Italian. And yet, it was the first time she'd seen two sturdy Middle Easterners go at it so casually.

No laughing, Isabel. It's his culture.

She pursed her lips to conceal a giggle.

"Isabel, come meet my friend, Asim Al-Bayati," Samir announced with chest-swelling pride.

"Wha—are you serious?!" she gasped in thrill. "I can't believe it!"

They chuckled at her childish reaction. Yet the scene turned a little awkward in an instant, when she extended her arm for a polite handshake. The Assyrian pulled his lips inward, glancing dubiously at their visitor. And it wasn't until he declaimed the words; As-Salamu Alaykum, that Isabel realized Asim was a Muslim.

"Oh! Sorry!" she said, drawing her hand back instantly. "Wa alaykum salam!"

"And where did you learn that?" asked a very impressed Samir.

"From your favorite TV series—Valley of Wolves."

Both men began laughing at her honest response.

"I teach her good, wallah!" joked Samir, addressing his friend.

Wallah?

The feeling of standing before one of the most intriguing characters in Samir's testimony was indescribable. He was the silent runaway, the brave hero of the Greek plains materialized in front of her—just as if he'd suddenly jumped out of the pages of her journal. However, meeting him was not the only reason she rejoiced inside. Now that he was present, she hoped to be saved from the cliffhanger of their journey into Europe, by adding his own version of events into her notes. But, of course, not before she'd reveal her own special surprise that day.

"So, what did you cook?" asked Samir.

"You'll see!" she said, excusing herself.

Back in the kitchen, Isabel served the stewed vegetables in a glass pan. And with her hands secured behind thick mitts, she carried it back to the table, followed by bringing a stack of warm flatbreads and two glasses of tea.

"Ok boys, lunch is served!" she called out.

The hungry bodybuilders approached the table, curious and eager, halting abruptly at the sight of the unexpected dish that was presented before them.

"You cooked dolma?!" exclaimed their special guest. "Wallah, Sam, you taught her good!"

Samir smiled faintly at his remark, but remained speechless nonetheless. He then sat down quietly, and invited Asim to do the same. Isabel's initial enthusiasm started to fade from her face, fearing she might have done something wrong by preparing that specific recipe. Still, as they began indulging in the savory taste of home, she noticed a nostalgic twinkle in their eyes that was reassuring. It was a great relief, one that was accompanied by sounds of delight slipping through their lips. But more than anything, she enjoyed watching them eat with extreme delectation, leaving no room for phony table manners. At one point, Samir even took away Isabel's fork, switching it for a piece of bread that he dipped into the stew.

"Take it like this," he suggested, holding the dripping chunk before her mouth.

She complied unhesitantly, closing her eyes as she savored her own delish creation right off her lover's fingertips. He smirked pleasantly, giving her yet another piece. And after the second bite, Isabel recalled some old times at many cocktails, where she'd stuffed her face with finger-food. She admitted that eating with bare hands was absolutely liberating, almost like having an intimate relationship with her meal without the need to use a cold piece of metal.

After the warm and filling dish, the men switched their tongue, and brought their chai back to the living-room. Isabel chose not to interfere, and from the kitchen she could clearly hear their rough Arabic, secretly wishing to understand their strong words. She wanted to join them, yearning to sit by Samir's side even if she couldn't take part in the foreign discussion. And though no privacy was requested, there was still something naturally authoritative about Middle Eastern men, which prevented her from marching in on their conversation.

Would they really mind?

After brainstorming for a good pretext, Isabel concluded that bringing a pot of fresh tea was the best excuse to step into the room.

"Excuse me," she whispered, placing the tray down on the coffee table.

The men glanced at her for a second, nodded gently, and then resumed their chat.

Ok, that went well!

Isabel then sat next to Samir, with folded arms and a pair of hopelessly perked-up ears. She had no clue of what was being discussed. But judging by their scowling expressions, and impetuous mannerisms, she could tell they were speaking of serious matters. The Iraqis fell silent for a moment, turning to face their spectator—who blushed instantly from being under the intense spotlight of their eyes.

"Thank you, Isabel," Samir said.

"Oh, you're welcome," she responded, interpreting his words as a polite request for her to retire.

"Hey, where you go?" he asked.

She paused. "I thought maybe you guys wanted some privacy, so…"

"No, why?" he added. "Come, listen to what happened with Asim."

"Why? What's going on?" she asked.

"Ah, well…I'm being deported," replied Asim, causing Isabel to drop right back to her previous position. She took a sharp breath, certain that she was about to hear yet another story of incomparable struggle—the third one that day, to be precise. The Muslim refugee then took a folder out of his satchel, drawing out a document.

"I came to the city this morning to see an immigration lawyer…" he continued.

Asim had been living in the Netherlands under temporary residency. And just like Samir, he had to wait around five years to apply for a permanent visa and the Dutch passport—which had long been their primary goal. But what Asim and tens of thousands of other refugees didn't know, was that there'd been certain changes in the immigration laws of the Netherlands—as well as exceptions in the asylum application process—for people coming from Iraq. These changes, however, varied in every refugee-hosting country.

"What kind of exceptions?" Isabel raised an eyebrow. "Didn't the war affect everyone?"

To answer this particular question, their guest handed Isabel a sheet with information on a policy known as *categorical protection*. In other words, it was a policy to protect minorities which were targeted for particular reasons; such as religious persecution or ethnic cleansing.

"Like Samir," she murmured.

"Yes, exactly," he added.

Regardless of the continuous insurgency and instability inside Iraq, there were many observable inequalities in the way asylum claims were being assessed.

This is so unfair...

Samir remained quiet at the time. He was analytic as usual, and probably uncomfortable for being unable to do anything for the man who once saved his life. Hearing all this gave Isabel strong, mixed feelings. She felt sympathy and sorrow for the Muslim community. But at the same time, an undeniable relief for the Iraqi Christians that were persecuted. Nevertheless, it was difficult to imagine that after such a long and dangerous journey, countless refugees would have to go back to where they primarily escaped from.

"My God...is there no organization that can help?" Isabel asked.

"I go to Belgium next week, I heard they are still taking applications there," Asim responded.

"I really hope they can help you," she added with concern.

"And if they cannot, then I try Germany. I don't stop trying, I swear in Allah."

Isabel suspired with admiration.

Asim added that he'd also been participating in several demonstrations across the Netherlands. It was an initiative to try catching the attention of both the media and the government, hoping to prevent more displaced people from being sent back. One of these protests had taken place outside of a refugee center in the town of Ter Apel, where hundreds of migrants from both Iraq and Somalia set up a camp in rejection to the forced deportations. Sadly, the fate of most of them remained just as grim. But despite the circumstances, Asim was a man who remained calm, with a heart full of hope and determination.

"What if they do send you back?" she queried.

"Then I come back, Insha'Allah!" he proclaimed. "Just I hope the Greeks don't make a higher fence!"

"Bring the boat, just in case!" added Samir, engaging his friend in a skit of dark humor. Isabel chuckled awkwardly, as this was surely no laughing matter. And yet, she was certain about one thing; if she'd ever have to define the word *faith* in one simple sentence, she'd say:

> *Faith is when a returned refugee crosses the same*
> *border for a second time, not giving up on the dream*
> *that awaits on the other side.*

Asim stayed for another hour. And for the rest of his visit, Isabel left both men to catch up and speak among themselves. As an enthusiastic admirer of Samir's story, she admitted that meeting his friend had been an honor, just as it'd been another eye-opening experience. It was, of course, inevitable for his testimony to also find its way into Isabel's mental rollercoaster of unresolved scenarios; Samir and his family, Ebele, Irina, Ulan, and now Asim.

"Hey, I forgot to ask; you got the job at that restaurant?" queried Sam, pulling her out of her heartfelt contemplation.

She sighed. "Honestly? I believe there are far bigger problems going on than my own. Please excuse me…"

Isabel locked herself inside the bathroom, hoping that standing underneath a warm shower could help wash off the stress of a long and atypical day. She couldn't stop meditating on the circumstances of all the people appearing on her path, as their faces kept on popping up inside her head.

Why is everything so difficult for them?

Nearly every day, Isabel would encounter a new person whose life perhaps hasn't been as privileged as hers. These were people she never expected to meet before, but who still managed to break down her barriers of ignorance. Through their stories she could get a glimpse of their reality. And she tried to be solidary, by pretending to at least feel part of their long-endured pain.

But why would they pull me so deep into their problems?

To know the truth per se did not bother her. On the contrary, she was sympathetic to all their causes. And yet, what was the use of being aware, if she couldn't change a thing?

"I can't…help them…" she sobbed.

I can't stop religious persecution. I can't stop sex-trafficking. I can't stop sectarian wars and terrorism. I can't stop foreign invasions. I can't stop racism nor ethnic cleansing. I'm nothing but a miserable spectator of the world's biggest disasters.

All of these realizations exploded inside her head at once, causing her to fall on her knees inside the shower room. She started heavy-breathing, unable to hold back a sudden scream of emotional pain and anxiety, as the running water kept on falling over her skin.

"Isabel! What happened?!" shouted Samir, pounding his fist hard against the door.

He then knocked for a second time, yet didn't waste another moment before kicking the door right in. His eyes flashed with fear, and his tongue unraveled strange phrases as he turned the faucet off, embracing Isabel's shivering frame in his arms.

"It's just too much..." she chanted continuously, holding onto him as though seeking his protection.

It may have looked like an endearing scene, but Isabel felt embarrassed by her vulnerability. She was aware that if there was anyone who knew about pain, it was the man holding her. And yet there she was; breaking down in his arms like a lost child—like a desperate and defenseless little girl trapped inside a woman's body. Samir couldn't figure out the reason of her distress, but he embraced her nonetheless. And in the same gentle manner, he wrapped a towel around her and carried her towards his room. He said nothing else, for Samir was a man of bold actions and few words. Instead, he placed her down on his bed, lying side by side to cover her nakedness with the warmth of his body.

"Thank you for being in my life," she whispered, curling up in a ball and closing her eyes.

"You don't need to thank me for anything," he replied.

"It's just so unfair..." she added in a soft breath, provoking him to tighten his grip around her waist. *Stop talking*, suggested the gesture.

But Samir's body soon began to speak a whole different language. It was loud, clear, and needed no translation. The enticing Assyrian started to press himself hard against her, and she panted desirous from the arousing sensation of his firmness. They lied intertwined in their infatuation for one another, yet rather ironically. Because moments back, Isabel was trembling from cold and anxiety, but now it was Samir who shivered from the fervor that consumed him. His breath faded into a long, choked gasp of longing. And her own body responded naturally to the persuasive signals coming from his. The yearning she felt was aggravating, nearly as much as her initial emotional strains. She turned around to face her lover, welcoming his parted lips in hers as she rolled over to sit on his torso. From above, she carefully studied his perplexing expressions, which clearly demonstrated lust, but also a deep rage she could not ignore.

How can he be so gentle at times, and still display such anger in his eyes?

Isabel wondered this and many other things; like what could have been going through his mind while he caressed her, while he lovingly traced her waistline with the back of his fingers. The tension that burned in him was not entirely carnal. And though he seldom explained it with words, she'd already learned to understand him and could decipher where his deepest anger came from. Samir was furious inside, and she'd perceived this from the precise moment they met. He was a man sick of being judged over his faith, his striking features, the language he spoke, or even for the blood running in his veins. He was tired of waiting for a piece of paper to give him validation, or some sense of identity inside of a strange world. Holland was a country in which Samir often felt lost, suffering over his family's disappearance in silence and solitude. The roughness he normally exhibited, was merely the consequence of all the emotional and physical wounds inflicted by fate. And that evening, Isabel strived to ease at least some of his pain, hoping that in her arms he could find enough pleasure and release, just as she did within his.

15

THE INTERVIEW: PART TWO

News about Isabel's relationship with Samir traveled rapidly, and soon reached the ears of all the students from the Dutch course, including the professor's. Some of them had long secretly placed their bets on the table, having expected her and the Iraqi to go out on a date, yet never imagining she would move in with him so quickly. Amaité had somewhat given them her own version of events, considering Isabel to be nothing but an opportunistic expatriate. And though her classmates didn't know the full story behind her decision, cohabiting outside of wedlock wasn't positively regarded in their eyes—especially not in the eyes of the Muslim students. For Isabel, it was almost like being in high-school all over again; dealing with individuals who demonstrated the same level of immaturity and lack of respect for whoever lived against the norm. This surprised her tremendously, because outside of that building, the Dutch were the most open-minded people on Earth. However, it seemed that in some particular matters, the clash of cultures was inevitable.

That same day, Mr. Pelengkahu asked Isabel to stay and speak with him after class. He wanted to know the truth of what had been going on; how she'd been living, where, with who. Speaking about herself wasn't something she felt eager to do at the time. But Ray's fatherly concern always inspired confidence in others. And though unreceptive to opinions or advice, Isabel still made an effort to explain part of her situation, and at the same time hoped to put an end to all the speculation.

"Seriously, I'm fine living with Samir. He's a good man," she asserted.

"Is he?" he queried. "I know you're working with him for the class project, and that's fine. In fact, I am also intrigued to learn his whole story."

"Ah, you and I both," she said with a smirk. "But he doesn't open up too easily."

"So how can you know he's a good man?" he asked boldly.

Her voice stuttered for a moment. "It's...just a feeling, professor."

"Alright then," he shrugged with a smile.

"And besides, it's just temporary," she added. "I'll move out as soon as I find a job."

Her last statement seemed far easier spoken than put into actions. It was just an old phrase, incessantly repeated by people of all ages who dreamed of a prompt independence. Mouthing these simple words felt good enough at the time. And still, Isabel had no idea where to find a common job that paid enough to cover the rent of an apartment in pricey Rotterdam.

Before taking the subway back to Delfshaven, she made a quick stop at the marketplace in Binnenrotte Square to buy incense and aromatic candles. Regardless of the many occasions she'd already been there, the experience was never dull. The market was an intriguing spot, replete with exotic faces and strange fashions. Behind every stand were men and women of various ethnic backgrounds—many of them vigorously yelling out the prices of fruits, vegetables, and other imported products they sold. There were also many kiosks displaying a vast variety of spices, clothes of all styles, beautiful scarves, elegant kaftans, and colorful carpets. It was almost like standing in the middle of a market in Marrakech.

Isabel explored every aisle. And when reaching the food section, her attention was caught by a crate of large, bright yellow mangoes.

"May I try a piece?" she asked the merchant.

"Yes, yes. Of course," he replied eagerly. "Very sweet and only two euro!"

"Mmm! Yes, these are great! Where are they fro— "

As soon as she read the labels on the crate, Isabel's words were cut short, and replaced by amused laughter. To her overall surprise, the mangoes in front of her had been imported from Puerto Rico.

"Well, look at that!" she exclaimed.

"Sorry, what?" asked the confused man.

"Oh! I mean, these come from my...ah nevermind! Here!"

Unable to explain herself without faltering, she proceeded to purchase two of the golden fruits, along with some of Samir's favorite snacks; bloody pomegranates, salted pistachios, dates, as well as other essential groceries.

"That's quite enough shopping for today," she told herself, after counting the last eighty euros inside her wallet.

Despite satisfied for being able to bring something to the table that day, the unemployed expat was unable to shake her financial concerns out of her mind. Isabel took comfort on being able to cook another meal out of her own earnings, admitting to be far too proud to ask Samir, or anyone, for a single penny.

As she was about to enter Blaak's subway station, her eyes were suddenly drawn towards the raciest and shiniest outfit she'd ever seen. It was hanging from the corner of the last kiosk, right at the end of one of the market's corridors. It was hardly a dress, but still captivating; composed of a colorful jeweled bra, with thin golden chains hanging under the cups, and a long turquoise double-slit skirt with a matching jeweled belt.

"Come take a look, it is for belly-dancing," said a turban-wearing vendor, standing vigilant behind the racks.

"Well, I'll be damned," she whispered as she stroked the soft fabric. "It's so pretty..."

Isabel examined the outfit for several minutes, enthralled by the sparkling stones attached on it. Her heart then began pounding hard at the thought of wearing it for Samir, that same evening, or every evening.

My very own Arabian Nights fantasy.

She giggled at the possibility.

"I give you best price, hundred euros," added the vendor.

"Oh...I...I don't have it, sorry," she replied.

He persisted, "How much money you have?"

Isabel froze, stuttering, internally telling herself not to do it. But then, she remembered Sarah's compelling suggestion. And the temptation of putting her romantic theory to the test was far more persuasive than her self-discipline. Without considering it for another minute, she took all the money she had and handed it over.

Isabel then pranced back to the apartment, feeling like she carried one of the world's lost wonders inside her bags. Samir was to return in a few hours, leaving her with more than enough time to prepare for her surprise. She placed two frankincense cones by each window and jasmine candles on the tables, in order to evoke the sensual vibes required for the perfect scheme of seduction.

I'll need more space...

She moved the coffee table against the wall, then closed the blinds to dim the lightning in the room. Using her imagination, she took all the pillows and blankets she found in the apartment, and tried her best to turn the area into a little private harem. She then made her way to the kitchen, where she prepared a platter of hummus and smoky *baba ganoush*. Once she was done cooking and decorating the place, it was time for her to become someone else than just the usually-introverted Isabel Alvarez.

Following a purifying shower, she remembered the oil flask that Sarah had given her, and decided to apply it on some of her most erogenous zones.

This counts as a special occasion, doesn't it?

Her shiny new costume fitted perfectly, and she couldn't resist shimmying her lower body the second she tied the noisy coin sash around her hips. Despite entertained embellishing herself, she glanced at the time on her phone and gasped, aware that Samir would be arriving in no time. Letting her natural waves down, she then rushed to enhance her large hazel eyes with the blackest liner, followed by adding a touch of plum gloss over her lips. She wore chandelier earrings, a dozen bangles on each arm, and silver rings around each of her fingers—considering that such a dance would be useless without the seductive swirls of adorned hands.

The strong scent of incense had long blended in the air, creating a warm aroma that inspired the luscious belly-dancer. She went on to place the food on a corner of the carpet, along with slices of Lebanese bread, fresh fruits, and a whole pot of sweet, hot tea. Lastly, she connected her phone to Samir's speakers, and browsed through her playlist for the perfect song to perform.

She sighed, "I should have thought of this two hours ago."

All of a sudden, she heard the downstairs door being shut. The sound caused her to flinch, as she only had a minute to begin her surprise act.

"Oh my God, oh my God!" she squealed, having no choice but to pick a song at random.

She then took a deep, soothing breath, and began moving her body to the sensual Arabian melodies.

"Isabel? What are yo—"

Samir's lips curved into a grin of delight, surprised by the mystical, yet familiar display before him. She first expected the Assyrian to sit by the carpet, and in pleasant repose indulge his eyes on her serpentine motions. But instead, he joined her exuberant performance, showing off some of his own peculiar customs. He clasped his hands together, rotating them in a way that allowed him to snap his index finger against the rest. This created a sharp clicking sound, almost as though he were playing an actual instrument.

That's actually kind of cool...

Isabel shook her shoulders and hips, allowing herself to be possessed by the ecstatic trance of the Middle Eastern beats. Arabic music took control of her mind and body with natural ease. It was as if the essence of her femininity had been awakened by the banging of the drums, and the clinking of the zills combined. She couldn't stop smiling for even a second, nor could the man she was dancing for. Pleasing him was now her biggest joy, and turning his bitterness into bliss had become her greatest ambition. She took him by the hand, and lead him to sit on the ground by the special corner she'd set up. And like an honored sultan in his own palace, Samir helped himself to the delicacies before him, keeping his much hungrier eyes fixated on his odalisque's alluring steps. She was his true awaited feast, her and nothing else, seducing him with her suggestive gestures. But then, he grabbed a full mango in his hand, curious, like he'd never laid eyes on the yellow fruit before.

"What is this?" he asked aloud, lifting a skeptical brow.

"Something new, try it," she replied, without pausing the synchronized banging of her hips.

Pressing his thumb into it, he discovered that it was tender, and grabbed a knife from the tray to cut off part of its peel. He then sunk his teeth deep into the pulp, causing its golden nectar to run down the side of his lips.

Savage, she grinned.

Isabel could hear a low, muffled moan of delight—his feral actions being as tempting to her as her coquettish sway was to his greedy eyes. Almost jealous of a piece of fruit, she turned around and slowly kneeled on the floor, taking her hair off her back, and looking over her shoulder with inviting glances. She then moved her arms in flowing motion, while gently bending backwards to perform the legendary belly-roll. The magical eastern melodies submerged her deeper into an ancient dream. And yet, Isabel didn't imagine that moments later Samir would be brushing his hot mouth over her bare abdomen. The entire world disappeared underneath his lips, and the ticklish sensation made her lose all focus from the inciting ritual of love. He then placed one hand under her arched back, pulling her body up against his. His strong embrace disarmed her, and the smoky scent of his body was the most gratifying aphrodisiac—like a mix of sandalwood and cedar, fused with the powerful pheromones that steamed out of his pores. His breath began accelerating, and his fingers found their way to the clasp of her beaded brassiere. He unhooked it with little effort, and tossed the piece of costume in the furthest corner of the room. Samir's erotic aptitude raised many questions inside her mind. But those same phenomenal skills also blocked her ability to find the answers of her inquiries. Nevertheless, Isabel realized, at the very end of their lovemaking, that something had changed in her.

She rested her head on his chest, like she was already used to. And he stroked her hair in the same tender manner he did every night. But for some reason, she didn't feel like herself anymore; she felt guilty. They'd turned the music down, yet the violins and flutes were still slightly audible through the speakers. The soft ballad playing in the background was melancholic, and it enabled Isabel's contemplative mood. She said nothing for several minutes, and neither did he. And it was in that exact tranquility that she believed to have figured out the cause of her uneasiness.

"Samir, can I ask you something?"

"Sure," he responded.

"Do you think that what we're doing is...wrong?" she stuttered.

"Doing what? Sex? he asked boldly.

"Yeah...I guess," she said, her cheeks reddening.

Samir took a deep breath, holding her by the shoulders, and lifting his body up along with hers. He then looked deep into her eyes, as if he were trying to find something he'd lost during the previous days.

"What happened?" he asked in a serious tone.

But the problem was not exactly what happened, but what she'd heard from her foreign classmates, concerning her open-minded lifestyle. She felt somewhat offended by their perception of her, and worried that Samir would consider her to be immoral as well.

"I mean...since you're from Iraq and all..." she shrugged.

The Assyrian stared at her wide-eyed.

"Ah, now I understand what you mean," he said. "And no, you're not. Don't care for what they tell you, ok?"

"Okay," she sighed calmly, as if having received godly words of approval.

But the moment Samir excused himself, Isabel suspected that he didn't quite tell her everything he had in his mind.

Cultural clashes, that's all this is...

He then returned to the living-room, wearing a tank-top and training pants. And in his right hand, he held one of Isabel's t-shirts and a pair of purple hot-pants.

"Here habibti, it's a little bit cold," he said, reaching out to hand her the clothes.

No, it isn't cold at all.

"I was perfectly warmed-up moments ago," she retorted. "What's the matter now?"

He sighed, speaking foreign words to himself, "Please, don't make problem, we don't need."

"What problem, Samir?" She got up and stood defiant before him. "My naked body is a problem all of a sudden?"

Without letting him add another word, she retired to the bedroom and slammed the door.

Liar, he's bothered by this...by us.

This assumption hurt her, but there was a fact that she already knew; Samir didn't think like Western guys. He was a traditional man, with values that could have seemed backward to most people on this side of the world, but they were legitimate values nonetheless. Ironically, it seemed that the women of his community were the ones enduring the most pressure, expected to behave in a more conservative way. The men, on the other hand, could get away with almost anything.

"I am a free, strong, independent woman," she said to her reflection in the mirror.

Isabel wanted to act like Samir's unspoken perception didn't bother her. And yet, her conceited words only displayed the usual ego-stroking defense mechanism of a feminist fundamentalist. In reality, it was merely a shield as thin as a layer of varnish, used to embellish her true feelings. Because no matter if she said otherwise, Isabel was indeed affected by these strict cultural ideals. She liked Samir's protective, fatherly attitude towards a woman. But it was clear that they both possessed colliding opinions when it came to relationships.

As she slipped into the clothes he'd picked out for her, she heard a different kind of music coming from the living room, easily recognizing George Michael's sensual voice—combined with a soothing piano melody.

Well, I really didn't see that coming.

She found Samir standing by the window, moving his head to the soft rhythm, and beckoning Isabel to get closer to him. He seized her waist in his strong hands, and she rested hers over his wide shoulders, coupling with him in a slow dance. His gallant deed surprised her at first, but then she recalled that it hadn't been the first time she'd witnessed the romantic side of him. Even still, before that night, she wouldn't have taken him for an admirer of 80's English classics either.

"There is much about me you don't know," he murmured in her ear.

"Yes, I can see that," she replied.

He engaged her in a long, amorous kiss. It was the kind of kiss that made her comprehend why she regarded his perception of her so highly. Isabel didn't tell him, but the longer their lips remained locked together, the clearer it all became; she was absolutely head over heels for him. Culturally-shocked or not, she'd fallen madly in love precisely with all which made him different from the rest, and his race played an important part in it. And then, there was the Arabic; a language so seductive in his mysterious voice, that it made her forget why they'd been arguing in the first place.

"You're wonderful..." she whispered.

"So are you," he responded, inviting her to sit on the carpet next to him.

"We can work in the interview now, if you like," he added.

His suggestion was everything she'd been wanting to hear that week. She eagerly opened her journal in the middle, exactly where they'd left off, impatiently waiting for him to begin moving his story-telling lips.

"Very well..." he sighed. "Athena...Athena..."

Just like fierce felinae, the refugees scurried for hours through the wilderness and the vast cornfields that surrounded them. They were being guided by their Armenian *coyote*, in search for some old train tracks that would lead them towards the town known as Nea Vyssa; a small village just twelve kilometers from the Evros river bank. As soon as they found the anticipated trail, they knew they were getting close and hastened their pace. It was around three in the morning at the time, and they'd been running restlessly under the freezing rain, marking the beginning of a dreadful winter in the region. Not a single establishment was opened, nor were there any lights on to be spotted. It was a critical situation because Samir continued bleeding out, in urgent need of medical assistance. Sarkis began banging on the window of an old cafeteria, calling out for help as he and Yasir supported the nearly-fainting man in their arms. From another side, the Iranian woman had fallen to the ground on the sidewalk—exhausted, numb, and soaking in both rain drops and her own tears of grief and heartbreak. Her deafening cries, combined with the men's unbroken shouting, created an atmosphere of hopelessness in the air. The Pakistani mother approached the widow, and attempted to comfort her. Along with her ethnic attire, she wore a blue dupatta over her head. It was still slightly damp from the rain, but she removed it nonetheless, and wrapped it around the young Muslim girl. She then offered her arms for an embrace, and together with her children she invited her to join them in prayer.

"But the Pakistani woman...she was a Christian, no?" Isabel interjected.

"Yes, but that was not the time to care about religious differences," Samir replied.

Indeed, what all the refugees wanted at that moment was to survive. But such a goal could only be achieved by them staying united, and throwing aside all of their ethnic or ideological divergence—whether they prayed in Aramaic, Urdu, Arabic, or Farsi. What was truly important was to love one another, as a family in the eyes of God. To imagine such display of faith and unity was both intriguing and inspiring. And it also showed that sometimes, it was under the worst circumstances where people made an effort to forget their disputes, and raise a white flag in solidarity with one another.

The town of New Vyssa—though usually swarming with immigrants who passed by after crossing the border—appeared completely deserted on that early morning. Only after another fifteen minutes of banging on the door, the owner of the café finally decided to come out. He was shouting, swearing, and shooing the group away from his business, up until the second he saw the badly-injured man. He then hurried everyone inside and closed the door, clearing out a table to help lie Samir on top of it. When they took off his jacket and shirt, they gasped in shock to notice that the wound had become infected; the tissue around it was swollen and covered in coagulated blood. The women started to cry once more at the sight, rapidly getting hushed by the Greek man assisting them. His name was Kostas.

The gray-haired proprietor instructed the women to find alcohol and clean towels under a counter, but they ultimately returned with a bottle of Arak from the bar. Nearly the whole group was required to hold the strong Iraqi down, as he jerked heavily and roared in pain the second Kostas poured the colorless liquor directly into the wound. Freeing his left arm away from his own brother's grip, Samir grabbed the Armenian smuggler by the collar of his shirt, threatening to kill him if he survived the morning. Despite that he was now trying to save his life, Sam felt that Sarkis' negligence was the reason why the rest of his family had gone missing. The angry Assyrian was then given analgesics, along with a shot of the heavy drink to try sedating him until he could be taken to a doctor—one that wouldn't inform the authorities of their illegal presence.

Kostas was a sixty-five year old man, who revealed to have spent over fifteen of those years assisting hundreds of stateless immigrants who continuously fell at his doorstep—starving, thirsty, and nearly dead from cold or exhaustion. He also confessed that Samir's wound was not the first border-police-induced gunshot he'd healed in his life. Though he admitted that the situation with asylum seekers was getting out of hand, and that his country was in no condition to continue receiving them, he was still kind enough to allow the small group to stay in an empty room above the cafeteria for that day. This could give Sarkis enough time to arrange the last part of his deal, making sure the guarantor would be waiting for the group down in Athens.

"How far was that town from the capital?" Isabel asked.

"Like nine hours in car," replied Samir.

The morning after, Sarkis had fortunately come in contact with the missing bus driver back in Turkey. He assured him that Samir's family, and rest of the refugees, had been safely taken to Athens through the main road, after some of the passengers desperately bribed the authorities. He was also given an address. Samir turned hysterical as he received the news, pressuring Sarkis to find them new transportation immediately. But it was not until midday that a suspicious van parked across the cafeteria. Kostas peeked through the window, and saw that the man stepping out of the vehicle appeared even shadier than the car he drove. He was broad and tall, with a shiny shaven head—sporting a brown leather jacket, jeans, and fancy aviator sunglasses. Sarkis sighed in relief as he saw him, realizing that it was their long-anticipated ride. He brought the whole group outside, and each one of them was given another change of clothes, forged passports of various European countries, and a whole discourse of instructions. For instance, the Muslim girl was told that at some point she would have to remove her hijab, if she wanted to cross the checkpoints unnoticed—a command she didn't take so well.

The pathway out of the small village was similar to that of a maze. They drove through a snake of neighborhoods, with houses that greatly resembled one another; with white and yellow concrete walls, orange gabled tops, and cozy terraces. It appeared to be a humble and typical area, not to mention an oasis for the uninvited. The road towards their destination was long, and the journey silent and dull. It carried on unchanging for many hours, and all they saw around were farms, glasshouses, and extensive crops that were still green and neatly mowed, even during the frigid season. However, not a single soul could be spotted for miles.

The land of the Olympians seemed camouflaged under a fog that was cold and grim, and as opaque as the fear in the hearts of some of the people inside the vehicle. But even though they knew they were fleeing towards an uncertain future, they were still rather grateful for not being pushed to walk for days in order to reach their meeting point—just as countless other immigrants did each month. On their way, they also drove by various villages; Kavyli, Orestias, Didymoteicho, and others around the Evros region. To the apprehensive asylum seekers, it seemed as though they would never reach the capital. A few managed to sleep during the rest of the way, but Samir wasn't one of them. He couldn't stop thinking of his parents and little brother, worrying about their well-being, and speculating on their current status. His only hope was to soon discover they were safe, somewhere within the large metropolis.

The tranquility of the countryside was later replaced by the loud honking of cars, and the roaring of motorcycles—all while their riders showed off their risky acrobatic tricks—drifting and cutting others, in an attempt to escape the infamous Athenian traffic jams. The clock had then hit midnight, yet the streets were anything but empty. Every corner was alive and packed with merry tourists, street performers, and waves of blasting music could be heard all around. Athens was yet another one of those cities that never lost its magic, in spite of the crisis or the time of the year. From afar, they could see the radiant Parthenon suspended gloriously atop the magnificent Acropolis, resembling a colossal, scarred nugget of gold. The infrastructure surrounding them was both modern and Hellenic. The roads were new, and many buildings had been recently restored, yet they made sure that their old, majestic look would never vanish.

After a few more turns, the group was then dropped off in front of Syntagma Square—located just across the Greek Parliament. That was the end of their journey together with Sarkis Nazarian.

"That was the last time you guys saw him?" Isabel asked.

"Yes, also Asim and the Pakistani people. After we got out of the van, they gave us a paper with different addresses, and we took separate ways."

"I see..." she said.

"All except Hadil, she stayed with me and Yasir," Samir added.

"Hadil...the Persian girl?" Isabel queried.

Samir nodded. "Yes, she had nobody else."

"Oh."

With the help of a pair of locals, the three newcomers walked for a while until they reached Patision Street; a section surrounded by short, porched apartment buildings, adorned with beautiful hanging flowers and colored awnings. Samir scanned the area, luckily finding a payphone to dial a number he was given. Five minutes later, a man identifying himself as Christos came out of a small restaurant nearby. He escorted the trio around the corner of his establishment, and through a narrow door. They followed the stairs until the second floor, entering an apartment where he sheltered around twenty other people, of all ages and genders. For most visitors, coming to this city represented the chance to jump from one museum to the other, followed by hitting the clubs and bars until losing their ability to walk in a straight line.

But that was not the case for asylum-seekers. Sadly, for them it signified having to share a cramped space with other homeless people, usually uncertain for how long. And for many, it even meant having to browse through the rubbish for a bite to eat, or something to sell.

Samir searched hopelessly through every room for any of his family members, nearly attacking Christos out of frustration. Fortunately, his brother managed to hold him back just in time to make him reason. However, the Athenian admitted to have seen his parents and brother just the day before, attesting that they'd gone out to seek help with the immigration authorities at Petrou Ralli Avenue. There was nothing they could do at the time, and Samir was irritated for having to wait until dawn to find his relatives. The three new immigrants then looked for a free spot inside the crowded room, on which they could attempt to rest. There were piles of dirty clothes on the ground, empty bottles, and some sheets. Even still, such conditions were still far better than those existing in most official refugee shelters within the country. Those inhumane detention facilities, truly represented a taste of hell inside a compressed space; for many were infested with rats, garbage, diseases, and human waste.

Samir soon started to groan in pain once again, and he was aided by Christos and his brother to lie down in a corner of the room. A Syrian woman who was among them, noticed the situation and approached them without delay. Her name was Amal, and to both their surprise and consolation, she used to be a pediatrician back in the ravaged city of Damascus. In an authoritative tone of medical urgency, she called upon Christos and instructed him to bring a bucket of water, clean gauzes, and any antiseptic to prevent her patient's wound from re-infecting.

"My God!" Isabel exclaimed. "If you would've stayed still, maybe you would've healed faster! You were lucky to find a doctor in such a place..."

Samir shrugged. "Yeah...maybe. Anyway..."

But Amal was not the only one holding a professional title in that crowd. Among them were also two engineers and a lawyer, and Hadil herself used to be a news reporter back in Tehran. In fact, there are numerous asylum seekers around the world who are fully educated, and who were law-abiding citizens with stable jobs and settled lives—long before they had no choice but to leave it all behind, and flee to safety away from wars, poverty and persecution. Nevertheless, none of them ever expect to find themselves roaming around cities where they are unwanted, or living in countries where their degrees and years of hard work signify absolutely nothing.

At daybreak, Samir and Yasir traveled for one hour in a bus, to the place where their family was rumored to have been spotted. To their further dismay, they witnessed as hundreds of people surrounded the immigration offices, all pushing and yelling in the attempt to get near its closed gates. All of them were waving documents above their heads;

mainly photocopies of their IDs, and applications for political asylum. It was a shameful display; a vivid example of the devastating humanitarian disaster, occurring right inside a civilized European country. All of a sudden, a fight erupted between two Afghan men, as one tried to take the space of the other in the queue. They ultimately ended up on the ground, striving to knock each other's lights out, while most of the crowd continued pressing forward unconcerned. The few security guards who stood by, also did nothing to interfere in the situation. And yet, in a matter of minutes, three armored vehicles of the EKAM— Greece's Special Tactical Forces—appeared on the scene, startling the anxious multitude. Entire teams of highly-geared officers, stormed out from the back of the black vans with their shields and batons ready in hand, and unhesitant to put them to use. Many men and women were beaten on the legs and arms, as the officers gradually and violently drove them away from the facilities. And that morning, only twenty applications were received through those dreadful gates. Twenty, out of several hundred.

"I swear in God, none of us expected Europe to be like this," spoke Samir. "They treat refugees worse than animals."

After these honest words, Samir remained silent and contemplative for a few minutes. Isabel shook her head in disbelief, and looked between her pages for further questions to ask.

"And what about...your parents?" she queried. "Did you see them there?"

"There were some rumors…" he continued.

Rumor had it that several families had been randomly selected by agents of an international humanitarian-aid organization. They were to be relocated to other Western countries, where they would be placed in proper asylum facilities, and have their documents processed. Samir hoped that his family was among the chosen, but nothing was certain.

He and his brother returned to Patision Street, and soon attempted to find any means of income. Fortunately for Samir, he'd learned how to make bread from his old father, and was given a job at Christos' restaurant—baking pitas and psomi loaves back in the hot kitchen. Yasir, on the other hand, spent long hours each day doing several tasks; salting the few icy sidewalks in the area, selling newspapers, and even polishing shoes at the public Square. They arranged to stay in Greece for a few months, until they could earn enough money for a plane ticket to Belgium—the country where his family was later rumored to have been sent to. However, one morning at around 9:00, a violent raid was carried out in all of Athens. Samir happened to be carrying a sack of flour through the back door of the kitchen, when he suddenly heard screams coming from the street out front. Dozens of police officers surrounded every road, seizing any illegal immigrants they found, and forcing them into buses leading to the dreaded detention centers. Samir dropped the bag on the ground and ran towards the main entrance of the restaurant, recalling that his brother was just across the street, cleaning shoes behind Agios Loukas Church. But as he attempted to step outside, he was rapidly grabbed and pulled back in by Asim.

"Oh my God! Where did he come from?" Isabel exclaimed.

"He'd been informed of the raid and went out to find us, but…"

Samir began shouting his brother's name, watching in horror as he was being handcuffed and pinned against the pavement, along with several other people. The Assyrian tried to push his friend off him, but was forcefully held down by the sturdier man, and pulled away from the sight of the merciless cops. Asim told him that there was nothing they could do for Yasir at that moment, stressing that they had to leave the area immediately. They then rushed out through the back door, leading to a side street where Christos waited for them behind the wheel of a car. They rapidly jumped inside the vehicle, but just before they drove off, they heard the familiar cries of a young woman. The three of them became alarmed to see that it was Hadil, being dragged away by an officer. Samir called out her name and she followed his voice amidst the chaos, jerking tremendously and crying out for his help. Convinced by the Iraqis that she had no one else to rely on, Christos cursed loudly in his native tongue, while reversing maniacally to retrieve the girl.

"Oh damn, you guys attacked the officer?" Isabel asked.

Samir smirked, "Not too much."

After a brief but demented chase, Christos managed to lose the authorities, arriving at an empty residence he owned in the seaside city of Porto Rafti—not too far from the main airport. They stayed there until the late afternoon, receiving instructions from the brave Athenian man who'd just saved their lives, and who'd expressed feeling ashamed of the way his own political leaders dealt with the refugee issue. Later on, the three runaways put together all the money they'd earned so far. And with further help from Christos, they booked three plane tickets to Amsterdam for that same night.

"Wallah, it was God's mercy they didn't notice we had fake passports," remarked Samir, as he made the sign of the cross over his chest.

"God's mercy?" Isabel asked dubiously. "It seems to me that it was more for Christo's mercy that you made it out of Greece at all."

Samir shook his head and frowned slightly, but respected Isabel's own opinion on the matter. She sensed that she'd offended him, and apologized for her incredulous mindset. Internally, she admitted that it was truly unbelievable how they'd made it out of the country unnoticed.

"So, what happened when you guys arrived?" she added.

"We did like they told us; we threw away our passports. After that, I called my cousins in Holland," he replied.

"And the rest is history," Isabel said.

Samir nodded, "Aiwah."

Aiwah...yeah...

"Wow..." she whispered in a deep state of awe.

Christos' selfless determination to help others, was both confounding and admirable. And without a doubt, every part of Samir's testimony was just as extraordinary. However, for people like Isabel it was difficult to understand why the Greek citizen so willingly risked everything he had in order to aid strangers—especially when he had nothing to gain from it. It was an observation to which Samir calmly explained that Christos loved to help people, precisely because he knew what it was like to be persecuted. His grandparents, from his father's side, had been fatal victims of the Christian-Greek genocide that took place during the Ottoman rule.

"Sometimes, when people are connected in suffering, they become a family," he added.

Isabel's eyes turned crimson from hearing such emotional words. She'd become uncomfortably speechless, and attempted to write down her last notes, realizing that she had but a few blank pages left in her journal.

"I don't know what I'm doing anymore," she spoke softly. "I...I need a minute."

Isabel plodded all the way to the kitchen, and poured herself a glass of water to try relieving her reactive anxiety. She closed her eyes and breathed systematically, until her pulse began to ease down back to normal. Never in her life had she experienced such high levels of inner stress. And it frustrated her to feel her emotional condition worsening, particularly throughout the time she'd been living in the Netherlands. She spent a few minutes staring out the window and towards the starry skies, reflecting on everything she'd been going through. Without even realizing, she began addressing her thoughts to God—wondering if He was really somewhere up there, watching over her and everybody else.

Isabel's mother had always been a faithful Christian, and nothing could ever change her mind about her convictions. She fervently believed that God was ever present in her life, and even her daughter's, no matter how obstinate she were. These assumptions were always unacceptable to Isabel, for she thought it unfair that a god would be merciful to only some parts of the world, while allowing the suffering and annihilation of millions of people—people who restlessly praised His name, regardless of the brutal persecution they endured. For this, and many other reasons, she continuously refused to be open to any religion, or to even consider believing in a deity. Amelia always said that Isabel had inherited her stubbornness from her father, who happened to be a fervid atheist of the far-left.

However, in the past couple of weeks, Isabel had been undergoing several experiences, all which had made an evident impact in her life. They had somehow worked like a seed that had been planted inside of her, and that was now beginning to germinate. Subsequently, it served to give life to a kind of hope she never had. This hope was plainly the encouraging idea, that perhaps there really was more to life than one's earthly existence. A she meditated on this, she could feel her mind fiercely battling her spirit, and it was more than what she could stand at that time.

"No! It's just not possible!" she shouted.

When she turned around, she flinched from seeing Samir standing against the doorframe, with his hands buried in his pockets. He displayed a look of concern on his face, somehow fearing that he might have been haunting Isabel with his own old demons.

"I'm so sorry...I didn't know you wer—" she sighed and turned her face away. "I feel so stupid right now..."

"Why are you talking like this?" he asked.

"I don't know! It's just...your story, and all these people, and then my mom, and this whole God craziness, ugh!"

She clenched her hands behind her head, and turned to face the window once more, feeling too confused and annoyed to even speak words that could make the slightest bit of sense. Samir's concerned demeanor had then intensified. But he approached the girl nonetheless, and embraced her from behind.

"Tell me what is really bothering you," he said softly.

He asked the same question a few times. But at the third repetition, his voice in her head had become faint and distant. She was not angry, but afraid. She was terrified to start believing in an actual fatherly figure who really loved her unconditionally, and who would guide and protect her—only to wake up one day, and discover he never existed, or that he'd chosen to abandon her.

Isabel turned towards Samir again, and looked steadily into his dusky eyes as he waited for an answer. The only audible sound throughout the entire apartment, was the melody of a slow and gentle oud coming from the next room. And yet, even with the thought-stimulating tune, she still couldn't find the right words to explain everything she felt at that moment—concerning both her spirituality and her personality—in a way that sounded logical. She diverted her gaze away from his, lowering it steadily as she ran her fingers down his sturdy shoulders, and over the lumpy, pink scar on his chest.

"I just wish I had your courage, Samir. I envy you."

The Assyrian squinted slightly, as though trying to figure out the meaning of her words.

"Envy me? For what reason?" he asked astonished.

She smiled.

In the back of her mind, Isabel did a rerun of her entire life—from her stage growing up in a safe place, to being able to study and pursuing a good career. She used to consider herself lucky with her cozy lifestyle, assuming that the only element missing was the love of a man. Now that she'd lost everything she ever worked for, she admitted to have gained an unmeasurable amount of knowledge about the world that she could've never acquired inside a classroom. Nevertheless, she admired Samir for more than just his ability to survive the violent persecution. Because despite the circumstances, Samir was proud of his heritage and his country, and he yearned to see the day when Assyrian people could have their ancestral lands back again. Most definitely, his strength did not reflect merely in the toughness of his body and character, but also in the flame of faith that burned within his heart.

"Patria o Muerte," she whispered. "When I look at you, I feel like I can truly understand the meaning of that revolutionary motto."

"What does it mean?" he asked.

"It means that you live under the right convictions."

He shrugged, still confused.

She then walked away from him, in her usual meditative mood. And just before stepping through the door, she turned her head to ask one last question that night.

"When you mentioned that your brother was in Turkey, and the whole immigration lawyer issue, did you mean that—"

"That he's still in prison there, yes," he spoke.

Isabel inhaled sharply.

"But I will get him out," he added with a firm voice.

She nodded, "I have no doubt of it."

16

"ANA BAYANOUKH"

It happened to be the hottest time of the year in the Netherlands. The constantly-shifting weather in the region managed to confuse even the locals, who appeared surprised to see how one of the rainiest countries in the world turned so terribly dry all of a sudden. The heat all around had become overwhelming, to the extent that even working-out was out of the question for Isabel. All windows in Samir's apartment remained wide open each day and night, in the attempt to catch some fresh breeze from the North Sea. Not to mention that cheap ventilators blew an air so warm that it was almost torture.

None of these conditions helped Isabel's cause, as she struggled with her Dutch skills to type down the last pages of her essay; *Rotterdam: The Whole World at the Edge of the Rhine*. Professor Pelengkahu had given the day off to both his morning and afternoon classes, so they could work on the final stages of their paper, and turn it in the very next day. Her essay was certainly going to be different, if not outstanding, from the rest of her classmates'. Each page that she wrote contained not only astounding stories, but fragments of real people's lives as well. Out of all of these, Samir's story was featured as the one causing her the biggest impact, due to her closeness with the protagonist. She was no longer ashamed to admit her affection for him—at least not to other people.

The star of her masterpiece had just returned from the gym that Thursday evening, looking sweatier from the heat outside than from his heavy routine.

"Ufff! Too many people at the gym today! You missed good training," he said while collapsing on the couch.

She looked at him skeptically from above her specs. "Aha, I doubt it…"

He laughed vigorously at her reaction, admitting to have been one out of the four mindless jocks who'd actually showed up at the fitness center that day.

"How is this, your project?" he asked.

"It's almost done. But it's so warm here I can't think straight anymore!" she groaned.

"Ah, I know what we both need…" he said in a suggestive voice.

Isabel turned to face him again. But before she could utter a word, he'd already pulled her out of her chair and thrown her behind his back.

"Wha—hey!" she protested, while being carried into the shower room.

Well, he wasn't lying…

Their overheated bodies intertwined under a cool stream, was all she required to recover her strength after a long and stressful week. Up to that day, she was still unsuccessful in finding a job, and the fact that her email inbox was swarmed with Lennert's threats, made her situation even more irritating. She wouldn't mention anything about her debt to Samir, however, for she knew that he had his own problems to solve. She'd also noticed that he'd been acting odd and secretive during those last few days—particularly that evening, just before dinner.

Isabel was preparing a Greek salad recipe she'd seen on the internet. And while she minced a block of feta, she could overhear Samir arguing on the phone. She tried to eavesdrop on his discussion, immediately cursing under her breath for not understanding a word of Arabic. The tone of his voice concerned her, for it was far louder than usual. And while the strange call lasted no longer than five minutes, it was replaced with Samir's heavy footsteps approaching the kitchen.

"Isabel!" he called out. The curious girl flinched at the rough sound of her name, causing her to drop a pint of plain yogurt on the floor.

"Why are you yelling?" she asked, groaning as she knelt to clean the mess on the ground.

"Sorry, sorry. But, uhh, we need to talk," he insisted.

Oh no, nothing good ever comes after those words.

Nervous to find out what he was about to communicate, Isabel followed him back to the living room, where they sat amidst a thick cloud of tension. He shook his head and stared down at his feet, keeping his elbows rested on his knees, and his hands clenched together.

"Samir, please say something, you're freaking me out!" she exclaimed.

"I'm afraid I will do something stupid," he finally said, scoffing.

Isabel squinted with confusion. "What do you mean?"

"I have a contact person in Istanbul, and he called me last week..."

He paused.

"And?!" she stressed

"My brother is not in Turkey anymore. They sent him back to Iraq, but they didn't tell me where."

"Oh no...Yasir—" she paused in sudden realization. "Wait...please don't tell me you're considering—"

"Isabel—"

"No!" she cried out. "No, you can't go back there!"

Unable to hold back her tears, Isabel threw herself in Samir's arms. He embraced her tightly, but she pulled back abruptly.

"Who was that on the phone just now? Was it your contact person?" she asked.

"No," Samir replied.

He held her hands in a gentle manner, turning his face away in concealed shame.

"I go out of town for some days, okay habibti?" he said.

Isabel drew her hands away angrily, and rushed towards the window. She placed her right thumb between her teeth and started biting her nail, as she looked out into the animated nightlife of Delfshaven. Samir then walked up to her, and placed his hands over her shoulders—but she shook them off in contact.

"Isabel, listen to me, please."

"Haven't you seen the news lately, Samir?" she murmured with a cracking voice.

"Yes," he breathed.

"Haven't you seen what they've done to Christians, to your people in Mosul?"

"Yes," he repeated.

Following Samir's perplexing words, Isabel took a moment to remind him of the current situation in his country—particularly in his city of origin—and of how Assyrians and Yazidis alike had been pushed out of their villages, under relentless death threats from a ruthless and vile militant group.

"Sam…" she sobbed, "don't go…please."

"Isabel, I'm not going to Iraq, at least…not now."

She turned her head towards him, looking into his eyes with a puzzling gaze.

"First I need money to find my brother, wherever he is," he said calmly.

Isabel's heart finally started pacing down, unsuspecting that Samir was about to reveal even more troubling and implausible ideas.

"That was Ali on the phone today, my friend from the gym."

"Oh? Go on..." she said.

"I go with him to Belgium for a job." he added.

"What kind of job?" she asked.

He smirked, "Just I drive him someplace, don't worry."

"So it's just a chauffeur thing?" she queried with a dubious tone.

He replied, "Something like that..."

Crossing her arms, Isabel turned her entire body around in a slow twirl, facing the tense-looking man before her while keeping her mouth open in disbelief. As he was about to move his own lips again, she began to chuckle, until the giggles transformed into a long laughter of irony. He tried to explain himself, but she wouldn't allow him to, it was no longer required. In her mind, she'd already drawn a sketch of all the possible jobs he could have been referring to. She felt, however, that if he could have it in him to disclose such ideas so openly, then it was only fair for her to unveil her most withheld secret.

"I love you, Samir," she said plainly, hoping that it would make him reconsider his plans.

A gush of air escaped through his lips, as though he'd been stabbed directly into his heart—not quite the reaction Isabel had been anticipating.

"Oh my God," she gasped, throwing her hands over her mouth, and storming out of his presence in overwhelming shame.

She locked herself inside the bedroom, collapsing on the bed with her face buried underneath a pillow. The jingle of keys and the slamming of the entrance door, could be heard outside of the dimly-lighted room. What was it about that particular confession, that it always left people absolutely petrified? After all of the wondrous moments they'd shared, Isabel had assumed those were words he would have welcomed happily. And yet, right at the end of her sentence, his expression transformed radically, like he'd been given the most inconvenient news of his entire life.

The lonesome night progressed much too silent and slow for Isabel to find any sleep. Many hours had to go by, before her restless mind had finally given out from exhaustion. Samir didn't return until early in the morning, but she didn't see him nor did she feel his presence. By the time she'd awakened, the sun had already risen above the city, but the mood inside the room was just as somber as the previous night. She jumped out of bed to look for him in every corner of the apartment, discovering that his gym backpack was gone, but that his favorite trainers were still lying by the door. She then placed her hand on her chest and rushed to check his closet, where she found several empty hangers. He'd left just as he'd informed he would. And as she checked her phone, she saw a text message that confirmed it;

I know you are angry with me, and I won't ask you to forgive me. Just I will ask that you try to feel like me. Imagine that is your father. What would you do if he was in danger? I come back after some days.

Good luck with your project.

In those few sentences, Samir managed to embody three points that left Isabel disconcerted beyond her current state of uncertainty. She knew, for instance, that he was up to something unlawful, and he was being honest about it. It was only natural for a human mind to judge him, without even considering his reasons. And yet, he wittingly used the empathetic and never-failing strategy of demanding her to walk a mile in his shoes, as a way to justify his decision. She was hurt that he would dare drag her relationship with her father into the issue so deliberately, knowing it was the one subject she was most sensitive about. Not to mention that, above all of this, he couldn't even come up with a proper response to her bold declaration of love.

At that moment, she felt an incredible urge to respond to his note with both anger and spite. But as she glanced at the time displayed on the corner of the screen, she remembered the essay she had to finish for that same afternoon. She had to think of a last sentence for her conclusion, and instantly remembered one of Samir's awe-inspiring quotes—which she re-wrote in her own way;

> *"Refugees don't want to be given handouts forever. We want to have a future in safety, in freedom and in dignity, just like everybody else."*

These words were absolutely perfect. And ironically, even while she was mad at him, the Assyrian still managed to impress her greatly.

Isabel made herself ready in less than fifteen minutes; wearing her gym clothes, a messy ponytail, and her large glasses. She then took the metro towards Blaak, walking for just a minute until reaching the city's Central Library. This was yet another awesomely and atypically-shaped structure in the city. It had a peculiar industrial look, proving once more that Rotterdam possessed some of the strangest edifices in the world. Professor Pelengkahu had arranged to meet the whole class at a café located within the six-story building. But before gathering with them, Isabel made her way to the top floor to get her project printed and bound. She handed her flash drive to the librarian on shift, and as she waited for her work she went on to take a look around the area. All study rooms were empty at the time, as most students in the country had already hung their backpacks to the flagpoles in front of their houses—quite an interesting Dutch tradition. Nonetheless, the few visitors that lounged around, reading or sitting behind the computers, reminded Isabel of those dynamic years roaming around campus. The familiar image even made her fantasize about the possibility of going back to college one day.

Perhaps it's time to think about a Master's degree, she thought as she ran her hand over the book shelves. *But in what?*

Her finished essay had amounted to twenty-five single-spaced pages, and she carried it proudly back downstairs to *café Dikt*. Part of her class was sitting at the bar, and they waved spontaneously as they saw Isabel walk in.

"There you are!" exclaimed Jamil.

"Oh my God, am I the last one to get here?" she asked worriedly.

Jamil and Pete scoffed in unison.

"Indeed, we're already at our third round of bitter," said the cheeky Englishman.

"What? But it's three in the afternoon!" Isabel said.

"This is Holland!" added Pete. "Come, let's join the rest upstairs."

The three of them then made their way up to the open terrace, where the rest of the students were gathered along with the professor. Isabel had pictured their last meeting a little differently—perhaps simply handing out the project, and giving everyone a polite farewell handshake. Instead, they all sat together for the rest of the afternoon, enjoying of the sunshine like it was a family barbecue at the local park. Isabel tried her best to share their enthusiasm, but she continuously fell back into her pensive mood; wondering where Samir could have been right that second, and hoping he was alright.

"Isabel!" called the instructor, dragging her out of her thought cloud.

"Sir?" she replied.

"Please share your future plans with us," he said. "You've been awfully quiet today, much more than usual."

She shrugged. "Honestly...I don't know."

"Aw, come on, you never tell us anything about you!" added Sarah. "And, where is Samir?"

The whole class uttered teasing sounds, just like little school children. Isabel was not particularly amused by the subject, and she chugged the last bit of her wine in a brusque manner.

"He's gone," she replied bluntly, followed by getting up from the table and directing her eyes towards her instructor. "It's been an honor, Ray Pelengkahu."

"Isabel, please don't leave like this," gently added the professor.

But without saying another word, Isabel grabbed her backpack and abruptly left the establishment. Her brash departure gave her a good feeling at first, but it didn't last very long. In her stomach she carried nothing but a handful of bar-stool pretzels, and the one merry drink Pete had ordered for her. She started to feel dizzy as she reached the metro station, panting and focusing her blurring vision through the crowded terminal. In there she found a bench, and sat on it to catch her breath. And holding her spinning head inside her hands, she tried to convince herself that she would be back at the apartment in no time.

"Well, well, well. You really look terrible," said a familiar voice.

When Isabel raised her gaze, she was both surprised and overjoyed to see her old coworker, Ebele, who'd just walked out of her shift. The former housekeeper made an effort to get back on her feet, to give her Ugandan friend a big, tight hug that lasted close to twenty seconds. The broad woman cleared her throat, but Isabel continued to cling onto her, just like a child would to her mother—and she sobbed.

"Oh, I'm sorry Ebele," she whispered, slowly letting go. "I just needed that hug so bad right now…"

"That's fine, honey. But what happened to you?" she asked.

They sat together on a metal bench, and Isabel recounted some of the most recent events in her expatriate experience. It didn't take long before Ebele noticed that she seemed ill and fatigued, and she confronted her about it.

"It's nothing—I was in a bit of a hurry today, and forgot to eat enough," Isabel explained.

"You forgot to eat? Are you for real?" Ebele responded with an astonished tone.

She rapidly browsed through her handbag, from where she drew out half a pack of saltine crackers. These were the same ones she normally ate for lunch each day, and she kindly handed them to the visibly-ravenous girl.

"It's not much, but you can have them," she added.

To anyone else, the gesture wouldn't have signified anything out of the ordinary. And yet, since Isabel was aware of the Ugandan's life story, she received the snack with teary eyes and a moved heart. She then unwrapped the salty biscuits anxiously, and stuffed her face as though she were delighting in cocktail quiche bites. The scene surprised Ebele so much, that all she could do was stare at it with a round-gaped mouth.

"Are you...feeling better?" she asked.

Isabel let out a sharp sigh. "So...much...better. Thank you."

"Honestly," added the hardworking maid, "after analyzing everything you just told me, I think you should really call your mother."

"To tell her that I've failed?" Isabel asked. "No. It's been only six months, I can't give up so soon."

"But who says that you've failed?" asked Ebele. "Besides, you don't have to give up on anything. Just ask her to send you some money until you can find a new job."

Albeit somewhat convenient, the idea of asking her mother for help made Isabel feel too powerless, and as dependent as a college freshman. She felt that it should have been her helping Amelia, instead of the other way around. She knew that Ebele did it for her own children, but it was a totally different, and incomparable situation.

"I wish I was more like you, always so strong and optimistic," Isabel said with admiration.

"Honey, I don't have a choice, but you do. You have a good life to return to—if you decide to go back, I mean," she replied.

Isabel shrugged. "Yeah, I guess you're right."

Shortly after, Isabel and her former colleague said their farewells, and got on different subway cars. It was a little past 18:00 by the time she arrived back to Delfshaven. But it was still bright outside then; clear enough to notice an unfamiliar individual desperately buzzing the button to Samir's apartment.

"Excuse me, can I help you?" she asked.

The person in question was a woman in her early thirties; with big, kohl-lined eyes, and a light-beige visage wrapped in a silk, golden veil. She glanced at Isabel in a strange manner, but disregarded her presence and continued to press the button on the panel.

"Hey! I'm talking to you. Why are you looking for Samir?" she insisted.

The mysterious female jumped at the sound of his name, and Isabel felt threatened immediately by this reaction—as if a switch of jealousy had just been turned on inside of her. In an impulse, she pulled the hijabi's arm away from the panel, and the girl jerked roughly.

"Who the hell are you!?" they asked each other at the exact same time.

The stranger appeared irritated, and began mumbling to herself in a tongue that was neither Arabic nor Turkish. And just as Isabel was parting her lips to ask her name once more, she came to realize that she already knew it.

"Wait a minute...Hadil?" Isabel asked with disbelief.

The woman's surprised expression was sufficient to confirm Isabel's assumption. On the other hand, Hadil was not amused by it.

"How do you know my name?!" she demanded. "And where is Samir?"

Isabel crossed her arms tightly. "He's not here. He will be back in a couple of days."

Hadil sighed with deep concern, as though she also knew about Samir's out-of-town job. Isabel scanned her from head to toe, with both curiosity and wonder, for she was also an intriguing character in Samir's story. Another thing she couldn't help to notice was her modest, yet chic manner of dressing up. She wore jeans, dark boots, and a black over-the-knee tunic top, embellished with golden oriental patterns around the collar and sleeves.

"And if you know he's not here, why are you here?" asked the Muslim girl.

"I live here," replied Isabel with a snobbish tone.

The dubious Iranian girl nearly choked at the bold revelation. "Here....with him?!"

"Yes," Isabel added while drawing out her keys. "Would you like to come upstairs for a cup of coffee, or tea?"

"Why would I do that?" asked Hadil.

"Well, as you may have noticed, the nosy neighbors are nearly hanging from their windows..." said Isabel.

The uninvited visitor hesitated for a moment, yet ultimately obliged to the invitation, noticing that Isabel's humorous remark wasn't far from the truth. When they stepped into the apartment, Hadil proceeded to uncover her head, gracefully revealing her long and curly auburn hair. Isabel had to gulp hard at the sight of the Persian's stunning beauty, but was even more amazed to see that she already knew her way around the place.

"Um, may I use the WC, please?" she asked politely.

"Sure, but I guess you already know where it is," Isabel inferred, strutting towards the kitchen.

There was a sort of competitive tension filling the air around them. And though she'd started to feel annoyed, Isabel did her best to appear unreadable. The awkward silence continued on as they later sat on the couch. Hadil sipped her tea in an elegant fashion, and Isabel held her coffee mug against her lips, while keeping her dubious stare fixated on the unusual guest. Throats cleared as one waited patiently for the other to break the iceberg, but there was only one subject blowing up in their minds that neither of them dared to address.

"Okay," breathed Isabel. "I feel we both have a lot of questions right now, so...I'll go first."

"Fine," the girl responded.

"What's your relationship with Samir, exactly—besides the whole Athens thing?"

Hadil laughed with childish mockery at the suggestive question. "What's my relation—" she giggled again. "You're the one living with him, perhaps I should ask you the same thing."

Isabel exhaled sharply and placed her mug on the table before her.

"Well, since you're so shocked, then I guess you and him are in fact—"

"Nothing," interjected Hadil. "I'm shocked because he's living with anyone at all, especially a woman. And then...well..."

"What?" Isabel stressed.

"Unmarried," the Persian added boldly. "Or...are you...?"

"No," Isabel scoffed, followed by explaining how she'd actually met Samir, and how she'd come to know about her. Their conversation shortly turned into an interrogation that quickly faded into a confession—for neither of them were ashamed to admit their legitimate interest in the Iraqi. However, according to the hijabi, none of them had a chance at establishing a solid relationship with him.

"What do you mean?" asked Isabel.

"Simple, you'd have to be one of them, an Assyrian," she explained.

Seeing that Isabel's bewildered mien wouldn't soften, Hadil placed her own cup down on the table, and gave her a brief lecture on Middle Eastern culture and marriage traditions. She spoke calmly and without stuttering, for she was no stranger to the strict rule of *not mixing with foreigners*—much less with those who didn't share an ethnic connection. In her particular case, Hadil knew she was never going to have a chance at something serious with him, due to the fact that she was a Muslim and he was a Christian.

"It can't happen, not after everything the Iraqi Christians are going through," she added.

Isabel smiled internally at her last statement. But a second later, she recalled that she was neither a Christian nor she had any legitimate connection to the Middle East.

"That explains it then," she murmured. "I actually told him that I loved him, and he just—"

"Oh no!" Hadil chuckled, covering her mouth with her hand. "What were you expecting?"

"I don't know, really," Isabel rolled her eyes. "But what about you? Did you ever tell him your...feelings?"

Hadil coughed phonily as her cheeks began to redden.

"This is really strange to talk about, I...I don't even know your name."

"I'm Isabel."

"Isabel...hmm, Samir never mentioned anything about you."

Her unfiltered words were as cutting as a sharp knife, so much that Isabel literally felt a puncture in her chest that stole the air from her lungs.

"But, don't get me wrong," continued the Persian, as she attempted to sweeten her harsh remark, "if you're living here, then you must be someone special..."

"Hmm, you're actually right," Isabel said.

"Oh?" the girl uttered with an arched eyebrow.

"This conversation is really weird," concluded the host.

The apparent rivals coincided in a brief and awkward snicker. But Hadil remained pretty reserved about her history with the fancied Assyrian. However, judging by her confident attitude towards the matter, it wasn't difficult to assume they'd been something more than just friends and border-crossing comrades. Deep within her tense poker-face, Isabel wondered if whatever they had was still going on—and if that was the reason why she'd suddenly appeared in Delfshaven at all.

"By the way," added the curious host, "you never said why you came all the way here. Don't you have his phone number?"

Hadil became pensive over the question, and studied Isabel's mien before giving her a legitimate answer.

"I assume you already know about Yasir's situation, yes?" the Muslim girl queried.

Isabel nodded immediately.

"Well, I'm the one who's been helping Sammy with contacting the lawyers and such…"

She paused.

Sammy? Are you kidding me?

"And…?" insisted Isabel.

Hadil exhaled sharply, then continued explaining that someone had notified her about Yasir's whereabouts. He was safe, and had been taken to a monastery in Kurdistan, along with hundreds of other refugees.

"I've been trying to call Sammy all day. But since his phone is turned off, I came here instead."

Come on, is she serious?

Shaking her jealous thoughts away, Isabel sank into the couch with an overwhelming sense of hopelessness. She knew that Samir was somewhere out there—doing who-knows-what—in order to get money to save his brother. Then again, even if he were conscious of the recent events, Isabel was sure that he would have gone away with Ali still, since without money he couldn't help Yasir anyway. Hadil stayed until late, attempting to contact Samir together with her host, yet having no luck. Meeting each other had been an odd experience, but the outcome had been positive enough for them to engage in a courteous and elegant farewell.

That night, Isabel lied in bed with her phone pressed against her ear, uselessly trying to reach the uber-complicated man to whom she'd recently confessed her love.

"An impossible love in a broken life," she whispered.

Isabel had been battling fiercely with her inner self; between romantic feelings, spiritual imbalance, and little sense of direction. But despite all of her mind-boggling experiences and life lessons, she was still inclined towards finding a solution to her own issues. There was no doubt that her concern for Samir and his family was genuine. And yet, it was in her own future where most of her thoughts were fixated.

"But what future?" she asked herself, considering her current circumstances.

However, something unexpected had occurred that afternoon. She didn't see it then, but the exact moment she placed her essay on Ray

Pelengkahu's hands, her presence in the Netherlands had become meaningless. It was as though she'd accomplished her purpose on that specific period in her life. It was also a realization that gave her a rush of alarming chills, and she laughed about it.

No, it can't be.

But it was. Deep inside, she suspected this also. Isabel eventually desisted from her persistence in trying to contact Samir. And instead, she dialed her mother's home number. It was around 20:00 in Amelia's time zone. And being familiar with the advanced hours at her daughter's location, Amelia answered her phone with a mildly frantic tone of voice. A mother's intuition never failed, and it was useless for Isabel to hide anything from her, though she didn't intend to. From beginning to end, she told her the absolute truth about everything she'd been through; the lies about her employment, the shocking stories of other immigrants, the clashes with Lennert and her debt to him. And lastly, she revealed the truth about her unforeseen relationship with an Iraqi refugee. Just as Isabel feared, her last confession managed to confuse Amelia's bilingual tongue, which went from shouting hysterical English remarks, to chanting the Spanish version of all the holy names in the Bible. It was at that very second when Isabel regretted going too deep into details.

"Ay ma' it's not like that, seriou—what?! He's not going to make me wear that, he's a Christian!"

"Oh?" Amelia paused her ranting. "Umm...like Protestant, or Catholic?"

"Mom, please! Listen to what you're asking!

"I'm just worried, dear! Imagine if he's from one of those false sects...ay Dios no!"

Isabel sighed with deep annoyance. "You know, it is exactly because of that mindset why the Church is so divided."

"Mi amor, I'm so—"

"This was a bad idea, we'll talk later," Isabel interrupted.

Overwhelmed with her mother's arguments, Isabel abruptly hung her phone up and slumped back into bed. She'd hope to receive some kind of guidance, or at least a seal of approval to stay and find a new purpose in the Netherlands. Unfortunately, Amelia's overprotective hysteria was completely discouraging.

If only he'd be here by dawn, lying next to me… she wished silently.

That Saturday, the local weather had fallen back into its habitual condition, matching the exact same state of mind of the antsy Hispanic girl. Lounging against the sofa—and holding a tea glass in her hands for a change—she could tell that she was about to endure a long, and rather slow day. It was one of those quiet days, where the only sounds that could be heard were the heavy rain drops crashing against the windows. She'd long given up on trying to reach Samir, yet continued to read his last text message until she'd memorized it—*Imagine that is your father*—and her father wouldn't leave her mind throughout the whole morning.

"What would I do?" she asked herself, as she reached out for her old journal.

Folded right in the middle of it, was the only letter her dad had ever written for her. She opened it and studied every word carefully, much more than the day she discovered the tattered sheet of paper. This time, she hoped to find some kind of hidden fatherly advice within the compelling sentences. And yet, the words penned down on that paper seemed more like orders, and a reminder of some sort of birth duty she never asked for.

"To help my people…which people?" she muttered with a scornful tone.

That particular possessive term was one she couldn't comprehend. After settling in the United States at such a tender age, Isabel had grown up to be impartial. And the fact that she never felt accepted in a group, made her believe that neutrality was the correct and most truthful way to live. She could see that any other option only created conflicts, separations, and most evidently, serious relationship issues. To her, it had always been hypocritical to speak about unity and equality among all people, but then run back to a certain group or community of origin at the end of the day. Ironically, she never expected that in her fervid attempt to be an unbiased individual, she would find herself alone, and with the strong perception of not belonging anywhere at all. But there was still the memory of those days, sitting among her culturally-diverse classmates, where she felt like she was actually part of something. And on several occasions, she'd even managed to see her class as a fraternity for expatriates like herself. On the other hand, she unconsciously ignored an important detail; each one of her fellow expats had a homeland which they longed to return to one day—even if just to visit and remember who they were.

But where do I go?

Without planning it, Isabel was gradually starting to see beyond the surface of her existence, recognizing that a life without national identity was a lonely path full of empty gaps. If a man couldn't tell where he came from, he would certainly find a bumpy road ahead, not knowing where to go, and perhaps unsure of what to become in the future. After all, everyone wishes to know their history at some point, and in different cases; children naively asking how babies are made, adopted kids growing up with the urge to find their biological parents, and of course, people who spend their entire life trying to figure out whether they are God's creation or protagonists in Planet of the Apes. But out of all these, she felt as if being aware of her cultural heritage was one of the most important conditions of all. Having grown up lacking this quality, ultimately translated into Isabel wrongly identifying herself as something completely unrelated to what ran inside her veins. Nevertheless, she didn't want to be identified as a United States citizen anymore. At least until she could find herself, she wanted to be seen as a citizen of the world; a woman without borders.

Solitude was a good spare time for the creative, but also a dangerous habit for over-thinkers like Isabel. Isolation lead her to submerge in deeper thoughts, until she ultimately and unwittingly crashed against inconvenient truths. Still, the truths she'd been discovering had little to do with her ethnic background. There was no way she or anyone could have questioned her obvious Latin roots. Her real problem was that she'd been feeling like an empty vessel—up until recent days. Reading between the lines of her dad's letter made her realize that, not only had she been separated from his love, instruction and guidance, but also from the promise of a significant life purpose. Suppressed inside her heart was a growing desire to discover her heritage. And she understood that she could only achieve this by finding her father, and open her mind to everything he wished to teach her. But Amelia had made a big mistake with her over-protective motherly behavior, and the most hypocrite of all. Her past as a left-wing activist was no secret, and she was proud of it. But the moment she became pregnant, Amelia made sure to keep her child away from the political controversies and the revolutionary movements. She found comfort in religion, and wanted to teach Isabel that Christ was the right path to follow, saying that the most important identity was as a child of God. But is it really so? Can't a man be patriotic at the same time that he strives to be a faithful believer? Did King David not defend his nation with the blessing of Jehovah? Did Colombian Catholic Priest, Camilo Torres, not die fighting for freedom and speaking against injustice? Amelia herself once said, with utmost boldness and security, that Jesus Christ was the very first socialist in history. So what happened?

An intelligent person should be able to differentiate between those who use the name of God to perform atrocities, and those who simply want to defend their patrimony and dignity, hopeful that there is a higher power backing them up in the process. Either way, Isabel understood that Amelia acted rather selfishly by keeping her away from her own father, with the excuse of protecting her from his expectations. And though she was no longer a child demanding protection, Isabel reached a point in her life in which she was in tremendous need of direction.

The quietness surrounding her in the apartment was turning as burdensome as her inner voice, which continued making up unanswerable queries. She needed someone to talk to—her friend, her lover—the only person inside her mind, the one who couldn't seem to reappear in front of her upon a simple wish. Contacting her classmates was her next idea, and apologizing to them sounded like a good excuse to be around them. But then, as she browsed through her phone contacts, she saw that she hadn't saved any of their numbers.

"Damn it," she groaned.

All of a sudden, her disappointment was replaced with a dash of hope, for she recalled the glossy business card Sarah had given her. Isabel raided her purse desperately, shaking it a couple of times, and dropping its contents all over the couch. Between euro coins, make-up, a wallet, bubblegum, her passport, a pen-drive, and three party flyers—commonly handed out around the city center on a daily basis—Isabel found, not only the card of the belly-dance studio, but also the bulletin of Rotterdam's most peculiar Church. She remembered having been enthusiastic about that Sunday's sermon on Christian Persecution, and her eyes shifted from one piece of cardboard to the other, while she considered both options indecisively. From one side, she was certain that a tantric dance session could take away all of her stress, and she truly needed it. While on the other hand, attending the Sunday service seemed like doing further research on a subject she'd somewhat covered in her essay.

I really need to relax...no more drama, no more persecution...

She grabbed her phone and started dialing the number on Sarah's card, but then paused just before pressing the little green tab on the screen.

"Alright...fine!" Isabel muttered, dialing one more time.

Her heart began racing as she heard the ring-back tone, which was replaced by a motherly greeting after the second ring.

"Hello Mei, it's been awhile," Isabel sighed. "I was wondering, what are you doing tomorrow morning?"

17

REDEEMED

"Do you know anyone here?" Mei whispered in her former neighbor's ear.

Isabel scanned the splendid and heavenly-lit nave inside Pauluskerk, in search of any familiar face. The service had not yet started, but most of the congregation was already sitting on the colorful chairs provided. There was a lot of chatter all around, giving the impression that all members were already acquainted with each other. However, as soon as the grand sounds of the organ filled the room, each and every person dropped their faces in reverent silence—including the entire Chen family that sat next to Isabel. The majestic instrument was located above, on the minstrel's gallery, with its shiny steel pipes almost touching the white ceiling, and its noble melodies so high they must have reached the heavens.

It was precisely at that moment when Isabel spotted the one cleric she was familiarized with—Minister Jansen—entering the room along with other Church staff. In the middle of the bright chamber was an oval-shaped table, and on it were several stacks of paper. These were later handed out to the whole congregation by the cleric and his assistants. As he approached Isabel's row, his face lighted up and he nodded complacently upon seeing her. He said nothing then, but as he went on to stand behind the podium, all eyes darted towards him.

"Blessings upon you all, friends and family, and welcome home to Pauluskerk. On this sublime morning we are truly rejoiced to have some special visitors among us; Miss Isabel Alvarez, and the Chen family, right over there."

Everyone in the congregation turned their heads towards the conspicuous guests. Isabel smiled, somewhat awkwardly, since stepping inside a new Church for the first time was always a little odd. On some occasions, she'd had the perception of being judged under the religious eye of a stranger. But that morning it was different. Many of the members approached her and her friends for a warm greeting. The men offered a polite handshake, and the women gave them a familiar embrace. The loving gestures reminded Isabel of the few times she visited her mother's Church—mostly during special holidays—but she didn't expect to receive the same treatment in a place where nobody knew her.

I guess not all Christians are crazy fundamentalists...

After a few sublime devotional songs, the children were escorted into another room for their Sunday school, and the toddlers were taken to the nursery. All attention was then focused on a preacher and missionary from the United Kingdom—commonly stationed in South Africa—who was invited to speak about the persecution. The documents that were given to those present contained information about various countries around the world, in which Christians were being harassed on a daily basis, if not murdered or jailed. North Korea was at the top of the list, followed by several Middle Eastern and Asian countries. Isabel scanned a partly-highlighted map that was provided, and was surprised to see that Cuba and Colombia were also in the list of countries where Christians faced hostility. The English preacher presented the congregation with plenty of facts, and historical information on how the persecution began—and whether it was for religious or political reasons. And he also criticized the international community, especially the Western Church, for not taking enough action on the matter. His assumption was, that perhaps they were afraid to get into a situation that would lead to controversy, or they didn't want to risk being attacked by the government for demanding justice.

"I am deeply ashamed," he proclaimed with a bitter tone, "because none of us here this morning truly represent what Jesus Christ went through. But all those people out there do, and we aren't doing anything to support them in their struggle."

His piercing words caused many of the members to stare down at their hands, while some even mumbled prayers of forgiveness. Isabel turned to glance at Mei, noticing that she was crying while Xiang embraced her tightly. She'd naively invited the Chens to the service, assuming they would have been interested in that morning's sermon. But bringing back bad memories was certainly not part of the plan. All of a sudden, Mei began to call out for her kids, demanding that she needed to hold them close. And less than a minute later, she was escorted to the kid's room by the staff.

"Xiang, I'm so sorry, this is all my fault..." Isabel whispered.

"No, Isabel, it isn't," he calmly replied. "Sometimes we just need to be reminded of how merciful God has been with our family. She will be ok."

Isabel sagged into her orange chair and exhaled in reassurance, then continued listening to the informative lecture. In the end, everyone joined hands in fervid intercessory prayer; for the needy, the persecuted, and for every human being in the world. As it was customary, the minister called upon those who wished to accept Christ as their Savior. At that point, Isabel felt her skin turn warm and flushed from the pressure of being stared at. She often disagreed with pastors who expected newcomers to step forward without delay, or without getting a chance to consider the implications of following a religious path. It was not the first time Isabel was placed in that awkward position. But she was a tough case, an analyst of everything, and a thinker who couldn't be easily convinced. And yet, for some mysterious reason, that morning she felt her entire body tremble in a strange and uncontrollable manner. Fearing to be experiencing one of her panic attacks, she sat back down and pressed her knees together, attempting to hold herself steady. She let out a soft laugh of irony. And when she lifted her gaze, she saw Minister Jansen walking towards her, while Xiang and the rest of the attendees slowly cleared the nave.

"Isabel...Isabel," he said, "why do you fight Him?"

"Eh, fight who?" she asked dubiously.

"The Holy Spirit. Why can't you give in?" he added.

Oh, it's a Him?

"Oh, come on," she scoffed. "I have an anxiety disorder, it's really not what you're thinki—"

"Really?" the clergyman asked. "What could possibly make you anxious in the house of God?"

You, interrogating me.

For as much as she brainstormed, Isabel couldn't construct a comeback clever enough to defend her viewpoint. She remained silent, standing up firmly and stretching her hand towards him.

"I just can't give into what I don't understand, Mr. Jansen."

The cleric shook her hand and studied her countenance meticulously, noticing that she'd tightened her lips to hold back her true emotions.

"Yet you felt His presence, and you know it was real," he said. "Besides, you also didn't understand what Christian persecution was, but you came here to hear about it, didn't you?"

"It's not the same thing, minister. Please don't try messing around with my logic," she countered.

"Did logic make you wake up early on a Sunday, and moved you to wear your best clothes to come to Church?" he added. "Or did logic make you invite your friends, who, from what I can understand, have inspired you in your search for truth?"

What?

"I...ahh," she uttered in confusion, "I just felt like it, that's all."

"It's a beautiful day outside, isn't it? You could have opted to do many other things today, yet you chose to be here—or felt like it, as you say," he added. "But what you felt was not a coincidence. God is calling you for this time."

Isabel groaned and threw her palm over her head.

Here we go...

"With all due respect, pushing your beliefs upon me isn't going to work," she contended. "With so many religions around, what makes you think you got the absolute truth?"

Unwilling to worsen their clash of ideologies, Isabel excused herself and began walking towards the exit, halting abruptly as the minister opened his lips once again.

"Nobody is pushing you to do anything, Isabel. But since you're so keen into using your reasoning, then consider this: In the past several months you've opened your heart to experiences that were totally unknown to you. You lent your ears to listen to the difficult situations of total strangers, and even established a close relationship with certain foreign man you never expected to meet. I can only wonder; why can't you give Christ the same chance?"

Isabel slowly turned around to face him, having her mouth open in wonderment.

"How could you possibly know any of this?" she stuttered.

The clergyman smiled warmly and let out a peaceful sigh. "I would like to pray for you, if you'd allow me."

Isabel nodded in a slow pace, keeping the same surprise plastered all over her face.

"Ok...I guess it's just a prayer," she whispered.

From the entrance of the room, the entire Chen family watched as Isabel stood before the cleric with her eyes closed. He quietly took a few steps back, followed by grabbing a tall glass bottle from a drawer inside the podium. He poured a small amount of the content in his palms, then gently placed his hand over her forehead. He spoke softly in her ear, and her lips began to move right after his. The prayer itself was inaudible from the door, but witnessing such a scene truly gladdened the Chinese couple that Sunday.

"Come, let's wait for Isabel outside," Xiang whispered to his family, as they walked away close together.

With two young children playing in the backseat of Xiang's car, the ride back to Delfshaven was anything but quiet. The Chinese family had planned to eat lunch at some restaurant near the harbor, but the contemplative Puerto-Venezuelan wasn't feeling up to engaging in more social activities that day. They dropped her off at Samir's place instead. And as soon as she went inside, she closed all the blinds in the apartment, undressed swiftly, and collapsed flat on the bed. Just as she was on the verge of falling unconscious, she became startled by her vibrating phone. Reaching out for it, she noticed a new email notification from her mother. After reading each line, she was pushed to rub her eyes to review the text all over again. The message couldn't have been clearer; Amelia had just transferred five-thousand euros through Western Union. Still unable to believe it, Isabel jumped right out of bed and immediately called her on Skype.

"Mom, where did you get all that money from?" she asked preoccupied.

"Well, hello to you too—and why are you in your underwear?" queried Amelia amidst a chuckle.

"Uh, I was in Church—I mean, I had a dress for Church, but I just—ah! That's not important! Please answer my question," Isabel insisted.

"Santo! Mi niña really went to God's house all on her own?"

Amelia started cheering joyously. While Isabel, on the other hand, could only roll her eyes and throw her head back in childish annoyance.

"Mom!" she shouted.

"Okay, okay, Mija!" Amelia said. "But don't worry about the money. Just settle that debt you have, so your mother can relax over here!"

"Alright, but I still want to know how—wait a minute..." Isabel gasped. "Ma'...where's your Cajiga painting?"

Isabel covered her mouth in horror, noticing the empty wall behind her mother—the one on which the Albizu portrait used to hang. She'd sold it without having second thoughts, stating that owning that painting had been a blessing.

"...because it served to help my most precious masterpiece," she said proudly.

Isabel's voice had gone dry, and her eyes teared from hearing such loving words.

"I really don't know what I'd do without you, ma'," she sobbed.

"I'm only sorry I couldn't stop the repossession of your car," said Amelia.

And yet, losing the BMW was the least of Isabel's worries then. She would have traded anything just to be able to hug her mother right at that second. And as she ran her hand over Amelia's streaming image, she realized how much she missed being around her.

"But, mom," Isabel spoke, portraying a sudden look of confusion, "my debt is only three-thousand euros. Why didn't you keep the rest?"

"Well, I want you to keep your options open," the mother shrugged. "You may use the rest to get around there for a few weeks until you find a job, or—"

"Or I can come home," Isabel added.

The jobless expat knew that it was only a matter of time before she would hear her mom speak these words. After all, it was the safest option; the last resort amidst a broken present and a highly uncertain future.

Isabel accepted the money, humbly, but with great relief. And right the following morning, she strolled down Schiedamseweg in search for the nearest Western Union to retrieve the heaven-sent cash. As soon as she walked out of the establishment, she juggled between mailing the money inside an envelope back to Lennert, or taking a subway straight to Blijdorp to leave it in his mailbox—ultimately concluding that both ideas seemed rather poor. She'd lost all trust for the Netherlander, and feared he would dare deny having received the payment. Instead, she sent him a text message and arranged an informal meeting for that same day, right at the stairs of the city's World Trade Center. Isabel didn't have to wait long by the flowing colored flags in front of the impressive glass building, before spotting the haughty and handsome European coming from the other side of the road. She noticed that he seemed impatient as he crossed the Coolsingel, glancing at his platinum watch, and fixing his impeccable grey suit just before opening his cocky lips.

"Miss Alvarez, we could have certainly met at a more private location, such as my place. However, I could never say no to a nice lunch with a beautiful woman such as you,"" he spoke self-confident.

"Drop the phony charm, Lennert," she retorted, handing him the envelope along with a hand-written release. "And there's no lunch."

Lennert stared at her with a dubious expression, but his mien softened rapidly as he looked inside the package.

"You may count it," she added while crossing her arms.

"No need," he said, signing the document. "Hmm, I guess things are going well with you...unless…"

He chuckled with mockery.

"Unless what?" Isabel queried.

"Well, I don't know...all this cash inside a lousy envelope makes me wonder; you didn't happen to join Holland's infamous underworld of pleasures, like most of you little Latinas, or did you?"

Without a bit of self-control, nor caring that they stood in the middle of the city, Isabel wiped Lennert's sarcastic grin right off his face, with a thunderous slap that managed to echo all over Beurs. Some marching citizens even slowed their pace to take a mental picture of the heated scene. Lennert, on his part, clenched his fists in anger as he turned around, and with a pulsating red cheek he stumped quietly the same way he came from. Isabel breathed heavily from both outrage and thrill, but felt proud of her instinctive and bold reaction nonetheless.

Upon returning to Delfshaven, Isabel saw her former classmate, Amaité, walking out of Yousef's store. She carried a bag of groceries in her right hand, and the usual skeptical look on her face. But her expression changed as she noticed her fellow Hispanic coming from the opposite direction. Isabel wanted to turn around and avoid getting her day ruined by Amaité's sarcasm. But this time, the Sinaloan had some news of her interest.

"Oye! Isabel!" she called out.

Great...

"Hey, how are you?" Isabel acted up.

"Fine. But did you hear about Samir?" asked the Mexican expat.

Isabel's heart skipped a beat at the sound of her lover's name.

What does she know? What happened? Is he okay?

Many questions appeared in her mind, but very few clear answers escaped Amaité's lips. She'd approached her with worrisome gossip; rumors of Samir being linked to a late-night police pursuit in Belgium. She'd heard about it in the morning news, and the entire district had been talking about the incident ever since.

Oh shit.

"Oh please, how can you be sure that he was involved in it?" asked Isabel.

"Because there's a video to prove it," she replied. "Watch the news."

Isabel was speechless, staring at the other girl with a gaze full of shame and sorrow. She didn't want to believe it, even when she already knew he was up to something. Amaité's attitude towards Isabel had taken a 180° turn that day, as she expressed being concerned about her fellow expat staying by herself inside his apartment. She even offered her own couch for Isabel to crash on, at her studio, not too far from the Assyrian's place.

"If the authorities go look for him and find you, you could get in serious problems, and Samir in even deeper trouble."

"Okay...thanks for letting me know. I'll think about it," Isabel replied unsure.

She then returned to Samir's home, having her earlier sense of achievement completely spoiled, and her mood dropped further as soon as she turned the TV on. There was a news report live from the city of Charleroi. The journalist was standing before an abandoned industrial site, where earlier that day an undercover officer had set up three foreign men, right in the middle of a false drug delivery. They showed footage from a hidden camera, attached to the disguised cop's jacket. Ali's face was clearly displayed on the screen, and in the background was another man she didn't recognize. Isabel sighed in a momentary relief. But seconds later, as the officer revealed his identity, the two men ran towards a vehicle across the lot; precisely where Samir waited.

"Oh no, no, no!" Isabel exclaimed, throwing her hands over her mouth, unable to look away from the TV.

The image had become unclear, for the officer had started running back to his car himself. And all that Isabel heard before the video was stopped, was the deafening bang of gunfire.

"This can't be happening," Isabel whispered, throwing her head back in frustration.

She suddenly heard a text notification coming from her phone, but groaned in disappointment from seeing that it wasn't from the person she'd expected. It was actually a message from Hadil. Because just like Isabel, the alluring Persian had been on high alert in case the impetuous Iraqi came in contact. Coincidently, she was asking Isabel if she'd seen the news that day—a question to which the Latina promptly replied;

I just did. I don't know what to say...

Isabel tried to divert her worried thoughts by preparing a delectable dinner for herself. She placed several bottles of spices over the counter, as well as some vegetables and half a pound of ground lamb. She'd decided to make *kofta* that night, just as Samir had taught her to. She later sat at the table—under candle light and amidst a slow melody of eastern flutes—imagining that any second she would hear the sound of his keys closing in, and his firm steps entering through the door. But her fantasies couldn't comfort her even in the slightest way. As she dipped her bread into the reddish sauce, a deep feeling of anguish started to hit her. She missed Samir badly, and not knowing his whereabouts was overwhelming. And yet, at the same time, she feared that the man she'd fallen in love with was probably being pursued at that exact hour. That assumption alone made her lose her appetite halfway through the dish, and she was soon overpowered by a disorienting headache. She went to wash her face in the bathroom, taking four paracetamol tablets she'd found inside the cabinet. She then lied down in bed, with her arm thrown over her eyes, and it didn't take long before the high dose of analgesics began to show its effects.

"Please God, just let him be ok..." she mumbled almost unconsciously, as she slowly submerged into a deep sleep.

18

RESIGNATION

Summer is known to be Rotterdam's most awaited season. It was the time of the hot Latin festivals, live Salsa performances, and many other cultural events. Isabel, on the other hand, was not exactly feeling up to attending any sort of social activities. Two weeks had passed since the moment she'd watched the alarming news about the set-up, but there hadn't been any updates on the case. She had not yet received any messages or calls from Samir either, and not even his cousins knew where he was. All of this caused Isabel to speculate on her lover's most probable outcome; imprisonment. And for as much as she wanted to continue searching for him, she knew that leaving the country to run strange errands had been his choice all along. However, the undaunted Hispanic woman did not stay with her arms folded during the past fourteen days, for she'd ultimately decided to accept Amaité's offer of moving into her place. She had also listened to Amelia's sensible words of advice, opting to leave the Netherlands once and for all.

Due to its minimalistic style, Amaité's small studio apartment resembled her personality perfectly. It was decorated with great simplicity, and the walls were painted with calm, neutral colors. Also, taped on the wall above her bed were several newspaper clippings about the decriminalization of soft drugs use, and a map with markings over the countries where marijuana had been legalized. It was all part of her thesis research, based on the economic development of Sinaloa. Past the Mexican's usual tough character, was a sensible woman who truly worried about the future of her hometown and the safety of the Sinaloan people. She'd grown up sick of the violence brought by the drug lords. But also expressed having mixed feelings at times, admitting that in many occasions the *narcos* helped the poor more than the government ever would.

"It's complicated," she would say.

But complicated or not, Isabel found Amaité's drive to help her people to be absolutely admirable.

On a bright morning of late July, Isabel Alvarez had checked her suitcases over three times, making sure that all of her belongings were neatly packed, and that her souvenirs and gifts were safely wrapped— ready to withstand the infamous airport staff handling. But before any of that were to occur, the enthusiastic traveler had someplace else to be that morning. Earlier that week, and just an hour after purchasing her plane ticket, Isabel received a surprising phone-call from Ray Pelengkahu. He joyfully expressed that the entire faculty had been blown away by some of the essays, figuring that such great works deserved some kind of merit and recognition. Isabel assumed that her current roommate had left early to be at the event. But considering that she had little time in her hands, she wanted to know if it was truly necessary to attend. Unfortunately, Amaité wouldn't pick up her phone.

I guess I'll have to show my face...

Before saying her farewells to the picturesque town of Delfshaven, Isabel went to take a last look at the building where she and Samir shared countless, unforgettable moments. She smiled at her loving memories, telling herself that even though what they had ultimately came to an end, she gained something wonderful out of it. With the Assyrian she felt to have gained wisdom, compassion, love, awareness, and many other priceless values. And as she looked up towards his window, Isabel flinched from the impression of having seen a silhouette move around for merely a second.

"I'm already hallucinating," she whispered as she walked away.

Once in Rotterdam Central Station, she secured her luggage inside a locker, and grabbed another metro towards the Central Library. The city was awfully crowded, more than usual, for the highly acclaimed Zomer Carnaval Street Parade was taking place on that day. It was a huge event, similar to Rio's Carnival—with incredible floats, extravagant dancers, and dozens of groups representing different countries from around the world.

I really picked the wrong day to leave this country...

When she arrived at her destination, she saw a banner above the entrance that surprised her. It read; Rotterdam: The Whole World at the Edge of the Rhine—the exact same title of her essay. It also featured a picture of the whole city, surrounded by a collage of world flags and a diversity of people in different traditional costumes. Isabel walked through the door rather sheepishly, curious of why they'd named the activity after her own work. But all of her questions faded from her mind the second she stepped inside the hall. Before her dazzled eyes was a vibrant, scenic display of spectacular pavilions, made in the shape of famous international structures.

What's all this?

"There you are!" exclaimed a joyous Jamil, who was wearing a traditional Chinese *changshan* in red. "Hey Sarah! Look who decided to show up!"

Their Kurdish classmate immediately walked out of a monumental booth, shaped and painted exactly like the marvelous Ishtar Gate. To Isabel's further surprise, the beautiful northern Iraqi had put on an outfit representing no more and no less than the Caribbean Island of Puerto Rico; a flowing, long blue skirt with horizontal white stripes, and a white off-shoulder blouse. She'd also adorned her beautiful black hair with a large, red daisy.

"Hey you! Sorry I couldn't find an *amapola*," she said, making a gracious turn. "What do you think?"

Isabel nodded happily.

"You look perfect! But I don't understand...what's going on?" Isabel asked.

"You don't know?" asked Sarah. "Your essay has inspired the multicultural community of Rotterdam, and it will be featured in the upcoming issue of The Xpat Diaries."

"The wh—what?" she stuttered.

"It's a magazine!" said Jamil.

Sarah then explained that their instructor was so impressed by the story, that he posted it on a social network and on his personal blog, thus drawing the attention of many community leaders. They felt it was the perfect time of the year to put together an event that would celebrate the diversity of cultures. They also realized it was an opportunity to educate people, by using real facts to clarify most common misconceptions about certain groups.

"And the best part yet," she added, "we're going to have a fundraising to help victims of human trafficking, as well as Holland's homeless people."

Needless to say, Isabel was completely dumbfounded by the impact her work had caused. Not wasting another minute, Sarah pulled her former classmate by the arm, and dragged her inside the Iraq-inspired kiosk. There were many guests present at the event—students, tourists, fellow expats, artisans, and musicians—all enthusiastic to take part in the cultural celebration. Every pavilion had staff offering basic information about each country represented. They also had a mini art gallery, wall-mounted flat screens presenting videos and images of the country's most notable locations, as well as a gastronomy booth with samples of some traditional dishes. It was like the wonderland of cultural integration—truly The Whole World at the Edge of the Rhine.

The two women hid behind a curtain, in a little corner they used for keeping props. And in there, Sarah kept a large rectangular box. From within, she revealed an exquisite emerald-green kaftan. It was one of the most enchanting dresses Isabel had ever seen; embellished with goldwork embroidery around the collar and sleeves, and completed with a delicate gem-decorated waistband and bejeweled flats.

"I wore it at my engagement party, and thought it would look great on you for this occasion," said the Kurdish woman.

Isabel remained speechless by the beauty of the outfit, and even more so by Sarah's lovely gesture. When Ray called her about a week back, he'd mentioned they were going to have a special gathering to speak about the projects. But never did she imagine he planned to turn the entire library hall into Epcot's World Showcase.

With the help of her fellow expat, Isabel slipped out of her casual shirt and jeans, to be gracefully dressed like an Arabian princess. When she walked out, her eyes glowed bright, almost matching her splendid attire, and her overly-thrilled smile highlighted the entire salon. And a minute didn't go by, before visitors lined up to take pictures with the beautiful woman in green—many even asking questions about the country she represented. A group of college students mentioned the Iraqi war, as it was expected, as well as other negative and unfortunate events that had occurred in the region during recent times. But rather patiently, Isabel shared details about the magic, art and history that constituted what Mesopotamia truly had been. She spoke about Iraq with plain nature, listing names of contemporary artists, actors and musicians, as though she were talking about her own homeland. She then guided the group before a smart TV, and using an application she showed them a video of the legendary Hanging Gardens of Nineveh— one of the seven wonders of the Ancient World. Isabel couldn't help to mention some of the great kings and epic warriors of that period, and encouraged the visitors to read about them in history books, but also within the Holy Bible.

"Even the Garden of Eden is said to have been located in this area," she added with pride. "So despite what we see now, I assure you, Iraq is simply...out of this world."

Isabel sighed with prolonged wonderstruck at the end of her lecture. She remained slightly spaced in her memories of her favorite Iraqi person, yet frowned immediately from realizing that she might not see him again.

"Please excuse me," she said to the baffled group, before making her way out of the pavilion.

Her eyes shifted in all directions as she desperately looked for Mr. Pelengkahu. She checked inside the little Taj Mahal, the Pisa Tower, even behind the walls of a cardboard St. Basil's Cathedral, finding most of her former classmates but no teacher. And then, right at the end of the lobby, Isabel saw a small wooden house—resembling the ones displayed on some of her mother's paintings. It was painted in pink, with an aqua-colored front door and window, and topped with a gabled zinc roof. It was completed with a white, wooden porch, looking like the perfect treehouse she always dreamed to have as a child. Isabel was so stunned scanning the structure, that she didn't even notice Ray and Amaité emerging from the inside, along with another group of guests. But as she took a good look at him, she had to gasp from amusement. He wore a long-sleeve *guayabera* and black pants with suspenders, and he'd even topped his head with a traditional panama hat.

"Like it?" asked the instructor. "Amaité helped us finish it earlier this morning."

"I don't know what to say..." Isabel replied softly. "This is probably the closest I've ever been to a typical Puerto Rican house."

"For now, vale?" Amaité winked at her.

Isabel nodded.

"Oh, hey! There's the journalist of the magazine, come, come!" hurried Ray, as he waved at a handsome Dutch guy in a grey UvA alumni sweatshirt—most likely an intern. He seemed excited to meet Isabel, but she remained confused by all the attention, and suggested that the entire class would be present for the interview.

"We were all given this assignment." she added. "And I believe everyone's story deserves the same merit here."

"The thing is, Miss Alvarez, your work went beyond just an interview about an immigrant's cultural integration," said the young writer. "You really saw people, listened to them, and captured their every emotion on those pages."

She shrugged coyly. "Yeah, but—"

"And," he interjected, "publishing your story in our magazine will help raise awareness, and give a voice to those who don't have one. I must say, Miss Alvarez, you would make a terrific journalist."

Hearing those last ironic and bittersweet words, caused her to swallow so heavily they must have seen a giant lump run down her throat. She smiled shyly, thanking him for the compliment, just before beginning with the questionnaire;

"What motivated you?"

"Are you still in contact with these people?"

"How long did it take to write the story?"

"How much research did you need to do?"

"And, who is Samir Ishmael? Can you tell us more about him?"

Isabel flinched at the last question, and Amaité rapidly stepped in to cover her.

"Um, how about asking her something about her own background?" her Sinaloan friend suggested.

"Ah yes, of course!" said the young man. "I was told you are half Venezuelan and half Puerto Rican, raised in the United States—how did it feel to grow up so uprooted?"

Isabel raised her brow at his typical Dutch honesty.

"Well...exactly as you've so directly put it, actually; uprooted," she answered.

He asked her to elaborate, and Isabel explained that the worst consequence of growing up away from her roots, had been her inability to fully integrate with her own people in the United States—unable to feel like she was part of the Latino community at all.

"Having that sense of belonging is essential," she added. "And when you feel that your identity has been taken away, you really need to return to your place of origin."

"So, are you planning to do that any time soon?" he lastly asked.

"God-willing," she replied with a pleasant smile.

After the interview, all of Ray's former students gathered with him in the middle of the hall to have their photo taken for the magazine. The event was far from being over, but Isabel wouldn't stay until the end. She checked the time on her phone, and rushed back to the Mesopotamian pavilion to change back into her travel outfit. She carefully placed the kaftan back in the box, and left a note above the cover, reading;

I went to find my lost roots. Thank you for everything.

Love, Isabel.

19

RUN

Back at the train station, Isabel picked her luggage up and made her way upstairs to the platforms. Her train arrived conveniently on time, not allowing her to consider turning back for even a second.

It was all a good experience...

Her cell phone wouldn't stop vibrating in her purse, but she wouldn't bother answering. She knew that Ray would be trying to reach her after noticing her absence at the library. She hoped, however, that Sarah would eventually figure out where she'd gone. But the calls wouldn't stop coming in, and it was beginning to annoy her. Isabel abruptly grabbed her phone out of her purse, with the sole intention of switching it off for the rest of the ride. And yet, all of her determination faded into a long gasp. Each and every call and text message had not been from her professor, nor from her former classmates, but from Samir. And just as she was about to call back, he beat her to it.

"Sam, where the hell have you been?"

The Assyrian avoided giving any explanation on his previous whereabouts. He demanded to know where she'd gone, expressing feeling devastated to have found his place empty, with nothing of hers except for her belly-dance costume folded atop his bed.

"I'm in a train, Sam. I'm going home," she sighed anxiously.

His breathing through the phone became heavier with each passing second, and he was only able to utter a broken "No" before hanging up.

"Hello?" Isabel asked.

But he was gone again, impulsively like every other time, making Isabel wonder if the call had been just another figment of her imagination.

Unless...

"Oh my God, it was him," she whispered, recalling what she'd seen near his window that morning. "He was really home!"

Isabel tried to call him back immediately, but there was no answer. She felt like she'd been stabbed in the heart again, right in the same old wound of his first departure. Because even if their relationship seemed like a fantasy without future, her feelings for him were real, and too strong to let go of.

But I have to let go, I have to move on...

As she arrived at the airport station, she took the escalators up to Schiphol Plaza, to print her e-tickets at the self-service check-in kiosk. And then, her phone started vibrating again—only this time the caller was unknown.

"He—hello?" she answered with curiosity.

"Hello, Isabel! This is Rami."

Samir, in an eager attempt to prevent Isabel from leaving, had come in contact with one of his cousins, who happened to be a security guard in Schiphol.

"Uh, hey, how did you get this numbe—ugh, why do I even ask?" she groaned and rolled her eyes. "What's going on?"

"Where are you right now? Ah, nevermind, I see you."

The thirty-something year old in blue uniform, walked up from behind and deliberately grabbed her suitcases, placing them on a baggage trolley—a bold action to which she protested.

"Are you really going to argue with an officer...at the airport?" he asked bluntly.

Before she could even react, the Iraqi's phone started ringing. And when she heard him speak through it in the Aramaic tongue, she immediately figured that it was Samir on the other line.

"What kind of childish scheme is this?" she argued. "I'm going to miss my flight!"

The tall, slim Assyrian then hung up and asked her to calm down.

"Rami, please...I don't know what he's trying to do...but I have to go."

"Not before you hear what he has to say," he replied.

"Which is?" she asked.

He sighed with frustration and started pushing the cart, "Just follow me, yes?"

Their stroll across the terminal wasn't long, but the place where Rami stopped surely managed to surprise her. Right there, in front of her confused eyes was the same enormous red and white checkered cube, where she and Samir saw each other for the first time over half a year back.

"He'll be here in fifteen minutes, please sit." said the conspiring Iraqi.

To make the situation even more uncomfortable for Isabel, the bold officer asked everyone sitting around the Meeting Cube to clear the area, adding that he was holding a "code red suspect" in custody.

"You've got to be kidding me," she murmured, taking an annoyed deep breath, while sitting back against the giant structure.

The longer people stared at her, the more she wanted to disappear. But each minute seemed to pass by at a snail's pace. Rami appeared impatient himself, aware to have been putting his own job at risk for helping his impetuous cousin.

This must be just a plot for me to miss my plane...

With that idea in mind, Isabel got back up and tried to play the sympathy card, explaining how difficult it was for her mother to put together the money for the ticket. Rami glanced at her for a moment, but turned his face away rapidly before reconsidering.

"Could you at least call him? It's been over twenty minutes already!" she demanded.

"Fine," he agreed.

But suddenly, as he was placing the phone next to his ear, he lowered his arm again and pressed the red button on the screen.

"Wha—why are you hanging up?!" she argued.

"Because he's running in our direction," he replied, signaling toward the main entrance.

The moment Isabel turned her head, and her hopeful eyes crashed into Samir's impassioned gaze, was the moment she wished to have booked an earlier flight. She hoped this, only because she feared that seconds later—when he'd press her body tightly against his warm chest—she would surely regret her decision to leave the country. And she wasn't wrong, since it didn't take much more than a whiff of Samir's scent for Isabel to drop all resistance. He truly looked like a man on the run that day, for his beard had filled in a little more than usual, his shoes were dusty, and he seemed anxious, afraid ever.

All of a sudden, two other security guards rushed into the main hall, becoming alarmed as they looked in Samir's direction.

"Hey! You there!" one of them yelled as he approached, causing both Isabel and Samir to flinch.

"Is the black Mercedes yours?" added the guard.

Isabel gasped, "You took the company car to come here?"

"It's faster than the NS Stoptrein," Samir joked, admitting to have left it in the middle of the front road, with the engine still on, and the driver's door wide open.

How did he even get a hold of it?

Rami cursed under his breath.

"I'll handle it," he added. "Give me the damn keys...and hurry up!"

Once they were alone, Isabel's smile started to fade from her lips, as she recalled all of the reasons why she'd decided to leave so promptly—one of them being the fact that Samir had disappeared.

"I...I thought you were in prison," Isabel said. "I was terrified."

"And what made you think that?" he asked.

"I'm not stupid, Samir, I saw you on the news. I know you were in Belg—"

He shushed her before she could finish her sentence.

"I see," Isabel scoffed. "Well, maybe you shouldn't be here."

"I had to see you," he whispered. "I had to come back for you."

Her heart rattled inside her chest after hearing these words. But she knew that he was vulnerable inside an airport, risking his last chance to be free just to speak with her again. She couldn't allow that.

"I should tell you this also, I met Hadil," she said.

His eyes widened immediately after hearing her name, "How?"

"She came by your place looking for you, on the same day you left, with news about your brother," Isabel continued, leaving Samir partly out of breath.

He muttered, "Is he...is Yasir..."

"He's safe, at a monastery in Kurdistan," she said. "We tried to call you many times."

Samir turned away from Isabel, placing his hands behind his head in frustration. He confessed to have lost his phone in the middle of a struggle with some cops, not having a chance to get it back. One of his partners had been shot in the leg during their attempt to escape, and only he and Ali were able to flee. They lastly drove all the way to Lille, where they found a spot to ditch their friend's car.

"We came back with nothing," he sighed. "Shit!"

There was a lot of regret in his voice—regret for not waiting for Hadil's phone-call, and for not listening to Isabel's advice in the first place. He never wanted to do what he did, he was not that kind of man. But he knew that even if he put together all his earnings as a chauffeur, he was never going to come up with enough money to get his brother into Europe. Samir was desperate to find his family, but was starting to feel hopeless before the current panorama in his life. In the middle of his talk, Isabel realized that she'd lost track of time, and that her plane was leaving in less than fifteen minutes.

"Samir, I really have to go..." she said hesitantly.

And as she grabbed the handle of the baggage trolley, Samir stopped her once again.

"Isabel don't go, please!"

"There's nothing for me here, Samir! I tried!"

"But I am here now!" he exclaimed, holding on to her arms.

"No! You need to leave this place, or else they will—"

"Not without you, habibti," he insisted.

Isabel struggled to hold her real feelings back, making a supernatural effort to appear indifferent.

"Besides, Hadil told me everything you refused to explain," she said.

He shrugged, "What?"

"Now I understand why you turned away when I said I loved you, or when you tried hiding me from Petros while we lived together," she added.

"Isab—"

"I get it. You can't be with a woman who is not Assyrian."

"Just let me I explain!" he shouted.

"Enough," she said, pulling her arms back. "Your words can't make me change my mind, I'm sorry."

"Can this...make you change your mind?"

Right at the end of his question, Samir did what Isabel never expected him to do, nor what she imagined any other traditional Assyrian would ever do. He reached into the inner pocket of his leather jacket, drawing out the same gold crucifix necklace his mother had given him.

"Our families are not here," he said with sorrowful eyes, "but I give you this gold, all I have left, if you accept me."

Onlookers stared strangely at the scene, not understanding what was happening between the detained Hispanic woman and the bulky Middle Eastern man. But Isabel knew exactly what it was, for she'd read stories about it.

Is this really...

"Isabel, you know what this is?"

"*Meshmetha*," she whispered. "Oh my God..."

"Yes!" he exclaimed with joy.

"But Samir...your tradition says—"

"I don't care! Stay with me, forever," he said firmly, deliberately placing the golden cross around her neck.

Her eyes started to fill up with tears, and a gush of air escaped her lips as she felt the metal caress her skin. The chain itself was weightless, but the meaning of the cross hanging on it was much too heavy at the time. She now had the option of losing her flight to stay behind as his betrothed, as his future wife. This was the only way serious relationships worked in his culture; with a prompt engagement. And in some cases, it was all priorly arranged.

But what about his family? And what about my dad? No, I need to go. I need to go now!

"No, habibi," she murmured, carefully taking the jewel back off. "We can't do this."

Samir became speechless, but his breathing was accelerated. He was surprised by Isabel's reaction, having expected her to easily agree to his last-minute proposition. At that moment, many things began to shatter inside of him; his expectations, his ego, his heart. Isabel placed the necklace back in his hand, and Samir looked at it for a couple of seconds before strongly clenching his fist around it.

"I hope for you a good life..." he said, unable to look at her in the eyes anymore.

"And I hope you find your family, at last," Isabel said. "Run Samir, and don't look back."

Samir figured that insisting would have only hurt them both. And in his mind, he admitted that she was right at least about one thing; he had to flee once more. Nevertheless, he somewhat felt remorse for allowing their relationship to flourish in the way it did, acknowledging there were far too many obstacles along the way. Isabel had fallen in love with a man trapped between two worlds—East and West—a man on an important mission, haunted by his rough memories of Mosul. On the other hand, Samir had accidently opened his heart to an incomplete and unsettled woman, not realizing that it was his own story which ultimately inspired her to seek the truth of many mysteries in life. He loved her dearly, as she loved him. But he now understood that he had to let her slip away from his present, so that they both could rediscover themselves, and build a future someplace else.

Good bye, hayati, her gleaming eyes said—just as Samir walked away, furrowing his eyebrows again, and gradually falling back into the cold character of his distrustful nature.

Shlama Elokhum

SOMEWHERE OVER THE ATLANTIC...

Even after the hardest airport farewells, it is expected for one to feel some kind of tranquility once sitting inside the plane. Sure, maybe in the first class section, but not all the way back here. At least I have an aisle seat. Still, it's such a full flight I almost can't breathe. And even though every other passenger is submerged in sleep, I can't seem to reach the same level of peace. I feel so sick...damn you anxiety.

Isabel sighs as she puts her pen down, placing it inside her new journal. She unbuckles her seatbelt and carefully makes her way to the lavatories, where she splashes water all over her tired face. Suddenly, everything starts to bother her; her makeup, her jacket, and even her boots. She feels cold sweat drops running down her shirt, just as a sharp pain pierces into her stomach. Leaning back against the door of the tiny room, she looks steadily at the toilet bowl, feeling her mouth salivating heavily, and a large lump growing inside her throat.

"Ay Dios mio..." she whispers.

ABOUT THE AUTHOR

Raised in Rio Grande, Puerto Rico, Isandra Collazo Rivera is a self-proclaimed citizen of the world. She's an enthusiast of international cuisine and foreign music, devoted to learn from other people's cultures, and sharing their life stories with the purpose of breaking down the walls of fear and prejudice.

She'd majored in Foreign Languages and Tourism with the goal of becoming a tour guide one day, but all of her plans changed when she felt a calling to serve the community within her Caribbean Island, as well as beyond its beautiful, white sand beaches. Committed to help bring change into the world, Isandra is now a Christian missionary, human rights defender, orator, and philanthropist.

With her debut novel; *Across the Border: Interview with a Refugee*, she hopes to raise awareness on many social issues happening today, and that way inspire others to raise a voice for those in need.

.